CW00494322

BEC McMASTER

DUKES ARE FOREVER

LONDON STEAMPUNK
THE BLUE BLOOD CONSPIRACY

Dukes Are Forever © 2019 Bec McMaster

Copyright notice: All rights reserved under the International and Pan-American Copyright Conventions. No part of this book may be reproduced or transmitted in any form or by any means, electronic or mechanical, including photocopying, recording, or by any information storage and retrieval system, without permission in writing from the publisher.
Dukes Are Forever: A Blue Blood Conspiracy Novel
Copyright 2019 © Bec McMaster

This is a work of fiction. Names, places, characters and incidents are either the product of the author's imagination or are used fictitiously, and any resemblance to any actual persons, living or dead, organizations, events or locales is entirely coincidental.

Edited by: Hot Tree Editing
Print formatting by: Cover Me Darling and Athena Interior Book Design
Cover Art 2019 © Damonza.com

ALSO AVAILABLE BY BEC McMASTER

DARK COURT RISING

Promise of Darkness

LONDON STEAMPUNK SERIES

Kiss Of Steel

Heart Of Iron

My Lady Quicksilver

Forged By Desire

Of Silk And Steam

Novellas in same series:

Tarnished Knight

The Clockwork Menace

THE BLUEBLOOD CONSPIRACY SERIES

Mission: Improper

The Mech Who Loved Me

You Only Love Twice

To Catch A Rogue

Dukes are Forever

LEGENDS OF THE STORM

Heart of Fire

Storm of Desire

Clash of Storms

Storm of Fury

DARK ARTS SERIES

Shadowbound

Hexbound

Soulbound

BURNED LANDS SERIES

Nobody's Hero

The Last True Hero

The Hero Within

OTHER

The Many Lives Of Hadley Monroe

Thief of Dreams

DUKES ARE FOREVER

LONDON STEAMPUNK: THE BLUE BLOOD CONSPIRACY

A compromising situation forced him into marriage. But has his wife been working for the enemy all along?

In a steam-fuelled world where vampires once ruled the aristocracy, a dangerous conspiracy threatens to topple the queen, and the Duke of Malloryn knows his nemesis has finally returned to enact his plans of revenge.

Malloryn can trust no one, and when incriminating photographs surface—of an enemy agent stealing a kiss from his wife—he is forced to question just why his wife, Adele, trapped him into marriage.

Is she an innocent pawn caught up in a madman's games, or is she a double agent working against him?

The only way to discover the truth is to seduce her himself...

Adele Hamilton may have agreed to a loveless marriage in order to protect herself, but that doesn't stop her heart from yearning for more.

Her husband promised her a cold marriage bed. He swore he'd never touch her. But suddenly he's engaged in a campaign of seduction—and the only way to keep her wits about her is to fight fire with fire.

The ruthless beauty has locked her heart away, but can she deny the passion that flares between them? And when the truth emerges, will she be the only thing that can save Malloryn's life?

Or the weapon his enemy will wield against him?

CHAPTER ONE

It was a kiss like no other.

The touch of his lips burned her, his hand sliding over her nape and bending her body into his embrace. Adele Cavill, the Duchess of Malloryn, drew back a hand and slapped the man, though her heart was suddenly racing and she knew for one desperate second, she hadn't fought him as hard as she should have. "Sir, you take too many liberties."

"I should like to take more," Lord Devoncourt whispered.

For a moment, she was almost tempted. Her lips still tingled. The sounds of the ball washed over her. "I'm no whore," she said firmly, "to cuckold my husband."

"No?" Devoncourt smiled, tracing her cheek with the back of her hand. "Then where is your fine husband? If you're such a loyal wife, why aren't you in his bed right now?"

Because I've never been in his bed. Adele bit her lip. *Never been kissed. Never been held. Barely even glanced at as I sit at our dining table each morning and stare at Malloryn over the baked kippers and extravagant repast.*

All her fault, of course.

She'd been the one to use the Duke of Malloryn's opposition to a recent trend amongst young blue bloods ruining girls for a single night of blood sharing to trap him into marriage. And she couldn't for one second deny she would do it all over again, if she had the chance. For the first time in years she was safe and protected from the blue bloods that'd mercilessly stalked the Echelon, hunting for those young debutantes that strayed from the glittering lights of the ballrooms.

With her reputation in tatters from one such incident, the only lord willing to take her as his thrall had been Lord Abagnale, a man who'd buried three of his previous thralls, and—it was rumored—had placed them in the grave himself.

Malloryn was her blessing, but he'd made it eminently clear that whilst she would bear his name, she would never bear his children or share his life. Indeed, she'd heard rumors of a mistress.

His bed, at least, wasn't as cold as hers.

He'd damned well told her to "make her own arrangements."

Those tempting fingertips cupped her cheeks. Adele looked up helplessly as Devoncourt stroked his thumb over her mouth.

"I think," he murmured, "your silence is answer enough."

His face lowered to hers, his warm breath brushing against her sensitive lips, bringing a sudden yearning to life within her breast. Not for the hidden meaning behind his words, but *this*.... She didn't think she could fight this, the careful tenderness of his touch. It ached in her chest, a longing to turn her cheek into his palm, to press it there and feel, just for one moment, what it was like to be cared for.

To be touched.

"I cannot," she whispered, because she'd made a promise in her heart to be true to her husband, a means of repaying him for the lie she'd told that had seen them married.

Devoncourt stepped away, his gloved hand falling from her face. "When you have thrown off the shackles of your morals, you know where to find me. I shall love you, Adele."

Love. What a mockery.

"I shall show you things that will make your heart beat forever with the sound of my name. I shall worship at your feet. All you have to do is say yes."

Auvry Cavill, the Duke of Malloryn, stalked inside the study he kept at 45 Hardcastle Lane, instantly soothed by the scent of leather and cognac. The headquarters for what he—and several of his compatriots—jokingly referred to as the Company of Rogues was becoming more of a home these days than his own.

Part of the reason for that had thick, golden ringlets, a figure more rightly suited to a Botticelli, and a clear adoration of extravagant silk gowns and feathered hats.

His wife.

With her devious green eyes and a streak of cunning that almost matched his own, Adele was the only person of his acquaintance who roused any sort of emotion within him these days. Malloryn rarely enjoyed being outplayed, and Adele had manipulated him into marriage with all the gall of a seasoned enemy general. He could almost have admired her determination, if he hadn't been the fox caught in her snare.

The woman was downright ruthless; all his friends had told him that.

But by then it had been too late.

How could one champion a cause, then protest otherwise when he'd been caught in the gardens of Lord Dalrymple's party with her? She'd practically thrown herself at him, making it clear they were in the prelude of something—whether a kiss or a bloodletting, he wasn't certain.

Sometimes he thought he hated her the most for that. He'd done his duty, by God, and if she expected anything more, then their frosty silences over the dining room table had swiftly taught her otherwise.

There was a swift rap at his study door, and for a second he flinched, taken unawares. His nerves were still recovering from Russia, though he'd be damned if he'd allow anyone to know that.

Malloryn shrugged out of his coat and glanced at the ormolu clock on the mantle. His nine o'clock appointment. "Come in."

Caleb Byrnes, one of his most experienced agents, pushed inside.

"We've finally found the operative we suspected had been placed within the Echelon." Byrnes slid a folder toward him, and then his cold blue eyes unexpectedly flitted over Malloryn, a hint of smothered humor within them. "He's an ex-Falcon who's been masquerading as the long-lost Earl of Devoncourt. Gemma recognized him from her days as a Falcon-in-training."

Devoncourt?

Malloryn had vague memories of the man from somewhere, though the acquaintance was fleeting at best.

As part of the ruling Council that served the queen, he was far too busy to attend every ball and function. Besides, his wife was always in attendance and Malloryn wasn't *that* good an actor, to pretend theirs was any sort of marriage. "And this amuses you?"

Byrnes laughed. "Oh no, it's not Devoncourt that amuses me. Keep reading."

It could be anything. Byrnes had the worst sort of humor Malloryn had ever encountered.

Sliding the file open, he examined the grainy sepia photograph of the man. Handsome, dressed somewhat foppishly, with the kind of smile ladies would swoon over.... He didn't look like an assassin, but perhaps that was the point. Malloryn let the photo rest. "What's his purpose?"

"We don't know."

Again that sensation that Byrnes hesitated.

"If you wish to say something to me, I'd advise you to simply throw it on the table."

"Look at the rest of the photos, Your Grace. Gemma took them. It was an unexpected lead."

"I thought she was keeping an eye on my wife after that incident at the wedding?" Someone had tried to murder Adele the day they were supposed to be married, and with Lord Balfour at large again, it made sense to protect those he'd targeted in the past. It was one thing to dislike Adele, quite another to allow someone to outplay him that way.

"She was."

A familiar sense of foreboding curled through Malloryn's innards.

Malloryn flipped the tumble of photographs into his hands and sorted through them swiftly. Devoncourt at his club. At a garden party, at the park..., kissing Malloryn's wife.

Malloryn stilled, his senses locking down. Thumbnail tracing the shadowy image of Adele, he simply couldn't believe his eyes.

A dozen emotions swirled.

But most importantly, he couldn't help noticing the way Adele wilted against Devoncourt's hard body, a hint of longing on her expressive face as she stared at the earl. It softened her features—those devilish eyes with their wicked tilt looked almost innocent, and that indecent mouth was parted with longing. It made her seem younger. Desirable. A woman destined for a tumble into bed.

In the next photograph, she slapped Devoncourt. But the look on her face.... Not entirely one of chagrin. Malloryn had never seen that particular expression cross her devious face.

Almost as if she longed for something more.

Byrnes was waiting, his arms crossed over his chest. His recent marriage had done little to soften the man, though Malloryn suspected Ingrid might actually be the more dangerous of the two.

"I'll deal with it," he said quietly and closed the file.

"Gemma's not certain what, precisely, she witnessed. It's evident this is not the first time they've met."

"A conclusion I'd reached myself, thank you." He looked up. "You're dismissed."

Byrnes took his leave. Malloryn leaned back in his chair and scratched at his jaw. He didn't throw the file or burn it. Which he was shockingly tempted to do. Instead, he steepled his fingers together and stared into the distance.

Was Adele merely a means for Lord Balfour to get access to him?

His old enemy had been thwarted by the Company of Rogues in Russia and would be out for blood. Malloryn had spent the past three months looking over his shoulder, just waiting for Balfour to finally reappear.

Or had Balfour already succeeded?

His blood ran cold. He'd never thought anything more of Adele's obviously desperate attempt to force him into marriage, and he'd never asked her why. They rarely spoke, if at all, and of frivolities only. If she was indeed a spy, then he had given her poor value indeed.

But the idea rankled. She could be dangerous to him if her allegiance was indeed suspect. How the devil could he know precisely what her game was or if she was achieving it?

Or was she waiting for some signal from her master?

You're seeing Balfour in every corner. Malloryn rested his fingertips against his temples. *Adele couldn't be one of his agents. She couldn't.*

But that little niggling feeling wouldn't go away.

He could hardly question her about it, regardless of which methods he chose to use—and there were many available to him. Malloryn had long since given up on any squeamishness, but torturing one's wife?

Flipping the file open again, he took a long, slow drink of his blooded scotch. None of the photographs interested him, particularly the one of her kissing Devoncourt. But the other.... That look upon her face. He stared at that for a long time.

He'd told her to make her own arrangements.

He'd given a callous shrug at the time and assured her he intended to make his own, though he'd been too busy, perhaps, to make good on his threat.

But the sight of her in another man's arms had the same effect as someone dumping a bucket of iced water over his head.

Why the hell did he care?

Because there might be an enemy in your house.

That had to be it.

"So you want to play games, my dear?" He threw the rest of the scotch back, the blood igniting his darker, well-checked urges. Igniting something inside him he hadn't felt for a long time; a dangerous kind of fury, of need. "Then let us play."

There were, after all, other means to find out precisely what his wife was up to.

CHAPTER TWO

Alex Carver grabbed a fistful of Adele's pearls and tried to strangle her with them.

"Goodness." Adele winced. "He has the grip of a sailor."

"His father, rather," her dearest friend, Lena Carver, said wryly, reaching forward to rescue her. "Will's lack of manners too," she scolded, pressing a kiss to the baby's chubby cheek as she untangled his grip on Adele's pearls and tugged him into her arms. "Stop being such a beast to Adele."

Despite her words, Lena was smiling as she turned and lifted the baby into the air. He gurgled and stared down at his mother as if she'd set the sun and the moon in the sky.

"He's growing so swiftly," Adele noted, rubbing at her throat tentatively.

"Verwulfen are like that." Lena brought him down into the curve of her softened body, tucking him against her shoulder. Her bronze eyes danced and Adele felt a faint stab of jealousy as she realized her closest—and perhaps only—friend was leaving her behind.

Lena had a husband now, a man who adored her with almost embarrassing fervency, and her six-month-old son, who was burbling up at his mother as he stuffed Lena's gold chain in his mouth.

The work they'd shared as part of the Society of Roses, to help protect young debutantes in need of a safety net from the blue bloods of the Echelon, had faded in recent times with the queen cracking down on certain activities. No longer were debutantes bearing the brunt of a blue blood lord's bloodlust. Several lords had been exiled from the Echelon for such behavior, one had even been executed, and the rest of them had very swiftly become the model of decorum.

There was no longer the need for rings filled with hemlock—the only means of defense one had against a blue blood in the grip of the blood thirst.

No longer a crop of frightened debutantes turning to Adele in the powder rooms of every ball and begging for help.

Adele looked into her teacup.

The Society had given her a sense of purpose in recent times. It helped ease the boredom of her days of constant tea parties, shopping expeditions, and wondering precisely what kind of woman her husband's new mistress was.

A *Mrs. Danner* someone had told her.

Presumably to replace the baroness, who'd been at his side for years, before her death several months ago.

No matter where she looked, it was clear her husband preferred the company of other women to her.

"I never thought I'd love someone as much as I love Will, but I cannot describe the feeling of being a mother," Lena continued. "It's like Alex's entire being lights up when I walk into a room. It's a lovely feeling."

"I'm sure it is."

Lena's smile faded. "Oh, Adele. I'm so sorry. That was unforgivable of me."

"Nonsense. You're entitled to your happiness. Please don't hide it from me just because I shall never know the same."

"You never know," Lena argued. "Sometimes I see the duke looking at you when he thinks you're not aware of his gaze. You might be surprised."

"Does his expression look a little like this?" Adele mimicked her husband's haughty, somewhat displeased expression, and then added a good dose of disgust for good measure.

Somehow her eyes ended up crossed.

Lena burst into laughter. "You almost had it until the end. Malloryn doesn't dislike you."

"You're right," she mocked. "That would require emotions and as far as I know, my husband doesn't suffer from them. How frightfully plebeian."

"He looks at you as though he doesn't quite know what to do with you."

That's because he doesn't.

I don't even know what to do with me.

Adele's gaze strayed to Alex as her smile faded. She toyed with the ring on her finger—her wedding ring.

Alex's hair had recently all fallen out, and Lena didn't bother with a bonnet inside, but something in Adele's chest gave a small squeeze at the sight of him. The baby adored his mother unconditionally.

What would it be like to be the focus of someone's world like that? To be loved, no matter what you had done or what type of person you were? She had little doubt about her own nature. People found her cynical and somewhat cold, but it was all she knew, the only way she had of surviving as a young woman.

"But then, I suppose we're not to speak of the expression on *your* face when Malloryn enters a room?" Lena added.

Adele's fingers froze on her ring. "What sort of expression?"

Lena patted Alex's back as she swayed to and fro, her eyes dark with sympathy. "Your spine goes stiff, your shoulders straighten, and you look like you're girding yourself for war. 'Scale this tower at your own risk. Nobody can touch me in here.'"

"That's because I'd rather lock myself away like Rapunzel than suffer my husband's presence."

Lena's voice softened. "Is that entirely true? I'm your dearest friend, Adele. I *know* you. I can see how much he vexes you."

"That's precisely the point: Why would I want his attention when it irritates me so much?"

"Do you know what I think? I think you *want* him to vex you. I think you want him to look your way and press his attentions."

"I think I would rather eat a cockroach."

"Do you know the most surprising aspect of being made verwulfen?"

The abrupt switch in conversation made Adele suspicious. "What?"

Lena's eyes narrowed as she leaned forward. "I can actually smell your nervousness when you lie. You're lying to me right now. And to yourself."

Maybe it was true.

And who else did she have to discuss this with?

The memories were eating away at her.

"There was an incident between us," she suddenly blurted. "At the Ivory Tower four months ago, when the queen was nearly assassinated."

"What sort of incident?"

"Someone had shot Malloryn—not that I blame them. Entirely. He has that effect. But he was bleeding so much. And I.... It's not the first time I've given blood to a blue blood. I just thought.... I couldn't just leave him there."

"You gave blood to an injured blue blood?" Lena's eyes widened. "*Adele!*"

"I know." She slammed the ring back on her finger. "It's the first thing we're warned against as debutantes. An injured blue blood is at the mercy of his craving. They're no longer entirely in control of themselves."

"He didn't hurt you, did he?" Bronze flashed in Lena's eyes as her own passion roused. To be verwulfen meant being subject to your emotions, and if she thought Malloryn had harmed Adele, it was quite possible she'd go after him.

Adele looked down into her lap, her cheeks heating. "No. It wasn't... like that."

At all.

She could still feel the press of Malloryn's lips to her throat. And the caress of his tongue. His hand on her breast, thumb rasping over her hardened nipple as he ground his hips between her thighs—

"It wasn't just the bloodlust that roused," she blurted.

Silence fell.

Lena's pretty rosebud mouth had dropped open. "Did he—?"

"*No!* He came back to his senses in time."

"But it was clearly a passionate interlude."

Adele squeezed her eyes shut. "He's never touched me like that before. He told me he never would. And I never wanted him to before that moment. But now, I cannot quite seem to forget it."

"Oh, dear."

"And then he disappeared for nearly a month, with a letter telling me not to worry. Nothing to bother myself over. But when he returned... it was as though nothing had ever happened between us. He avoids me. I avoid him." She curled her fingers into fists. "But I wish to God he'd never touched me. Because now I know he is not merely made of ice. I was content with our agreement before then. I would have remained content. But now I *know*. And it is torture."

"Aha."

"Aha, what?"

"That's why I catch him looking at you so often with that indecipherable look on his face." Lena eased onto the sofa before her, placing her hand over the top of Adele's. "So what are you going to do about it?"

"Going to do? Why, nothing. Malloryn despises me."

"That is not the Adele I know. She would be taking no prisoners. You should seduce him."

"The Adele you know would prefer not to have her husband laugh in her face."

"Did he seem disgusted when he realized what had occurred?"

"Well, no. He seemed slightly horrified he may have hurt me. Then he lectured me about how dangerous it was. And then he realized the queen was under attack, and what happened may as well not have happened. I assure you, it hasn't cost *him* a moment of sleep."

Lena frowned.

"I told you: The man feels nothing." Adele shook her head. "You're my dearest friend. I know you want only the best for me, but trust me... there is no hope my husband desires me."

"Was he aroused at the—?"

"*Yes*, but I assume that was a product of the circumstances. Most blue bloods do rouse when their bloodlust rises."

Alex gave a whimpering cry, screwing up his face as he gummed at Lena's chain.

"Well, I still think there's a chance you could—"

Alex promptly cast up his accounts all over his mother's gown. Adele jerked her skirts out of the way in surprise.

"Oh, Alex." Lena gave an exasperated sigh, staring at the state of her gown. She rolled her eyes and transferred him to her other shoulder as the baby settled, evidently feeling much better.

"Is he ill?"

"No. He's a great big glutton, is what he is." Lena patted his back gently, her gaze softening as she looked at him. "It happens occasionally after he's fed."

That sounded ghastly.

And yet her friend still smiled. Adele couldn't quite understand it. "Perhaps I'd best take my leave and let you change. I've dwelled here long enough."

And she recognized the look in Lena's eyes.

Her friend was not going to change the subject, not anytime soon.

"Oh, it's no problem at all," Lena replied, raising her voice. "Nurse?"

The door opened, and the nursemaid appeared. "Yes, mum?"

"Could you please see Master Alex to the nursery? I believe he needs changing. I'll be along as soon as I've cleaned myself up."

The nursemaid bobbed a curtsy. "Yes, mum."

"I should go," Adele murmured. "Thank you for the tea and scones."

Lena pointed a finger at her even as she bent to try and clean her hem. "Don't think I'll forget about this. I intend to pursue the topic."

"Excellent." Adele fetched her hat from the table where she'd left it. "The very thought of my husband desiring me should prove humorous, if nothing else."

And the idea of seducing him?

Well, that was simply ludicrous.

Adele stood on the portico of Lena's home and stared blindly at the gardens, still picturing the baby's face in her mind and the look of adoration on his face.

I want one.

What an utterly ridiculous instinct. Somehow she breathed out a laugh.

"Fuck whomever you want, Adele, but don't bring any bastards home to my house. There are limits...."

Which meant the only way she would ever conceive a child was with her husband.

And that was never going to happen.

Imagine even presenting Malloryn with such a proposition? She could almost picture the look of horror on his face, and despite herself, a faint smile tugged at her lips.

"Aren't you maudlin today," she muttered to herself, shaking off the ill mood. "Feeling sorry for yourself is the least effective use of one's time. You made this decision, after all. And you can bear the consequences."

Still smiling at Malloryn's imagined horror, Adele took her leave, walking into the brisk London air.

Maybe she'd ask him for a child one day, just to see his eyes pop out of his head.

She'd wait though, until his disinterest in her was really beginning to prickle....

The taste of coal smog thickened the air, and she hurried to her carriage, clapping a hand to her black-feathered hat as the footman handed her up into it.

In the gloom of the interior, it took her a moment to realize she wasn't alone as the door slammed shut.

CHAPTER THREE

Adele clapped a hand to her chest in surprise as a pair of long legs stretched out in front of her, leading up to an opened newspaper. She would have gasped, but the golden signet ring on the man's finger was very familiar. She watched it every morning as her husband idly tapped the breakfast table whilst he flicked through the daily news, much as he was now.

Speak of the devil and he shall appear....

"Your Grace," she blurted. "What are you doing here?"

The newspaper lowered, a pair of cool gray eyes assessing her.

"I was in the area," Malloryn announced in the clipped tones he usually owned when speaking with her. "The coachman assured me you wouldn't be long."

"Did you wish to speak with me?"

"Not particularly." He rapped his cane on the roof. "Carry on, James."

It shouldn't have stung as much as it did. She looked out the window as the carriage lurched into action. "I'm sorry I took the coach then."

Malloryn leaned back in his seat, carefully folding his newspaper. "Do you make a habit of visiting the verwulfen ambassador's wife?"

Oddly enough, he seemed more curious than anything. That would be a first. "She's my dearest friend. I come here most Wednesdays."

"It's Friday."

I was lonely. Instead she smoothed her skirts. Pull yourself together. It's just your husband.

"Lena's planning a ball," she said with a noncommittal shrug. "She wanted my opinion on something."

She'd never felt more uncomfortable in her life than she was trapped in a carriage with him. At least the dining table was over twenty feet long. Much easier to deal with him when they engaged but briefly over twenty feet of polished walnut, with the saltcellars and cutlery arranged between them, arrayed like soldiers in the field.

Especially with the heat of Lena's foolish declarations echoing in her ears.

Seduce him, indeed.

"Going somewhere?" he asked.

"I was on my way home."

Her husband tapped the roof with his cane. "Malloryn Court."

"You were going home too?"

It was the middle of the day. He was rarely out of bed by now, his blue blood nature more prone to haunting the moonlit hours. Fashionable London didn't come alive until at least midafternoon, when the bloodthirsty aristocrats of the Echelon awoke and squinted fiercely at the glare of sunlight.

Malloryn studied her before dropping his attention to where he began to tug at his gloves, one finger at a time. "I lied. We need to speak, Adele."

The words froze her. Divorce? It wasn't unheard of, and Malloryn had made it quite clear this marriage wasn't to his satisfaction. An unpopular precedent, but he had the queen's ear. It could be arranged. And he wouldn't be affected by the scandal as badly as she would be.

Maybe this was revenge.

Maybe this was what he'd intended all along.

What the hell would she do for her sister, Hattie, if the money dried up? She could take care of herself. Somehow. But Hattie was only seventeen and still legally under their parents' roof. If Adele couldn't come up with the money to pay her mother off, Lady Hamilton would sell the girl to the highest bidder.

"Of course," she managed to say. "What would you like to speak of?"

If he divorced her, she'd be shamed. Her parents would never take her back now. What would she do? Go to Lena? But Lena had her own husband, her own life.... Blood and ashes, she hated being beholden to someone like this.

"—about time in a man's life to begin thinking of an heir...." His words finally penetrated, and she realized she'd frozen almost in terror.

Then her mind caught up to what her ears had just heard.

"An heir?" she blurted. He wanted to lie with her? To... to.... A baby? "With me?"

Every single jesting thought she'd had earlier about proposing such a notion sprang immediately to mind.

Only it wasn't Malloryn who was staring at her in horror, but vice versa.

"You are my wife." His voice softened. "And you owe me a rather large debt, Adele. I have done my part in this farce. It is time for you to do yours."

The word farce echoed in her ears. "Of course."

"You don't have to look so aghast."

"It's called surprise, Your Grace." She tried to regain her feet after he'd pulled the rug out from under her. "I thought you told me you'd never kiss me? Never summon me to your bed?"

Dark, silky lashes flickered over his eyes. "Begetting an heir doesn't require kissing. Nor a bed, if one is being technically accurate."

"I see."

She couldn't help thinking of Devoncourt in that moment.

The kiss she'd spurned because she owed more than she could possibly repay to the man sitting across from her.

She wouldn't regret denying Devoncourt, though she couldn't help resenting the fact she wanted to replace that memory with one shared with her husband.

It was not to be, of course.

How unnecessary kissing was, it seemed.

Even if a part of her ached for it.

Even if she couldn't help wondering what her husband's kiss would taste like.

He'd be an expert at it, no doubt. If there was one thing she could grant him, it was that Malloryn ruled his body with inherent grace. Each step he took was leonine in its intensity. Powerful. Controlled. He perfected everything he touched. He would not let the art of kissing escape his repertoire.

"Nothing to say?" Malloryn mused.

"Only that I am grateful not to be the recipient of your practiced attentions." She feigned a shudder. "It spares me the need to pretend to enjoy them."

Heat flashed in his gray eyes. Other than that he didn't

move. "I thought you quite enjoyed kissing?"

"What is that supposed to mean?" Her eyes narrowed.

"Nothing."

"And Mrs. Danner?" The words seemed to come from nowhere. "Your mistress?"

Malloryn arched a brow. "What of her?"

"I am not going to share my bed with two people," she somehow found herself saying. "If you're going to ask me to submit to this, then I hardly see why you should need her."

"It's not a matter of need, so much as a matter of want."

The words were like a knife to the chest. Mrs. Danner, the mysterious brunette she'd once caught a glimpse of, was evidently more to his tastes than his own wife.

What did you expect?

She stared furiously at her own hands. He had all the power in this relationship. Who was she to say he mustn't keep a mistress after the way they'd begun this blasted marriage?

She was Adele Cavill, the Duchess of Malloryn. That was who.

"Well, then you are going to be left wanting," she retorted, looking at him heatedly from beneath her lashes. The shock of his request was dissolving. Time to take matters into her hands. She'd learned enough over the years to know she wasn't going to simply lie back and surrender without a decent negotiation. There were things she wanted in life. "You want an heir? Then I want her gone."

A considering look. "I shall see her pensioned off."

"I also want an increase to my pin money," she added. Her mother's demands were growing shockingly vulgar of late, but paying the woman off was the only way to keep her younger sister, Hattie, safe.

"Shall I double it?"

"That's quite generous."

"Anything else?"

"Don't tempt me, Your Grace." Adele smiled through gritted teeth. "You may think me uncommonly mercenary for demanding such things, but you're not the one who is going to have to bear this."

"Bear this?" For the first time, he seemed intrigued. "You think me an ogre?"

Hardly that. He was stunningly, unfairly handsome. "I think I married a man who despises me and has no reason to be gentle with me. It's not the most pleasant of experiences, but I'm sure I will endure."

"Endure?"

"Don't worry. I'll lie back and think of England."

His lips twitched. "How considerate of you."

"Or perhaps I'll think of diamonds," she replied, toying with the pearls at her throat to keep her hands occupied. "Great big diamonds, offset with emeralds perhaps. To match my eyes."

"Is this part of the negotiation?"

"Maybe."

Malloryn rested his chin in his hand, his legs elegantly crossed at the shins as he considered her. Something heated the normally dark canvas of his eyes, and there was the faintest edge of a smile lingering about his lips. "Oh, I don't think you'll be thinking of England—or diamonds—Adele. Grant me some credit. I don't think you'll be able to think of anything else at all."

His voice was a purr, and the way he said her name as if caressing it with his tongue, made her swallow as she reassessed him.

It was possible she hadn't fully considered the idea of what an heir would entail. Indeed, the first thought that had sprung to mind had been a baby, looking much like young Master Alex in her head.

Now, she was beginning to think of the step she had missed in this equation. The actual begetting.

She knew enough to know what would happen. Every debutante worth her salt learned what flesh rights were. The ultimate aim of every debutante was to be taken as a thrall by an aristocratic blue blood, but though the exchange sold her blood rights to her lord, her flesh rights were her own, to give away if she chose, or not at all if she did not. It was rarely spoken of in polite company, but though debutantes might be innocent of body when they went to their new masters, of mind they were not.

There had been books detailing the physical effects of a consummation and what precisely a man appreciated.

There had been anatomically correct diagrams that made her eyebrows arch.

There had been gorgeously painted pictures that Adele had blushed to peruse, though the wicked little part of her had noted over one hundred different pictures, and therefore positions. Some of their names had made her tutor stammer and Adele had frankly stared, trying to work out precisely how, and what, and where....

And now all she could see was herself in those images. On her hands and knees, wearing not a stitch, with her husband taking up residence behind her with a turgid staff ready to plunge inside her.

Oh, God.

Her gaze came back into focus as she realized she was staring at her husband. Or more precisely, at the insolently lounged figure who would possibly lie atop her quite shortly. Her breath hitched. Malloryn made a harem pasha look rigid. There was always something vaguely relaxed about him, yet she caught hints of tension there now, in his thighs, in his hands, and about his soft mouth.

Their eyes met, and Adele found herself blushing for perhaps the first time in a decade. All of a sudden, her dress was too tight.

"Are you actually blushing?"

"No," she blurted, though her cheeks felt hot enough to cook an egg. "I'm just surprised. And... curious."

"Curious?"

"It's not as though I do not know what to expect. I attended all the lectures."

"You're untouched." He didn't look entirely pleased with this deduction.

Go to hell. She knew what the world thought of her. "You sound surprised, Your Grace."

"I was not the first man to be caught alone in a garden with you," he replied. "You were quite well known for it."

Not by choice. "Consider me an inexperienced expert of men's desires and what they want from me. I know the value of a woman's virginity. Without it, I'd never have been married. I went to great lengths to preserve my innocence."

"Yes, but it's one thing to know of such matters, and quite another to experience them."

"Don't worry, Your Grace. I am prepared to suffer through the entire affair."

His eyelids lowered, as if he considered something. "I thought you were jesting, but you honestly think I will hurt you."

And just like that, any sense of desire dried up. She felt sick.

"Perhaps you do not know what it was like for a debutante before the queen overthrew her husband." A bitter laugh broke free. "Of course you do not. You're a duke, you're a blue blood, and you're a man. You've never experienced a ball where you're little more than a young girl just ripe for the picking. If I'm untouched, then it's not for lack of lords trying. You're the predator. You have no concept of what it's like to be prey, to have very few means of protection but to submit and hope they do not hurt you too much when they take your blood...."

Adele looked away, fighting the urge to say more as she stared out at the passing London streets. He was still watching her. She could feel it. And she wanted to hit something, suddenly, at the memory of everything she'd thought she had buried.

Malloryn shifted, and it was like a snake suddenly striking. Adele flinched, but he had only reached out toward her, gesturing for her to take his hand.

"Come here," he said.

Where? She looked at him blankly, but he caught her fingers in his own and gave a tug. Adele slid across the intervening carriage space and found herself on his lap.

"I am not going to hurt you." He still seemed affronted by the idea.

Adele's spine remained stiff.

It was the closest she'd been to him since... well, that time in the Ivory Tower.

"I am the Duke of Malloryn, and no woman who's ever been in my bed has left it wanting."

"Even me?" she challenged.

Another long, slow, steady look. "Especially not you."

"Please. Don't exert yourself unnecessarily."

"And now I know you're untouched." The faintest of smiles played at the corner of his lips. "It would not be exertion, Duchess. In fact, I think I would enjoy it."

Her heart started beating a little quicker. "You would?"

Reaching up, he began to undo the buttons at her

throat. "I have been remiss in my duties, I see. I was quite irritated by your ploy. I never wanted to know why you were so desperate to marry me."

"It certainly wasn't your pretty manners or your charm," she said, swallowing as he continued down each button, slowly spreading the collar of her high-necked green frock open until the smooth, pale skin of her chest was revealed.

Malloryn glanced up from beneath his dark lashes. He was shockingly beautiful, in an unsettling, masculine way. He always had been. And then he smiled. "Wasn't it? Nor my obscenely large bank account? Or the oak leaf laurel I wore?"

"Any duke would have done," she replied, pressing her hands lightly against his shoulders for balance. The shock of cool air against her bare skin made her nipples harden. Adele shivered as he brushed the back of his thumb against her throat. "Any lord would have done. Anyone kind. Or someone like you, who was not kind, but staunchly opposed to the new fashion of blue blood lords simply taking what they wanted, instead of agreeing to a proper thrall contract where a debutante would be protected."

"Someone like me," he murmured, leaning toward her with an intense look in his eyes. Just before his mouth met her skin, his gaze dipped, and then the shock of his cool lips against her throat made her fingers clench in his shoulders.

She'd had lords force her down onto her back on cold stone benches in a garden, where but feet away swirled dozens of dancers inside a ballroom. She'd had them slash at her throat to drink her blood, and she'd fought and cried, and in the end none of it had mattered. She'd grown hard instead. Let them do what they wanted, while inside she pretended it would all be over soon, and her agile mind tried to find some way—any way—to escape this life of hers.

Then she'd found it.

She'd found him, and a rash decision had seen her throw herself at him, at his mercy, at his reputation. And wonder of wonders, he'd actually married her. She'd been safe for months, and it was a wonderful feeling. One she couldn't begrudge him credit.

She'd thought she could do it again, simply allow a man—her husband—to take what he wanted from her body and her blood, but what she hadn't expected was the faint stirring lash of his tongue against the thumping pulse in her neck. His teeth pressed firmly against her skin, a silken threat, and then his hand was sliding down over her breast.

It was happening again.

Adele ached everywhere. It was a horribly confusing emotion, for she had expected pain, expected to endure a little bloodletting and perhaps some groping.

She was wrong.

On all counts.

Her lord husband did not intend to drink her blood. His bite mark soothed instantly as he eased away from her, swiping his tongue over the flushed imprint. Adele shifted with a gasp. She liked the feeling. She liked the stroke of those slow fingers over her soft flesh. It was all a tease. A kiss against her throat, then lower, dipping into the hollow there. Another one painted against her collarbone, then lower. Lower... always lower. His lips brushed against the lace of her stays, and he licked her again, a long, slow swipe that left her breathless.

"Relax," her husband whispered, his breath stirring against her wet skin.

"What are you doing?" she whispered back, and realized his hands were curling around her wrists.

Slowly Adele found herself being lowered onto her back on the carriage seat. She kept her fists clenched in front of her chest when he let her go.

"Testing my theory." Malloryn straddled her hips, pinning her skirts with one knee and leaning heavily onto one hand over her. With the other hand, he brushed the back of his knuckles against her barely restrained breast. "What are you thinking about, Adele?"

"You're going to ruin my coiffure!" she blurted.

"Really?" Malloryn mock frowned. "Oh, I see I'm going to have to work harder than this then."

He curled over her, his shirt straining over the hard planes of his chest.

Malloryn's lips trailed across the sensitive skin of her throat, tracing little butterfly kisses there even as his thumb rasped against the turgid press of her nipple in slow, teasing circles that made her want to press her knees tightly together.

An odd sort of yearning swept through her. She was half-tempted to turn her head, to brush her mouth to his. He'd never truly kissed her. He'd promised he never would.

But all she could taste was Lord Devoncourt stealing that kiss from her, and she wanted, suddenly, to replace the memory with one of her husband.

Wishful thinking. His hands and mouth might be wreaking havoc across her willing flesh, but this had nothing to do with tenderness or stolen kisses.

"What's wrong?" he whispered, glancing up at her as his breath whispered over her skin.

Adele released the breath she'd been holding.

"I was wondering what I was going to buy with my newly increased pin money," she managed to say with a husky voice.

The smile on his mouth held all sorts of wickedness. "Maybe you can buy new undergarments, once I'm done with these?"

She looked down sharply.

Malloryn met her eyes as he tugged the edge of her bodice down, his perfect white teeth sinking into the scrap of lace that hemmed her chemise. The sharp ripping sound it made cut through the roughened exhale of breath.

And then he was tugging both her bodice and corset lower, revealing the flushed pink of her nipple.

His hot mouth closed over it, and Adele stifled a moan at the shock of sensation. Oh, God. She shifted uneasily, careless of her gown and hair, her fingers curling into claws as she fought the urge to touch him.

She wanted to rake her nails over his shoulders and arch her spine.

She wanted to thrust her breast into his mouth.

To beg.

To move.

But this was a game of wills now, to see how long she could defy him.

As Malloryn's tongue laved her nipple, she couldn't stop a small gasp from escaping her. The second he heard it, he flashed her a devilish smile, his lips wet and slick.

"Diamonds," she gasped.

"Great big ones, I'm sure," he replied, his breath against her wet skin punctuating each word.

Fingers stroked up her thigh, tugging her skirts toward her waist.

"Your Grace," she gasped, grabbing his wrist.

"What's wrong?"

"What are you doing?"

"I thought you were the expert, what with all the

lectures you attended. Besides"—his weight pressed firmly between her thighs as he cupped her hip and rocked against her—"this isn't the first time I've had my hand up your skirts. Only this time, I'm lucid."

The Ivory Tower. The bloodletting. The soft, exquisite pull of his mouth on her throat as she tried to save his life....

"Not in the carriage!"

"No?" His fingers traced mesmerizing circles across her garter. "Why not?" he whispered in her ear. "No one will see us."

Adele squirmed. Restlessness itched through her, demanding to be assuaged. Her corset clamped tight around her ribs, and the hot ache between her thighs became a loud demand.

"Aren't you curious?"

Yes.

Rolling onto one hip—and trapping one of her legs beneath him—he brushed the back of his knuckles against her drawers, pressing them directly against where she ached the most.

Adele captured his hand, her cheeks hot and no doubt red.

Their eyes met.

But she didn't push him away.

"How are those diamonds now?"

She said the first thing that came to mind. "Shiny."

"Mmmm." His knuckles brushed against her, and Adele's spine arched as she pressed into his touch, silently demanding more. "I'll bet they are."

The tips of his fingers breached her drawers, and then there was nothing but skin on skin.

"You're so wet," he whispered, stroking through the lush folds between her thighs. "I think you're lying about your diamonds, Adele."

"You don't know how much I adore diamonds," she managed to gasp.

"I think I know something you might enjoy even more than their glittering allure." His thumb traced teasing circles around her sensitive flesh.

"Oh?"

She sank her teeth into her lower lip as an exquisite sort of tension twisted through her lower abdomen. It was becoming harder and harder to pay attention to the words. All she wanted was for that touch... to move... slightly....

"I think if I replaced my fingers with my mouth right now, you'd love it," he whispered.

Adele's eyes widened in shock.

And then his fingers brushed over her, circling that sensitive nubbin like the lash of a tongue.

And his mouth lowered back to her breast, lips capturing her nipple, tongue teasing the rigid point.

It felt like there was a line tied directly between her clitoris and her breast.

His finger slid inside her, curling, just so. Stroking her lushly. "There's a part of me that wants to make you beg, Adele. Would you? Beg me for more?"

Those dangerous fingers held her right on the edge.

Adele's fingernails curled into the velvet of the carriage seat, and she bit her lip furiously, determined not to surrender.

But then his thumb joined the party, finally, finally pressing small, teasing circles against her.

Mouth and fingers and oh, God, what was she doing?

What was she thinking?

Have to... stay focused.

"Beg, Adele."

She shook her head, bit her lip harder.

But it was only prolonging the inescapable.

Malloryn's touch lightened, as if to hold her there, right on the edge.

Forever.

"Please!"

"As you wish."

A soft cry escaped her as the pressure increased, and she bit into her knuckles as pleasure rampaged through her. Adele lost all hint of herself as she writhed beneath him. Sweet gods. He was merciless, stroking her through each and every shudder. Watching her expression, the intensity of his eyes darkening as his eyelids hooded.

She clung to his shirt. Thrashed beneath his weight.

"Stop!" she finally gasped. "Please, stop!"

"Too much?" he murmured as he withdrew his hand.

Adele buried her face in his shoulder as her husband rested atop her. She couldn't look at him. She could barely move, a shudder tearing through her as her heart pounded.

How on earth was she to ever look him in the eye again?

"How many diamonds were there?" The self-satisfied purr in his voice made her want to commit bodily violence.

"So many I thought they were stars," she replied hoarsely.

And he laughed, as if her refusal to capitulate—even now—tore amusement from him. "Those weren't the diamonds, Adele."

"You don't know that."

Malloryn continued laughing even as he tugged her skirts down. Not a single lock of hair was out of place, and as she watched he took his handkerchief from his pocket and wiped his fingers dry.

She buried her face in her hands.

Good gods.

How mortifying.

How... intense.

Even now, she was filled with such languorous release, she felt like she'd drunk two bottles of champagne by herself. She couldn't have moved to save herself, but luckily, she didn't have to.

"Well." Even Malloryn sounded surprised as he eased off her. "I was beginning to think my recollections of what happened between us in the Ivory Tower were remnants of the bloodlust. Or insanity."

All she could see was the looming shadow of his body as the carriage eased to a halt.

"Insanity?"

Was that her voice, so low and rough?

He shot her a dark, mesmerizing look. "Shall we not be honest for once? We can call it the effects of the bloodletting—upon both of us—but something happened that day. Something neither of us has been able to forget, no matter how much we tried."

She was destroyed. A mess. And her husband looked almost immaculate.

He swayed onto his knees, peering through the window. "Oh, how unfortunate. We seem to be home." There was a maddening twinkle in his eyes as he tugged at the sleeve of his coat, forcing it to settle perfectly against him.

"Home?"

"You appear monosyllabic, my love."

Argh.

"You took me by surprise."

"With my proposition? Or what just happened? Still thinking of diamonds? Or emeralds?" His voice was a purr of pure masculine contentment.

"An entire choker of them," she whispered, refusing

to cover herself. Two could play at this game, and she hadn't missed the telltale bulge pressing insistently against her thigh. "Maybe I'll wear nothing but my diamonds when you visit my chambers. Would you like that?"

This time, it was his turn to look at her intently.

There, she wanted to crow. Take that, you arrogant ass.

"Maybe you can teach me how to beg," she whispered, and let her gaze shift lower, to where his erection trained against his trousers. "Perhaps I'd let you. Would you like to see me on my knees, Malloryn? Wearing nothing but my diamonds?"

Adele rolled upright, tugging her gown into place.

Inch by inch, he'd put himself back together, though she doubted he'd been truly undone. Her words seemed to stir some devil within him, however.

"Perhaps we can discuss this inside in more detail?" A muscle flexed in his cheek as the footman opened the door. "Tonight."

She smothered a small, victorious smile. "I shall be all aquiver."

Malloryn stared at her for a second longer, then disembarked.

"Oh, and Adele?" He paused in the middle of the carriage doorway, reaching inside his waistcoat pocket for something. "This ends. Right now."

With that, he handed her a photograph of her kissing Devoncourt.

CHAPTER FOUR

"You look particularly pleased with yourself," said a sultry woman's voice behind him.

Malloryn turned away from the window of the Company of Rogues' safe house, where he'd been idly tapping on the sill and pondering the events that had occurred in the carriage. He hadn't meant to take it so far, so swiftly, but Adele roused his temper—and his competitive instincts.

And, if he was being particularly honest with himself, his lust.

Lie back and think of England, indeed.

How on earth did she get to him so easily?

They'd spent months living in the same house, seeing each other only from a distance, and yet he could always sense her. Adele's perfume lingered in empty rooms, and everywhere he looked she was causing some sort of disruption. Even if it was just to shuffle the books in his private library, a place he'd asked her not to enter. She would move things deliberately, and at first he'd assumed it was to plague him, but now he had to wonder if she'd been looking for something.

"Should I not be?" he asked, glancing at Gemma's face. The beautiful spy was the one in charge of the Company of Rogues in his absence. "Nobody's tried to kill the queen in the past four months, London appears almost peaceful, and the Company of Rogues has been blessed with not one, but three recent marriages, with another soon to come." He feigned surprise. "In fact, it seems you and Obsidian are the only ones ruining the Rogues' almost perfect score."

"It's not cricket, Malloryn. Obsidian and I will marry when we are ready. It's not as though I have any sort of reputation to ruin, nor do either of us intend upon children." Gemma rolled her eyes and poured both of them a brandy. "And since when are you a proponent of marriage? I thought there was a universal ban upon Rogues frolicking with other Rogues?"

"Since when do the lot of you listen to me?" He accepted the brandy. "I stopped making edicts when it became clear every single Rogue was doing his or her best to flout them."

He'd formed the Company of Rogues over seven months ago in order to discover the mysterious mastermind behind a spate of attacks in London.

They were the best of the best in their respective fields, but following his rules was not one of their talents.

"Speaking of marriage," Gemma drawled, "Byrnes tells me you received the photograph."

Ah, there it was. He'd wondered how long she could bite her tongue.

"Yes."

"The entire encounter *may* have been innocent, Malloryn. She did slap him."

"I don't tend to believe in coincidences when it comes

to any of Balfour's agents."

Gemma gave him a steady look. "Byrnes said you'd take care of it. Does this mean you're planning a little light interrogation? Cuffs and all?"

"It's not as though I can lock my wife in a dungeon and demand answers. There are other means to get the truth." His eyes narrowed. "What else would you recommend?"

"No, no. Cuffs and caresses it is. It's just... seduction's not your usual style."

"Not as far as you're aware, no." Not his usual style, but not completely outside his realm of experience. Malloryn preferred to keep his assignations simple. Or he had, in the past. It had been months since he'd been with a woman. Before his marriage, in fact, though his recent spate of chastity had little to do with Adele. "I told her it's time to begin thinking of an heir. She won't think anything of it."

"And how goes your endeavor?"

Only Gemma could get away with such personal questions.

Though they didn't speak of it, he thought of her as the little sister he'd never had. Gemma had seen him at his worst, and despite her penchant for gossip, she'd kept the state of his recent issues from the other Rogues.

"I'm uncertain. Adele's a cunning adversary when she wants to be. And even I need more than a few hours to break her down."

"I shall be all aquiver."

He didn't know what to make of that statement. One moment Adele was playing the coy virgin, and the next she was challenging him.

The taste of her bare throat lingered, even now. He didn't know how the hell he was going to get through the next couple of hours. He'd forced himself to take his leave once he saw her safely home, but his cock hadn't seemed to understand.

Intolerable.

The bloody woman drove him insane.

"And if she's *not* involved in this plot? What then? Adele might have expectations in regards to your sudden change of heart."

She'd better not. "I'll deal with such a matter if it arises."

Gemma cut him a chastising look. "I just find it difficult to believe your wife is a spy owned by Lord Balfour. He *did* try to have her killed on your wedding day."

"And if I wanted to plant an operative in my enemy's house without having him doubt her, the first thing I'd do is stage an incident to make her appear a target. If Balfour truly wanted Adele dead, I'd have found her lying in the middle of her bed with her throat slit. Instead, his assassin kidnapped her and led you a merry chase, where we just *happened* to rescue her in time. Convenient, in my opinion."

"She saved your life in the Ivory Tower."

"All the better to worm her way into my trust."

"Well, for someone who's supposedly an enemy agent in your bed, she doesn't appear to have made much progress getting in there."

Malloryn peered down his nose at her. "Have you been examining my sheets every morning?"

Gemma shot him a sweet smile. "I don't have to. I know what a man looks like when he's only had his hand for company for several months."

My God. "We are not *ever* discussing the contents of my bed." It came out as a faint growl.

"Why not? It might do you some good to get a little action. You've been so tense even Byrnes is tiptoeing around you, and Obsidian—of all people—said you need a good f—"

"*Gemma.*"

She was outright grinning at him. "Prude. It might do you good. Ease a little bit of that pressure. You've been wound tighter than a corkscrew ever since you married her."

"My tension has nothing to do with Adele and everything to do with Balfour."

"Of course." Her drawl contained entire syllables of sarcasm. "It has absolutely nothing to do with the fact your very beautiful wife gets your back up in a way no woman ever has."

"Because I want to throttle her?"

"Because you very clearly want to do more than throttle her, and it drives you crazy. Because you can't control her. Because she challenges you. Because the second you get your hands on her I will place good coin on the fact the results are going to be... explosive."

"If I get wind of even a single bet placed on the outcome of this situation—"

"You won't," she promised. "Get wind of it, that is."

This was what he got for putting together a group of spies. Malloryn pinched the bridge of his nose. There'd been a flurry of wagers about whether he'd even get Adele to the altar or not.

"Don't you have something more important to attend to?" he growled. "Rather than interrogating me about my wife?"

Silence filled the study.

Gemma wet her lips and produced an envelope. "Actually, I was trying to ease my way into this conversation. A letter arrived for you several hours ago."

He stared at it.

The abrupt change in subject was somewhat jarring,

which meant Gemma was nervous.

Even before he reached for the letter, an odd sense of foreboding filled him. Gemma had been trained as a child assassin. It was rare to ever see a sign of nerves about her.

He turned the envelope over. "You did an excellent job of replacing the seal. This almost looks untouched."

"That's because it is."

Malloryn looked up, all of his senses coming to high alert. He had few qualms about the state of any personal correspondence that came into this house. If Byrnes wasn't somehow listening in to his conversations, then Gemma was probably rifling through his mail.

His butler, Herbert, made sure to intercept anything of note he wanted to keep private.

"Herbert found it sitting on your desk. None of the other Rogues placed it there, and there's no sign of a break-in. It simply appeared, and we have no idea how it got there."

Flipping one of his knives out of his sleeve, he slid it beneath the seal and plucked the letter out.

Dearest Auvry,

Did you miss me?

It's time to bring this game to an end.

There was no signature.

There didn't have to be.

He knew the handwriting as well as he knew his own, and a chill ran down his spine.

After four tense months, Lord Balfour had finally resurfaced.

"Balfour is back," Malloryn said as he seated himself at the head of the oval table that housed the rest of the Company of Rogues. Ten pairs of eyes looked back at him attentively.

Gemma ruled the team in Malloryn's absence, along with her lover, Obsidian, a *dhampir* assassin she'd lured from Balfour's side; Liam Kincaid and his wife, Ava, who were a contradiction of brawn and brains; Byrnes and his verwulfen wife, Ingrid, could hunt anything—including vampires; Charlie Todd could pluck the eyes from a man's sockets without him noticing, though his fiancée, Lark, might almost be better than him; Herbert, the butler who'd once been his personal assassin, fussed as he tried to pour tea for the ladies; and there at the end was Jack Fairchild, munitions expert and Malloryn's secret weapon against Balfour.

Most of them had been handpicked by himself; an elite team of blue bloods, verwulfen, and mechs who were at the top of their respective fields. Spies, thieves, bounty hunters, mechanical geniuses, and two Nighthawks who'd spent years tracking criminals and hunting murderers.

Lark was the only Rogue Malloryn hadn't personally vetted, but considering the fact she'd played a large role in rescuing him from Balfour's clutches in Russia, he'd welcomed her to the Company.

Besides, she and Charlie made a dynamic team. He wasn't about to look a gift horse in the mouth.

"It's about bloody time," Byrnes said, his eyes lighting up. "As much as I enjoyed the break after Russia, I'm tried of looking over my shoulder and second-guessing every clue I find. Is it Balfour? Or am I just seeing things?"

"The question is," Ingrid growled, "where is he?"

"More importantly, how did he get in?" Kincaid had turned into an overprotective bear of late, since his wife's delicate condition had become common knowledge among the group.

"It won't have been Balfour," Gemma argued. "He'll have sent one of his agents."

"Excellent." Byrnes grimaced. "Jelena or Dido?"

Malloryn had known it was coming and managed to control his flinch at the mention of Jelena's name.

It was the dreams he couldn't control.

"Dido," Obsidian muttered. "If it were Jelena, she wouldn't have been able to restrict herself to just leaving a letter. She'd have left a body."

"Preferably Malloryn's," Byrnes noted.

Gemma glanced at him as if to gauge his reaction, but Malloryn ignored her. She alone knew how deep his scars following Russia went.

Charlie leaned back in his chair. "Lark and I think we found the point of entry. There's a faint chisel mark under the latch in the attic window. Couldn't have been there long. This morning, I'd imagine."

Malloryn arched a brow. "Herbert?"

The butler looked chagrined as he added blood to Ava's tea and replaced the small flask in its ice bath. "You have my abject apologies, Your Grace. I noticed nothing amiss."

And if one of his best assassins hadn't noticed an intruder, then no one would have.

"Hardly your fault." Malloryn drummed his fingers on the table. "So... it seems Balfour wants me to know he's back, which means he has plans afoot. He'll have been here in London for weeks—possibly longer—no doubt. And he won't have made this move unless he was fully prepared to restart the game. He'll be miles ahead of us at this stage."

"We destroyed his London base and the *dhampir* who were working for him here," Gemma mused. "But that doesn't mean he doesn't have allies remaining in London."

"We just don't know who," Ingrid said.

"Yet." This from Byrnes.

"We know his targets, however," Malloryn said. "Myself, the Duchess of Casavian, Lord Barrons, and the queen. We'll start there."

"You're last," Obsidian said, glancing up from his thoughts. "He wants you to see London burn, so he'll go after one of the others first."

"And the Ivory Tower's impenetrable," Gemma added, "which means the queen should be safe."

"Technically, it's not.... He penetrated it the last time he was in London," Charlie replied, heat flushing up the back of his neck as he glanced at Gemma.

Balfour's men had planted a mind-controlling device in her brain, and activated it when she was within reach of the queen. With her skillset, she'd been within inches of assassinating the queen when Obsidian, Byrnes, and Ingrid managed to stop her.

She'd also come very close to killing Malloryn himself.

"We cannot afford to presume the Ivory Tower is safe, but we're prepared to counter the neural stimulating device now," Malloryn said softly as Gemma flinched. Concern went both ways. She had her nightmares; he had his. "But Gemma's correct. The least-protected targets are Lord Barrons and the Duchess of Casavian.

"Which is why Byrnes and Ingrid will be setting up a team of Nighthawks near Barrons's household. Get a team in place to protect the household and then return. I'll need both of you shortly." Malloryn tossed the letter onto the table, and it slid to a halt in front of Charlie. The lad examined it. "While the rest of us are going to start tracking down Balfour."

"The paper's of excellent weight," Charlie said. "Good ink. Fine tip on the nib used to compose it. You'd find this sort of equipment in any blue blood lord's study."

"We always knew he was using several aristocrats to plot his coup. They're the ones who were most disenfranchised by the revolution three years ago. All Balfour needs to do is stir up old resentments, and they'll flock to his cause."

They'd be the ones who were most likely to have access to the Ivory Tower, where the queen resided, too.

"Do you think any of the Sons of Gilead survived your cull?" Gemma asked. "We cut off the head of the snake, so to speak, but there were a lot of noblemen who were involved—or sympathetic—who simply faded into the background once Lord Ulbricht died."

Lord Ulbricht and his cronies had formed the SOG as a means of overthrowing the queen. Unfortunately, Lord Ulbricht met a bad end and the cause disintegrated.

Old resentments, however, died hard.

"Most likely. Byrnes and Ingrid reported dozens of masked blue bloods in attendance at Lord Ulbricht's estate when they went in undercover. I only managed to get my hands on thirteen of them, and none of them were members of any prominence or knew anything important. They were all executed, but the others remain among the general populace."

"So the SOG might rear its head?" Kincaid asked.

"That's one option, yes."

Like a bloody hydra.

He had more enemies than he knew what to do with.

"There is one last avenue to pursue," Malloryn said. "A recent development."

Both Byrnes and Gemma looked up.

"Devoncourt," Gemma said.

"One of Balfour's ex-Falcons has been sighted masquerading as the long-lost Earl of Devoncourt. We don't know what his intentions are, but I don't believe in coincidence. If he's pretending to be one of the Echelon's lords, then he's doing it for a reason. I want to know what that reason is."

"You want Ingrid and me to kidnap him?" Byrnes asked.

"Falcons are trained to resist interrogation," Gemma said. She should know. "Far better to watch him from a distance. He may lead us to other Falcons, or possibly reveal certain former SOG members. We don't want to reveal our hand too early."

"Precisely." Malloryn pushed back in his chair. "Gemma, I'm putting you in charge of tracking Devoncourt. Discreetly. I will let the queen know the threat is back, and tighten our security at the Ivory Tower."

"And your wife?" Gemma asked.

He ignored the speculative looks on everyone's faces. It was clear they were well aware of Devoncourt's interest in Adele. If he pressed the matter, he'd no doubt find a betting book somewhere in the bloody house.

"I will continue my efforts to learn what part my wife plays in all of this. If—as you say—Adele is innocent, then Devoncourt was sniffing around her for a reason. I want to know why. Adele is either a cunning knife at my throat, or an unwitting pawn in danger."

His tone left little doubt which one he suspected.

"Dismissed."

CHAPTER FIVE

"May I have this dance?"

It was Malloryn's voice, though Adele had not expected her husband to be in attendance at Lady Rutherford's masked ball.

Adele stilled, all of her senses narrowing in upon the presence suddenly at her back. Orchestral strings shivered through a waltz in the distance. Feathers and gold sequins flashed past as the masked inhabitants of the ball swept in graceful figures before her.

But the pair of them might as well have been alone.

She could think of no one else.

The flutter of her fan increased, though she refused to look at him. "Considering yesterday's proposal and your mysterious absence last night, I thought you'd forgotten me."

"Hardly. If I'd had any hope of succeeding in such an endeavor it would have been months ago." There was a wry edge to Malloryn's voice as he stepped closer. Her skirts stirred against her stocking-clad calves. "Try as I might, I can never quite manage to get you out of my mind, Adele."

A shiver went down her spine.

She didn't turn, even though she could feel his cool breath on the back of her neck. Nobody was watching her here, tucked away in the corner of the ballroom, but she couldn't help feeling as though she danced the edge of scandal.

Ridiculous.

Malloryn was her husband, after all.

"You give a good impression of it," she retorted, trying to slow her fan and look disinterested.

A fingertip brushed against her back, rippling over the taffeta of her peacock-colored gown. "Did you wait for me?" her husband murmured, his voice soft and indecent.

Adele closed her eyes. *Yes, damn you. All night.*

"Not at all," her mouth said.

"*Liar.*"

Somehow, she knew he was smiling. "What do you want?"

Malloryn held out his gloved hand as he circled her. She couldn't stop her gaze from lowering to his stern mouth, though the black hawkish mask hid his features and its cascade of feathers disguised his coppery hair. A bird of prey. How eminently suitable.

"A dance, Adele. Consider it an apology for my absence. I've been seeing to some business."

"You never apologize."

"Perhaps it's time for peace between us. Dance with me."

"Do I have a choice?"

"I've probably earned that." The faintest of quirks crossed his mouth. "You could deny me. Nobody knows who I am right now, so the gossip would be minimal. Though I warn you, the consequences might be dire."

"What sort of consequences?"

He brought her gloved hand up to his lips, and his voice turned to liquid heat. "Try me and find out."

Adele glanced around, but the idea of dancing with him intrigued her. They'd never danced. Barely even conversed in a rational manner. Peace.... What a fascinating concept.

It didn't make her lower her guard entirely.

She accepted his proposition with a careless shrug that extricated her hand, and set it on his arm. Far safer than having it beneath his lips. "Don't think I'm afraid of your consequences."

"No?"

"Intrigued," she admitted. "I've never seen you dance."

"I generally prefer not to."

"And now you're offering to dance with *me*," she mused. "One might say that's somewhat suspicious."

It all had to do with Devoncourt's kiss, she was sure of it.

But what to make of it all?

Malloryn had told her to make her own arrangements, yet his reaction yesterday when he tossed the photograph in her lap belied the instruction. And now, here he was, showing up at a ball and asking her to dance with him.

Curiouser and curiouser.

If Adele was a foolish young debutante, she might almost have thought him jealous.

But she'd long given away such ridiculous notions.

Her husband was up to something.

His gray eyes heated behind the black velvet of his mask. "Well, if I don't make a move, some other young buck might."

"There'd be more rumors swirling if people knew it was *you* holding me in his arms, than some handsome stranger."

"You think me handsome?"

The thought clearly amused him.

"To lie would only make me seem an idiot. You're a veritable product of Michelangelo's imagination, and you know it." Her fingers squeezed the muscled flex of his upper arm, which was hidden beneath his coat. "Carved of chilling perfection, radiant with an unearthly strength and power. Just as cold as *David* himself and twice as untouchable. Indeed, one would expect to find more warmth in the statue's caress."

"Mmm." His head lowered, his lips brushing the curls in front of her ears. "But we both know that's not the truth, don't we, Adele?" His thumb stroked the pulse in her other wrist, a lash of sensation. "Or do you not recall yesterday afternoon in the carriage?"

Her pulse started to race. Of course she recalled it. How could she not?

The memory of his touch had haunted her all bloody night long, whilst he was off seeing to "some business."

"Perhaps I should remind you?"

"Perhaps we should dance?" she blurted.

There was that smile again as he led her onto the dance floor.

She'd never dared dream of finding herself in her husband's arms—dreams were for foolish girls, not those who'd tasted the darkness that could be found in one of the Echelon's ballrooms.

And yet, it was startling to realize how easily she fit there.

"Considering you prefer not to dance, you're very good at it," she admitted in a begrudging tone. Of course he'd mastered the art. He took the lead with a control and mastery that left her no choice but to keep up.

"My mother would have been pleased to hear that. She spent a fortune on dance tutors when I was a youth."

Adele's curiosity pricked. She'd been all through Lady Hammersley's *Guide to the Peerage* and could trace his origins as well as she knew her own.

A minor son of the House of Malloryn, he'd surprised the entire Echelon when he'd steadfastly climbed his way to the head of the house upon the death of his father. Or murder, if one was being accurate, though the killer was never named.

There were several ways one could legitimately inherit in the Echelon: have the good fortune to be born as the eldest son of an eldest son; or duel your way to the top.

She'd heard rumors of a dozen duels fought to clear his path, alliances between cousins against him, betrayals, attempted assassinations he'd somehow survived.

And when his cousins all fell, Malloryn was the only one left standing.

The youngest duke to ever sit on the Council of Dukes.

Ruthless.

Dangerous.

And yet, utterly loyal to his queen.

But it was the little things she didn't know about him—that he'd had a mother who'd insisted on dance lessons for her son, despite knowing he'd most likely never inherit anything of value. She must have dreamed of great things for him, but Adele wondered what had driven him to survive those bloodstained years where he nearly lost everything.

"You're quiet."

"Just thinking," she admitted.

"A dangerous thing, in my experience. What are you thinking about?"

"How little I truly know of you."

He swept her through an elegant turn, his gloved hand resettling on her waist even as his thumb stroked her hip. "I thought it was the title that mattered. Not the man."

"The title is what every debutante dreams of. But the man intrigues. Everyone likes a good mystery."

"What do you want to know?"

Why did you agree to marry me?

He'd asked her a similar question on the day of their wedding.

And when she'd trapped him—running breathless and bloodied out of the gardens of a ball, straight into his arms—he'd maintained it was a matter of his honor being besmirched by her claims that he'd done it to her.

But he was the Duke of Malloryn.

If he could survive a dozen bloodthirsty cousins, then he could survive her lies.

And yet he'd allowed the engagement to stand. He'd done his duty and married her. And while their marriage was a thing of locked bedroom doors and aloof greetings in the hallway as they passed, he'd never actually punished her for the lie.

"I want to know—" Her courage failed her as they swirled between dancers. "—what your mother was like."

Malloryn's left brow flickered in surprise. "She was a baron's daughter who married into the ducal line. My father was far down the line of inheritance, but it was a good match between them. They seemed happy together. She died of consumption when I was sixteen. My father was inconsolable."

That was all very good, but.... "And how did her son fare?"

Their eyes met, and she saw the faint tightening of his mouth. "As well as could be expected."

A polite disengagement.

He may have decided to seduce her into bed—or whatever game he was playing—but the message was clear: she was not welcome behind those walls.

She would never be welcome.

Somehow, Adele managed to paste a smile on her lips. "Well, she would be pleased to know her lessons have not gone to waste. One could almost think you were born to play the role of duke."

A slight hesitation. "It was not what my parents aspired for me, but forced on me by circumstance."

There'd been a woman, she'd heard.

Another lord's thrall.

And the girl had died, and Malloryn swore bloody revenge and set about taking it on his own terms.

"And what of you?" he asked. Lights glittered as they twirled in elegant circles, but all she could see was the watchful glint of his eyes. "From what I understand, you haven't seen your mother in months."

Adele fought to contain her instinctive stiffening, but he noticed. He always did.

"It seems she and my father did not welcome the news of our marriage," she admitted carefully. "There is no love lost between me and my mother."

Or my father, truth be told.

But where Sir George Hamilton seemed content to pretend he'd never laid eyes upon her, Adele's mother was a different story.

The only time they spoke was when Lady Hamilton wanted more money.

Did Malloryn know of those exchanges?

Her sister's peace and virtue in exchange for cold hard pounds?

"And here I thought I'd managed to escape family

dinners with the in-laws," he said. "I thought your parents would be thrilled to have landed me."

Adele took the opening he gave her and smiled in return. "Believe it or not, Your Grace, you are not universally adored."

"No?" Despite the mask, she was certain one eyebrow arched faux mockingly. "What conspiracy is this?"

"Perhaps you would earn the hearts of others more easily if you smiled more."

"You like my smile."

"So brilliant for its rarity," she responded, with the faintest flirtatious shrug. "Is that not the way of precious things?"

"Like diamonds, for instance?" His gaze dipped to the elegant array that dripped into her cleavage. "Though one would doubt their scarcity, considering how positively aglitter you are tonight."

He swept her beneath his arm, and then she was back in his arms, slightly breathless. This time he drew her closer, and she couldn't escape the brush of his thighs against her skirts or the stroke of his thumb across the inside of her wrist.

"You seem intrigued by them. I thought I was the one with the obsession with diamonds?"

"You can only blame yourself," he whispered. "All I can think about is your parting words of yesterday. What was it you said? 'Maybe I'll wear nothing but my diamonds when you visit my chambers....'"

She'd rarely been so bold before. Adele fought to conquer the blush she could feel heating her cheeks.

He held her too closely now, and she caught the flash of speculative glances thrown their way.

"People are watching us," she whispered.

"I know."

Malloryn spun her under his arm again, his palm resting but briefly on her silk-clad waist. By the time she waltzed back into his arms, they'd escaped the press of dancers, and he'd somehow maneuvered her under the arch of ivy that led to the gardens.

Away from the ballroom.

"Why don't we go someplace private where we can escape their prying eyes?"

"How convenient, Your Grace."

"I thought so myself."

Adele rested her hand in his, some part of her missing his touch on her waist. "I only agreed to a dance."

"I'm trying to convince you it would be in your interest to accompany me further."

Adele shivered as his voice lowered. "In my interest?"

"You haven't yet accepted my apology. I thought to earn it instead."

"How?"

She looked at his mouth, barely inches above her own. The same mouth that had been on her breast yesterday afternoon. As if the memory conjured the sensation of his touch, Adele felt it again, her nipples hardening behind the crush of her corset.

"Don't look at me like that, my dear." A whisper of pure temptation. "I'm not going to ruin the surprise."

Malloryn's voice had always been a weapon. She'd heard actors on stage with less control than he wielded. One second his mouth caressed her name, made her think of silken sheets and the heated lash of his tongue; the next it was a cutting whip, flaying the skin off someone who'd crossed him.

But now....

Lucifer tempting angels to sin.

"Are you going to allow me to steal you away to the

gardens for a midnight rendezvous?"

Somehow she found her breath as he took a step back into the shadows of the arch. "Should I? I'm still not entirely certain I should forgive you."

"I dare you," he replied, holding his gloved hand out to her with a merciless smile curving his lips. "I'll make it worth your while."

And Adele, damn her better sense, couldn't stop herself from taking his hand.

She was clad in cobalt blue with a peacock mask dripping feathers, and her hair gleamed like pure gilt in the lantern-light.

Think what he might about her, Adele was born for moonlight and silk, stolen kisses and whispers, throaty laughter and lies. In other circumstances, Malloryn might have pursued her.

He wanted to unearth that pale, creamy skin and reveal the flawless curves beneath the silk. He wanted to pin her to his mattress and fuck his way into her, making her scream with pleasure. He wanted to bind her wrists behind her back and leave her helpless to his whims.

It was what he disliked most about her: his inability to deny that some dark part of him found her irresistible.

It was the way she always challenged him.

It had to be.

"You think to ravish me in the garden, Your Grace?" Adele fanned herself, glancing around at the greenery as if disinterested. "First the carriage and now this. Do you have some aversion to beds?"

Malloryn tossed his mask carelessly aside as they reached the folly, and stepped toward her. Lanterns were strung throughout the trees, leaving her radiant and glowing. "Perhaps I can't resist you long enough to wait."

The faintest of laughs escaped her. "Tell me, is any woman actually foolish enough to fall for that ruse?"

"Is it so impossible? You're the most beautiful woman inside that ball."

Despite the fact she was possibly an agent of his enemy, he didn't deny the truth.

Adele speared him with a look. "Now I *know* you're up to something. You despise me, Your Grace. You've made no attempt to mask your opinion of me—until now—which means you have an ulterior motive."

"I don't despise you."

"You give a fair approximation of it."

"I despised your tactics in bringing me to heel." He considered her. "You've always been beautiful. I state it as a matter of fact, not flattery. And... you did save my life when I was shot."

It was the first time he'd ever truly touched his wife.

Blue bloods could heal from practically anything, but when Balfour put a mind-controlling device inside Gemma and she'd shot him, he'd been bleeding so badly he couldn't pursue her when she went after the queen.

Adele—of all people—had happened upon him and given him her blood, though the first he'd known of it had been when he came out of the ravening rush of the craving and realized he was clasped between his wife's thighs. His mouth had been on her throat, the coppery taste of her blood wetting his tongue, and his hand had been working its way up her thigh.

He had very nearly deflowered his wife on the floor of the Ivory Tower.

"It's not as though you were actually dying, Malloryn." Adele rolled her eyes, but he caught the faint stain of pink that swept her cheeks. "You made certain I was aware of that. Giving you blood helped accelerate your healing, but it didn't save your life."

"Did I say that?"

"You did."

"Then I was an inconsiderate fool."

Green eyes narrowed and she pressed a hand to his chest, stepping forward until they were barely inches apart. "What are you up to?"

His gaze fell to her lips. Those soft, rosy lips. He'd never tasted them. It was easier to play the part of besotted lover than he'd have imagined. "As I stated, I need an heir."

"Then throw me down on the bed and have your way with me. I believe that is how it works, does it not? And yet, you're actually attempting to"—for a second her facade slipped, impregnable insouciance giving way to confusion—"seduce me."

"You don't trust a gentle touch."

"I don't trust *your* gentle touch."

And yet, she wanted it. He could read it in the softening of her body and the way she leaned into him—even as she leashed her body's physical needs. To win her over, he would need to enrapture that cool, rational mind too—because she'd seen right through his physical flirtations.

Clever girl.

"You're right. I have no need to make such efforts." Malloryn's lashes half-shuttered his eyes. "And yet, my conscience dictates I make them. I am not the sort of man who *throws* a woman down on his bed and simply takes what I want, like some sort of barbarian. I am the Duke of Malloryn."

"Ah, arrogance." Adele tipped her chin defiantly. "Now that I can believe. I would hardly call it conscience.

You don't have one."

Despite himself, a smile brewed. "Be careful, my dear. For if that statement was true, you would be in a great deal of trouble right now."

"What would you do to me?" Adele bit her lip. "*Chastise* me?"

He stared at her. *Was she...?* She was. She was daring him. Practically flirting, if one didn't notice the calculating gleam in his eyes.

Malloryn leaned closer, until their breath mingled. "Like I said, I'm hardly a barbarian. I could think of other ways to make you rue your words."

Adele's gloved hands came to rest upon his coat. "I think every blue blood is part barbarian deep inside." Those hands slid lower, pausing over the flat ripple of his abdomen. She looked up, dark lashes fanning across her cheeks as her voice softened. "You all call it your primal side. Your craving. Your hunger. And you leash it, and think it obeys you. But it's still there, Malloryn." A thumb stroked inside his coat, inside his waistcoat. "I wonder what it's like when you let it off the leash. All that civilization stripped away from you. Your raw desires given sway. I wonder.... What would he be like?"

Good lord, she was actually attempting to turn the tables on him.

He felt that touch stroke lower, as if her silken-gloved hands actually curled around the thickening length of his cock. The words, the touch, the glance—all designed to intrigue and inflame.

Adele Cavill, you little devil.

If he'd been a lesser man, she'd be wrapping him around her little finger.

"You don't want to meet that side of me," he whispered back. "He doesn't play nice."

"Doesn't he?" She took a step back, her expression alight in a way he'd never seen before. "Maybe I don't want him to play nice. Maybe... the thought of unearthing the true Duke of Malloryn intrigues me. No more masks between us. No more twisted words. No more games. It would be interesting. And I think I could trust *him* more."

Malloryn captured a fistful of her skirts, holding her there. His knuckles strained within his glove. "There's a reason I leash my darker instincts, Adele. That man is ruled by his passions. He's a little dangerous."

"Perhaps I like a little danger?"

Inch by inch, he tugged her closer. "Do you?"

She certainly enjoyed driving him insane.

"I must admit you had me at odds and ends yesterday in the carriage," she said. "But I have been thinking about your proposition. Why now?"

"Why not?"

"Because you've never glanced my way before."

He sensed the doubt in her words and paused to consider how to play this. "If you think I haven't glanced your way, then you should think again. Every day your laughter echoes through the house. Your perfume haunts my library. I can hear the water dripping off your skin when you bathe—"

"Even through the locked door between our rooms?"

"*Especially* through the locked door."

"You're the one with the key." She glanced up, and he could sense her battling arousal in her efforts to keep a clear head.

Malloryn smiled. "Maybe we should unlock that door. Maybe tonight you should wear nothing but your diamonds when you retire."

"And if I do, are you even going to make an appearance? Or am I going to be left wanting again?"

So she *had* awaited him last night. His smile softened, became a little dangerous. "I don't know. I think I like the idea of you waiting for me." Brushing his knuckles against her bodice, he heard her faint gasp as they rippled over the hardened edge of her nipple. "Waiting and wet. Desperate for my touch."

Adele stepped back, her eyes glittering.

"Now it begins to make sense." She circled him. "This is a game to you. It's not merely your sudden requirement for an heir."

"Everything in life is a game. It's simply a matter of who plays it best."

"You think you can make me enjoy this, don't you? Did you imagine I would surrender? Did you think I would melt beneath your touch and beg you for more? I suppose I must seem the ultimate challenge. I don't like you. You don't like me. Did you imagine you would steal my heart?"

"I didn't think you had one, Adele. Isn't that what you said once?"

He turned his head to watch her. Skirts gave a silken rustle as she came back to the front.

"But you want me to beg," she whispered, her eyes glittering with heat. "Don't you?"

For a second, he felt an answering heat swell within him too. He'd thought this would be a challenge, but no more than any other woman who guarded her heart. It had seemed a forgone conclusion. He was the Duke of Malloryn, an expert in both understanding the base desires of a person and wielding such desires with a metaphorical lash. Adele would surrender. A fun game while it lasted, but not a long one.

But the challenge in her eyes....

She'd read him too.

And she knew exactly which buttons to push to ignite

his own sense of curiosity.

"Yes," he whispered as she settled directly in front of him, her shoulders squared. "I want you to beg. I want you to scream with pleasure, my dear. I want to own you."

"You couldn't," she shot back, "even if you engaged all of your prowess. My heart does not rule me. I will never allow any man to own my happiness, or my desires."

Now it was getting interesting.

He stroked the back of his gloved hand down her bodice, barely touching the silk. Adele's breasts lifted as she smothered a swift intake of breath.

But it was there.

And they both knew it.

"Are you daring me to try?"

She set one hand to his chest and pushed.

He stepped back.

"Be careful, Your Grace, that I do not consider my own attempt. I'm not the only one who can fall."

Malloryn captured her hand and held it there, where she could feel the thump of his heart. "I should like to see you try."

A breathless moment extended as they beheld each other.

Adversaries always.

But for the first time he felt something else between them. He'd been furious when she'd first trapped him into marriage, but there'd always been a tiny little part of him that had been intrigued.

Nobody got the better of the Duke of Malloryn.

But Adele had.

The constant sparring between them grated at first, and yet he had to admit it had become a little bit of a game between them. Now this....

He had a horrible feeling he might have finally met his

match in this woman.

Lifting her gloved fingers to his lips, he brushed his lips there, soft and decadently slow, even as he never took his eyes from her.

"What are you suggesting?" she murmured.

"War."

"Isn't that what we've been engaging in all along?"

"Not like this." He slowly turned her wrist, mouth whispering over the thin black silk that hid her pulse point from him. "Carnal warfare. The first to surrender loses. I'll even allow you a head start. You dictate how far each encounter goes."

"That's too kind of you."

"You're the one who said you were innocent," he pointed out. "It seems I have an unfair advantage."

His cock strained against the placket of his trousers. He'd said it to give himself the luxury of extending this chase between them—to give himself time to discover if his wife was innocent or dangerous. But the flex of his cock warned him: Adele was dangerous in more ways than one.

Because he wanted her.

Here.

Now.

And desire was possibly the only thing that could undo him.

"Innocent of pleasure, perhaps. Not of men's desires. Or their arrogance. I accept your deal. You were right," she said with a devilish smile. "You did make this worthwhile."

Then she set her hand against his chest and pushed insistently.

"But since I am in control of our game, it seems I must decline tonight's advances. Tonight *you* can go unfulfilled."

He trapped her hand there. "You don't accept my

apology?"

"I'm fairly certain I didn't hear one."

Her smile glittered as brightly as the diamonds around her throat.

"'Til tomorrow then." Malloryn couldn't deny it wasn't disappointment that filled him, but interest.

He allowed her to escape.

"Dream of me," she whispered, backing away from the folly, lantern-light gleaming on her blue skirts. "All alone, wearing nothing more than my diamonds."

Why had he ever thought inexperience took away her edge?

"I *will*," he promised darkly.

And then she turned and dashed away through the gardens, glancing back over her shoulder, just once, to make sure he was watching.

Malloryn felt his weight shifting forward, the predator within him drawn to chase her. To capture her. To win. Adele's silvery laughter caught his ear as she read it on his face.

And then she was gone.

He crushed his fingers into a fist and forced himself to rein his darker urges in. Every part of that act had been choreographed to an inch, designed to intrigue him. And she'd succeeded. If they'd been dueling, then she had drawn first blood.

He could practically sense the jaws of her trap woven carefully around him. What a dangerous, dangerous woman.

He'd never been more convinced she was working for the enemy.

CHAPTER SIX

Adele felt breathless as she clutched her skirts and dashed up the stairs back to the ballroom. An odd mix of victory, curiosity, and challenge filled her as she left her husband staring after her, and her cheeks ached from smiling so much.

For the first time since their wedding, she finally felt as though she held a little of the power between them.

And he'd *given* it to her.

Thoughts of Malloryn so distracted her that she hurried into the ballroom and slammed directly into a firm male body.

Hands caught her forearms and a husky laugh escaped her assailant. She was two seconds away from panicking when the scent of Devoncourt's familiar cologne caught her attention.

"If it isn't my favorite duchess," Lord Devoncourt mused, though his eyes flashed dark for a second, and he reached up to brush his thumb against her mouth.

Adele jerked her face away. "What are you doing here?"

Oh, God. If Malloryn followed her there'd be bloodshed.

She could still hear the chill in his voice when he cast that cursed photograph in her lap.

"This ends. Right now."

"When I saw your husband lure you into the gardens I thought all was lost, but here you are, rushing away from him as if you had the hounds of hell on your tail."

Nobody was watching them, but she couldn't afford to be seen here.

And she owed Devoncourt the truth: that while his flirtations had made her feel, for a moment, as if someone cared, they could not continue.

She grabbed his sleeve and hauled him into a nearby alcove. He wasn't even wearing a mask, as if he wanted the world to see him act so familiarly with her. "Are you *trying* to ruin me?"

"Trying, my dear. You've led me a merry chase."

Rough hands captured her face and his lips loomed close. Adele twisted her face away, her heart hammering as Devoncourt's mouth mushed wetly against her cheek.

"Unhand me, you idiot," she whispered, shoving against his chest. Every hint of desire she'd felt in the gardens with her husband shriveled up. *What was he thinking?* "My husband will kill you if he sees you."

Devoncourt staggered back, his brows drawing together. "He knows?"

The second his lips quirked, she realized he wasn't entirely displeased with the notion.

"He knows," she replied, then dragged her silk glove against her saliva-wetted cheek. *Really.* "He was displeased and insisted it go no further."

Devoncourt's smile held an edge she didn't like. "Malloryn can go to hell." His eyes focused on her again.

"It's not as though he's ever given a damn about you, Adele."

"I'm quite aware of his feelings toward me, thank you very much." *Probably more than you yourself are.* Adele mimicked a smile. This needed to end. "Devoncourt, while I am fond of you, you caught me at a weak moment the other night. I owe my husband a debt I can never repay. I do not intend to cuckold him."

"So you'll play the dutiful wife, even as he flits about town with his mistress."

Her smile died. "That is between me and Malloryn."

"Did he threaten you?"

You don't have to look so happy about it. "No. He simply insisted I end this flirtation. Think what you like of him, threats are not Malloryn's style."

Though she'd never expected seduction to be his style, either.

Devoncourt took a step closer, shadows obliterating half his face. "Be careful, my cherub. You wouldn't know what your husband's style is."

"Considering I spend most of my days in his home, I would like to think I have some idea. Malloryn doesn't care for scenes. And he certainly isn't violent. Particularly with women."

Cold and distant, perhaps.

But never cruel.

She might find herself starved of affection as his wife, but she'd never outrightly fear him.

"Isn't he?" Devoncourt leaned closer to whisper in her ear, "Do you have any idea what your husband gets up to of nights?"

"I'm not an idiot. I've heard the rumors. He promised me he's ended it." And she trusted her husband's word of honor, if nothing else.

"Poor, sweet cherub. He's pulled the wool over your eyes quite neatly, hasn't he?" For a second, his smile seemed almost a sneer. "I wasn't talking about his mistress, my dear. You know nothing about the duke. You have no idea what manner of man you married. I only thought to protect you, Adele."

What on earth was he speaking of?

She wanted to look down her nose at him, but a hint of unease trickled through her. What did she really know of Malloryn? Devoncourt spoke as if he was up to something nefarious.

"Protect me from what?"

"What's coming." His eyes hardened as he brushed a finger against her mouth again. "Why don't you ask your father about Malloryn's extracurricular activities?"

"My father? What does my father have to do with any of this?"

Sir George Hamilton had been unhappy upon her engagement, to be sure, but he'd never said anything else to her.

"Just ask him."

If there was anything she disliked more than being ignored by all of the men around her, it was when they spoke over her head like this.

"If you have something to tell me about my husband, then pray tell me. I dislike innuendo, Devoncourt. It smacks too much of insubstantial rumor, and I've been the victim of said rumor in the past. I don't appreciate it. Nor do I appreciate this attempt to put doubts in my mind. What do you know of Malloryn?"

"Just... be careful, cherub. Malloryn's made many enemies in the past few years. One day that's going to return to bite him, and that day might be sooner than you'd like. I wouldn't care to see a woman as beautiful as you torn down with him."

And then he was gone, and despite her bravado she couldn't help frowning.

Just a little.

Because while she might have defended her husband, she couldn't deny the truth: Malloryn wasn't spending his nights in *her* bed.

"She's late," said a cold, hard voice in thickly accented English. "You should have sent me, instead."

"If I'd sent you, my dear, you'd have brought me Malloryn's head, and I'm not quite ready to take it. Death is too kind an alternative for what I have in store for him."

Lord Balfour leaned against the stone pillar in the half-ruined tower, silently surveying the night. The old church had been burned during the prince consort's reign when the consort banned the practice of any faith that condemned blue bloods as soulless monsters. From here he could see half the city, including the elegant marble tower where he'd once ruled from on high.

This city was mine. And now I am but a rat scurrying about the shadows, gnawing at the corpses.

His lips pressed thinly together as he chastised himself for the thought. Weak men gave into their emotions and played their cards too early. It was impatience that had brought him so low in the first place.

Just remember, it was a rat that brought London to its knees all those years ago, during the plague.

"The death I would grant him is not kind one," Jelena said.

There was a flicker of movement in the shadows at the base of the church. A glint of gold as someone slipped through the rubble.

"I am tired of games," Jelena continued. "I want blood."

He'd have to let her off the leash soon enough, for her temper could be dangerous once roused. A little bloodletting and she would subside, like a cat that had finally filled its belly.

But he couldn't allow the claim on Malloryn's life to go unchallenged.

Balfour looked at her.

A cold blue eye locked on him, the other shrouded behind a black leather eye patch. She'd always been his most loyal *dhampir* agent—fanatically loyal, if he was being honest—but ever since Malloryn escaped her clutches in Russia and turned the tables on her, Jelena had thirsted for the duke's death with a vengeance.

"Patience," he murmured. "Malloryn must suffer."

"I can make him suffer. It will not be quick death."

Taking a step forward, he set his hand on her hair, gently stroking it. "He hurt you. I understand. But that sanctimonious prick has been a thorn in my side for years. I died at his hand." Balfour brushed fingertips across the corded scar across his throat, where Malloryn had cut him. "And I was reborn like a phoenix into this new life, this new body. But his death is *mine*. And mine alone. I owe him that. Mind you do not forget it." He grabbed a fistful of her silvery hair and forced her to look at him. "Do you understand?"

"*Da*, Master."

When he released his grip, Jelena bowed her head.

Footsteps echoed on the stone stairs.

Balfour patted her hair gently again, and then turned to greet his second-in-command.

"You're late." Jelena's insubordinance put a chill into

his tone.

Dido swept into the tower, looking for all the world like a fairy-tale princess in her gold gown and heavy velvet cloak. Albeit one who could rip your throat out with her teeth if she willed it. "Malloryn had his little bitch at the ball. I had to extricate myself carefully, as she was watching both exits."

"Gemma Townsend?"

"Who else?"

"And?"

"It appears the duke has taken your bait." Dido tossed her glittering gold mask on the ash-scarred table in the center of the tower. "Townsend was shadowing Devoncourt, and Malloryn's attention was fully focused on his wife. He was practically panting over her."

Interesting.

From what he'd heard of the marriage, it had been an alliance and nothing else. The duke and duchess lived separate lives, and his spy in Malloryn's household reported that the duke despised her.

"Is his interest in Devoncourt or his wife?"

"Difficult to say." Dido tossed the cloak from her shoulders. "Perhaps he's interested in the wife because of Devoncourt's sudden attentions to her."

This was why he'd sent her.

Jelena wouldn't have noticed the difference. Nor would she have cared.

"Definitely a situation to watch." He couldn't dare hope Malloryn would fall for the girl. That would be a gift from the gods. "And how did your meeting go?"

A faint sneer graced Dido's lip. "He'll be difficult to control but he has the influence of his peers. They prefer him to the other candidate you proposed."

"Then remove Darlington from the equation and give

Sir George my encouragement."

"He wants to know how you intend to bring the queen down."

Balfour paused. "My, my, he has grown big for his boots. Tell him that if he wants to know my final plans for the queen, then he needs to prove his loyalty. The latest shipment of explosives is due to arrive. Sir George owns three warehouses down by the docks. Tell him I'll be using those warehouses."

"I'll enjoy that," Dido said. "He thinks I'm beneath him because I'm a woman."

"Most of the older Echelon does." More fool them. Balfour had long since learned women could be the most dangerous of species. "Excellent. While Devoncourt and his wife divert Malloryn's attention, why don't we see if we can push forward with the Prometheus project?"

"And me?" Jelena demanded, like an overeager puppy.

"It's time to send Malloryn another message," he said, turning to her. "Would you like to spill some blood, my dearest?"

"Anything to report?"

Malloryn slung his coat off his shoulders and draped it over the back of his chair as Gemma followed him inside his study at Hardcastle Lane. He poured the pair of them a drink.

Gemma tossed her mask down on the desk. "She met with him again."

Malloryn froze, the brandy halfway to his lips as he tried to sort through the implications of her statement. "My wife?"

"With Devoncourt." Gemma slumped into the chair

opposite him in a spill of bronze taffeta. "Perhaps I was wrong. Perhaps she is working for Balfour. They seemed quite intimate as they withdrew to a small alcove. I couldn't get close enough to hear what they were saying, alas, but it was shortly after she returned from the gardens."

Where Adele had practically challenged him to seduce her.

Malloryn set the brandy down on his desk and tugged at his cravat to loosen it. *Well. And here I thought matters were proceeding according to—if not quite the plan, then certainly proceeding.*

A hundred questions circled through his mind, but what came out was, "Did he kiss her again?"

An uneasy expression crossed Gemma's face. "I don't know if it was precisely a kiss. Strands of ivy hung over the alcove and I couldn't get too close. But he grabbed her face and leaned in, and... something happened."

Son of a bitch. "Devoncourt's starting to irritate me."

"He may have just been whispering in her ear."

I may just strangle him with my bare hands.

"Don't even think about it. He's our only lead to the remnants of the SOG," Gemma pointed out, interpreting his expression accurately. Her blue eyes narrowed. "You're not actually jealous, are you?"

"Of course not." Malloryn threw back the entire glass of brandy. The burn of it cleared his mind. "But it's one thing to challenge me, quite another to try and blatantly seduce my wife in front of me."

"Oh, of course." Her eyes twinkled as she sipped at her glass. "We can't have that, can we? You only have yourself to blame. You told her—"

"I know what I told her. We have reached a new agreement."

"Oh?"

Malloryn set the glass down. "First one to submit."

Gemma burst into a laugh. "No wonder you've got your britches in a twist. My, my, all is not going according to plan?"

"Actually, this works perfectly," he mused. "It gives me time to work out Adele's loyalties without having to push her into bed."

"I shouldn't have thought it would be a problem? You're clearly attracted to the girl."

Attraction wasn't the problem. It never had been.

Others may have been indiscriminate with their bed partners over the years, but he'd never been comfortable flitting from bed to bed. He'd suffered enough betrayal in his lifetime to warrant a natural caution when it came to taking a lover. He desired trust, in the least, and preferred a mutual friendship, if he could find it.

He had none of those aspects with Adele.

Only pure, carnal desire.

Challenge.

An odd sense of grudging respect.

"This is merely a means to an end," he replied. "I need to know Adele's loyalties, not... whether we are well-matched in bed."

"You should find out." Gemma shook her head. "It's been months since you've even glanced at a woman. It worries me. I know you still regret what happened to Isabella, but it wasn't your fault. You cannot simply lock yourself away like a monk, just because Balfour's a threat to anyone who gets close to you."

And there it was.

The other reason he didn't dare get too close to another woman.

The baroness had been at his side for years. First as a friend, and then as a lover, and now, as yet another weight upon his stained soul. He'd tried to protect Isabella by ending their arrangement, but it had been too late.

Balfour had used his neural stimulating device to make her betray the Company of Rogues, and then kill herself.

"*I love you*," she'd said, and they'd both known he didn't feel the same. He'd seen the fire in Isabella's eyes die as she realized she'd never been more than a friend to him. Seen it fill her from within with bitterness.

Guilt. What a familiar taste it left in his mouth.

"Watch me," he murmured.

Gemma shot him a long, slow look. "You've never spoken about it."

"What is there to say? Balfour killed her because he thought he could hurt me." *He succeeded.* "Until I have his heart in my hand, nobody is safe and I cannot allow any distractions."

"You—"

"I need to speak to the queen," he said, pushing to his feet and swaying just slightly.

"You need sleep."

He shrugged back into his coat. *What little of it I can manage to snatch....* He wasn't tired enough to guarantee himself a dreamless slumber if he tried. And with Balfour arisen from the shadows and Jelena lurking out there somewhere, he doubted even exhaustion would allow him such.

"Unfortunately, there's no rest for the wicked."

"Are you still having nightmares?" Gemma said, stepping directly in his path.

He glanced toward the door. She was the only one who knew. He'd like to keep it that way. "They come and go."

Sympathy softened her face. "If you wanted to talk about it—"

"I do not."

A sigh escaped her, and she reached up and fixed his collar. "Then go warn the queen. And try not to murder Lord Devoncourt before we've extracted what we can from him. Or at least, try and understand precisely why he bothers you so much first."

Malloryn strode through one of the hidden tunnels that led into the queen's apartments at the top of the Ivory Tower.

The sound of merriment echoed within, but he had a good idea of her schedule and knew who her companions would be.

As he slipped out from behind a tapestry, he saw Sir Gideon Scott rise to poke the fire. The leader of the Humans First party was a stout man with gray at the temples of his dark hair and a dashing moustache. That he'd attached himself to Alexandra so soon upon her return from Windsor spoke of machinations.

The man was no doubt up to something: Some new law or rule he wanted to discuss in private with the queen. They were never far from each other's side these days, and Malloryn couldn't help wondering what they were plotting.

Several of the queen's attendants sewed and cleared platters, providing an escort for the queen.

One nearly dropped her platter when she saw him appear out of the shadows. "Your Grace!"

"Ah, my Lord Stormcrow." The laughter faded from the queen's eyes as she caught sight of him. "You look particularly dire."

Sir Gideon looked up sharply. "Malloryn."

He exchanged polite greetings with the room and bowed to the queen. As he rose, their eyes met.

Her Highness's smile never faded, but she clapped her hands, capturing the attention of her ladies-in-waiting. "It seems my holiday at Windsor has left me with a mountain of paperwork to sign, no doubt. I shouldn't wish to bore my ladies. You may all retire while Malloryn drones in my ear."

The three ladies-in-waiting curtsied and left the room.

Sir Gideon did not.

"What news?" the queen asked briskly.

Malloryn waited until the doors were properly closed. "You received my missive?"

The queen's hands paused in the middle of pouring herself tea. "I did not."

"Balfour is back."

A breath hissed between Sir Gideon's teeth. "You're certain of this?"

"I do not speak unless I am certain." Malloryn produced the letter from within his coat. "He left this on my desk. In my house."

No need to explain which precise house he referred to.

The queen's expression gave nothing away as she read it. "So Balfour has risen from the ashes once more. I do wish you would do something permanent about that sometime soon, Malloryn. I grow weary of looking over my shoulder."

"If he was so easy to kill, I would have done it. He's a cockroach."

"Then he means trouble?" Sir Gideon looked worried. "You think he'll make another attempt on the queen's life?"

"In the least. I've sent orders to have the guards doubled."

The queen made a vexed sound in her throat. "Let me guess..., you're here to convince me to cancel a certain number of my forthcoming engagements."

Malloryn didn't bother to lie. The queen knew him too well. "Yes."

Alexandra pushed to her feet, her skirts swishing around her ankles. "My fifteen-year anniversary is coming up."

"I know."

"No," she snapped. "No. I will not put it off. It's been nearly fifteen years since that bastard murdered my father and put me on my throne. Four years since I became queen in truth and not just name. I will not cancel my celebrations just because my husband's little lackey wants to take my crown. We've been planning this for months. The people are looking forward to the parade. Sir Gideon assures me it's vital they see me out in public, and not locked away up here like a spider toying with their lives. There's been so much unrest—"

"Most of it stirred by Balfour," he reminded her. "And as much as the people might wish to see their queen, I daresay it wouldn't do public morale any good if someone put a bullet through her head on the parade route."

She narrowed eyes at him.

"You think Balfour will make his play for revenge during the queen's celebrations." Sir Gideon stroked his moustache thoughtfully.

If he wanted Alexandra to consider what he was proposing, he'd need Sir Gideon's cool head on his side.

"Why would he not? It's very public, very visible. It would make a great spectacle and holds a certain sense of theatrics. I don't think he'll be able to help himself."

"Gideon?" the queen whispered.

"We can cancel the extraneous events," Sir Gideon proposed. "The parade will be more difficult, and the ball is meant to bring the Echelon back together. It's not just the human races who resent the lack of progress in recent times."

"Hang the blue blood aristocracy," the queen snapped. "They've caused me nothing but grief. Now. *And* then. And they're the prime cause of said lack of progress."

"Does this include me?" Malloryn asked coolly. "Lord Barrons? Lynch?" He saved the best for last. "Your dearest friend, the Duchess of Casavian?"

The queen's lips thinned.

"You are their queen too," he reminded her. "And while it frustrates you to see their rallies against your new laws, you cannot hate them all. You cannot crush them completely, or you are no better than your husband was."

Alexandra drew back as if slapped. "You dare?"

"Speak the truth?" he pointed out. "Blue bloods have the same right to exist as humans do. You will never weld this country together if you resent one and not the other. Change is happening. And yes, it is slower than you may like, and yes, there are always going to be teething problems with each new law we introduce, but if you take this stance then you play directly into Balfour's hands."

The queen paced like a cat backed into a corner. "Gideon?"

"For once I agree with Malloryn," Sir Gideon replied.

She turned on Malloryn, and he knew he'd won. "I will cancel all the parties and the fireworks. The parade will go on as planned. The ball will stay. In the meantime, find that bastard and bring me his head."

Malloryn met Sir Gideon's eyes as he bowed. "I will do my best."

"Do better than your best, Malloryn. This time, I want no failures."

CHAPTER SEVEN

The war began on a Wednesday.

Malloryn would always remember that, afterwards.

It began at midafternoon when he was dressing for the day, meticulously knotting his cravat with half a mind as he played through the queen's demands for her forthcoming anniversary parade.

A sound caught his attention.

The flurry of movement next door.

Maids' murmurs. Heels coming and going, as if in a mad dash.

And his wife's voice. "Get rid of it all."

Malloryn met his valet's eyes.

Simmons looked away swiftly.

The servants all knew the duke and duchess kept separate bedchambers. The door between had never been breached, and he'd never intended it to be.

He completed the cravat—a task he never allowed Simmons to do—but his attention kept returning to the door as a maid gasped in shock behind it.

What the devil was going on in there?

"Has my wife broken her fast?" With blue bloods sleeping through most of the day and carrying out their revelries at night, London society had evolved to fit their schedules.

But sometimes Adele was out of bed early enough in the day to have it still be deemed morning.

"I believe she has, Your Grace. She's been about for several hours."

"Causing mayhem?"

Simmons coughed politely into his hand. "I believe it could be considered so. Will that be everything, Your Grace?"

Malloryn dismissed Simmons with a wave of his hand and moved toward that bloody door. He paused a moment before he turned the key. There was only one, of course, and it resided firmly upon this side.

There was absolutely no reason doing this should make him feel as though he crossed an irrevocable line. It was just a door. But he paused all the same. With a soft click, he eased the door open, encountering mayhem.

The duchess's chambers were in an uproar. Silk and velvet swathed everything. Hats cascaded across the divan and the carpets. Feathers and gowns adorned the bed.

And in the center of it all stood his wife, gowned in an exquisite concoction of seafoam green that made her look pure and innocent, all soft ruffles and a gauzy bodice overlay that hid the smoldering curves that were her best weapon. Curly hair bound back in a loose chignon. Breathtaking, to be sure, but... hardly the sort of battle visage he'd expected. Innocence wasn't the sort of thing to entice a man like him, and she'd made it clear she intended to bring him to his knees by fair means or foul.

Four maids stared at him with wide-eyed horror.

Adele hadn't noticed. No, she was too busy flinging

her armoire open and considering the contents.

"Good grief," she said, hauling out a filmy nightgown she dropped on the floor. "What was I thinking?"

Adele tossed something behind her, and he caught it before it hit him in the face, glancing once at the four maids in dismissal. They bobbed a hasty deference and practically fled, and that was when his wife finally noticed him.

She spun in a swirl of green skirts.

"A little early for spring cleaning, isn't it?" Malloryn opened his bare hand.

Silk. The palest of pinks, edged with frothy white lace. A frilly little peignoir with lace so thin across the bodice it would be...

See-through.

Aha. There was the first strike. His gaze slowly shifted back to Adele.

She blew a curl off her forehead, hands on her hips. "Did you know, I actually thought I would need a wedding trousseau. I wanted to please you." She rolled her eyes. "I promised myself I would be the best wife you could imagine. I would strap myself into pretty white corsets and lacy chemises that would make the veriest maid blush. I would do my duties, lie back and think of England—"

"You do think of England quite a lot," he mused. "A sacrificial martyr on my altar?"

"It sounds silly, doesn't it? What would the Duke of Malloryn do with such an insipid creature? She was becoming quite maudlin, but I'm tired of playing that Adele. She was a fool who miscalculated rather badly. It's time to become the new Adele."

"Oh?" He belatedly discarded the garment—if it could be called such a thing—into the trunk with all the others.

The impression of the silk lingered against his skin.

"Do tell," he murmured, sliding his hands into his pockets. "Does this new Adele have a certain agenda?"

"She might. I've made an appointment with Lena's modiste, Madame Lefoux."

"Madame Lefoux?" He failed to understand. "I've never encountered her name, I'm afraid."

"A pity. Every husband should know Madame Lefoux's efforts at least once in their lives."

Malloryn's gaze sharpened upon her at the sultry sound of her voice.

"Ah," he said, as Adele swanned closer. "That kind of modiste." His gaze raked her from top to toe. There was something different about her today; a new kind of confidence. And he still wanted to get to the bottom of her appearance. There was something... out of place about it. "Is that a new gown?"

"This old thing?" A strange light filled her eyes as she reached for his collar. "No. I've worn it many times."

"It looks... different."

"That's because I'm not wearing a stitch underneath it," Adele whispered as she began to fix his cravat.

Tension slid through him.

Two could play at this game.

"An excellent opening salvo," he admitted.

"I've been thinking," she murmured. "You said I was in control of how far matters between us went."

"And? What did you decide?"

"You've never kissed me."

His smile slipped. *Unlike Devoncourt*, he wanted to say, but the surge of emotion that came with the thought was a trifle bothering. "I kissed you the day we married."

"The barest touch of your lips to mine."

"And that's what you desire most? Right this second? A kiss?"

A kiss was intimate.

Unnecessary for what they planned.

It seemed an odd request. But he could see the answer in her eyes. *Yes.* She wanted that kiss. She wanted his kiss.

Was that the angle he could work to win this game between them?

"I will trade you," he said. "A kiss on your lips in exchange for a kiss elsewhere."

Those green eyes sharpened. "Elsewhere?"

"Wherever I desire."

He watched the turmoil race across her expression. Need. Want. And yet, suspicion.

"Why do I feel like I'm walking into a trap?"

Because you are, my dear.

"You've already kissed me elsewhere." A hot blush stained her cheeks as she no doubt remembered that interlude in the carriage.

"But not everywhere," he pointed out. "I promise you will enjoy it."

"I'm sure I will. One kiss," she finally conceded. "For another."

"Wherever I choose."

"Only if your kiss is worth it."

Malloryn smiled. "You like making rules."

"I like being in control. You've always been the one who made the rules between us." Adele eyed him with a challenging glint, and he realized she expected her kiss now.

Malloryn stepped forward, his nerves thrumming with anticipation. "You place such a high price on such a simple exchange. One would think you'd never been kissed."

"A dozen times," she admitted. "But never by my husband."

Malloryn stroked his thumb across her mouth. All pretty and pink, glistening with moisture. It was the type of mouth that could hypnotize a man, if he wasn't careful. His voice dropped. "Then he is a fool."

"I like to think so too."

A breathless laugh escaped him. Every time he thought he had control of the situation, she would surprise him.

"I've never kissed my wife either. I've thought about it. Sometimes."

In the dark of night, when he listened to her breathing on the other side of that door.

More than once he'd woken from fevered dreams of Russia, desperate to turn his mind from such nightmares. He'd refused to allow the servants to leave a lantern burning at night to still the dark, and those moments where he woke—disorientated and confused—were the worst.

She'd been his escape.

Even as he feared to reach out and find himself locked inside the Iron Maiden Jelena had put him in, he would hear Adele's soft breathing. If he concentrated, he could make out the slow, steady throb of her heart. An anchor in the dark. A means to remind himself he was safe, in his bed, in his house.

Not alone.

And as the panic surged, a crushing wave seeking to drown him in the darkness again, he'd use anything to force it back. Even memories of *her*.

"Now I know you're lying," Adele chided.

"No. I'm not." Malloryn realized his finger pressed against her lip and he hadn't moved. "I don't want to think about kissing her," he confessed. "But sometimes, in the middle of the night, I do. I think about that time in the tower, when I came back to myself with my lips on her skin. I think about the soft gasps she made. The way the skin of her inner thigh felt like silk beneath my fingers."

He ran the pad of his thumb across her lower lip in a hypnotic action. Back and forth. So soft. A shiver ran through her, but Adele merely parted her mouth, and, never taking her eyes off him, sucked on the end of his thumb.

Heat flared through him.

His cock had long since roused, but as he felt the sharp edge of her teeth, it flexed eagerly.

"And sometimes I've wondered if her mouth is as soft as it looks," he whispered, fingers stroking her cheeks as he leaned down and replaced his thumb with his mouth.

Adele's lashes fluttered shut as she tilted up to him. Their lips met, the barest of touches, a replay of the kiss he'd granted her on the day of their wedding.

But this time he pressed deeper.

Took more.

He stole the breath from her lungs with a gentle, devastating caress. The taste of her morning's lemon tarts was still on her tongue, and he sought to drink it from her mouth, as if he could steal that too.

Palms slid up his chest as Adele opened beneath him. It was intoxicating, how swiftly passion burned to life between them. He felt like he'd been waiting months for this, hard and aching in his bed, while the door provided sturdy barrier between them. The soft slick of her tongue darted out, touching his. He'd meant this to be a seduction of the senses, but for the first time, he realized it wasn't just Adele who was being seduced.

The words had gotten to him too.

Because they'd been the truth.

She exhaled, and he tasted her breath in his mouth as he slowly licked her tongue. Adele wilted against him, soft arms sliding around his neck as her breasts were crushed against his chest.

And there was the craving, rising in his veins, wanting, demanding.

The darkness of his very soul seeking release.

A growl escaped him as Malloryn slid one hand down the smooth flex of her spine, finding the curve of her bottom. She, too, hadn't been lying. She was wearing not a stitch beneath the silk. Fingers sinking into such luscious flesh, he ground her hips to his, relishing in the feel of her soft body against the fierce ache of his cock.

Adele's eyes went wide as she drew back from the kiss with a gasp, her lips passion-swollen and as pink as raspberries. He had only to track her swift downwards gaze to realize he'd surprised her.

She might kiss and flirt like the devil, but she'd been honest: She was an innocent through and through.

And he needed to get a hold of himself.

Eyes glazed, he rested his forehead against hers. "I believe it is time for *my* kiss."

"Do you think you earned it?"

"I know I did." He pushed closer, brushing his lips against her cheek, and trailing them across her ear. One hand slipped the cap sleeve of her gown from her shoulder. "But you can try and deny it."

Adele shivered. "Do your worst then."

She had no *idea* what he intended.

Brushing his mouth across her bare shoulder, he slid his hands down to her hips. And then he hauled her up into his arms, and strode toward the bed.

"What are you doing?" she squeaked.

He tossed her down on the bed and knelt between her thighs, his knees trapping her skirts as he leaned over her. "You just threw down your gauntlet. I am merely returning the favor." A smile escaped him. "Did you think it would be that easy? An exchange of kisses?"

"No." Her eyes seemed a little wild.

Oh, this was going to be fun.

"What are you planning?"

"Use your imagination, Adele." He bent lower, breath whispering across the lace of her décolletage. "Maybe I wanted to see whether you were telling the truth, my dear."

"About?"

"Whether you were wearing a stitch...."

Capturing her knee, he dragged it up against his hip. Her skirts fell to her knee, leaving nothing but her stockings beneath his palm.

"It's the middle of the day!"

"Yes." He slid her skirts up slowly, so slowly. Thumb catching on her garter, he stroked back and forth, enjoying both the feel of the material and the sudden look on her face. "Won't the maids be scandalized?"

"You said—"

"Anywhere."

"Yes, but...." Her eyes widened. "But...."

He pressed a finger to her pretty rosebud mouth. "My choice, Adele."

A heated shiver ran through her as he dragged that finger down over her stubborn chin and throat. Hooked it in her bodice and tugged the garment lower, until her nipple threatened to escape.

"Here?" he whispered.

She lay utterly still, barely breathing, as if to see where that finger would end up.

"Or here?" He kept going, their eyes locking, as the fabric covering her abdomen shirred beneath his stroke, lower, lower—

There.

Adele froze.

And then her thighs clamped on either side of his

hips, and that breath finally escaped her, as if she realized there was no escape.

"You wouldn't," she gasped.

"All pretty and pink, just like your mouth. I wonder if it will taste as sweet?"

Malloryn tugged at his cravat, drawing it loose from his throat.

She watched every movement he made as shock gave way to sudden curiosity.

Capturing her hands, he knotted the cravat around them, and then glanced at the scrolled iron headboard. Perfect. Malloryn bound her wrists over her head and then eased back onto his knees as he surveyed her.

"What are you doing?" She arched her spine to look over her head at where she was tied.

"You're the one who wanted the barbarian. So now he is throwing you down on your bed and tying you to it."

"I never said—"

"Oh, I know." Malloryn lowered himself over her, hovering on his knuckles. "But you've mentioned it once or twice now. I think the idea isn't as appalling as you pretend it is. You were right, my sweet." He nipped at her lip as he confessed, "There is something inside me that enjoys the idea of ravishing you. But there's something inside you that wants to be ravished. I could see it in your eyes. I can hear it in the rush of your breath. And if I stroked between your thighs right now, I'm sure I would feel it." His voice grew a little rough. "You're wet, aren't you, Adele? So. Damned. Wet. I want to taste it on my tongue."

Another half-strangled squeak wheezed from her.

Malloryn smiled as he brushed the back of his fingers down her cheek. So pretty. "You wanted a kiss. Will you let me kiss you *there*?"

She took command of herself with a firm hand,

glaring at him boldly. "You're the one playing the ravishing barbarian. I thought he'd simply take what he wanted."

"Ah, ah, ah," he chided. "Say it. Will you let me kiss you there? And just so you are forewarned, my dear, it will be an exact reenactment of the one I bestowed upon your mouth."

Her clever little mind raced, but he could see the moment she capitulated. Or was it capitulation? For she looked at him with a boldness he'd not expected. "Never let it be said that I renege on the deals I make."

He barked a laugh. "No, never."

Under his touch, the slither of her silk skirts whispered up her thighs. The only thing she wore was her stockings, he saw immediately. White silk stockings with pretty pink garters. Ribbons and lace. Decedent and sensuous, in a place that only he would ever see.

"Were these for me?" He suddenly wanted the answer to be yes.

"Who else?"

But she swallowed and watched as he slowly, slowly slid her skirts higher. Pausing just before the apex of her thighs.

"Show me," he whispered, for the fun wasn't only in giving her pleasure, but making her concede.

Inch by inch her thighs widened, even as her breath caught in her chest. Adele closed her eyes at the last moment, the hem of her skirt hiding her from view.

"Wider," he whispered.

And, blushing prettily, she spread her thighs, revealing all.

He wanted to devour her.

He wanted to make her scream and beg, and concede this first round in the war between them.

Brushing his lips against her thigh, Malloryn breathed

in her scent. A flinch went through her at the touch, but not one of denial. Instead, he heard her breathe in....

And then hold it.

"You're so beautiful," he whispered, his tongue darting out to taste her skin as he nudged her thighs wider.

He pressed a gentle, nuzzling kiss to her damp flesh.

"Malloryn." A single word. A moan.

Not quite a plea.

Not yet.

It would be.

Adele's spine arched, her thighs trembling as she clearly fought the urge to close them. Malloryn looked up the length of her body, delighted to see the heated flash of her green eyes upon him.

"Did you like the stroke of my tongue against yours?"

Her head thrashed back against the pillow, and she strained at his cravat. "Absolutely not. It was horrid."

Defiant until the end.

He laughed. "We'll see if you like this better then?"

Thumbs spreading her, he lowered his mouth and claimed her, his tongue plunging into the warm, wet heat of her. Adele cried out, her thighs clenching around his head, but there was no stopping him. Not now.

It was an echo of what they'd done with their mouths. A deep kiss, right at the heart of her, tongue lashing over the swollen, aching quiver of her clitoris as Adele gasped, and cursed, and writhed in her bonds.

Shock gave way to pleasure in her voice.

She was begging now, lifting to meet him, her hips arching. Splaying a hand over her abdomen, he pushed her down, and looked up the length of her body to see the damage he'd done written all over her expressive face.

Biting her lip, she threw her head from side to side. "Oh, my God."

Suckling her heated flesh, he gave himself over to the taste of her. Let himself take what he wanted in hungry, claiming caresses. Soft, helpless cries tore from her lips, urging him on.

He wanted her undone.

He wanted to punish her for going to Devoncourt last night after she'd challenged him in the garden.

He wanted to make her forget any other men who'd ever crossed her path....

His. She would belong to him and him only by the time he was through with her. Malloryn slowed, the rasp of his stubble branding her thighs as he pushed her right to the edge and felt it quiver within her.

Her fingers clenched and unclenched in their bonds, and her wrists strained white as she gasped and looked down, passion-drenched eyes bleeding a stormy, turbulent green.

Their gazes caught and held.

The shock of connection made him ache viciously as he nuzzled against her slick flesh. He wanted her to see him like this. Wanted her to know who brought such ruin upon her. Enemy agent or no enemy agent, he was suddenly determined to bring her to wrack and ruin.

But first....

"Say 'please,' Adele," he whispered, blowing cool air over her heated skin.

For a second he thought she wouldn't do it. Submitting wasn't in her nature. And he kissed her slowly, fingers sliding into her wet sheath as he tortured her with the promise of pleasure and never quite gave it to her.

"Please."

The word was torn from her.

"Oh, God. *Please!*"

Her release was just as wild and unfeigned as it had

been in the carriage. Malloryn captured her hips, holding her spread beneath him as he licked and suckled and pushed her through a firestorm of passion.

A scream forced its way free of her as she came.

God, he wanted to tear his trousers open, free his straining erection, and plunge into her wet and willing body. He stayed with her through every ruinous moment, loving the helpless quakes her body made as he nuzzled her and ate at her.

And then she was collapsing back onto the mattress in a sprawl of sweat-dazed limbs and trembling aftermath.

Mine, he thought, with a dark smile.

He rose to his knees, ignoring the insistent press of his erection as he wiped his mouth. The musky taste of her stirred the darkness within him. His heart pounded, and all the blood rushed through his veins. *Take her*, whispered his hunger. She was right there, spread open like a flower beneath him.

But he hadn't won yet.

And he wanted her to know he'd beaten her at this little game.

"Delicious," Malloryn whispered as he tugged her skirts back down. "You make the prettiest noises."

"You bastard," Adele breathed, but it wasn't in fury. No, she looked soft and rumpled and delightfully undone.

It was difficult to see her as a ruthless spy while she lay on the bed like this.

Difficult to see her as anything more than a breathless wife just experiencing her first taste of passion. He very much wanted to explore further.

"Tell me," he murmured, leaning over her and stroking his finger across her lower lip, "which kiss did you prefer? Yours? Or mine?"

Adele bit his finger, her eyes dangerous. "Tell me," she

rasped, her voice low and smoky, "how much do you want me to ask for more? Since I control how far this goes?"

Malloryn held his breath.

And then he smiled.

"It would be too easy."

Leaning down, he painted a whisper of a kiss across her swollen mouth, his tongue licking hers, before he broke free and drew back.

"I believe that is check. And mate. Have a lovely afternoon, my sweet." Malloryn tugged his cravat free from the bedhead with a small smirk. "Give my regards to your modiste. This was my round."

CHAPTER EIGHT

Modiste be damned.

Adele fumed as she paced the parlor of Lena's house, her skirts swishing around her ankles.

It was becoming quite apparent she was outclassed in every way that mattered when it came to seducing her husband. He had— And then she'd—

Her breath caught. Oh, God. She could still feel his hands and mouth on her skin. Still hear her soft gasps and desperate pleas.

How mortifying.

How frustrating.

How... insanely pleasurable it had all been.

"What on earth are you doing?" Lena's voice rang from the doorway. "Adele, what is it? You look beside yourself."

"I need help," she said, knotting her hands into small fists. "I couldn't think of anyone else I could turn to. Especially not with this small problem I am facing."

"Of course." Lena swept toward her, clasping her hands. "You know I will always help you. What is it you need?"

Oh, God. She hated even admitting this. "I am facing a slight marital issue I had not anticipated. I have started a war with my husband, and he's destroying me."

"What?" Lena's voice rose, her eyes flaring bronze as her protective instinct rose.

"Not like that. I need tactics. I need knowledge."

"About...?"

"How do I bring my husband to his knees? How do I—" The words choked in her throat. "You and your husband are quite familiar with each other. I see the way Will looks at you—as if you set the sun in the sky. You are his everything. You fill his whole world. And he gets this sort of look on his face whenever you smile at him, and I *know* what that look means. It's as if there's no one else in the room when he looks at you like that. No one else in the world. How do you do it? It's becoming quite clear my lessons in flesh rights are ineffective. I know what goes where and what Malloryn would expect of me, but I have little idea in how to truly drive him crazy."

Lena blinked. "You want to *seduce* the Duke of Malloryn?"

"Yes." Adele released an unsteady breath. "I want to ruin the man. I want to drive him to his wit's end and leave him a panting, pleading husk. It's your own damned fault. You set this in my head the other day and then he.... He set his first piece into play, so to speak."

Instantly, Lena's eyes flashed with heat. "This is going to require some instruction."

"You'll help me?"

"To bring Malloryn to his knees? I would enjoy nothing better. The man's insufferable."

"You don't know the half of it," she muttered.

Lena was already turning, leading her toward the door.

"Come with me. This calls for champagne."

"'Allow your husband or master to insert male appendage into the feminine vessel. Discomfort can be eased by overzealous application of Madame Vexley's Liniment for Young Ladies internally, though it is advised to apply such ministrations before attending your husband, in your private toilette. A gentleman prefers discretion and one does not wish to insult him by indicating less than fervent ardor on your behalf. Apply....' Good grief." Lena smothered a laugh. "I feel like I'm reading a cooking manual. I've never had to use Madame Vexley's Liniment. And Will's the very antithesis of discretion."

"What the hell is going on?" asked a loud male voice. "I can hear the pair of you gigglin' all the way down the street. And I heard me name?"

"Will!" Lena cried, sitting up with a happy little smile. "And Alex. My two favorite men in the entire world!"

Adele nearly spilled her glass of champagne as she hastily reached forward to flip the cover of Mrs. Hathaway's *Obligations in Marital and Flesh Rights* closed. The illustrations and sermons within the book seemed far too prudish for what she'd thus far encountered with her husband, but Lena had been pointing out discrepancies.

Much to their mutual amusement.

The verwulfen ambassador dwarfed the room, his broad shoulders straining against the cut of his shirt. He'd discarded his coat somewhere, his necktie hanging open and the top buttons of his shirt undone. Will Carver always seemed uncomfortable in society, but in Lena's sitting room, with his son draped over his chest and shoulder, he looked seemingly at home.

Bronze eyes raked the table between them and the ruin of a platter of little teacakes, scones, jam and clotted cream. "Enjoyin' ourselves, are we?" he growled, though the edges of his mouth kicked up. "It's barely three in the afternoon."

Lena waved her champagne flute at him. "We're plotting mayhem. Mayhem requires champagne. Besides, I knew you had Alex for the afternoon."

She pressed a half dozen kisses over Alex's chubby cheeks, and the baby immediately reached for her.

"Who's the recipient of said mayhem?" Will asked, trying not to drop the lad.

"My husband," Adele said, pointing her empty champagne flute at him. "You're a man. Can I ask you a question?"

Will grimaced. "I ain't gettin' involved in any marital disputes. Especially not Malloryn's."

"You know him!" Adele was delighted. Or perhaps that was the four glasses of champagne she'd consumed.

"I've had that pleasure."

"So has Adele," Lena snickered.

Will clenched his eyes shut and then tilted his face upwards, as if praying for divine intervention.

"Malloryn made a deal with Adele," Lena continued. "He would set his mistress aside, on the grounds that Adele would provide an he—"

"*Any*way," Will said, patting Alex on the back. "Look at the time, me boy. Let's leave your mother and her friend to their plottin'."

"Don't you dare. You're here to provide a male opinion on matters."

Will muttered something that sounded like, "I'd rather jump into an entire pit of snakes, thanks very much."

"Just listen. I volunteered your services."

"For what?"

Adele bit her lip. "There's a slight problem I'm having. It's not uncommon knowledge that my husband spends his nights away from home, but we made an agreement—"

"Stop right there," Will warned. "It ain't any of my business."

"Oh, Will. Stop being such a prude," Lena chided. "If this were the Warren, you'd be all up in Blade's secrets, regardless of your antiquated notions."

"This isn't the Warren. And Malloryn ain't Blade."

"Agreed," Adele said. "He has much better taste in waistcoats than the Devil of Whitechapel, to begin with."

"Waistcoats aside—"

"Lord Devoncourt said I didn't know what my husband was getting up to of nights. Indeed, he was almost nasty about it," Adele blurted. "But Malloryn promised he'd set his mistress aside. And yet, he's always off somewhere at night. I don't know where he goes."

"And I said what we needed was someone who could track him," Lena said. "Like Will."

"Will could," her husband replied, "but Will ain't goin' to do anythin' of the sort."

Lena turned big brown eyes upon him. "I hate seeing Adele so out of sorts. I know you don't want to get involved, but what if this isn't merely the result of Malloryn dallying with a mistress? What if he's in some sort of trouble? You heard what Adele said. Devoncourt practically threatened him."

"If there's one thing I'm certain of, it's the fact that Malloryn is more 'an capable of handlin' himself."

"*Please?*"

Adele watched with fascination. She could practically see the fierce verwulfen rogue turning into a little puddle of mush at his wife's feet.

What would it be like to have a man so enamored of her that way?

"I will make it worth your while," Lena whispered. "No application of Madame Vexley's Liniment required."

"What the hell is Madame Vexley's Liniment?" he growled, as if to maintain his fearsome reputation.

"See," Lena told Adele pointedly. "I told you it's hogwash. Completely unnecessary."

"You do not wish to know," Adele advised, when the verwulfen ambassador looked as if he was going to pursue said topic.

"Adele was there for me during my confinement, when I was so worried Alex was going to be born with the loupe," Lena said, touching his arm. "She was the one who defended your name in society when Lord Maddesley was trying to claim you were nothing more than a beast. I owe her, Will."

"Fine," Will growled. He tipped his head to Adele. "I'll follow him tonight. But if I catch wind of a mistress, then I am done with this mad plan. Understood?"

"Understood. Thank you!" she said, her shoulders slumping in relief.

Finally.

She'd have some answers.

Even if they weren't necessarily the ones she might desire.

CHAPTER NINE

It was Byrnes who brought Malloryn the news.

There was a body in Clerkenwell, and the Guild Master of the Nighthawks had requested his presence.

Unusual in itself, for the Nighthawks were comprised of rogue blue bloods that'd never been accepted into the Echelon. They were London's law enforcement, and a dead body was something they dealt with on a regular basis.

Which meant there was something out of the ordinary about this one.

Malloryn took a hack through the hubbub of the late afternoon street, accompanied by Byrnes, who was uncharacteristically quiet. Only the cracking of Byrnes's knuckles broke the silence.

A wall of Nighthawks had cordoned off the street ahead of them, so they were forced to disembark and walk the rest of the way.

He could scent the blood before he even arrived.

Garrett Reed, the Guild Master of the Nighthawks, strode forward to meet them, wearing his harsh black leather body armor. Though young, he held himself with the confidence of a man who knew what he was doing, and Malloryn had been one of the first dukes on the Council to approve his posting.

"Your Grace."

"Master Reed," Malloryn said, tilting his head.

"Byrnes." This greeting was a touch more effusive.

The pair of them clasped hands—old friends—as Malloryn peered impatiently past them.

"Garrett. I hear you need a little help solving a case?" Byrnes drawled. "Getting rusty in your old age?"

"Hardly." The Guild Master's mouth thinned. "But we thought you'd want a look at this one."

"Why?" Malloryn asked.

The Guild Master and his wife were aware of the work the Company of Rogues undertook.

This had to be Balfour's doing.

"Because it's a message for you, Your Grace," Garrett said. "This way."

He led the pair of them past a doctor, waiting with his mortuary trolley, and the crime scene investigator who'd replaced Ava at the Nighthawks.

Fog clung to the alleyway, and blood scented the air.

The stale scent of death filled Malloryn's nostrils as everything fell quiet. He'd seen death in many incarnations, but he knew this one would be bad, judging from the way several of the Nighthawks wouldn't meet his gaze.

"We don't know who she is," Garrett murmured. "But we will."

Malloryn knelt in the alleyway beside the dead girl's body, fog wafting away from his knees as he examined her and the crime scene. He'd been wrong. This wasn't vicious or overly violent, but strangely clean. Almost economical. No, it wasn't the manner of death that had made the others drop their eyes.

Barely hours old, judging by the congealed blood staining her white gown. She'd been shot right through the heart somewhere else and placed here, for him.

He looked at her face then.

Smoothed the black hair from her forehead so he could get a better glimpse of her.

Heart-shaped face. Blue sightless eyes, staring forever into an overcast sky. Pretty white gown that reminded him of something a debutante might wear.

It was like looking at a ghost.

Even now, seventeen years later, guilt flayed him like a lash, and Malloryn closed his eyes for a second.

After all this time, it was difficult to conjure Catherine's face, but he saw the flash of her smile, the haunted blue of her eyes. Saw them widen as Balfour turned his pistol from its lock on Malloryn's chest to settle upon her.

Crack.

He flinched as the memory of the pistol firing cascaded through him. It was the same memory that had haunted him for years; the moment Balfour set this vendetta into play forever.

Oh yes, it was bad. But no one watching would ever understand why.

It should have been me.

"Do you know her?" Garrett asked, looming over Malloryn's shoulder.

"No." Malloryn opened his eyes. "I know who killed her though."

Tense silence echoed through the alleyway as the pair of Nighthawks standing on guard shifted uneasily.

"Who?"

"An old friend," he replied, leaning down to examine the body. There was a calling card clutched tight in her hand.

His calling card.

No wonder the Guild Master had contacted him.

Malloryn plucked it from her fingers and straightened slowly. "Who found her?"

"A lamplighter," Garrett said, dismissing the nearest pair of Nighthawks, leaving only the three of them. "Called it in around dawn. Thinks he might have heard a shot, but he wasn't certain and I doubt he truly heard a thing."

"It didn't happen here."

"No. Not enough blood. She was placed here deliberately, where someone would find her."

"Can you smell the killer?"

"I'm picking up traces of gunpowder, mechanical oil, and hints of bergamot. But no personal scent, which means it was either a blue blood or a *dhampir*," Byrnes said, squatting beside the girl and examining her fingernails. "She's not upper class."

"No."

Bergamot. He almost flinched again. Jelena had dabbed the oil at her pulse points. The scent of it made his heart beat a little faster, though his senses weren't as highly refined as Byrnes's.

"So she could have been just a girl plucked off the streets," Byrnes murmured.

"Why her?" Garrett asked.

"She looks a little like Gemma," Byrnes said pointedly. "Think Balfour's going to go after her? She did ruin all his fun in Russia, after all."

"It's not meant to represent Gemma," Malloryn replied, locking all the pain, all the panic deep inside him.

Byrnes's gaze sharpened.

"It's meant to remind me of Catherine Tate. You were right. It is a message for me. But what is he trying to tell me?" Malloryn slowly unfolded to his full height, glancing down at the calling card. "We know he's back. He left a letter on my fucking desk. So this is a threat. Or a taunt."

"We need to keep an eye on the female Rogues?" Byrnes asked. "After all, he did want Obsidian to put a bullet through Gemma's heart and leave her on your doorstep."

Malloryn's mind raced. "He wants me to suffer. He wants to take away every last thing I care for. All the Rogues need to watch their backs. I daresay this won't be the last time we find a body."

The Guild Master waited, arms folded across his chest nonchalantly, even as his sharp blue eyes took in everything. "So Balfour is back and now he's killing young women with black hair?"

"Unfortunately, yes. I may need you and your men before this is done."

"You have them," Garrett replied, without hesitation. "I'll set Perry to try and track the killer."

His wife was the best tracker the Guild had to offer, but she also had two young daughters now.

"Tell her to take others with her and watch her back. She's looking for a *dhampir* woman with silvery blonde hair, an eye patch over one eye, and a scar on her cheek. Track the killer, but don't engage. She's lethal."

Byrnes sucked in a sharp gasp. "Jelena."

"Bergamot," he murmured. "I'll never forget the scent."

It haunted every single one of his nightmares.

"In that case, maybe I should join Perry?" Byrnes's expression hardened. "You might need a *dhampir* to counter her."

Malloryn nodded.

"Find her," he said, locking down the sharp fury that

bit at the back of his throat. "If we find Jelena, then we find Balfour."

"Yes, Your Grace," they both echoed.

This time, Lena came to her.

Adele led her into the gardens behind Malloryn House, where they could have some modicum of privacy. "Will was successful? He tracked my husband?"

She hadn't seen him since that moment in her bedchambers, beyond a brief note saying he had "business" to attend to. The question of precisely what he'd been up to last night niggled through her brain like a worm spreading rot.

"You wouldn't know what your husband's style is."

Devoncourt's words bothered her more than they should.

Because I know my husband likes games and he played me like a fiddle. What if this entire act is a game?

What sort of business required Malloryn stay out of all hours?

"Yes." Lena squeezed her hand, and her entire demeanor made Adele swallow. "I'm sorry, Adele. So sorry. Malloryn led him a merry chase across half of town, but Will managed to track him. There's a small, discreet house in Hardcastle Lane in Clerkenwell. Malloryn went in the back door as if he knew the place well. Will doesn't know what Malloryn was doing there, but there were several others coming in and out, and... a woman. A very beautiful woman with black hair."

Adele's heart fell. "He told me he'd let Mrs. Danner go."

"It wasn't Mrs. Danner. The butler called her Gemma.

Gemma Townsend."

That lying wretch.

Adele turned around abruptly, pressing her knuckles to her lips. She couldn't believe she'd ever let him touch her. Kiss her. Press her down on the bed and ravish her, the way he'd done....

And the entire time he'd been lying to her.

Though technically, she supposed it wasn't lying. He hadn't been with Mrs. Danner, but no wonder he'd been able to promise her—with a completely straight face—that he'd ended things with the opera singer.

"It might not have been an assignation." Lena curled her arms around Adele's waist and rested her chin on her shoulder. "Will doesn't know what it was. There were other people there—"

"He told me he was seeing to business," she snarled, leaning back into Lena's embrace. "Matters to do with running the *country*."

"Well, at least you know." Lena kissed her cheek. "I'm sorry."

"I'm not." Adele broke away from her, pressing a hand to her forehead. "At least I haven't completely humiliated myself by attempting to use some of your seduction techniques upon him." She shook her head. It could have been worse. "Though perhaps you might be able to teach me to shoot a pistol?"

"I hope you're joking."

"Of course."

Perhaps.

"What are you going to do?" Lena asked.

Adele paced across the grass. The not knowing was the worst part. Perhaps this Gemma Townsend *was* another woman in her husband's life. But what if she wasn't? What was he doing there? Why did he seem so familiar with the house?

And why the hell had Will called it a merry chase?

"Did he know Will was following him?" she asked, banking her anger into hot little coals in the grate of her soul.

"I doubt it."

"And yet, he took a circuitous route to his destination as if he believed he might be followed."

Lena nodded. "He was definitely trying to give someone the slip. He went into one of his clubs and then slipped out the back fifteen minutes later and into a waiting hackney. If Will wasn't on the rooftop, he'd have missed it."

Hmm. Adele's pacing slowed. Hardcastle Lane, she'd said.

"Did you happen to have the precise address?"

Lena's eyes narrowed. "Just what are you planning?"

"I think it's time to demand some answers," she replied grimly.

She'd been expecting a raven-haired beauty to answer, but as the door to 45 Hardcastle Lane jerked open, Adele came face-to-face with an impeccable butler.

Who blinked at her.

"I'm sorry, my....?"

"I am here to see my husband," she said, lowering her dripping parasol and taking a step up onto the lintel as if to enter. Rain darkened the skies behind her, but it suited her mood.

The butler didn't move. "Your husband...?"

"I'm told he visits here," Adele said boldly. "You may know him as Malloryn."

She might as well have set fire to his well-ironed tails. The butler's gaze suddenly focused on her intently, as if he hadn't recognized her before, and she could have sworn a line of sweat sprang up down his spine. His eyes had that look.

"Your husband," the man repeated stupidly.

"I know he was here last night," Adele growled, taking the chance to duck under his arm and into the entry. "And I know the lady of the house is a rather remarkable brunette."

There was no sign of anyone else, but what did she expect? A lady's petticoat draped over the armchair in the parlor? A pair of stockings hanging from the light fixture?

"Y-Your Grace." The butler stopped just short of grabbing her, his hands twitching in midair. "You cannot— You can't just—"

"I'm not supposed to be here?" she asked icily, turning on him with a hint of the wrath boiling in her veins. "Oh, I daresay I'm not. Malloryn would prefer me tucked up at home with no idea what he's up to at night. Where is he?"

A scalded sound echoed in his throat, and he looked beside himself. "It's not.... You can't.... He's not here."

"You're lying."

"I'm not!" He tried to usher her toward the door without actually laying hands on her. "If you'll just wait a moment, I'll, ah, I'll send for your carriage and—"

"I am not going anywhere until I see Malloryn." Adele stepped right up into his face. She was done with being toyed with. "So either you fetch him or I will."

CHAPTER TEN

The message reached Malloryn at his club, just as he was about to corner Barrons about cancelling the queen's celebrations completely. He'd need Barrons's vote if he had any hope of pushing this through council, for the queen was determined to keep her parade and her ball despite the dangers.

Urgent assistance required. Intruder apprehended at HQ.

It stopped him in his tracks.

Herbert's impeccable handwriting held an unusual flourish, as if he'd either been in a hurry, or somewhat flustered. He'd even sent the message with an errant newspaper boy, which was a breach in security protocols.

Herbert was never flustered.

He was unflappable in any situation, and yet the note seemed to disprove that theory.

Herbert was in a flap.

Malloryn demanded his coat and scarf and headed for the door with sharp, rapping strides. It had to be Balfour. The snake had finally reared his head. Or maybe Byrnes had had some luck tracking Jelena, despite the fact he and Lady Peregrine had lost the trail yesterday. Summoning a hack, he gave terse directions to Covent Garden, where he slipped into the morass of people on the street. A brief detour through a house advertising "French Lessons" in the window, and then a hurried set through a series of alleys, and he was entirely certain he'd lost any tail that might have been given him.

Ten minutes later he was standing out the front of 45 Hardcastle Lane.

The entire Company of Rogues awaited him in the foyer, and Ava was kneeling beside Herbert, who sat with his head bowed on the bottom step of the staircase, a cool rag draped over the back of his neck. Gemma's skirts swished as she paced, and the second he entered, relief broke over her expression like a sunrise.

"What happened?" he demanded.

Movement shifted upstairs, sharp heels rapping on the floor of his study. Malloryn's gaze shot upwards, then he took in Herbert's face—the way his butler couldn't quite meet his eyes. There was a faint trace of foreign perfume in the hallway, something that smelled like...

...a woman?

Malloryn shrugged out of his coat, handing it to Charlie as his mind raced. "You said there was an emergency."

They all looked at him, no doubt gauging his temper accurately by the looks on their faces.

Then Byrnes snorted, a slight laugh escaping him. "There was a break-in. We've managed to contain the perpetrator—your wife—in the study."

"My wife."

What the hell was Adele doing here? And why were half his agents arrayed in the parlor like they were too afraid to go upstairs?

"It wasn't easy," Byrnes reported, still laughing at him, goddamn him. "She put up one hell of a struggle, and we weren't certain just how far we were supposed to subdue her... being your wife and all."

That still didn't answer the questions he had. Why the hell was Adele here? Suspicion slithered through him. He'd swallowed her story about the big bad Echelon taking advantage of her, but had he been played? Maybe she was a plant. There could be no other reason she'd be here. Could there?

That kiss sprang to mind again, doubt curdling his insides.

"And why is my wife in my study?" he asked, once he was certain he had his emotions under control.

"Well," Gemma started, "She—"

Byrnes held a hand up, silencing her.

"Oh, no," he said, with a nasty-looking grin. "We're not allowed to spoil this one. If the duke wants to know why his wife is here, then perhaps he should ask her? We'll wait."

"She was looking for a Mrs. Danner," Ingrid suggested helpfully.

"Or me," Gemma replied pointedly. "A Mrs. Townsend who was keeping you company."

Malloryn's gaze shot to her, then lifted steadily to the roof as a half dozen conclusions drew themselves. Mrs. Danner? His fake mistress? His cover? Why would—

A sudden memory of Adele's glare regurgitated itself. "You want an heir? Then I want her gone," she'd snarled, in a most un-Adele-like way.

And he had the sudden sensation that something was going on, something that had nothing to do with the SOG, or Lord Balfour, or the fate of the country.

His mind made one of those brilliant leaps of conclusion it sometimes made, and the result ended up somewhere around the vicinity of oh, fuck.

"Herbert?"

"Yes, sir." The man's cheeks reddened, as well they should, damn him.

"May I ask how my wife got in here?" He paid the man a small fortune to keep the house safe, after all.

"Ah, I let her in, sir, and claimed the master of the house was away. But she was armed."

"Armed?" His voice sounded cold and flat. "Adele was armed?"

Herbert cleared his throat. "Hemlock, sir. I didn't expect it."

Hemlock.

He made his way toward the stairs as he digested this. Of course. Those bloody rings that were all the rage among the latest crop of debutantes.

From what he'd learned, his bloody wife supplied them.

"Careful," Byrnes called. "She's already taken one of us down. I should absolutely hate to see her unman you too. Charlie took a tray of brandy up to her, and we heard something smash about ten minutes ago. I suspect she's not feeling very wifely round about now."

"Is she ever feeling very wifely?" Kincaid joked.

"Are we taking odds?" Charlie stage-whispered. "Who wins this bout? The duchess? Or Malloryn?"

"My money's on the duchess," Kincaid shot back.

"Seconded." Byrnes and Gemma.

"And me," Ingrid added.

"Damn it." This from Charlie.

Only Herbert spoke up for him.

Malloryn shot them all a scathing look and started

tugging his gloves off as he took the stairs slowly. They could be useful, he told himself, as the muscle ticked in his jaw. Especially Byrnes. There was a reason he put up with the man, after all. "Herbert, if you want to redeem yourself in this situation and save some face, then I would suggest you see the house cleared of this pack of gossiping rabble, and then take up station outside until I give the order it's safe to come back inside."

"Yes, sir," Herbert barked, even as Byrnes made a disappointed sound.

Then Malloryn went to corner his wife.

CHAPTER ELEVEN

The door opened and closed with a quiet click.

Adele didn't bother looking up from the board she'd been perusing, with its variety of notes, photographs, and red string pointing from one photograph to the other. She knew who it was.

"I didn't know you missed me so much," her husband said into the stillness.

A shiver of anticipation went through her, but she swallowed it down. The last time she'd seen him, he'd had his face buried between her thighs. And her treacherous body replayed a succinct memory of that sensation, leaving her lips, her thighs, and even *that* area he'd kissed tingling.

Gathering herself, she turned around.

And was undone once again.

The wind had tousled Malloryn's hair, and his piercing gray eyes locked on her with a dangerous intensity. She rarely saw him in a relaxed state; his attire was usually impeccable, his hair combed and pomaded. Even when he'd tied her to the bed and had his way with her there hadn't been a button out of place, which was frustrating, to say the least.

He tossed his scarf over the back of a nearby chair, perusing her with a coolly detached sort of curiosity that roused all her ire.

"Well? Did you find what you were looking for?" Malloryn asked, and it was almost a taunt, as their eyes locked.

Adele took a steady breath, her fists clenching. Anger had sustained her on the carriage ride here, but it had evaporated in the brief two hours she'd been locked in the study, as her mind started working. She'd been played for a fool, and she did not enjoy the sensation. Worse, she'd made a fool of *herself*. The new Adele had been a concept that invigorated her, and yet she saw immediately there'd been traces of her old self left behind.

A hint of naiveté.

A slightly breathless feeling of hope.

She would not make that mistake again.

"No opera singers hiding under my desk?" Slowly, he tossed his gloves on the nearest chair and took a step toward her, moving with predatory grace. "No perfume on my coat? No undergarments belonging to some other woman in my drawers?"

"I haven't checked the drawers yet. The map of London and all the photographs of dead men sidetracked me. I knew Lord Ulbricht was missing, thanks to the *London Standard*, but I see he's been accounted for. Did you bury him yourself?"

"That's what I pay others to do."

"I see." Adele captured her skirts and swished around the desk, keeping it between them as she moved. Nervousness lit along her spine. She wasn't precisely certain what put that look in his eyes, or what he intended to do with her. None of this was what she'd expected, but she was starting to put the pieces together. "Just why do you have a photograph of the bomb scene from our engagement party on your map?"

"Maybe I planned it."

Adele's eyes narrowed. "It's not your style."

"Oh. What is my style?" Malloryn undid his cravat, dragging it from around his throat and curling the strip of linen around his fist. The movement was oh-so-precise and hearkened back to the other morning in her bedchamber when he'd bound her wrists to her bed. Probably meant to intimidate her, but then she was starting to understand this man. Starting to learn all of his tells.

The second she let him intimidate her was the second she let him play her. She'd grown up under her father's thumb; Malloryn was good, but he had nothing on Sir George Hamilton.

With a smile, she stopped by the brandy decanter and poured herself a drink, nursing it as she leaned back against the bookcase. "The bombing was far too messy. Your style is a knife in the dark, isn't it? It's a disappearance that cannot be accounted for—rather like Ulbricht. And there's never, ever, any messiness left behind. You hate it when I rearrange the saltcellars on the dining table" —which was precisely why she did it so often— "and you have to put all the books back in their right place after I've been through your library and left them lying around. And interrupting your daily schedule makes that muscle in your jaw jump, just like it's doing now." Lifting the brandy to her lips, she sipped it, the fiery liquor scoring her mouth. "You like the queen. You keep the pin she gave you after you helped her overthrow her husband in your desk drawer. You like the Duchess of Casavian and her husband, Lord Barrons, and they were directly in the path of that bomb. Which brings me to the conclusion you didn't plan it." She looked at the board, at the map, all those pins, and felt again the revelation she'd discovered earlier. "You're trying to find who did."

It made sense.

He *had* been taking care of business, after all.

Someone was taking all of Malloryn's neatly ordered plans—his precious London, the city he'd fought so hard to bring to order—and casting chaos into its midst.

"Those people downstairs.... I remember them from our engagement party when that vampire suddenly appeared. And from our wedding, when someone tried to kill me. They stopped it all from happening. They're working for you. They're trying to hunt the people behind all of this." She was breathless. "That's what you're doing here, isn't it?"

Silence.

"You put all of that together... from a map?" he asked incredulously.

Malloryn wasn't the first person who'd underestimated her. But it infuriated her suddenly. Her father had scorned her mind and forced her into her preordained role as a thrall. Her mother had never offered her a chance to escape. She'd always known she was more than what they'd tried to make her.

And somehow, in the last week, she'd begun to feel as though her husband believed it too. "Did you *think* me an idiot?"

Malloryn blinked. Then those gorgeous eyes became half-lidded again, as if he was sorting through possible answers in his mind. "No. Never that. How did you find me?"

"I asked a friend of mine to follow you. I thought you were with.... The letters that kept arriving at the house at all times of the day. The constant 'something came up' or 'business.' I thought you were still seeing her."

"Her." Her husband stared at her, his eyes calculating and only his fingers twitching slightly as he caressed his cravat. Slowly, he let it drop. Then he crossed his arms over his chest. "Her, who?"

"Your bloody paramour—" She paused. Malloryn wasn't stupid, and he looked cautious now. That wasn't a denial, but more of a sounding out. "Who else would you have thought I suspected?"

Was there someone else?

"I have many contacts. I just wasn't certain who you were referring to."

"Contacts? Like the women downstairs?"

"The women downstairs work for me," he replied. "And if I even looked twice at any of them, I'm sure their husbands would take askance at such a thought."

Something wasn't right here. Her husband was known for playing games, for dictating the narrative about his life. "*Was* there even a Mrs. Danner?"

"There is a Mrs. Danner onstage at the Capitol," he replied calmly. "A very voluptuous brunette with a known temper. I send her flowers once a week, and spend at least one evening out on the town with her before we 'retire.'"

"Retire?" She hated how stupid it made her sound.

"Giulia goes to bed and reads, and I slip out her back window where no one can see me."

The floor dropped out from under her. "You let the world believe you were having an affair with an Italian *soprano*?"

"Is it the world that has you so bothered, or is it you?"

"You let *me* believe you were having an affair with an opera singer."

Just to be clear on the matter.

"I didn't let you believe anything. You reached that

conclusion yourself. It was convenient for me to have a reason to disappear at times. Mrs. Danner played into that illusion. I paid her quite handsomely to be discreet and to make reference to me, and in return I got to slip quietly about London when people think I am elsewhere."

Adele's mouth fell open. She had been played. And right on the heels of that realization came other conclusions. The photograph with Devoncourt. The begetting of an heir. The sudden interest her husband took in her.

It left her breathless.

If he'd wanted an heir, he would have bedded her. But no, he'd been amusing himself with her. Whispering promises of seduction... and fulfilling none of them.

There were too many doubts suddenly rearranging themselves into suspicions in her head.

"You didn't want a child from me, did you?"

Barely a flicker crossed his face, but she had the sudden feeling he was cautious. "I'm a duke. I require an heir."

"You didn't want an heir, did you?" Adele stabbed a finger toward him. "That was an excuse. This whole game was a joke to you. Seduce me? Ha. Something about Devoncourt set you off. Who is he? What is he to you?"

It had to be Devoncourt that had roused her husband's interest. All this had occurred in the wake of that damning photograph.

Malloryn's gaze grew narrow again. "Devoncourt works for my enemy—"

Adele barely heard him. "Oh, my goodness." She pressed her fingers to her temples. "Oh, my goodness." None of it had been true. "I cannot believe I actually thought you suddenly interested in me, after so many months of indifference. I'm an idiot."

"You're not an idiot," he replied carefully. "You're quite an intelligent young woman. I've always known that—"

"I *am* an idiot," she declared. "I actually thought...."

That you wanted a child with me.

Her heart threatened to punch its way through her ribs. The image of the baby she'd begun daydreaming about, the one with little Alex's face, was suddenly ripped to shreds. And it hurt. It hurt so badly she thought she was almost going to cry. And worse, she'd actually begun to soften toward her husband. He'd kissed her as if she were made of spun sugar. He'd charmed his way into her bed with one flicker of his perfectly arched brow.

He could have bedded her if he'd desired. She would have let him.

She'd wanted him to do it.

All of it was a lie.

A means to test her allegiance. A way to twist her around his little finger while he worked out her loyalty. She felt like she wanted to throw up.

Or throw something.

"Adele?" A silky smooth whisper.

Don't you dare call me that. Adele slammed her walls up, protecting her poor, battered heart.

"Say something."

She wanted to say *everything.* But the sudden seething rage inside her choked off the words, leaving her shaking with fury.

"I came here expecting you to throw something at me."

That did it. Adele drained the contents of her brandy glass, not willing to waste good liquor, and hurled it at him.

Malloryn snatched the glass out of the air. They stared at each other. "I'm a blue blood," he pointed out. "I'm faster than you, Adele. You can throw anything you like at me"—he examined the glass—"though I do note Charlie gave you the lesser set of glassware."

"The lesser set of glassware?"

He didn't even care.

"He must have been anticipating fireworks."

"*Fireworks?*"

And suddenly she was filled with the urge to ruffle those elegant feathers. To make him act like he *did* give a damn. Anything. All she wanted was for him to shout at her, just once. Some bloody sign of emotion that might make her feel not so alone in this.

Reaching behind her, she found the decanter of brandy. Malloryn's eyes widened as she lifted it.

"Perhaps we should test your phenomenal reflexes then?"

She hurled the decanter, which he caught. The stopper tore loose though, half the brandy splashing across his chest before he righted it swiftly and set it aside. There were three more glasses that she threw at him in quick succession, and Malloryn snatched them all out of the air.

"Adele," he barked, juggling glassware like a professional.

Her back was up, her breath coming in short, sharp gasps. "I thought you were gadding about behind my back with your bloody opera singer," she shouted, flinging the silver tray at him like a discus. "I let you—" Her words choked off as a flood of embarrassment swept through her. *I let you kiss me all over. I let myself....* No. She stopped the thought right there, ignoring the aching twinge in her chest at the memory of how she'd felt when he looked into her eyes and slowly, slowly kissed her mouth.

She did *not* care about him.

She *hadn't* been entertaining stupid, foolish daydreams about her husband sweeping her away to the country where they could lie in bed all day and whisper idiotic love words to each other—

"Let me what?" His mercurial gaze sharpened as he dumped all the glassware on a shelf nearby.

Still unruffled. Still wearing that faint, supercilious mask, one eyebrow arched.

That was more than she could take.

Books came into her hands and she flung them at him, one after the other, depleting the bookshelf in swift succession. Malloryn had an armful. His eyes narrowed as he glared at her over the top of it. "Adele. Stop. I'd expect this from—"

"*From?*"

"A highly strung Italian soprano!"

"I'll give you 'highly strung!'"

More books. She was throwing with all her might now. Malloryn cursed under his breath as he dropped everything he held, trying to capture the encyclopedic tome she'd slung at his head. He glared at her as all the books tumbled into disarray at his feet, his shirt creased and drenched in brandy, one coppery curl draping across his forehead. Disarray achieved.

Finally.

Adele tossed one more book at him, almost a taunt, and then the mask shattered. He strode across the study with predatory intent, and she suddenly realized she was in trouble now.

This time the scurry of lobbed objects was made as she tried to flee. If he got his hands on her—

"Yes, 'highly strung'!" Malloryn accused, ducking beneath a paperweight. "Are you *trying* to kill me?"

"You're a blue blood," Adele shot back, darting around the desk and glaring at him over it. "You're so much faster than I am," she taunted, batting her eyelashes at him. "You can survive almost anything—"

"I'm not sure a barrage of books counts," Malloryn snarled, launching toward her. "Or you. Sometimes I wonder if I'm ever going to survive *you*!"

Adele squealed and darted the other way. "Well, I don't exactly have a pistol right now! It's the books or nothing, and I—"

"You'd what?" A hand snagged in her skirts. "You'd like to shoot me?"

Adele hammered at him as he swept her back into his arms. Too late. She was caught now.

"I wouldn't waste the bullet!" She couldn't resist trying to escape. She was so damned angry. "You lied to me."

"I wasn't certain if you were working for the enemy," Malloryn finally snapped. He turned her toward him and Adele kicked him, stubbing her toe against his shin.

"*Me?* Working for your enemy? What did you think I was? Some kind of spy?"

An icy, impenetrable look came over his face. "I—"

She couldn't help herself. She laughed right in his face. "Then I'm not the only idiot here, it seems. Perhaps you were too clever for *yourself*? How does that feel, Malloryn? Talking yourself around in bloody circles every time you meet someone? Questioning their loyalty. Standing there alone—"

"That's enough." She'd scored a point though.

"Is it?"

"I think," he stated, "that I don't know half of what goes on in that pretty little head of yours. You decimated Lord Abagnale when he tried for your hand. You had me bound at the altar before I could even blink. You set up a black market trade among the debutantes of the Echelon, running hemlock rings to them beneath the noses of suspicious mamas and blue blood lords everywhere—"

"So it makes sense I would be working for the *very men* I despise?" Adele countered. "The elite lords of the Echelon who want to take the world back to the days when they ruled it and the rest of us were just prey?"

Malloryn froze.

"I don't think you were thinking at all," she taunted, wriggling furiously. "Let me go."

"No."

Adele struggled harder. "Let. Me. Go."

"*No.*"

"I see the barbarian has managed to stake its claim on you!"

"That's enough."

Adele fought to free herself.

"I said, that's enough." He slammed her back against the wall, breathing hard as he captured her wrists above her head and pinned her there.

There was no way to escape. He was stronger than her. Faster. His temper thoroughly roused. The pair of them glared at each other.

"You are a fool, Your Grace."

His eyes narrowed even further, which somehow seemed impossible, but he was clearly thinking again. "You wanted a child."

There was no way in hell she was admitting any of *those* thoughts to him. "What I want is for you to get your hands off me, right this instant."

"Yes, but we don't always get what we want, do we, Adele? Now what?" he taunted. "Are you going to hemlock me too?"

"I only had one dose."

"Poor Herbert." His lips kicked up.

"Poor Herbert, my foot."

There was only one weapon left to engage. She meant

to escape, but it was clear her husband overpowered her physically. Which left only her mind. And—

Adele kissed him.

There was a moment of frozen shock as Malloryn absorbed the action without responding. For a second she thought he was going to reject her, that it had all been one stupid game to put her in her place, and make a fool out of her—

And then he threw himself into the abrupt change in dynamics, his mouth capturing hers with a hungry snarl.

It was a kiss to put all others in their place. A kiss with no design, beyond a statement: *You are mine.* A clash of tongues and teeth, and hard, heated hands that forced her to yield. But yielding was not in her nature, and she bit his lip as if to warn him she would not be conquered. Not by him. Not by this.

A growled—utterly un-Malloryn—sound escaped him, and then he slid one hand under her bottom and hauled her against him, his hips pressing into the warm juncture of her thighs.

His tongue delved deeper, caressing hers.

And she met each stroke with her own unabashed response, unleashing all her fury and hurt in each breathless kiss. Taking what she wanted, damn him.

Malloryn's hips ground against hers, his erection lining up right between her thighs. Right *there.* He thrust against her in an almost mindless simulation of the physical act of consummation.

It set every inch of her on fire, until Adele was grinding against him, her hands sliding through the dark coppery strands of his hair, fisting there and mashing her mouth against hers.

She wanted to climb inside his skin. To drink down every last inch of him. To consume him. She wanted to throw all caution to the wind and pretend none of the lies mattered. Suddenly there were too many clothes between them. Too many barriers.

But the most insubstantial was the one around her heart.

For if she were being honest with herself, it wasn't just the thought of a child that had begun to lure her into her husband's arms.

And it hurt, because some part of herself had began to feel something for him and—

Adele tore her face to the side, away from his dangerous mouth.

Away from those tempting thoughts that beckoned her down a dark road that only ended in heartbreak.

Both of them were panting. Trapped against each other. Tangled by way of flesh and clothing.

"Look at me," he whispered.

No.

"Adele." A soft word. A word that pierced her through and through. "Adele, look at me." She was almost strong enough to deny him, until he added, "Please."

She looked. Heaven help her, but she looked.

And enough of the mask had slipped for her to see a faint, unguarded glint in her husband's eyes. One that showed her he wasn't quite as certain as he seemed.

They stayed there for long moments, and she realized his chest was heaving, almost as much as hers was.

"Are you happy now you've destroyed the order in my study?"

No. She wouldn't be happy until she'd destroyed the order in his heart. Her gaze slid over his shoulder, then back to him. "The desk still looks untouched."

A heartbeat.

Then a devilish smile that made her stomach drop

almost to her feet.

"We could fix that," he purred as he leaned closer and rubbed his cheek along hers, his whisper a caress against her ear. "Lady's choice, of course."

A thrill ran through her.

Adele closed her eyes.

She wasn't seriously thinking about this, was she? He'd lied to her and tricked her. But it was all out in the open now, and as he rocked against her, she felt the insistent press of his erection.

That wasn't a lie.

Their marriage might have been built upon cool, slashing words and disdainful looks, but it was becoming quite evident there was heat there too. Desire. Need. Ever since that bloody day in the Ivory Tower when she'd saved his life and he'd nearly taken her right there on the floor, she couldn't seem to look away from him.

Something within her had bloomed to life that day, and Adele wanted it.

Why not take this one thing for herself?

It didn't mean anything more than that.

Soft lips found her throat, brushing against her grandmother's pearls.

"Do you want me to fuck you on my desk, Adele?" Malloryn nuzzled her throat, stubble rasping against her sensitive skin, and she flinched a little at the rough sound of his voice, of *that* word.

All those years pretending she was unaffected. All those years of burying her fire, her fury, hiding it all behind a mask of cool disdain. It wanted to erupt from her skin. She felt not at all herself as her nails dug into his shoulders and he made a slight hissing sound of gratification.

Malloryn wasn't promising a damned thing except pleasure.

And more....

For the first time she realized he was offering her something else: the opportunity to take what *she* wanted from him.

Fingers turning into little claws in his shirt, she arched her throat and moaned as his teeth bit down sharply. Not just pleasure, but unabashed pleasure. Uncontrolled. Untamed. A little dangerous....

And Adele made her decision.

"Make me your wife," she whispered.

Malloryn drew back and looked at her, face-to-face with her. She felt like she could fall into those gray eyes forever as she sought to find the truth of the man behind them.

Then his lashes fluttered shut as his mouth melted against hers in a kiss that would have had her begging him, if she hadn't already conceded. She didn't want soft and sweet. She wanted ruin. Adele bit his lower lip, sucking it into her mouth. A growl echoed in his throat, and then he was moving.

One hand blatantly cupped her bottom, and he hauled her thighs around his hips. Adele clung to his collar as he turned and strode toward the desk.

The hard muscled flex of his hips surged against her, and she could feel the rampant press of his body between her thighs. Adele gasped, one hand slamming back upon the desk for balance as he bit at her jaw.

It was all happening.

So swiftly she could barely think, let alone react. But oh, gods, how she wanted it.

Malloryn pulled back, soft fingertips trailing down her throat and décolletage. She could almost sense him reining himself in, but that wasn't what she wanted at all.

She needed him to remain unbalanced.

"I hate your composure," she snapped, grabbing two fistfuls of his shirt and tearing.

Buttons shot everywhere.

"And I hate the way you make me feel," he growled. "I want to ruin you."

"You couldn't, even if you tried."

"We'll see." Malloryn captured her mouth, his lips firm and punishing. There was no sweetness to this kiss. Only hunger. Only absolute dominance.

Adele yielded with a low moan.

Her palms slid against his chest, but there was no time to explore. She dug her nails in, wanting him to feel her urgency. Needing him to know it too.

Then he was shoving her skirts up, tearing at the lace in his haste. The insistent press of his fingers found her through the slit of her drawers, and for the first time his touch gentled. The stroke of his fingertips was like a velvet lash that lit her nerves on fire. No hiding how wet she was. The second he'd slammed her back against that bookcase, something had started aching low in her abdomen.

Their eyes met.

His touch slowed, thumb pressing insistently against her clitoris until her nails curled into claws on the mahogany desktop. *Oh, God.* Even now he sought control. Even now he could play her body like a lute.

Adele grabbed a fistful of his hair and dragged his mouth back to hers. Her other hand darted between them, finding the firm press of his erection. Buttons.... More wretched buttons. She tore them loose, and then her palm was curling around velvet-sheathed steel.

Malloryn groaned into her mouth, thrusting into her palm. Sharp teeth bit her lower lip, as if to prove she wasn't wholly in control here, but he let her learn him. Let her circle the swollen, heated head of his erection with her thumb, just as Lena had directed.

The soft touch of his own fingers had slowed.

Adele's heart soared. Not so in control. Not now.

Then he was pressing forward, the firm head of his erection nudging against her slickness. A thrill shot through her; a luscious little mix of nervousness and desire. *Yes.* She threw her head back as teeth raked down her throat, sending sensation slicing through her.

The tip of him breached her. Then he withdrew. Used his cock to rub exactly where she needed it. A tease. The whole damned thing was a tease.

Adele bit her bruised lip, her hips begging him for more.

"Please," she whispered, exulting in his lack of composure.

Malloryn eased inside her again, and this time he wasn't drawing back. Adele clung to the remnants of his shirt, fighting the instinct to tense. She'd felt his length and size and for a second wondered how on earth she was to manage this....

And then he surged to the hilt, a harsh breath escaping him.

Finally a wife in more than name.

It wasn't precisely painful.

No, it was the strangest, fullest sensation she didn't think she'd ever be able to describe. Adele sank her teeth into her own lip as he rocked against her, a ricochet of heat and pleasure spearing through her.

Dark eyes met hers as he looked up. The blackness of the craving swept through his irises, stealing away the stormy gray. There was only hunger there now. A desire to claim.

"Are you all right?" he clearly forced himself to say, the muscle in his jaw locking tight.

Adele pressed her lips there, her lashes fluttering half-shut over her eyes as she caressed his face. "I thought you promised me ruination? Don't stop now."

The next thrust caught her almost by surprise.

Malloryn lifted his face to the ceiling, as if trying to fight his darkest impulses. Every muscle in his throat stood out in stark relief, his shirt torn open, revealing the reddened marks she'd left on his skin.

Gently she lured his mouth to hers with small kisses painted across his throat and jaw. Every inch of his body was tight with restraint, and she shivered restlessly as she clenched her hips around his, riding him through the next thrust. And then the next.

There. The little quiver in his jaw.

A breath escaped her as he worked her harder, his hips flexing sleekly even as his mouth opened over hers.

Kissing him like this felt like all of her was melting. No more finesse. She felt the muscles beneath her hands quiver as he pumped his body into hers, crushing her shoved-up skirts between them.

Malloryn hauled her chest to chest, his mouth hot and frantic. Corset straining around her heaving ribs, she slid a hand to his nape as she bit at him, and sucked and licked.

He'd lied.

I will never kiss you, Adele, whispered through her head as the duke's tongue tangled with hers.

I will never make you my wife in truth.

But here he was, thrusting inside her with brutal intensity as she gasped and moaned, her nails digging into his shoulders.

And I will never love you.

It was that last one that challenged her.

Nothing she'd ever learned in her flesh rights lessons had prepared her for this.

Submit, and it won't take very long.

Lie back and count to a hundred, if it helps take your mind off matters.

Even in moments such as these, remember, at all times, that you are a lady. Please your lord. Submit. Be graceful. Never let him see your discomfort.

But submitting to Malloryn's carnal invasion held nothing of propriety in it.

She lost track of time. Of everything but the heated slam of flesh against hers. There was hair in her hands. His hot, ravaging tongue in her mouth. A thumb pressing insistently between them, working over that little spot between her legs that made her want to scream.

Sweat and panting and hard, echoing thrusts that rocked her back against the desk. Adele gave herself over to the feelings inside her. Restlessness strained within her. God, where he was touching her.... Her sex clenched, and she threw her head back, words tumbling from her lips. Words like "please" and "oh, God" and "harder."

And then she was shattering around him, white-hot pleasure obliterating her world.

"Malloryn!"

The animalistic scream that escaped her sounded like it came from someone else. She no longer cared if it wasn't ladylike.

As if he'd been waiting for that moment, Malloryn unleashed himself. Teeth sinking into the corded muscle between her throat and shoulder, he slammed her back into the desk. Again. And again. And again.

Until she was crying out, her body spasming around his as a groan escaped him and a gush of warmth flooded between her thighs.

Malloryn collapsed atop her, his weight pressing her down into the desk.

Gasping for breath, shuddering for a return of her senses, she simply held him as she tried to put herself back together. Her hips ached where they were wedged around his. There was a sticky mess between her thighs.

"God help me, but you drive me crazy," Malloryn whispered, lifting his head from her shoulder.

Adele lay flat upon the desk, panting for breath as she tried to regain her composure. She ached, but it was a pleasant, hazy ache; an aftermath more than pain.

The duke pushed away from her, dragging his trousers back into place as she slid her trembling hands through her hair. Good gods. What had just happened?

She was no longer a virgin.

Malloryn was no longer merely her husband in name only.

And while he'd proven himself master of her body, he'd been completely undone in his own pleasure. Nobody had won. He broke her, and she broke him, though the little flutter in her chest signified a troubling significance.

The little flutter that said, *please, touch me again.*

A whisper in her soul that yearned to be held.

Did she dare reach for him? Did she dare hope that Malloryn could ever look at her the same way? Did he feel it too? A connection, no matter how tenuous it seemed.

Today had proven he wasn't immune to her.

The only problem was that to breach Malloryn's defenses, she had to risk the utter destruction of her own.

This wasn't over yet.

But could she ever reach the heart of the untouchable duke?

CHAPTER TWELVE

Somehow Malloryn picked his way through the mess on the study floor, finding the decanter—curiously safe, until he remembered that was the first thing she'd thrown—on the shelf nearby. The glasses had met a less successful fate, taken down by an errant book.

Malloryn turned, plucking the topper from the decanter, as he surveyed the state of affairs.

The study was destroyed. His desk desecrated—he'd never look at it again without thinking of her, and it was becoming difficult enough to focus on his work without thoughts of Adele intruding as it was.

As for his wife....

This had not gone the way he'd planned.

None of this had been expected.

Adele was cool, rational cunning, a woman who deliberately toyed with him every time she rearranged his dinner table. Someone who arched a brow at him as she pushed her metaphorical chess piece across the mental playing board between them, her eyes telling him, *"Your move."*

Not a book-throwing harridan. Not a woman who raked her nails down his back as he made her scream with pleasure. And he wasn't the type of man to throw a woman down upon his desk and fuck her without a single thought beyond the all-consuming drive to be inside her.

He looked at her then.

Finally.

All torn skirts, tangled hair, and flushed skin. Her ravaged mouth. The bite marks on her throat and shoulder. There was no hiding what had happened here.

Fuck. She was driving him insane. Malloryn tilted the decanter to his lips and swallowed half the brandy before he could rearrange his thoughts well enough to contain them.

When he lowered it, Adele was still blushing.

"I didn't hurt you?" he asked with a rough voice, and that was yet another serious problem. He never lost control like that.

"No," she whispered, and her cheeks grew even pinker. "It was...."

It was.

And he'd liked it. That thought burned behind his ribs. He'd liked every single moment of what had happened between them. Liked shoving his way under her skirts. Liked the gasp she made when he curled his fist in her hair and—

Malloryn rubbed his chest, feeling dangerously unhinged. This wasn't him.

Or not the man he'd made himself into.

The last time he'd felt like this he'd been seventeen, in love, and blind to the world around him. When he'd lost everything and stood in the ashes of what Balfour had made of his life, he'd finally understood what his father, now dead, had been telling him all these years.

Emotions were weaknesses. Love was a ticking time bomb, an Achilles heel. And he could never, ever, allow himself to feel like that again.

Two facts arranged themselves in his head: Adele breached something inside him, left him shambling for control.

Adele was dangerous.

She undid everything he'd made of himself and stripped him raw. He couldn't think when she'd grabbed him by the shirt and kissed him, and that was terrifying, especially right now, when Balfour was out there again, trying to destroy him.

He'd survived the last time Balfour came against him.

Barely.

He couldn't afford to give in to weakness now. *Any* kind of weakness.

"Here." He helped her to her feet, locking instantly on the brief wince that narrowed her brows. "You *are* hurt."

"No." Adele collapsed against his chest, looking up at him with pleasure-dazed eyes. "Just a little weak-kneed and—"

Her face suddenly blanched.

Fetching his cravat, he offered the rumpled linen to her. "For the mess."

Face flaming, she turned around and tidied herself as best she could, whilst he pretended to fix his shirt in the reflection in the window.

It wasn't often he forgot himself.

He hadn't been so careless since he was a lad, unwilling to bear the consequences of a child.

Did it matter though?

She was his wife.

And yet, he found himself thinking of that other child. The one who'd never been given a chance to draw breath.

The one Balfour had murdered in the womb. Two lives stolen with the cost of a single bullet.

Yes, it damned well mattered.

It wouldn't happen again—and he would just have to hope nothing came of this... altercation.

"Turn around," he said, taking Adele by the hips and maneuvering her.

Tendrils of blonde hair escaped her neat chignon. She'd lost a button somewhere, and several others were undone.

He had no idea what to say to her, except.... "This wasn't what I planned when I came up here."

Adele burst into laughter, and damn him to hell, but he couldn't resist a smile. The bloody woman would be the end of him.

"I don't think this was what I planned either."

"*You* kissed me," he pointed out as he fixed her buttons.

"You had me pinned to a bookcase," she protested. "I didn't know what else to do."

"It was... effective."

"So I noticed." Her cheeks were still that pretty pink he couldn't quite reconcile with Adele. "It never occurred to me I could end an argument with you in such a way."

His lashes obscured his eyes. This couldn't happen again. "I wouldn't recommend it."

"No? I enjoyed myself. You seemed to have no complaints." Adele reached out and smoothed her hands down his bare chest. "I owe you a shirt."

Malloryn captured her wrists.

Adele's flirtatious smile slipped from her pillow-shaped lips, as if she recognized the silent rebuke.

Malloryn stepped away from her, buttoning the only two buttons that were still affixed, and trying to recompose himself.

"Brandy?" he offered, as she sank into the stuffed armchair and fixed her skirts.

Green eyes locked upon him. "Did you know, if I couldn't feel the ache of your hands and teeth imprinted on my body right now, I'd begin to think you an automaton. And yes, I would love a brandy."

He handed her the glass and hesitated. "I'm not a machine, Adele."

"Oh, I realized that." She sipped her drink and gave him a long, slow, heated look. "Sometime between the bookcase and the desk. I think I like you best when you let yourself off the leash."

Time to perform some damage control. "This can't happen again."

"I see. I cannot say I didn't expect you to begin putting up walls the second you got your breeches buttoned." Her voice softened. "You can't pretend it didn't happen."

"It's got nothing to do with you and me."

She paused with the glass to her lips, and there was the flash of intelligence in her eyes that so provoked him. "And here I thought we'd be stepping quite neatly around the topic that brought us to this situation."

"As you've made clear, you're too intelligent to be left in the dark. It would be dangerous if you started asking questions of the wrong people, and I daresay, knowing you as I do, that you wouldn't be content to let matters lie."

"You assume correctly," she replied, with a challenging tilt of her head.

"I have enemies, Adele." Malloryn leaned forward, resting his forearms on his thighs. "One in particular who would like to see my head removed from my shoulders. He's made no qualms about the fact he will remove any obstacles between us. Nor is he squeamish when it comes to striking down those close to me."

Her lashes obscured her thoughts. "Like the baroness."

The name was a whiplash of guilt across his seared nerves.

"Yes," he managed to say, though he was momentarily blinded by the sight of Isabella's vacant eyes staring sightlessly at the roof as she lay in a bloodied tangle on the carpets of the Ivory Tower. "She's not the first woman I've cared for that he's struck down. But she *will* be the last."

He'd promised himself that as he took one last look at Isabella in her coffin before he gently closed the lid.

Balfour would only hurt those close to Malloryn. Keeping his friends and those he cared for at arm's length was the only way to protect them.

"Our estranged relationship is your best protection," he said. "Everybody knows we don't care for each other."

Adele took a long, slow swallow of her brandy before responding, "Who is it?"

And here came the crux of the problem. The less Adele knew, the less she could repeat. Though he'd clearly made a mistake in regards to her loyalties, he wasn't entirely certain if he trusted her.

But he walked a fine line of leaving her unaware of the danger around her, if he didn't at least warn her.

"Lord Balfour."

"*Balfour?*" She nearly dropped the brandy. "He died in the revolution. You cut his throat and buried him—"

"Not deeply enough, it seems." Malloryn sat back in his chair as he considered her. "You've seen my maps, my photographs. He's behind everything, though he's content to hide in the shadows as we speak. He wants revenge upon all those who destroyed his power during the revolution. The queen. The Duchess of Casavian and her consort. Me."

It was quite unnerving to see her take such facts and quietly compute them. "Are you certain it's truly him?"

"Considering he had me kidnapped and taken all the way to Russia the other month, yes, I'm certain."

"Kidnapped?" Adele frowned. "You sent me a letter saying you were in Norway."

"Gemma forged my handwriting and signature."

Again, she glanced away. "I should have guessed. It seemed overly familiar."

Bloody Gemma. Meddling in his personal life.

"So where is Balfour now?"

"I don't know." He shrugged. "That's what I'm trying to discover."

Adele drummed her fingernails on her empty glass, staring into the distance. "You think Devoncourt has something to do with him. You said he worked for him."

There was that dangerous intellect again.

An odd surge of curiosity rose within him. He'd underestimated her several times and couldn't afford to do so again. Despite the frills and taffeta, Adele could be a dangerous adversary if she so chose.

He didn't like walking this knife's edge with her.

But he couldn't deny it intrigued him.

"The man you know as Devoncourt is not truly an aristocrat. According to my sources, he's a former Falcon of Balfour's masquerading as the long-lost earl. He was on the edges of the SOG movement before we killed and arrested the ringleaders—" She looked momentarily baffled, so he quickly explained the SOG to her. "We think he's using his false status to gather those former SOG members who faded back into the populace once Ulbricht died. I wouldn't be surprised if he was one of the ringleaders who referred to themselves as the Rising Sons. I'm fairly certain he knows where Balfour is."

"He's been charming me for months." Heat filled her voice. "That bloody bastard. He kissed me."

"I'm aware."

The curt tone of his voice drew her attention.

"Well, you certainly weren't interested in kissing me." Adele's lips thinned. "And now I'm not even certain if he was. I hate being made a fool of." Pushing to her feet, she paced the room, looking thoroughly vexed. "But what did he want with me? Was I merely a plaything? A means to draw blood from you without a direct confrontation? A *jibe*?"

"He could have been after information."

"Because I know so much," she said, a little bitterly.

Malloryn didn't respond. He'd said it only to be polite.

"So what now?" Adele demanded, turning on him in a rush.

He'd have to remember that: She might be furious, but she thought swiftly on her feet.

Rather like the night she'd trapped him into marriage.

"Now? I put you in a carriage and send you home. Life goes on as if this.... None of this happened. Stay away from Devoncourt, but continue your life as usual. I would encourage you to make a disparaging remark or two about me in public. Laugh and dance. Flirt. Spend half my fortune—"

"In short, be a good little duchess and bat my eyelashes at people."

He paused, warned by her tone.

"Damn it, Malloryn! I could help," she cried, her eyes flashing with determination. Despite everything, he couldn't help rousing again at the sight of her like this. All fierce and determined, a warrior in silk. "From the sounds of it, you have no idea who might be an SOG sympathizer or a Rising Son. You're rarely seen in society. Too high and mighty to hobnob with the rest of the elite, according to most sources. But I know the Echelon like the back of my hand.

"And if *Lord* Devoncourt belongs to Balfour, then why not let me get him right where you need him? He thinks he's charming me—"

"You are *not* getting involved," he said sharply, pushing to his feet. "This isn't a game, Adele. This is dangerous. The last thing you want to do is make yourself a target."

"My entire goddamned life since I entered the Echelon has been dangerous. Do you think this is the first time I've faced a man who could kill me? Why do you think I got involved in trading hemlock rings in the first place? It was the only means I had of striking back—"

"While I won't pretend I don't know what you're speaking of, this is a little different than dealing with privileged lordlings who think they can take whatever they want." He forced his tone to harden. "You were there when the baroness shot herself. Balfour put a mind-altering device in her head. He made her kill herself and she knew it. She knew there was no hope of saving herself even as she pulled the trigger. I will not add your name to my list. No. My final answer is no—"

"But—"

"And if you continue arguing, then I will simply ensure you have not the means to put yourself in danger."

"What are you going to do? Lock me away?"

"If. Necessary."

Adele's teeth gnashed together. "Argh. You're just like my father. I am not some insipid little debutante with fluff in her head—"

He moved toward her. A swift yank and he drew her back against his chest, locking one arm across hers as he captured her chin and tilted her head up. "If I had a knife to your throat, right now, what would you do?"

Adele's chest heaved. "I would hemlock you."

"Alas, I'm fairly certain you would have tried that the moment I walked through the study door. You have no hemlock. You're human. You're not strong enough to fight me off, and if I wanted to kill you right now, I could." He let his grip on her chin soften, his fingers stroking down her throat. "I know you're intelligent. It doesn't mean a damned thing when Balfour or one of his agents has a pistol to your head."

He released her.

Adele staggered out of his arms, and touched her throat gently, her lips pressing together.

But her expression looked troubled.

"I won't have your death on my conscience," he warned. "And while you might know the Echelon's waters better than I, I have an entire network of information-gatherers who are out there right now, working to locate Balfour. Go home, Adele. And forget everything that happened here."

"Including what occurred between the pair of us?" she challenged.

"Especially that."

"Just that easily?" Adele arched a precise brow. Not so long ago, the twitch of said brow would have made him want to clench his jaw. Now all he wanted to do was capture her chin and claim that pretty, impertinent mouth and kiss the hell out of it.

How things had changed.

He felt slightly off-kilter, as if the world had shifted on its axis while he wasn't looking.

"As will you, no doubt?" she murmured, searching his gaze.

"As will I."

It was a lie.

But she clearly believed it, for the light in her eyes died. "As you wish."

CHAPTER THIRTEEN

Fury rode her well into the next day.

Adele rose early, and for the first time in days she didn't bother to ask if her husband was at home.

No. He'd be about saving the world and searching for a dangerous blue blood mastermind who wanted to destroy London. And while she respected that he knew the sort of dangers involved, she couldn't help resenting his instructions.

Go home. Forget everything. Be a good little duchess.

For a moment yesterday, when he'd explained what he was involved in, she'd almost felt as though her husband was treating her as an equal.

For a moment she'd hovered on the verge of something more than this weary life.

She'd been ablaze with excitement—until Malloryn quite firmly set her back in her place.

All her life, her father had cursed her for not being born a son—or ignored her as unimportant because she lacked the necessary physical requirements. It wasn't until she turned fourteen and started drawing attention from young men that Sir George Hamilton had begun to realize he had an asset on his hands.

Prized for her beauty, and not her brains. Stuffed and shoved into gasp-inducing corsets, her hair heated into torturous curls, and her manners critiqued at every turn, she'd become his most valued possession.

Her father didn't want to hear what she thought. He wanted her to capture attention. He would point out a young fellow in society and tell her to make her introductions. Adele would smile and flirt, and lead said target back to her father, where suddenly she was forgotten again.

In hindsight, she longed for those days when her father had forgotten her. It might have been better than when he realized what value she truly had. Or her body, rather.

But yesterday, as she'd sat in Malloryn's study, her body aching with the aftermath of all that had occurred, she'd felt something new blossom within her.

He hadn't merely told her to mind her business, or ignored her questions. He'd revealed quite dangerous secrets, and she'd begun to believe he might see some value in her.

And then, the second her heart started beating faster at the thought that she could help, he'd swiftly disabused her of that notion.

She'd been told not to get involved.

She wasn't *going* to get involved.

But the second Adele finished breakfast, she sent for her writing set and locked herself away in the library.

The SOG had been a group of disgruntled blue bloods longing for a return to the old days, according to Malloryn.

She'd heard them speaking, of course, but she'd never known there was a name for them. Or a group. She'd thought it merely a gathering of fat old windbags who'd whine into their blud-wein about how they weren't allowed to molest and take what they wanted from young society ladies anymore.

Or the many younger blue bloods who had never had a chance to be such predators and resented the stolen opportunities.

"Poor devils," Adele mocked, as her nib moved across the paper and she listed every single lord she'd learned to avoid over the years.

Who were Devoncourt's cronies again?

Not the older blue bloods that'd once been in power, but the younger set that'd been the most dangerous of all. She hadn't liked that about him, but he'd assured her they were harmless.

Or defanged, he'd said, with a wry little smile.

Ha. Ha. Ha. Adele had laughed politely, for she was an expert at playing the game.

She hadn't trusted Devoncourt—she never truly trusted any blue blood—but he'd been polite and charming. And worse, he'd paid her enough attention that she'd begun to think him harmless enough.

He'd even set one or two of his little lickspittles into place when they'd treated her condescendingly.

Now that she knew who he was, she could see right through his ploys.

By the time the morning's sunlight began to brighten into midafternoon, she'd compiled a good four dozen potential SOG members; another dozen or so who were too brainless to be involved, but might have kissed enough boots to be useful; and several dozen other young blue bloods who she was fairly certain weren't involved.

And she'd circled the top five potential ringleaders or influencers.

Malloryn might not want her involved, but perhaps she could help in some small way.

With a sigh, Adele collected her pages and headed for the door. Who was she fooling? Whether he wanted her insight or not, at least she felt like she'd contributed.

As if to spite her, Malloryn was just making his way up the stairs when she strode into the hallway. For a second their eyes locked, and she was right back there in his study in Hardcastle Lane, staring into his eyes as he slowly kissed her.

A rush of heat went through her, and curse her treacherous body, but a shiver of tension curled deep in her abdomen.

"Duke," she said coolly, to cover the reaction.

"Duchess." He paused, his gaze sliding slowly over her. "You look like you've been up to some mischief."

"I wouldn't dare."

"Somehow I find that difficult to believe. You live for such mischief."

The teasing way he said it hearkened back to the flirtation of the previous couple of days.

Adele did not take the bait. "If you'll excuse me, I have matters to see to. You want to find your SOG?" She slammed the pieces of paper against his chest. "Then I suggest you start here. It's a list."

Swishing past him, she summoned the nearest housemaid for her hat and day jacket.

"Where are you going?" Malloryn demanded, following her down the stairs.

"I'm fairly certain I have some jewelry to purchase. Maybe a little mindless giggling on Bond Street with some of my friends? Or if I'm really lucky, a thrilling encounter with the milliner."

"For a second I thought you were referring to your

new modiste," he mused. "The one you spoke of the other day."

Adele paused in the entry as the maid slipped her day jacket over her shoulders. Was he referring to—?

He was.

It was as if the yesterday hadn't happened.

Flirt with other men, he'd told her. Make a disparaging comment or two in public. But right here, right now, he was the one flirting with her, as if nothing had changed. As if they could both pretend in private there was something more between them.

She was growing so tired of playing pretend.

Malloryn lounged on the stairs, his hands in his pockets and no sign of the papers she'd given him. His eyes glinted with challenge, but what was the point, really?

"You thought wrong," Adele told him, tipping her chin up. "I canceled my order. It seems there was no point in it. And I thought it was what you would want."

And then she smiled at the maid and accepted her hat as the door opened before her.

Adele did not look back.

It *was* what he wanted.

But as the door closed behind her, Malloryn realized he was staring at it. And both the maids had noticed.

He tilted his head in recognition to them, then turned and moved toward his library.

Adele's perfume filled the air. It always did. No matter where he went in this damned house, she haunted him.

Slowly, he drew the papers she'd given him out of his waistcoat pocket and smoothed the crumples from them.

The second he started down the list he realized she

might just know what she was talking about. There were columns detailing the most likely candidates. Little notes decorated each name, scathing indictments of each lord and what they liked to get up to in their spare time.

Lord Higginbotham—liked to bathe in blood to keep his skin youthful for the never-ending stream of handsome young footmen he replaces each month. Is currently being investigated by the Nighthawks for the disappearance of at least two of them.

The Earl of Carstoke— frequently rants about how one used to be able to toss a handful of coin to a girl on the street as repayment and nobody would dare bleat.

Lord Abriel—cannot attain "permanence" without putting his hands around his mistress's throat. Resents the fact bruises upon one's thrall are now frowned upon.

How the hell did she know that?

That Society of Roses project she'd started. It had to be. The girls must all talk, and Adele kept track of everything. If she'd been of a mind to resort to blackmail, she could most likely bring the entire Echelon to its knees. He suddenly wondered just what was discussed in the powder rooms of a ball.

Keeping her out of this was for the best.

But he couldn't help crossing to the window and watching her ascend into the carriage.

She'd surprised him more than once in the last few days.

"Well, that's enough about me. What have *you* been up to?" Hattie asked, finally running out of things to say.

Making war and then love with my husband. And now it seems we're back to war.

"Nothing in particular," Adele replied, granting her

sister the same vapid smile she'd mastered when she was twelve. "Trying to decide what to wear to Lady Haynes's ball."

The distraction worked. Hattie instantly started babbling about her newest silk gown.

Hattie's cheeks had lost their smooth plumpness of youth, and at seventeen, she was starting to truly blossom into a stunning young woman. Adele might have been as vibrant and innocent at that age. She honestly couldn't remember it. Instead, she felt like she'd been cursed with cynicism from the day she was born, her exterior hardened by her first bloodstained glimpse of the world around her.

Adele glanced down into the depths of her hot chocolate.

She wasn't the only one who'd noticed the way Hattie had bloomed. Several blue blood lords had asked Hattie to waltz at the last ball they'd both attended, and she'd seen them circling the young girl like vultures.

Hattie had even begun to mention Lord Seymour's son in the sort of voice that left her slightly breathless.

She didn't, however, mention Lord Corvus.

Adele wondered if that was to spare Adele's feelings, or whether her sister honestly wasn't aware of his lordship's interest in her. Lady Hamilton had been paid more than handsomely this month, which meant she had to hold up her end of the bargain and refuse to let the bastard anywhere near Hattie.

"Oh, look at the time," Hattie suddenly said. "You should have stopped me. I've spent the entire afternoon filling your ears with gossip."

"It's happy gossip. Reminds me of my days as a debutante." Gathering her reticule, she pushed to her feet. "But I should be going. Cook will want my help planning next week's menu."

She kissed Hattie on the cheek, pausing as she saw the shadow watching them.

Sir George Hamilton loomed in the doorway of the parlor like a behemoth, his heavy brow shadowing his eyes. She didn't know how long he'd been there, but she didn't like the way he looked at her.

He was supposed to be out this afternoon. She'd checked with Hattie before she came.

"Father," Adele greeted with a tilt of the head, one adversary to another.

Her father's lips thinned beneath his neatly trimmed moustache. "Fancy seeing you here, Adele." He stepped forward and pressed his dry lips to her forehead, though she knew it was merely for show. He'd given up on her years ago. "I wasn't aware Harriet was meeting you for tea this afternoon."

Interpretation: You're not supposed to meet with your sister. I thought we'd discussed this?

He turned hard eyes on Hattie, who wilted beneath his gaze.

"Blame me," Adele said swiftly, stepping between them so she'd face his ire, and not her sister. "I begged her to let me come."

"She told her mother she had a case of the megrims. Lady Hamilton would never have gone out if she'd known it was a ruse."

"It was my idea."

The muscle in his cheek ticked. "I don't doubt that. Since you're here, you may as well spare me a moment of your time. My study?"

Her smile faltered. "As you wish."

Hattie followed them to the door, and Adele squeezed her hand to assuage her sister's nerves. Everything will be okay. Sir George couldn't hurt her anymore, but Adele could still feel her sister's stare between her shoulder blades at every step along the staircase to the second level.

Sir George wasted no time.

The second the door to his study shut behind her, he turned on his heel abruptly. "Your mother tells me you disapprove of Lord Corvus's intentions toward your sister. You are not to meddle."

I daresay Lady Hamilton forgot to mention the part where I pay her two hundred pounds a month to keep his lordship's paws off my sister.

Dealing with Sir George was another matter.

"Corvus is only circling Hattie like a vulture because he knows how much it gets under my skin," Adele hissed. "You're the one who wants to throw her to the wolves. Do you possibly imagine he is interested in a match with her? He'll ruin her."

"This vendetta you have against him—"

"Vendetta?" Her voice rose. "How dare you?"

"It cost me a great deal to keep Corvus off my back after your little incident," he warned. "If you upset him again—"

"If I upset him?" She couldn't restrain the heat in her voice.

"You drew his blood."

"He deserved it." Adele turned in a whirl of skirts, pacing to the window. "And if you think I shall ever forget how you made me apologize to him, then you should think again."

Of all the indignities she'd suffered under this roof, apologizing to her erstwhile attacker was the worst.

"Lord Corvus is a powerful man—"

"So is my husband." She wasn't above throwing Malloryn's name around when it came to riling her father. "I don't think he'd approve of your machinations with

Hattie if I told him the truth."

Sir George's face mottled. "Your husband wouldn't give a damn. Do you think I am unaware of his lack of concern when it comes to his wife? Rumors abound, my dear, of how your husband avoids any balls you attend."

Adele steeled herself. "Malloryn is too busy with matters of the realm to attend most of the Echelon's balls. But of course rumors abound. Of course it's my fault. You probably started them yourself."

"The last thing I want to do is bring more attention to you and this household," Sir George yelled. "You dishonored this house once, and I will not have you bringing the murk of your past back into the light."

"How was marrying the duke a dishonor? No member of this household has ever striven so high!"

"High?" His voice raised several octaves. "Malloryn's a traitor to his class. He ought to hang."

"I'd be careful how loudly you say those words, Father," she replied coldly. "Because they smack of treason."

A sharp rap came at the door, cutting the tension between them.

Visibly seething, Sir George turned to the footman at the door. "What is it?"

"There's a messenger here, sir. You wanted to be alerted immediately the second he arrived."

Sir George cut her a sharp look. "We are not done yet. Stay here and don't touch anything. I need to see to this."

"I think I've heard enough, thank you very much." She gathered her skirts.

"Well, I haven't finished talking. Lord Corvus and I have come to an agreement, and you will abide by it."

Adele froze. "What kind of agreement?"

Sir George bared his teeth in a smile as he strode

toward the door. "As I said, stay here. And you will find out."

CHAPTER FOURTEEN

An agreement with Lord Corvus....

If Sir George had dared make a rash decision over Hattie's fate, Adele was going to kill him. She hastily rifled through the papers on his desk, trying to find some sort of letter or document pertaining to Corvus.

Damn it. Nothing.

Adele turned, her fingertips pressed to her temples, when she saw the fireplace.

And her breath caught as she saw something she'd never truly noticed before.

There, right in the heart of her father's study, was the rising sun emblem of the SOG—according to Malloryn.

Every inch of her stiffened.

"Malloryn's a traitor to his class."

Why had she not seen it?

Oh, she'd known Sir George despised her husband, but he was careful about the sorts of opinions he allowed to grace public air. She hadn't even bothered to put his name on the list she'd given her husband.

But what if he was an SOG sympathizer?

Creeping closer, she pressed her fingers to the sun embossed in the black steel of the fireplace like a *fleur-de-lis*. The emblem depressed into the setting, and the fireplace groaned.

Drawing her hand to her chest sharply, Adele took a step back.

Had the fireplace moved?

Reaching out, she pushed it, and the fireplace began to turn, revealing a small hidden room behind it. Gray light streamed through a dirty window, highlighting a battered old desk and several shelves covered in heavy, leather-bound volumes and sundry other items. A mechanical ship held pride of place on the desk and she knew if she looked closer, she'd see *HMS Hamilton* engraved on the tiny nameplate.

Sir George had earned a knighthood from the prince consort for designing a new type of recurring mounted gun to be used by naval forces, one year before the prince consort was overthrown. She'd never understood it. Many other manufacturers designed important things, but her father had been granted a title for it.

If there was any memory Sir George worshipped, it was that of the moment he'd been raised into the Echelon. No longer a mere second son of a second son of some poorer House, far from the grace of the ruling duke, but a titled man himself.

They'd even named a ship after him, which seemed abundant, even to her, though now she had to wonder.

What else had he done for the prince consort?

Or had he somehow been involved with Lord Balfour? Everyone knew Balfour had pulled the prince consort's strings, so the knighthood must have been his idea.

It fit.

It fit together all too neatly.

Her father was a traitor.

As if drawn by magic, Adele crossed to the desk. She wasn't supposed to get involved, but she had to know the truth.

Sir George had never been neat, but the sheer number of papers strewn across his desk surprised her. She flicked through them methodically, trying not to disturb them too much, even as she kept one ear on the door.

There were several maps of London, with various locations clearly marked upon them in red ink.

A letter addressed to Thomas Mowbray, demanding a bill of sale for what seemed to be a household automaton. Or several hundred of them.

Schematics to some sort of device or invention she couldn't quite make heads or tails of.

But it was the small list of ingredients beneath it that caught her attention. Or to be honest, one item on the list in particular.

Nobel's Blasting Powder.

While she had little knowledge of chemistry, the term "blasting" sent a chill down her spine. That was an explosive, wasn't it? TNT?

What was her father doing with a list of explosives on his desk in what appeared to be a secret study?

"He's SOG," she whispered out loud.

He had to be.

It made too much sense.

Oh God. What was she going to do? This would ruin Hattie. She'd long since stopped caring what happened to either of her parents, for the feeling was clearly mutual, but Hattie was the one thing she'd fought to protect all her life.

Adele's head jerked up as she heard raised voices coming nearer.

Her father.

She hastily shoved everything back into place, and then examined the desk to see if it looked like someone had been in here.

Darting through the secret entrance, she put her back to the fireplace and tried to force it back into place. Inch by inch, it groaned closed. Her father's voice was louder. Damn it. Adele gave an almighty shove, and the fireplace hissed shut with a sharp click and a whuff of exhaled air.

By the time the door opened, she was seated in the same chair she'd been in when Sir George left. His gaze shot to the book she was holding, which she abruptly closed before pasting a smile on her face. "Sorry. Just had to touch something."

He'd have expected nothing less, even though sweat chilled her spine.

"Now, where were we?" Sir George snarled.

But for the life of her, Adele couldn't focus on what he was saying.

How the hell was she supposed to stay out of it now?

"Ah, Duchess. What a pleasant surprise. I didn't expect to see you here."

The words hauled Adele out of her private reverie as she scurried down the stairs leading down from her father's townhouse. Adele paused, one hand lingering on the railing, as the Earl of Devoncourt appeared in front of her.

One of Balfour's Falcons.

Adele's heart leaped into her throat.

"My family lives here," she managed to respond. "Why on earth would you be surprised to see me visiting?"

A smile softened Devoncourt's mouth, but it didn't

quite reach his eyes. She'd never noticed that before. "My apologies. I thought you and your father were at odds."

Such a suggestion had never come from her mouth.

What had her father said about her?

Adele arched a brow. "You thought wrong. I won't say he was pleased to hear news of my marriage, but he's accepted it now. And I was here to visit with my sister. Not my father." When one was caught out, the best way to deflect was to attack. "Though I must say, I'm surprised to see you here. I know you and my father are friendly, but calling at home?"

Was he the messenger her father just had to see?

Had her father told him she was visiting?

Had he waited for her to emerge?

After all, she'd forced herself to sit through another ten-minute lecture on how Sir George respected Lord Corvus, and if Corvus wanted to court his daughter, then Hattie could make no truer match.

"We do some business together. Nothing of interest to you, I'm sure."

Adele bared her teeth in a smile. "Ugh. Business. How dreadfully dull. If you'll excuse me? I probably should be going. I'm going to be late. There's a new hair style my maid wishes to practice for Lady Haynes's ball."

Nothing was better designed to make gentlemen back away from a conversation than mention of gowns and toiletries.

"Surely you can spare me a moment? I wanted to speak to you about something."

"What sort of something?"

"Walk with me," he murmured, offering her arm. "And you'll find out."

Adele didn't disguise the furtive look she sent down the street. How was she to avoid this? "I don't know if that's entirely wise."

"Only to the park across the road," he replied. "Your husband can have no qualms about that, can he?"

"You don't know Malloryn very well if you think that," she replied dryly, as she accepted his arm.

"Ah, so I was right." Devoncourt's blue eyes softened as he stroked his hand over hers. "It was not by your design to give me the cut direct the other night."

What the hell could she say?

Malloryn had warned her away from Devoncourt, away from all of this, but she couldn't quite admit to Devoncourt why.

Adele let herself smile somewhat bitterly. "Apparently, while my husband might have no interest in touching me, he's quite territorial about other men venturing too close."

"Typical."

"Precisely my thought," she said.

"Did you ask your father about Malloryn's... nighttime escapades?"

"And have him throw my marriage in my face? I think not, my lord."

Devoncourt seemed to be trying to read her expression. "You should have, you know. You might have learned a thing or two about him."

"You seem awfully interested in my husband," she chided, rapping him on the arm with her fingers.

"One always studies one's opponent. And I never know when I may learn a deadly weakness to exploit."

"Are you going to fight a duel over me?"

"Perhaps. Would you like that?"

"What young woman isn't flattered by such attentions?" she replied smoothly.

Devoncourt's thumb brushed against her palm; an indecent gesture that sent a shiver through her. Despite what she might think of him, he was good at what he did.

"Would you meet with me again?"

"I am meeting with you," she pointed out.

"Privately?"

"I've told you—"

"He doesn't have to know." Devoncourt boldly tucked one of her curls behind her ear, his heated gaze darkening. "I know you spend your nights alone, cherub. All alone in that big house while your husband gads about London doing... whatever he damned well feels like doing. It's not as though he keeps track of your schedule, does he? You could slip out for the night. Tell him it's a ball."

She'd promised Malloryn she'd stay out of this, but what if she could somehow twist Devoncourt to her plans?

Malloryn had already admitted he had nothing in regards to the SOG.

"What did you have in mind?" Adele whispered, looking up into Devoncourt's cerulean eyes.

This time his smile touched every inch of his face.

Reaching inside his coat, he produced a gold-rimmed invitation embossed with a rising sun.

Her gaze locked on the logo.

"What is it for?"

"A secret gathering. A masquerade, of course. There'll be music. Dancing. Little alcoves where one can steal away privately, if one has the need for it."

"A ball?" she replied cynically.

"Not a ball. It's a little more... exclusive. A little more like the old days, when blue bloods were allowed off their leashes."

"That sounds dangerous."

"Oh, it is," he purred. "But not for you. All I want to show you is another side of life. You have no liking for your husband, do you?"

"He's a cold, merciless prig," she said mechanically.

"And your marriage is barely that."

"So you keep saying."

"What if you could free yourself from such a marriage?" His voice lowered.

"The last thing I want is a divorce." Her heart started beating a little faster. Because she knew he wasn't speaking of divorce at all.

And suddenly the stakes were higher than they'd ever been.

What if someone was plotting Malloryn's murder?

Could she get Devoncourt to tell her more?

"There are other ways to end a marriage," he replied, "And as I said, Malloryn has many enemies."

Her heart skipped a beat.

It wasn't an outright confession, but when it came to someone murdering her husband, she wasn't about to take any chances.

"The only other way that I can see is widowhood." Each word came out slowly. "I'm not quite certain I'm ready for that, and all it entails. He isn't... cruel."

Devoncourt seemed to hesitate. "There are rumors he's very fond of his mistress. A love match, they say."

She didn't bother to keep the bitterness out of her voice. "He wouldn't be the first aristocrat to prefer his mistress's bed."

"Yes, but she's been saying she doesn't expect him to be at your beck and call for very much longer. She'll have him all to herself."

"What does that mean?"

Devoncourt gave her a frank look. "All he has to do is declare you mentally unfit, my dear. He owns you. And it's common knowledge the marriage didn't come about of his own volition."

Despite the fact she knew he was lying, a shiver ran down her spine. "You're saying Malloryn might lock me away?"

It was a very real fear every woman in the Echelon faced.

Her father had even threatened her with it, if she didn't apologize to Lord Corvus for slashing his face with the little knife she carried up her sleeve.

"You would be out of Malloryn's way, and he would be free to spend his nights where he willed it."

No point reminding Devoncourt that he himself had told her that her husband was already spending his nights where he wanted. He must think her an utter fool. Anger stirred, lashed to a tempest by both Malloryn's request that she forget all this nonsense, and now Devoncourt's dismissal of her intelligence.

"What should I do?" she whispered, making her eyes very big and very round.

His hand immediately softened against her cheek. "I would protect you, cherub. I promise I would love you if you let me—"

"A lot of men have made me promises. Why should yours be any different?"

Devoncourt seemed momentarily taken aback.

Sorry, it seems I haven't quite swallowed your lies completely, dearest. "You ask me to put my faith in one man when I dare not trust another? You have no claim over me. No power over him. You ask me to walk into ruin with no guarantees of my safety. How can I beat the Duke of Malloryn? How can you destroy him? He's so powerful."

"He's not completely invincible." There was a faint snarl to his voice.

"You think you can bring him down?" Adele bit her lip. "But how? He has the queen's ear."

"Come to my gathering. There are many others like me and you who are ill-satisfied with the way life currently stands. Powerful men. And women. They could help you."

"For what price?"

"We all need a little help," he murmured. "You have the perfect bargaining chip. My friends want to see Malloryn and his ilk cast down. You're in a prime position to assist them. And in return you gain your freedom."

"Widowhood?" she whispered.

A smile. Devoncourt lifted her hand to his lips. "Perhaps."

"But what would I have to do?"

"Just come," he whispered. "Meet them. See what they have to say."

"I don't know...."

"You'll be safe, I promise." He set the invitation in her hand, and curled her fingers around it. "But make sure you bring the invitation. It will grant you my protection. No blue blood will touch you if you bear my mark of protection."

There was a hard lump in her throat.

Adele responded with a saucy shrug, playing up to the image of what he expected her to be. "I'll consider it." She tucked the invitation inside her bodice, knowing she drew his gaze. "Though I won't offer any guarantees."

Devoncourt laughed, setting his thumb on the middle of her lower lip for a heated second. "That's quite all right, my dear. The fun is in the chase."

And from the look in his eyes, he thought he had her on the hook.

CHAPTER FIFTEEN

Going to Hardcastle Lane was out of the question.

Malloryn had made it clear she wasn't to be seen there, and if Devoncourt and his allies were watching the safe house, then her cover would be blown.

So Adele sent a message, and settled into his library to wait.

Hours ticked past.

She tried to still her nerves by flicking through the books he'd piled beside his reading chair. Darwin's *The Descent of Man, and Selection in Relation to Sex*. *Frankenstein* by Mary Shelley. *The Origins of Bio-Mechanics* by a Thomas Shelby. Sedgwick's *Travels Through the Orient.*

She'd expected *The Prince* by Machiavelli to be more his style, but as she continued perusing the pile, she realized Malloryn didn't seem to have any sort of style at all.

Beyond curiosity, it seemed.

Sharp heels rapped on the hallway floor outside, and Adele instantly set *The Count of Monte Cristo* back into place. She'd recognize that impatient stride anywhere and practically launched to her feet.

Where had he been?

She'd said it was *urgent*.

Malloryn burst through the library doors, a palm splayed against each door. He wasn't the tallest man she'd ever seen, but his mere presence seemed to swallow all the oxygen in the room. Malloryn drew everyone's eye, simply by existing.

He held her brief missive up between two fingers. "What the hell were you doing with Devoncourt?"

"Flirting," she replied. "And trying to get him to tell me everything."

"Flirting." A cold, hard word. He turned abruptly toward the brandy decanter, as if he needed a moment to gather his emotions.

"It's the only weapon available to me at times."

"I thought I told you to *stay away* from him. Did you not hear a word I said?" he snarled, turning on her so angrily that brandy sloshed over his sleeve.

"Quite. You were most specific about what you wanted me to do."

"Then why the hell did you disobey me? This isn't a game."

"Oh, silly me. That's precisely what I thought it was."

The swish of skirts had followed him inside the room, but it was only as a woman coughed discreetly that Adele realized he wasn't alone.

His protégé, Miss Townsend, seemed slightly amused as she took in the scene. "Why don't you let her speak, Malloryn? As much as I'm enjoying the byplay, she did say it was urgent. In my experience, your wife's not an idiot."

"Thank you." Adele tipped her head toward the voluptuous brunette, though she wasn't entirely certain what to think of the woman.

"You're welcome."

Adele turned to Malloryn. "Just in case you were interested, I didn't seek Lord Devoncourt out. I.... He was.... Goodness, I should probably start at the beginning." *But how?* She pressed her fingers to her temples. "It started this afternoon. I went to see my sister—"

Malloryn looked at her incredulously. "Adele, I don't have time for—"

"Can you *please* let me finish?"

He shut his mouth.

"My father wanted to see me. Something about Lord Corvus officially applying to court Hattie as a thrall, and how I wasn't to make a fuss about it. He was called away for a moment, leaving me alone in his study, and I realized there was a rising sun symbol embossed on his fireplace. Out of curiosity I examined it and the fireplace swung open, revealing a hidden study behind it."

Now she had his attention. Malloryn suddenly looked lethal as he leaned toward her. "The fireplace just happened to swing open?"

"There was a small latch. It caught my eye, and then my curiosity."

"And?"

"There's a secret study hidden behind the fireplace. I spent years in that house and I never even knew it was there," she blurted. "I didn't get much time to examine the place. I knew Father would be returning at any moment. But I saw maps of London on the desk inside, with little red crosses marked over certain places. Hardcastle Lane was one of them. The opera was another. The Ivory Tower. There were some factory schematics underneath it. More detailed drawings that appeared to design some sort of device. I'm not mechanical-minded, so I have no idea what it is. A detailed list of supplies, including large quantities of Nobel's Blasting Powder—"

"Explosives," Miss Townsend said abruptly.

"I think so. I barely had time to look at any of it. But I think... I think my father's involved in your Rising Sons. He's always hated you and was furious when I told him we were to be married. It made no sense at the time, for what father would not desire his daughter to be made a duchess? But now? After this? The only reason I can find for such intense dislike is that he's involved in the Rising Sons and he knows exactly who you are and what you do."

"And if he has maps and plans in a secret study in his house, then it's highly likely he's one of the masters behind the scheme," Miss Townsend murmured.

"Describe the study, and the fireplace," Malloryn demanded.

So Adele did.

"You're thinking this is a job for Charlie and Lark?" Miss Townsend asked, when she'd finally finished.

Malloryn paced by the window, scrubbing a hand over his mouth. "Yes. I need to know what Sir George is up to."

"There's more," Adele said. "You're not going to like it."

"I don't like any of this, particularly the part about you sneaking around your father's study when you suspected he's working for my enemy."

"I couldn't help myself. The rising sun symbol was right there in front of me." And she'd *needed* to know. All those years of sanctimonious lectures. All those times he'd told her women and children should be seen and not heard. The expression Sir George had worn when she'd told him the Duke of Malloryn had compromised her and then offered marriage. *I am done with you*, he'd said, as if he'd simply closed the book on their life together.

But some part of Adele wasn't done with him, and the second she'd seen that symbol every inch of her had run hot and cold. *Ignore me now, you bastard.*

"What was I supposed to do? Pretend you hadn't enlightened me? Twiddle my thumbs and try not to wonder if my father is involved in a plot against the queen? If I did so, then you'd be no closer to finding the Rising Sons."

He had no answer to that.

"I think you're enjoying this." Malloryn slid his hands into his pockets, his gray eyes glittering.

Adele couldn't resist a small smile. "Only a little."

"Go on," he said.

"This is where Devoncourt comes in," she said. "As I was leaving I encountered him on the stairs. I don't know why he was there. It did strike me that he might have been following me, but I think it more likely they're coconspirators. He knows my father. They're quite friendly. It's how we met. He was circling around Hattie, and I didn't like it."

"So you were flirting with him." Malloryn gestured, as if to say, *very well, get on with it.*

Reaching inside her bodice, she withdrew the crumpled invitation. "Devoncourt wants me to go to a private soiree with him tomorrow night."

She'd expected him to be furious.

If anything, Malloryn's expression only tightened. "Why?"

"Because he thinks you're going to suffer a seeming accident sometime soon, and I'll be left a merry widow, or somesuch. I might be lonely, judging by the sympathy dripping from his voice. I may have given the impression I find you cold and distant, and he assumed I was looking for more entertaining companionship."

"Namely him," Miss Townsend mused.

"It did seem that way," she replied. "He always asks about you. Wants to know where you are and what you're up to. And in the next breath he's hinting that you're madly in love with your mistress and there are rumors you're planning on casting me aside, or locking me away in an asylum. Anything to drive a wedge between the two of us."

"Oh, he's good." Miss Townsend seemed impressed.

"I'm going to kill him." Malloryn said it without an ounce of heat in his voice, and yet there was a flash of something in his eyes. Something Adele couldn't quite decipher.

But then, sometimes it seemed understanding her husband would require an entire university degree.

And even then, she thought she might not know the full extent of him.

She wanted to.

"No, you're not," Miss Townsend chided. "He's the best lead we've got. Once he's led us back to Balfour, you can beat the claret out of him, or whatever you damned well like, but not before."

Again that hard gaze pinned Adele. "Did he say *why* he wanted you to attend his private soiree?"

"Use your imagination," she replied tartly. "I'm fairly certain it's not to dance with me."

There.

There was that hint of *something* moving through the mosaic of grays and greens that made up his pupils. A hint of violence barely restrained. A sliver of the darkness of the craving within him.

The predator.

A whisper of both trepidation and excitement thrilled through her. For a second she thought she could almost put a name to the emotion she saw, but then Malloryn shut down before her eyes, and it was gone again.

Cool. Rational. Implacable.

Malloryn, once more.

"He indicated that if I wanted to rid myself of you, then there were certain powerful people who might be able to help me. As long as I gave them something in return. Maybe I'll be able to recognize some of the others in attendance."

Plucking the invitation from Adele's fingers, he examined it. "Angel's Fall. You do realize this is a gaming club partly owned by Lord Corvus?"

She'd been ready for it. "You don't say?"

Malloryn rubbed his thumb along the invitation, as if chasing after the last hints of her body heat. "This is not the sort of place you should attend. Angel's Fall is dangerous at the best of times. Fortunes are won and lost in the gaming rooms; blue bloods beat each other bloody in the underground fighting pits; and there's a private auction room for gentleman of certain tastes to buy young ladies *intacto*."

Intacto...?

"Virgins," Malloryn added, reading her expression. "Whether willing or not, they're all virgins."

"That's horrific."

"Yes. Unfortunately, the club is heavily policed by several rogue blue bloods, and bidders must go through a ruthless process to prove they're not the sort to squeal to the authorities. The queen has sent Nighthawks in several times, but the auctions vanish as if they never existed. All I have is rumor and innuendo, and it's not enough to convict any of the lords involved. I've tried to get a man on the inside twice, but they've both disappeared."

She had the sickening urge to track Lord Corvus down and punch him in his perfect white teeth. "I shouldn't be surprised."

"No?"

"With Corvus involved, I'd expect only the most vile

of atrocities."

Malloryn's gaze locked on her. "Any reason you have a seeming vendetta against the man?"

"Nothing you ought to know."

He'd made it clear he was interested in tracking down the blue blood nobleman who'd assaulted her the night she'd forced him into a proposal, but Corvus wasn't the sort of man one crossed.

Not even Malloryn?

For a second she was tempted to tell him the truth. But he was dealing with enough mischief as it was. And Devoncourt, Balfour, even her father, were more important than handing a set down to the vile miscreant who'd stalked her through the Echelon.

She had to tell herself that twice.

"Adele," Malloryn warned.

"He's courting my sister. I don't trust him. Is that not reason enough?"

"Corvus is precisely the sort of character who's at the top of our list of Rising Sons." From the glint in Miss Townsend's eyes, she hadn't missed the faint flicker of distress on Adele's face. "He has a liking for pretty, innocent young girls. I could lure him somewhere private. See if he has anything of interest to say."

"He's dangerous," Adele warned. "At least as dangerous as Devoncourt, I would think."

"So am I, Your Grace. I can see to it that he'll never bother your sister again."

"Not yet." Malloryn tapped the invitation against his thigh. "This appears to be a private salon. If we can get an agent inside, we may be able to learn more about the Rising Sons."

"You've tried twice," Miss Townsend reminded him.

"Yes, but we never had an invite."

Adele plucked the invite from his fingers. "And you don't have one now. This has *my* name on it."

"Mask required," he pointed out. "All I need is a pretty little blonde, and I can get my hands on one of them with a click of my fingers. I have dozens of pretty little blondes at my beck and call."

Adele was taken aback.

Miss Townsend's eyes widened. "You're all charm. Remind me how you thought you were going to seduce your wife again?"

"By lying to me." Adele smothered the brief flash of hurt in her breast. "That's how he did it. He minced some rather pretty words several days ago. I think I prefer this sort of brutal honesty. At least I can trust it."

"I wasn't referring to personally putting my hands on—"

"I would quit while you're ahead," Adele said icily.

Malloryn's gaze promised retribution.

"I can find a female agent in one of my networks," he stated slowly, "who resembles you."

"There's one little problem with your plan," she said. "I was invited. You were not. If you send someone in using my invite and they're discovered, Devoncourt will know I'm working against him. Right now he trusts me. He thinks he's going to twist me around his little finger. The second your agent opens her mouth he'll know she's not me. And he'll know you're onto him."

"Unfortunately," Miss Townsend said with a beatific smile, "your wife speaks the truth."

"Since when are you in Adele's corner?"

Miss Townsend linked her arm through Adele's elbow. "Since she married you, Malloryn. Someone has to bring you down a peg or two. And I'm enjoying every moment of it."

He stared at the pair of them for long seconds, and then shook his head. "Fine. But if you enter that gaming club, you're not going alone. And you will obey every instruction I give you, or I'll rip that cursed invitation into little pieces and toss it in the Thames. Along with the pair of you."

Miss Townsend gave an amused huff as he stalked away. "Well, someone certainly has his britches in a twist. I wonder who it could be?"

And she gave Adele a disconcerting wink.

Malloryn smuggled Adele into the safe house later that night—in a trunk.

In all her dreams of being involved in the conspiracy, it wasn't what she'd expected, but as he guided her up the stairs into the private dining room that had been converted to some sort of briefing chambers, she couldn't help feeling breathless with excitement.

It wasn't so much being a part of this—she wasn't stupid enough to relish the danger she faced.

But it made her feel useful. Wanted.

And the fact her husband was taking her seriously softened any sorts of feelings she might have had about that *"I have dozens of pretty little blondes at my beck and call"* comment.

"Adele, you've met the rest of the Company of Rogues at various times," Malloryn said, gesturing to the eleven strangers who were seated around the table. "And it appears everyone here is aware of my wife's identity, considering the vast interest we've all taken in her ever since the wedding was announced."

That was definitely sarcasm.

Adele shot him a sideways glance. "Vast interest?"

"A delight, Your Grace," said a tall, handsome blond youth who seemed of an age with her. "The duke's referring to what happens when a company of spies discovers their leader is getting married. I'm Charlie Todd. I brought you brandy the other day."

"Oh, yes. He of the inferior set of glassware."

Charlie darted a glance toward Malloryn. "Should I know what that means? What's wrong with my glassware?"

"You don't have any glassware," said the young woman at his side.

"To your left is Obsidian," the duke continued, "then Kincaid, Ava, Byrnes, Ingrid, Lark, Jack, and you'll recall my butler and chief of security, Herbert. You made quite an impression upon him the last you met."

The twinkle in his eyes made her want to stomp upon his foot.

"I'm terribly sorry, sir," she said to the impeccable butler. "I was somewhat out of sorts the other day when I accosted you."

The butler tilted his head toward her. "Quite all right, Your Grace. The duke has a habit of putting anyone out of sorts on the best of days."

"It's lovely to meet you," said Byrnes, in the sort of voice she immediately found suspect. "Officially."

His face seemed familiar. "You were at my engagement party."

When the vampire had attacked and everything had turned into utter chaos. Adele's mother had been on the verge of ending the engagement right then and there, and if not for Malloryn's friendship with the queen, she may have.

Byrnes patted the hand of the tall, statuesque brunette sitting beside him. "One of Balfour's first attempts to kill your husband. Ingrid and I lured the vampire away, and then we blew up Tower Bridge. I can still hear Malloryn's lecture ringing in my ears."

"I thought your hair was black?"

Byrnes ran a hand through his silvery-blond locks. "Slight run-in with an insane enemy agent who wanted to transform me."

"Byrnes and Obsidian are evolved blue bloods," Malloryn told her. "We call them *dhampir*, and they're what occur when a blue blood enters the Fade and doesn't turn into a vampire."

The Fade was the final, irreversible end stage of the craving virus, when one usually devolved into a mindless, bloodthirsty vampire. Nobody had escaped that fate. "But how did—"

"Nearly twenty years ago, a Dr. Cremorne began performing illegal experiments upon blue bloods to see if he could halt the tide of the Fade. He managed to create an elixir that could transmute it instead," said the blonde woman at the end of the table in an excited tone usually reserved for university lecturers who'd been granted a captive audience. "It didn't reverse the Fade, but it created an evolved blue blood instead of a vampire. *Dhampir* are—"

"Thank you, Ava." Malloryn hastily cut her off, Adele noticed. "I'll explain it in more detail later, if you wish. Suffice it to say, *dhampir* are faster and stronger than blue bloods, and almost impossible to kill. Balfour has several of them working for him. We have two. And one last guest to introduce."

"We do?" This from the hard-eyed man he'd referred to as Jack, who wore a breathing apparatus slung around his throat.

Malloryn glanced toward the door as a woman entered, as if she'd been waiting for her cue. "Ah, Mrs. Herbert, how good of you to join us."

The woman was tall, brunette, and had the sort of face one would skip over in a crowd. "My pleasure, Your Grace."

Adele's eye did not skip over her.

Her mouth dropped open. "Clara?"

"Your Grace." Her maid tipped her head toward her regally.

It took a moment to sink in.

"My maid is one of your spies," she said to Malloryn through gritted teeth. "When were you going to tell me?"

One of his eyebrows arched. "It slipped my mind."

"How strange," Adele continued, "that my previous maid gave her notice almost three months ago, and despite having four potential maids apply for the job, only one of them showed up to interview. Her references were absolutely impeccable too."

"Of course they were," he replied with a straight face. "I forged them myself. It was shortly after I returned from Russia, and I realized you might be a target. I needed someone close to you who could protect you if need be."

"Let me guess? Our butler, Richards, spends his nights breaking into your enemies' homes?"

"Don't be ridiculous. Richards is eighty, if he's a day. He's merely the butler. But two of the upper footmen could kill a man with nothing more than a toothpick in at least six different ways."

"Only six?" Miss Townsend mused. "I could do it in at least twelve."

"Wait, wait, wait, wait." All four feet of Byrnes's chair hit the ground as he leaned forward and stared at Adele's maid. "Did he call you Mrs. Herbert? As in *the* Mrs. Herbert? Our Herbert's wife? The mysterious Mrs. H?"

The woman in the center of this entire furor blinked at him. "Aye, Byrnes. And I've heard all about you and your sense of... humor."

Byrnes shot Herbert a look.

"He's hilarious," the butler said, with an absolutely straight face. "And yes, this is my Clara."

His face softened as the spouses shared a look.

"Oh," said the hulking brute Malloryn had called Kincaid. "Our Herbert's in love."

"It appears to be contagious," Malloryn said distantly as he rifled through several sheets of paper.

"Well," Byrnes assured him, "you're the last man standing, so to speak. I wouldn't be worried at all if I were you."

Kincaid snickered, then blinked as his wife appeared to kick him under the table. The rest of the ladies looked murder at them, and an awkward undertone of silence filled the room.

"I'm not worried," Malloryn replied. "Love is a weakness I can ill afford at the moment."

It wasn't that the statement hurt; it was that he said it so coolly, in front of them all.

"Malloryn," Miss Townsend growled in faint rebuke.

"It's quite all right," Adele made herself say, wearing the thin smile that had seen her through several Seasons of vitriol she pretended she couldn't hear. "The duke and I have an understanding. And one would need a heart to be at risk of losing it."

"One should not throw stones when one lives in a glass house," Malloryn returned. "I was not named Ice Princess of the year, three years running."

"No, they tend to call you something else. It rhymes with that 'old trick.'"

It felt like the early days of their marriage, all over again.

"Is anyone else having any luck fading into the

furniture right about now?" Byrnes asked in a loud whisper.

Kincaid winced.

And Adele found herself blushing furiously as she lowered her eyes. Old habits died hard. If she'd been called an ice princess behind her back, it was only because she'd had to be in order to protect herself.

What, then, was Malloryn's excuse?

"Fine. We'll discuss this later. In private. Is there any chance we can concentrate on the matter at hand?" Malloryn asked. "Tomorrow night, my wife is going undercover at Angel's Fall. Since you're all well known to Balfour's agents, I have no choice but to send her in alone with Clara. Meanwhile"—he stabbed a finger toward Charlie and Lark—"the pair of you are going to break into Sir George Hamilton's private study and discover just what he's up to. Gemma's going with you, just in case. Any questions?"

Byrnes raised his hand.

"Any questions that do not pertain to Clara and Herbert's marriage? Or mine?"

Byrnes slowly lowered it.

"No, Your Grace," several of the Rogues chorused.

"Right, then let's go over the plan," Malloryn announced, unrolling a map that appeared to be of the gaming club in question.

Adele didn't ask how he'd gotten it.

CHAPTER SIXTEEN

"Allowing you to do this goes against all my better instincts," Malloryn murmured as he fitted a small brass device inside Adele's jeweled hairpin. A tracking beacon, he'd explained. Just in case something went wrong.

"I didn't know you had better instincts."

Silver eyes met hers, and then a rare smile touched his mouth. "There she is."

"*She?*"

"My tart-tongued bride. The one who gives as good as she gets."

"I wasn't aware I'd ever been anything else?"

"You've been a little quieter the last couple of days." He tilted her head, settling several blonde curls over her ear to hide the pin.

She'd never seen anything like it, but Malloryn had produced an entire array of gadgets and devices to assist in her endeavors. He'd clipped a listening device just inside her bodice, through which he—and several of his so-called Rogues—could hear everything that was said in her vicinity, even if they were a hundred yards away.

She wouldn't be able to communicate with them, but they'd know if she found herself in trouble.

"I was angry with you," she replied, glancing to where his Rogues were fitting themselves out for a stealth mission.

They'd set up their surveillance base on a rooftop several houses over from Angel's Fall. He'd even brought the butler, who was tuning the radio phonograph through which they'd be able to listen.

"You weren't angry," Malloryn murmured. "I've seen you angry before. You throw things."

"That was one time."

"It was memorable." His eyes crinkled with humor.

"You're going to remind me of that frequently, aren't you?"

"Forever."

If we have forever.

She bit her lip as she examined his face. His concentration was absolute, allowing her unrestricted access to his thoughts and emotions.

"About what I said yesterday in front of everyone—"

"You don't have to explain." Adele cut him off swiftly. "We were barely on speaking terms a week ago, so I never…. Love is not something I've ever anticipated. People of our class generally don't find it, and marriages are built on far less presumptive measures."

"Like honesty?" he murmured, looking down into her upturned face. "I shouldn't have said it. I haven't been sleeping well of late, but that's no excuse. Sometimes.... They push me too far. There was a bet leading up to our wedding about whether we would make it to the altar or not."

"Who won?"

Malloryn suddenly looked tired. "I did. Considering

our aborted first attempt, nobody knows the precise time and location of the actual ceremony."

"Should I expect to be interrogated about it?" she murmured.

"I don't think anyone would have the balls."

"I think your friend Byrnes would."

"He's not my friend."

Adele arched a brow. He seemed a different man around his Company of Rogues, and though the banter clearly drove him crazy, it also seemed to anchor him somehow. "If he does ask, I'll lie."

"You'd do that? For me?" The barest of smiles touched his mouth.

"You did just apologize."

"Truce?" Malloryn murmured.

Adele gave a careless shrug, but he stopped it with the faintest brush of his fingers against your cheek. "There is one last thing I wanted to talk to you about. I saw your expression when I introduced Mrs. Herbert."

"Well, yes. I wasn't expecting my maid to be spying on me."

"If it's any consolation, I put her into place to protect you," he pointed out.

"And you haven't used her services to keep an eye on me in the last week, when you thought me working for the enemy?"

He didn't bother to reply.

She knew the answer, and his face said it all.

Adele breathed out a laugh. "Look at the pair of us. How are we going to make this marriage work?"

"I don't know, Adele. I don't know. I cannot even promise you complete honesty," he admitted. "I know too many dangerous things—things that could get you killed if someone thought you knew them too."

"I don't expect you to blather in my ear about council secrets and the state of the realm," she said crossly. "I understand you cannot. But… I would appreciate it if you would not outright lie to me. If you cannot tell me something, then simply say that. And warn me the next time you intend to produce some spy in my household. Please."

"My apologies. I'm not used to this."

"This?"

"Being married," he admitted, "in anything other than name. Or sharing my thoughts with others."

Adele looked him directly in the eye. "Your Rogues all jump to attention when you bark at them, but I am not a Rogue, Malloryn. I expect—"

"Technically…." He trailed off.

"Technically, what?"

"They voted you in yesterday."

Oh. The idea took her aback, and she felt a flush of what could possibly be described as joy. "But you…. I thought you didn't want me involved?"

"Did you think *I* had any sort of say on things around here?"

"I think you're trying to distract me," she pointed out.

"Adele." Malloryn straightened, looking decidedly deadly tonight in black leather. There was no sign of the icily controlled duke she'd thought she'd married. "I'm sorry for the way this played out. I'm sorry I deceived you. If I hadn't thought you were working for my enemy I would never have—"

"Touched me," she whispered.

Something flickered through the depths of his gray eyes, though she'd always had trouble deciphering which precise emotion he felt.

If he felt anything at all.

"That's not entirely certain," he finally said. "I wasn't lying the other night when I said you were beautiful. Or when I said sometimes I think about kissing you. And you vex me constantly. Especially of late. One of us would have broken sooner or later, and exploded. And then I think we'd have ended up in bed either way."

An apology—and a compliment—was the last thing she'd expected. Adele wet her lips. "I'm sorry I began our marriage the way I did. I lied to you and the Echelon, and I forced you to marry me. It wasn't.... I didn't do it deliberately. Or it was, but not... premeditated."

"I know." His eyes hooded. "You've hinted in the past that someone hurt you and you saw me as your way out."

"You didn't believe me."

"I didn't want to believe you."

A small smile burst over her mouth. "You're starting to make me nervous, Malloryn. All these nice things you're saying. Apologies. Peace. Are you worried you'll have me on your conscience if this all goes wrong?"

"No." His expression hardened. "Because nothing *is* going to go wrong. Clara will be accompanying you, and she's an expert at hand-to-hand combat. You know what you must do?"

Adele rolled her eyes as the intimacy of the previous moment evaporated.

"I show my invitation. I giggle. I flirt. I do nothing to make Devoncourt suspicious. You're going to be listening in, so my role is to act the wide-eyed ingénue and see what he'll say to me. I'm to identify any lords I recognize, and see what they want me to do in regards to you. And then I'm going to have a violent reaction to the champagne and be forced to withdraw early."

"And don't go anywhere alone with Devoncourt."

"What if he expects a kiss?"

"Then play coy."

"I've been playing coy with him for months. He's just invited me to a secret masquerade. You yourself said how dangerous this is if he discovers I'm playing him false."

There. The faint tic of the muscle in his jaw.

"It's just a kiss," Adele whispered, though she couldn't let him know she didn't give a damn whether Devoncourt kissed her or not. No. She wanted to know if her husband would even care. "How else am I to wrangle the truth out of him? I can hardly wrap him around my little finger in public."

"*Adele.*" A growl.

"And you've been kind enough to teach me how little I knew of kissing. I'm sure I've mastered the art by now. He won't know what's hit him."

"I wasn't aware you were planning to go in there to kiss him."

"Well, I can hardly arm wrestle him into submission. Or tie him to a chair and question him. How did you think I was going to try and get answers from him?"

Silence.

A thick, weighted silence.

She couldn't resist torturing him a little more. "Don't worry, Malloryn. He's kept it fairly chaste until now. I'm sure he'll suffer in comparison to your expert ministrations."

"I don't know why I let you talk me into this."

"Do you know what I think?" Adele whispered.

"What?"

His face was so close to hers, she could almost taste his breath against her lips. Byrnes, Ingrid, Herbert, and Clara hovered nearby, but the pair of them might as well have been alone for the way the air thickened around them.

"I think," she said, tilting her lips almost to his in a

taunt, "that you don't want me anywhere near Devoncourt. And it's got nothing to do with him being an ex-Falcon."

"Do you know what *I* think?" He banked the smoldering heat in his eyes with pure willpower, but the look he gave her was no less dangerous.

"What?"

"I think we're no longer talking about Devoncourt kissing you. Are we? Do you want me to kiss you, Adele?"

There. There it was.

He hadn't touched her since the other day in the study.

She shrugged. "We're on a rooftop. I'm about to embark on a dangerous mission. It hardly seems the time or place."

"When it comes to kissing you, it's never the time or place."

"Admit it. The idea of me kissing Devoncourt bothers you."

Malloryn's eyes darkened with heat as his fist curled in a handful of her skirts. "Is that what you want of me? To admit I'm jealous?"

Yes.

"I don't think I have to be," he purred.

Sliding a hand around her nape, he hauled her mouth to his.

Adele gasped, and the slight parting of her lips gave him the opening he needed. The hot, slick glide of his tongue stroked hers possessively. She could feel that touch in other areas, her nipples hardening as his other hand splayed over her bottom and ground her hips against his.

All those cool, arrogant looks he gave her....

The careless quirk of his brow....

It melted away in a firestorm of heat as Malloryn kissed her as if this was their last moment on this mortal coil. She'd always thought him cold and dispassionate, but the second he put his hands on her the mask melted away, leaving her with the man beneath.

Her back met the wall, the pitted brickwork pricking at her spine. But all else was forgotten as she felt the demanding press of Malloryn's erection grinding against her belly. And suddenly she was back in his study, splayed across his desk as he took her with passion and fury.

Heat slicked between her thighs, and somehow she slid her hand beneath his coat, working it down between them.

His mouth softened as he captured her hand before she could enclose it around his erection. A nip at her lower lip. Then another, as he eased the fury of the kiss. The faintest of laughs escaped him.

Malloryn tore his mouth from hers, breathing hard.

"Now, now, Adele. You're going to blow your cover if any of the Echelon see me fucking you here, on a rooftop opposite Angel's Fall."

Adele wilted in his arms, resting her forehead against his chest, her fist curled in his shirt. *Good God.* He'd stolen her breath. Stolen her wits. Left her shaking and ruined, her mouth blistered with the mark of his.

Her only consolation was the fact she wasn't the only one undone.

She could feel the tension in his body; the hard press of his hips to hers. And there was the throbbing pressure of that hard length grinding into her hips. No matter what he told her, a part of him wanted to toss up her skirts right here, right now; she'd stake her life on it.

Adele looked up challengingly. "Was there a point to that? Beyond acting like a possessive devil? You only proved my argument."

"Go to him with the taste of my kiss on your lips,"

Malloryn whispered in her ear, and a shiver ran through her. "Do what you must to maintain your ruse. But be careful. And call for me if you need me."

The flicker of disappointment lit within her. She didn't want permission. She'd wanted him to say no. "So you don't care if he kisses me?"

Stepping back, he traced his thumb across her swollen mouth and cast her a well-satisfied smile. "Devoncourt could kiss you a thousand times, Adele. I don't think there's anything for me to worry about, is there?"

Damn him.

"This isn't over," she warned.

She'd never seen that sort of smile on his face as he backed away. The years sloughed off him, leaving him winking at her with a remarkably boyish twinkle in his eyes. "It's just a kiss, Adele."

CHAPTER SEVENTEEN

"You came."

Adele took a glass of champagne from a passing tray and sipped it, the bubbles tickling her dry throat as she examined the darkened room. Angel's Fall had been built in a newly restored church, and the watchful eyes of stained glass angels looked down upon the gaming tables as their denizens committed to sin. "You doubted me?"

Devoncourt leaned closer, his mouth curling into a satisfied little smile. He'd found her the second she entered. "You've been a touch inconsistent in the past, my dear."

"Is that not a lady's whim?"

A kiss to the back of her hand. "I never quite know what you're thinking, cherub. I must admit there's a certain sort of challenge involved in bringing you to heel."

Cherub.

Ugh.

For once, she was quite grateful for the way Malloryn had never used such sickly sweet words on her.

He didn't need to.

Just the way he said her name made her shiver a little.

"Adele."

As if there was a wealth of meaning in the word. A challenge. A certain sort of possessive claim.

"If you think you're going to 'bring me to heel,' then I beg you, pray think again," she said, rapping Devoncourt's knuckles with her fan. "I belong only to myself, and I don't think I like your assumptions."

"Forgive me," he said smoothly, backing away with tempting smile. "Hopefully what I show you tonight will make up for my appalling lack of manners."

Blond, foppish Devoncourt, with his devastating blue eyes and wicked smile. A part of her couldn't quite believe he was one of Lord Balfour's most feared assassins.

But perhaps that was the point.

He had the easy manner of a charming scoundrel, a way of soothing a nervous young lady's fears when it came to blue blood lords. Nobody would expect a knife to the throat, not from him.

"This is my companion, Clara," she said, gesturing to her former maid.

"So pleased to meet you, my lord," Clara said, sounding almost breathless with excitement as she dipped into an elegant curtsy. From maid to lady with but a simple change of clothes.

"Does she have a last name?" Devoncourt didn't look happy with the turn of events.

"She does, but is this not a masquerade? Nobody knows anybody else's identity. I thought that was part of the fun?"

"The invitation was for one."

Adele drew back, as if a little shocked by his curt tone. "Yes, but I cannot simply gad about London unchaperoned. This is a dangerous part of town, my lord. She won't breathe a word of what she sees here, I promise.

She just.... I'm not the only one who wants to escape my world. All we wanted was a night of fun."

"I promise I won't get in the way," Clara said, with a flutter of her fan. "Adele said there might be *dancing*."

With her neat brown chignon and the dashing cut of her gown, Clara looked like she was ready to kick her heels up.

"Fine. This way," Devoncourt murmured, flicking his fingers at a nearby fellow in a plain back mask. "Perhaps my friend may entertain yours?"

Adele glanced over her shoulder. Clara placated her with a smile, graciously accepting the stranger's embrace as he swept her into a fast-paced waltz.

"You're unhappy with me," Adele said.

"No, I'm just.... I don't like surprises."

"I promise I'll make it up to you," she breathed, and then glanced around the glittering chamber. Dozens of masked men filled the space, as well as several scantily clad women.

It seemed like a mockery of a ball.

But no debutante wore her gown cut so low, and several of the women wore watered silk that clung to every curve in an indecent way. One had a golden leash about her throat, which was lashed to the wrist of a portly gentleman who looked like Lord Brummel.

Devoncourt intercepted a footman and took two glasses from his tray. "Here."

Adele clinked her half-full glass against his in chastisement. "I've barely finished this onc."

"Then drink up." He seemed to have cast off his surliness like a cloak. "I want to celebrate."

Adele paused. Then she tipped the glass to her lips and drained it. "What are we celebrating?"

"You. Me." He smoothly replaced her empty glass

with his full one. "That fact your husband isn't here."

Adele made herself laugh. "Well, I could hardly bring him, could I? Malloryn has such a dampening effect upon a gathering. It's the supercilious way he peers down his nose at you, I think."

A little part of her enjoyed the fact her husband would be listening to every word.

"And where is he tonight?" Devoncourt murmured, slipping one hand onto the small of her back as he guided her into the edges of the ballroom.

"Malloryn? Why the hell would I know? You were the one who reminded me he wasn't spending his nights at home." She let her smile thin. "Or his days."

"It bothers you."

"Of course not." But she looked away sharply. "I don't want to speak about him. Not tonight. Tell me about this place. It's *so* exclusive I hear even Lord Buxton was denied membership. He's as rich as Croesus. I cannot believe he was turned away."

A flicker of frustration darkened Devoncourt's brow. "Unfortunately, you cannot merely buy your entrée."

"No?" She feigned surprise. "That must ruffle some feathers."

"Oh, it does."

"What are the requirements for membership, then? Can ladies join?"

"Unfortunately, it's strictly a gentleman's club. Members may invite those of the opposite sex for the night, but only blue bloods are initiated."

"Like the Echelon in its peak?"

Women had been mere chattel when the prince consort reigned; denied the Blood Rites where a nobleman's son was judged by his peers and found worthy of receiving the craving virus, and thus near immortality.

"Similar. Angel's Fall provides a place to play for those who find themselves reduced in status."

Her ears pricked.

She was right.

The members of Angel's Fall were all blue blood nobles who longed for a return to the old ways. The perfect recruitment ground for the Rising Sons. And if they were lucky, there would be membership rolls listing the current members.

Hopefully, Malloryn would be smart enough to make the same connections she had.

"Who makes these rules?"

"The founding four. They call themselves the Four Horsemen."

Someone had a high opinion of themselves. Adele stifled a giggle in her champagne. "The Four Horsemen? It's starting to sound like some sort of occult society, and not a club at all."

"They intend to bring about a new age," Devoncourt said. "The heralds of the Apocalypse."

"Can I meet them?" she asked. "This all sounds so dashed exciting."

"Alas, their identities remain unknown. We only know them as Death, War, Famine, and Conquest."

"It's rumored Lord Corvus owns a share in the business," she murmured. "Is he one of your Horsemen?"

He looked at her sharply. "Where did you hear that?"

"I make it my business to know what Corvus is up to." Her throat was suddenly dry. Adele finished the rest of her champagne in a hurry. "Is... is he here?"

"Gadding about in the bowels of the building," Devoncourt said. "Why?"

"Oh, we just.... We had a run-in once." *When I hemlocked him in Lord Abernathy's garden.* "He's not very fond of me."

"Ah, that explains why he seemed surprised I'd invited you. I assured him you were under *my* protection. He won't come near you."

"Well, if he's a Horseman, then how are you meant to deny him?" She made a pleased sound when she saw the flicker of frustration on his face. "You're a Horseman too, aren't you?"

And no doubt the one who'd set this all into motion.

He turned it all around on her. "You ask a lot of questions."

"Well, of course I do," Adele replied. "This all sounds so lurid. It's almost straight out of a gothic novel."

"You do realize that if you repeat any of this to anyone…." Devoncourt covered the silken threat with a smile.

Adele let the feathers of her fan brush against his lips. "Who am I going to tell?" Her voice dropped sadly. "My only friend, Lena, left me behind when she married that hulking brute verwulfen of hers. Nobody else listens to me. You're the only one who ever pays me such courtesies." She suddenly pressed her gloved hands to hot cheeks. "Oh, I'm so sorry. I'm babbling and dominating the conversation. Mother always told me I should let a gentleman speak, and I promise I will. I think that last glass of champagne went straight to my head. Do you think we can get some fresh air?"

Devoncourt looked like he was regretting inviting her. "Of course. This way."

He offered his arm and led her through an archway draped in decadent red velvet curtains.

"Where are we going?" Adele murmured, toying nervously with her emeralds. Though she knew Malloryn was listening to everything she said, she couldn't stop herself from worrying a little. She'd meant a balcony.

"Somewhere private."

He led her to a small garden alcove at the rear of the building. Glass windows lined the ceiling, offering a view of London's night sky. Lush vines trailed up the walls.

"What a lovely garden," she said, hoping Malloryn would hear. "One would never know an orangery was tucked away back here at the rear of the building."

"This place was a monastery, once upon a time," Devoncourt said. "The monks grew vegetables here, but we've made some small adjustments. This is our Garden of Eden."

And you're the snake.

"That's better," Adele murmured, as the noise died to a lull.

"Is it?" Devoncourt pressed her against a tall, marble column sheathed in ivy. Instantly, she set her hand to his chest with a warning quirk of the brow, but he merely smiled and captured her hand, lifting it to his lips.

"He's not here, cherub. No one to see. No one to hear."

"I know. Maybe I'm being *whimsical* again, my lord."

"Or maybe you're playing games."

There was a faint hint of warning to his tone.

"Aren't we all?"

"What did Malloryn say to you in the gardens the other night?" he suddenly asked. "He seemed quite intently interested in you, despite your claims of indifference."

"You were watching?"

"A friend mentioned it. She said you seemed flattered by his attentions. You encouraged them."

Adele pushed past him, sucking in a sharp breath. All the hairs down the back of her spine lifted. "It's not that."

"No? It's clear he's pursuing you."

"He noticed your flirtations," she said, thinking quickly. "He didn't approve of them. It seems even Malloryn is like a dog with a bone when it comes to other gentlemen sniffing around my skirts."

"You like his attentions."

How much had he seen of that moment in the garden?

"I don't... dislike them," she admitted carefully.

"And yet you're here."

The dazzling smile he shot her seemed charming, but dark edges of distrust glinted in his eyes. Pushing off the wall, he stalked toward her.

Adele didn't dare take a step back. He was already suspicious. "You invited me."

"I didn't think you'd actually come," he said, brushing a lock of hair behind her ear. "Why did you come, cherub?"

"Because I was curious. I was home. Alone. Once more. What do you want me to say? He ignores me all the time. I hate it. The only time he's ever paid me any attention has been of late. After you kissed me."

Devoncourt stilled. "Ah, so that's your game. You think if you encourage me, then you'll bring him to heel."

Adele gave a careless shrug. It seemed everyone thought her a heartless flirt who flitted from one man to the other. She might as well use the reputation. "I want a child. Malloryn's indifference concerns me. I find myself in a somewhat precarious position. You wouldn't understand. You're a man. I have a role to fulfill and my husband makes that role rather difficult. I cannot risk him setting me aside just because he won't…."

She bit her lip.

Devoncourt's suspicion softened. "I could give you a child. He'd never know."

"Unfortunately, he would," she replied, with a wry

smile. "He's never touched me. I need him to believe the child is his."

"Ah." Devoncourt brushed his knuckles against her lips. "So you use my attentions to prick at his jealousy. You are a clever girl."

"It's not like that." Leaning into his touch, she closed her eyes and let him stroke her cheek. "I do enjoy your flirtation. It's just…, one step too far and I cross a dangerous line. You were the one who said he might lock me away. You understand?"

"Perfectly."

Adele turned her face into his palm and pressed a kiss there, her heart beating rapidly. "If I can seduce my husband, then perhaps…. Perhaps I could enjoy your flirtations more."

"Only then?"

"I couldn't risk it."

Someone cleared their throat.

"Ah." Devoncourt backed away from her. "I'd like you to meet a friend of mine."

Adele turned in a swirl of skirts, determined to do her part. This was where she would be approached and asked to do something by one of the other members of the Rising Sons. Hopefully, the mastermind behind them.

The woman who stepped out of the greenery wore a long black velvet frock coat, with a cravat tied at her throat. Her silvery hair had been bound back into an elegant chignon, and she carried a gold-handled cane.

Adele's heart started beating faster.

Whoever she was, she was a blue blood.

No human woman had skin as pale as that, or hair without a hint of color to it.

To recover her shock, she fell back on the manners that had been drilled into her as a young woman. "How do you do?"

"As of right now? Excellent." The woman smiled, capturing Adele's gloved hand and lifting it to her lips, her voice dropping into a purr. "I have been waiting to meet you for a very long time, Your Grace."

"This is the Lady Dido," Devoncourt said, gesturing to the stranger. "You did say you wanted to meet the Horsemen. Well, she is Death, and she rules here in Angel's Fall. She rules us all."

"This is the Lady Dido…."

Malloryn froze. He leaned closer to the detachable phonograph as Devoncourt's voice came through the speaking tube.

"Is that—?"

Malloryn held a hand up, quelling Byrnes's question instantly.

"What are we going to do?" Ava asked, looking pale as Dido laughed gently at something Adele said.

Indecision flooded through him.

He'd never hesitated to make tough calls in the past.

The rest of them stared at him.

"If we go in there," Kincaid warned, "we risk ruining this entire venture."

"You can't go alone. The place is filled with dozens of blue bloods," Ingrid pointed out.

"We could lose this lead on Balfour," Byrnes said.

"Fuck Balfour," Malloryn snapped. He'd promised Adele she wouldn't come to any harm.

His first instinct was to extract her immediately, but how was he going to do that when Dido was standing right in front of her? Dido would slit Adele's throat the second she saw him.

"We wait," he said quietly, his heartbeat pounding. "Dido may not know Adele is working for us. Byrnes, I want a visual on Adele. She said she's in some sort of orangery at the back of the building, with glass walls."

"On it." Byrnes vanished.

"Herbert, do we have confirmation of where Clara is at the moment?"

The butler frowned and pressed his fingers to the earpiece he wore. "Still dancing, I believe. She was trying to extricate herself, but the gentleman would not take no for an answer."

"He'll regret that."

Herbert nodded. "He will."

If Adele kept her head….

She could do this. She thought swiftly on her feet. And she was intelligent enough to see the trap yawning around her.

Malloryn had to keep telling himself that.

"Devoncourt, could you fetch us both another glass of champagne?" Dido asked. *"I thought I could have a little chat with the duchess, woman to woman."*

"Thank you," Adele said politely, though he heard the tension in her voice.

"Devoncourt tells me you're interested in escaping the yoke of the Duke of Malloryn?"

"I don't know if I would dare, my lady."

Good. Nice and noncommittal. A breath eased out of him.

"It's a woman's lot, is it not? To suffer under a man's control."

"This is the world we were born into."

"But you are here to discover if you can find some way of escaping him. Poor little soul. Love hurts," Dido mused. *"A woman is better off without it."*

"I've never expected such emotions to afflict me, to be honest. I never expected anything more than to make a thrall contract."

"And marriage to a duke was beyond your expectations." Dido sounded almost motherly. *"Besides, one would need a heart to be at risk of losing it."*

One would need a heart....

Their previous argument leapt to mind, and everything within Malloryn locked down cold. This was a taunt. Somehow Dido knew exactly what had been discussed in the dining room at Hardcastle Lane.

They'd searched the entire house after someone left a letter on his desk, but there must be listening devices planted somewhere.

"She knows." The words sounded hollow and distant. "We need to get her out of there. Now. Herbert, get Clara into position."

"I would, Your Grace, but there's nothing but static coming through that line."

Damn it. What was going on in there? "Ingrid?"

"Byrnes can see her," Ingrid replied, "He says they're only talking."

"Devoncourt said you wished me to assist you in some endeavor?"

Right to the point.

He leaned forward, knuckles digging into his thigh.

"Oh, yes. I was hoping you would be the key to my plans to bring Malloryn down."

"The key?" Adele asked. *"In what way?"*

"But that is where the problem lies," Dido said patiently. *"For I cannot trust you, it seems."*

"I assure, my lady, I'll breathe not a word of—"

"You don't have to," Dido interrupted. *"Because Malloryn is listening to every word we say. Isn't he?"*

"Pardon? I'm not quite sure what—"

"You lie very well, but you're working for him. You have been all along. But Malloryn's not the only one who can listen in on conversations. And there is someone who's been dying to reacquaint himself with you. Lord Corvus, if you will join us?"

"Lord Corvus?" Adele gasped, and there was a muffled sound of voices he couldn't quite hear.

"I trust our negotiations are complete, Corvus?"

"I am more than well satisfied."

A scream echoed through the phonograph. The sound of something crashing. And then Malloryn was on his feet and moving toward the edge of the rooftop.

"Let go of me!" Adele cried.

Adele trembled before no one. But *someone* had hurt her, someone had made her so afraid for her life that she'd seen marriage to him as a blessing somehow.

She'd refused to tell him who it was.

Malloryn wasn't a gambler, but he'd have bet good coin that someone was Corvus.

"We're coming with you," Ingrid said, ripping her coat off and tossing it aside. "And don't bother arguing."

One last scream echoed through the device, and the color faded from Malloryn's world as the predator within him awoke. "Then make sure you stay out of my way."

Adele spun around as a patch of shadow detached itself from the gloom near the far wall. Lord Corvus. Her nightmare. Her gaze shot to his face as he lowered his mask; those sharp cheekbones, hawkish nose, and the bottomless pits of his eyes.

This time Adele didn't bother hiding her fear as she took two steps away from him. Heat flooded in from her extremities until her heart was a rushing, pulsing engine that throbbed with it.

The passage to the gaming room stood behind her, but she'd never make it in time.

Not with Dido watching her with an amused smile as she sipped her champagne.

"Well, well, well," Lord Corvus drawled. "I promised we'd meet again, my dear, and here we are." His hungry gaze raked her from head to toe. "Here *you* are. In my own domain."

Where had he come from? There was only a wall of ivy in that corner.

"Lord Corvus," she blurted.

The sinister lord took a step forward into the gaslit circle of light, his dark wig and brows gleaming like a raven's wings. "Did you know, Devoncourt actually thought he could keep me away from you, even whilst he flaunted you beneath my nose."

Adele took an uneasy step back. They knew she was working for Malloryn. She had no means to defend herself beyond her hemlock ring and her little knife. No means to run. All she could do was hope Malloryn had heard this.

And that he would come for her.

"I trust our negotiations are complete, Corvus?" Dido stood, slipping her gloves back on.

"Devoncourt won't be happy," he mused. "This thwarts his plans."

"Such a shame," she mocked.

"Then I am more than well satisfied."

Corvus lunged toward her, and Adele fled, sending an enormous urn crashing to the ground. A hand snatched her skirts, and then strong arms wrapped around her, dragging her back into an unbreakable embrace. She screamed and kicked, but it was to no avail.

"Let go of me!"

Corvus slammed her against the nearest wall as Dido vanished into the gloom.

"I've been wanting to get you alone for a very long time." He brushed his cheek, where her little knife had scored the pale skin once upon a time. Thanks to the craving virus, there was not a blemish there, but he'd promised he'd return the favor. "I owe you for that debacle in Abernathy's garden."

"I apologized," she whispered.

"But you were never punished for it. You owe me satisfaction, my dear. And I've come to collect."

CHAPTER EIGHTEEN

"You want to slip the lock? Or shall I?" Charlie whispered.

Lark gave him a look that could best be described as, *are you serious?*

"Fine. After you," he said, cupping his hands and hoisting Lark ten feet up the wall.

The toes of her rubber-soled shoes slipped into cracks in the brickwork, and she hauled herself up the side of Sir George Hamilton's house like a spider. His position gave him an excellent view of her backside in her tight leather breeches—

An elbow drove into his ribs, and he barely managed to contain an *oof.*

"Concentrate," Gemma whispered.

"I was."

Her arched eyebrow spoke volumes. It was frightening how much she and Lark had in common.

Charlie winked at her.

"Think you can handle this?" he murmured, offering her his cupped hands. "Breaking and entering isn't really your style."

"Oh, you sweet boy," she breathed. "I was running across rooftops before you could even crawl."

Then she was scampering up the wall after Lark as if to prove it to him.

Charlie lunged at the nearby brick wall, his foot striking halfway up it. He pushed off, twisting in midair, and caught the edge of the window on the second story. It took mere seconds to join the ladies on the ledge just below the window Adele had marked out as Hamilton's study.

Lark cracked the window, pausing to see if anyone had heard.

A dog's howl echoed through the neighborhood, but other than that, there was no outcry. Not that he'd expected it. Obsidian was keeping watch on a rooftop across the street and hadn't reported any guards set on the house. Either Hamilton was a bit player in this entire scheme, or too arrogant to believe he'd ever be brought low.

Lark found the sun symbol on the fireplace and pressed it. A faint groan of stone on stone, and then the fireplace swung open, just as Adele had described.

Darkness loomed behind it.

An odd sense of foreboding filled him.

There wasn't a lock that he and Lark couldn't pick, but Gemma was here for one reason and one reason only: with her memory, she could practically reproduce anything she saw on a piece of paper.

"Adele said there were maps," Gemma breathed. "I need light, Charlie."

Charlie shook the phosphorescent glimmer ball to brighten it again. The ghostly green glow cast just enough light across the small private study to see that someone had cleaned the desk.

No map. No schematics.

"He's locked the desk," Lark whispered, already kneeling in front of it with her lock pick. A faint click and she eased the draw open.

There were papers inside. A hollow leather tube to protect something large. Lark handed him the tube, then started rifling carefully through the papers.

He eased a roll of schematics from the tube and unrolled them across the desk. Sharply drawn lines furled across the paper.

It looked like the small control chip they'd removed from Obsidian's head several months ago that had forced him to do Balfour's bidding.

"Is it—?"

"No." Gemma frowned at the specifications. "It's not the neural regulating implant. I examined the one they took from my head. This is different." She ran her fingers across the paper, tracing the name at the top. "The Prometheus Project. I wish we'd brought Kincaid or Jack. They might be able to recognize what it does."

"Can you draw it for them?"

"I should be able to recreate it, yes."

Charlie took a step toward the bookcase, and the floorboard beneath his foot depressed.

Downstairs came the sudden loud bonging of the grandfather clock, just once. Easing his weight back sent the noise crashing through the house again, and he took three swift steps away from the loose floorboard.

All three of them looked at each other, and then Charlie tugged his pocket watch from his pocket. "It's twenty minutes past the hour."

Gemma swiftly rolled the schematics back into place and slid them inside the tube. "He's rigged the study. Hurry. We need to put everything back."

A low grinding sound echoed through the room.

Shit. Charlie lunged toward the fireplace and jammed his boot between it and the wall. Something clicked, as if the mechanism was trying to force it closed.

"Gem," he rasped, wincing as the bones in his foot creaked.

Gemma slid to the ground at his feet, peering down into the solid iron turntable the fireplace rested on. She drove a knife between the cogs, and Charlie managed to ease his foot free as the clockwork mechanism groaned.

"How the hell do we get out of here?" There was no window in the room.

"Can you reverse the clockwork mechanism?" Gemma asked, thrusting the glimmer ball low so he could see the mechanism.

"I can barely fucking see it."

"Reach through the door and see if you can depress the sun symbol," Lark hissed.

Charlie did, groping in the darkness. Instantly, the fireplace ground to a halt.

The glimmer ball was fading into darkness as Lark hastily returned everything to its right place. She shoved the drawer shut and locked it.

"How strong are you?" Gemma asked.

Charlie threw his shoulder against the fireplace, and it creaked wider. One inch. Two. The strain was immense.

"Can you fit?" he gasped.

Gemma tried to wedge herself through. "Half of me."

It was the top half causing her trouble.

He jammed his boots against the fireplace as it strained to close, forcing the gap to widen. Gemma vanished into the main study.

"Lark!"

His fiancée dashed toward him, sliding between his legs and through the narrowing gap. Charlie threw himself clear and the fireplace groaned as it closed with a hollow, resolute *thump*.

Lights were flickering on in the house as Gemma slipped out the window. Footsteps hurried up the stairs. He snatched a gold paperweight off the desk and shoved everything else to the floor, to make it look like they'd been ransacking the main study.

"Just like old times," Lark said, flashing him a grin as she followed Gemma.

Just before the study door flung open, Charlie threw himself through the window, hitting the ground and rolling.

Dogs set up barking.

The window sash slammed up and someone shoved their head through the opening. "Stop! Thieves!"

But the three of them were well away.

"Let go of me!" Adele cried, trying to kick Corvus in the shins as he hauled her through a narrow passage hidden behind a veil of ivy, and into the dark.

He'd stripped her hemlock ring from her finger and found the small knife she had hidden up her sleeve.

Without them, Adele was as good as defenseless.

"You don't want to cross my husband! He knows I'm here. I told him I was going to come and if I don't return home—"

"You think Malloryn gives a damn about you?" Corvus snarled, shoving her up a flight of stairs. "You're a means to an end, Adele. And you'll be returned to your nice, safe warm bed in the end. A pity it won't be in one piece."

She tried to dart under his arm, but he slammed a palm straight into her chest. The blow winded her, and then a hand closed around her upper arm and she was dragged up the rest of the stairs and thrown through a small door.

Every inch of her ached as the door slammed behind her.

She couldn't breathe. Couldn't escape the clasp of her corset around bruised ribs. But somehow, the sound of that lock clicking shut sent a chill down her spine, and she forced herself to scramble onto her knees and turn to face her worst nightmare.

Corvus's cloak flared around his boots as he stalked toward her.

"Did you think you'd escape me forever?" he demanded. "Did you think Malloryn was the answer to your prayers? I'm a patient man, you little slut. No one has ever drawn my blood before, and I'll be damned if you think you can get away with it."

"He'll kill you," she rasped as he slammed her back into the desk. "Malloryn will not let this stand!"

"He's not going to be a problem for much longer. I was going to wait another week until this was all done, but with Devoncourt flaunting you right in front of me, the opportunity seemed too good to resist." Gripping her chin in one hand, he forced her head back, baring her throat. "Stop struggling, you cursed bitch."

Never.

She strained to see what he was doing.

Dragging his bleeding kit from inside his coat—the little case every blue blood carried to bleed their thralls—he slapped it on the desk and tugged it open. Steel gleamed beneath the gaslight, and Adele kicked furiously.

Not like this.

She'd escaped this life by marrying Malloryn.

Six months of freedom from the worry of being

stalked by those like Corvus, who didn't give a damned whether she protested. A tear leaked from her eye as the razor edge of the flechette he held sliced across her vein, and hot blood splashed free.

The press of his body ground her against the desk, and then his dead fish mouth was locked around her throat, taking what did not belong to him. Adele raked her nails down his arms, but she might as well be wrestling with steel cables.

The kit.

Her hand flung out, reaching blindly as she gave a low, whimpering moan. Somehow her hand closed around one of his little knives.

Adele drove it into his eye.

Corvus screamed, rearing back from her with one hand clamped over the wound. Adele jerked away from him, but then his good eye locked on her, and she knew she was in trouble.

He lashed out with his blade, and the knife scored across her upper arm as she flailed backward, smashing into the desk. Slipping on the hem of her skirts, she went down, flat on her back, as Corvus advanced.

"I will kill you," he promised as he leaned over her.

And then there was something moving in the cathedral-like rafters.

A shadow opened dark wings above her, like a fallen angel plummeting from the heavens.

Adele thought she was seeing things, but as Corvus knelt to grab her, she realized it wasn't an angel.

It was Malloryn.

Malloryn.

He landed on the desk, boots slamming onto the timbers as Corvus's knife jerked against her shoulder in surprise. A single kick and Corvus's entire weight was flung back off her. Adele gasped, clutching at her bloodied throat as Malloryn went after him.

"Your Grace?" Byrnes appeared out of nowhere to help her to her feet. Behind him, Ingrid watched the fight with molten eyes.

"I'm fine." Adele dashed a hot tear from her eye, her hands shaking violently. There was blood all down the front of her pretty gown. On her hands. On her breasts.

Her blood.

"Allow me," Byrnes murmured, spitting on his fingers and then smearing his saliva quite liberally across the gash in her throat.

A disgusting gesture, but a kind one. The chemicals in his saliva would coagulate her blood and force the wound to heal.

"Here." Ingrid dragged her leather coat off and draped it around Adele's shoulders as Corvus's breath slammed out of him. "Don't watch."

"I want to."

The violence in the fight shocked her; she'd only ever seen Malloryn reclining in his library chair, or stalking the edges of a ballroom with watchful eyes. Even among the Company of Rogues, he was the one who gave the orders from the comfort of his safe house.

But Corvus was the one with the knife now.

It didn't seem to matter.

Malloryn didn't even bother to draw his own, and still he was beating the daylights out of her attacker. He dodged a lash of the knife, capturing Corvus's wrist and twisting it violently behind his back as he took the knife off the bastard. A fist to the back of the head drove Corvus into the wall, and he coughed teeth. A second blow slammed the lord's head into the stone with a sharp impact.

"He's going to kill him," she whispered.

"Malloryn knows what he's doing," Byrnes said. "He's cool, calm, exceptionally rational…."

He trailed off as Malloryn buried the knife up to the blade in Corvus's throat. The lord gagged, trying to pull it free, but it was driven right into the wall, pinning him there.

"You were saying?" Ingrid asked.

"Not so much fun when they can fight back, is it?" Malloryn tore Corvus's shirt and waistcoat right down the middle, baring his chest.

"I think the duke has been under a little bit of pressure of late," Ingrid said dubiously, hovering on the balls of her feet. "He's going to kill him."

"You want me to stop him?" Byrnes asked incredulously.

Adele closed her eyes. If Malloryn ended Corvus right here and now, she'd never have to look over her shoulder again. But.... "He knows something about Balfour's scheme. He seemed to think Malloryn wouldn't see the week out."

"Damn it. Easy now," Byrnes said, easing forward with slow, carefully placed steps. "Take the knife out of his throat, Your Grace. We don't want to kill him."

"Speak for yourself." Malloryn drove his hand beneath Corvus's ribs, right through his flesh. Corvus screamed, the sound muffled by Malloryn's other hand.

This time Adele looked away.

She found her face buried in Ingrid's shoulder as the other woman clutched her there.

"I have my hand around your heart, you bastard. I can feel it pulsing. I could rip it right out of your chest—"

"But we don't want to do that, because he might have valuable information," Byrnes soothed. "Trust me, Your Grace. I'm as shocked at this moment as you are. Me, being the voice of reason. Let his heart go. You can kill him later."

"Please," Adele whispered. "Please don't kill him just yet."

There was nothing of the Malloryn she knew in her husband's face.

His eyes were given over entirely to the hunger. Obsidian irises seemed to suck in every last vestige of light, until they were nothing more than black pits in the chiseled frame of his face.

"We don't have time, Malloryn," Ingrid said. "Dido could appear at any moment. Herbert's trying to extract Clara. We have to leave."

Malloryn's jaw locked tight.

And then he jerked the knife free of Corvus's throat, and the bloodied lord slumped to the ground unconscious.

"Deal with him," Malloryn said, turning away, his sleeves absolutely drenched in blood.

Byrnes flipped Corvus onto his front and hastily bound his arms behind him with his belt. "He's bleeding quite badly."

"He'll survive." Something dark and bloodthirsty settled over Malloryn's expression. "Blue bloods can survive almost anything, after all."

"All trussed up." Byrnes hauled Corvus to his feet. "Let's go."

"Not yet!" Adele gasped, and met Malloryn's blackened eyes. "Membership rolls! There must be a list here somewhere with all the names of Angel's Fall members. This is Balfour's recruiting scheme."

"I think Devoncourt will realize you're involved if his membership list goes missing," Byrnes said.

"They already knew."

Ingrid surveyed the spatter of blood on the floor. "But if we set fire to the place he won't know what we've taken."

"Good point." Malloryn started toward the lantern in

the corner and set it on the desk. "If we find that list, we don't need Devoncourt," he said, tugging open drawers and rifling through sheaves of paper with his bloodstained hands. "I'll have proof enough to get a warrant passed through council. I can shut the Rising Sons down in one night and cut Balfour's allies in half."

Adele slammed an enormous ledger open, her heart skipping a beat as she found a list of names hidden in a secret compartment cut into the back of it. "Here," she said, her voice rising. "I think I've got it."

Malloryn tore it from her fingers, his expression tightening. "This is it. Let's get out of here."

He paused by Corvus. "And bring this prick. I'm not done with him yet."

"Are you all right?" Malloryn demanded as he helped Adele inside the carriage. Ingrid took one look at the pair of them and then shut the door, granting them some privacy.

Adele's hands shook, and her eyes were wide. She reeked of blood and smoke. "We succeeded in our endeavors, and that's all that matters. We have the list now. I'm fine."

"You're not fine." He reached out and took her hands in his, trying to rub warmth back into them. He could just make out the lick of flames in the distance, where Angel's Fall burned. So much for subterfuge. "I should never have sent you in there. You're untrained. You can barely defend yourself."

"That's why I have you," she whispered. "We weren't to know it was a trap. And you rescued me."

But what if I didn't make it in time?

He closed his eyes and fought the thought down, as

the craving whispered through his veins. He was still raw and on edge, struggling to rein in the darkness inside himself. He'd never lost control like that, and there was a rather bothering sensation that lingered in his chest.

One that wanted to stop the carriage and rip Corvus down into the street where he could finish what he'd started.

One that insisted he hold her, just so he could feel the heat of her body against his and know she was safe.

One that demanded he claim her.

Right here.

Right now.

Fighting against the urge was taking everything he had in him, and he needed to have his head about him. Maybe if he just granted his hunger a little taste of what it wanted, it would be easier to restrain. Malloryn gave into the lesser of several evils.

Slipping onto the bench beside her, he eased her onto his lap. Adele rested her head on his shoulder with a grateful sigh. "I knew you were there. I knew you would come."

The utter belief in her voice left him a little breathless.

But it was the contented purring of the darkness inside him that left him on edge.

Troubling.

"So that was Dido," she whispered.

"Yes." He pressed a kiss to her hair, breathing in her familiar perfume. The tension in his chest eased a little more. "Can I ask you a question?"

Adele glanced up.

"It seemed as though Dido made a deal with Lord Corvus. He would grant her... something, in exchange for you."

Every inch of her stiffened.

"Is he the one who hurt you?"

He didn't need to know the answer. It was there in every line of her body. Adele burrowed her face back into the warmth of his coat, closing her eyes. "Yes."

Then he's a dead man.

"You'll never have to worry about him again," he promised, and for a second he was looking at a gray-tinted world as the craving roared through his veins. So much for controlling it.

Her fingers stroked the collar of his coat, and her voice was very small when she asked, "What are you going to do to him?"

Rip his fucking head off.

But that was not the correct answer. That was not what the Duke of Malloryn would do. It was what the monster inside him—stirred to protective lengths somehow—wanted to do.

Malloryn leaned into the caress of her fingers, easing out a steady breath.

Why did she affect him like this?

It was more than the usual protective urge he felt toward women.

More than Balfour's hovering presence.

No. This had everything to do with Adele, and nothing to do with Balfour's plots.

"Malloryn?" she whispered, brushing her thumb against his lip.

"I'm going to ask him a few questions," he managed to say. "And then I'm going to see that he is guillotined very, very publicly."

There was one nice thing about being friends with the queen.

"He'll hate that."

"I know."

"Good," she said, a little viciously.

But nothing about this situation was ‘good'.

What the hell was wrong with him?

CHAPTER NINETEEN

"Go to hell, Malloryn." Corvus spat a mouthful of bloodied mucus at him as Malloryn strode inside the cell he'd been granted inside Thorne Tower, home to political enemies, traitors, and criminals of the important kind. "I'm not going to tell you a damned thing."

The muscle in Malloryn's jaw ticked. Corvus had been the one who'd molested Adele the night she trapped him into marriage, and she'd managed to escape only by using a knife on him.

But he was no longer in the grip of the craving. No longer ruled by the hunger and the heat of his emotions.

Somehow, holding Adele in his arms all the way home had managed to soothe the raging beast inside him, so he could damned well start thinking again.

Malloryn knelt down, a fresh set of trousers pulling taut over his thighs as he eyed the bastard. "I think you will."

"I think he will too," said Byrnes, tossing a knife up and down nonchalantly. "Indeed, I'm willing to bet good money on it."

Gemma *tsked* under her breath. "Boys. There's no need to make threats. I'm sure Lord Corvus understands the gravity of the situation he's found himself in. The queen wants the head of any traitor, after all."

"She don't need to know he's even in here," Byrnes murmured.

Lord Corvus sneered. "I'm an earl. If you touch one hair on my head, the entire Echelon will be up in arms. You think you're so high and mighty? You think the queen's name cows *me*? Well, you're going to get what's coming for you soon. There are those of us right beneath your nose. You'll never see them coming. You'll never know—"

"You mean all the lords listed on these pages?" Malloryn tugged the membership list out of his coat and proffered it elegantly.

Corvus froze.

"It was very considerate of you to write them all down for us. Saves me the hassle of having to torture my way through your cohort." He glanced at the first couple of names. "Coded, of course, but Gemma managed to crack it in under half an hour. Sloppy work, Corvus. Adele mentioned the Four Horsemen, and I see you've even given me *their* names too. Practically giftwrapped. The leaders of this little resurrection of the Rising Sons, I presume?"

"Conquest," Byrnes snorted, looming over the sniveling lordling. "He named himself Conquest. Who does that?"

"Conquest had another name," Gemma murmured. "I think 'Pestilence' suits the earl better."

"I think I'd rather be Devoncourt," Byrnes said, "though titling yourself as 'War' is a little self-congratulatory."

"And my dear father-in-law, Sir George, is

masquerading as Famine. There's only one Horseman's name that's not listed." Malloryn examined the lists. "Was it Dido who gave you such names? Or should I say, Death?"

A white mottling settled over Corvus's pale expression. "It's too late, anyway. You won't stop it now."

"Stop what?" Malloryn tucked the papers back inside his pocket. "Maybe I can offer you a deal. Tell me what Balfour plans, and I'll make this very quick for you." He leaned closer, letting Corvus see some of the rage within him. "I don't want to. I want to make it slow and painful, considering you dared lay hands on my wife, but I always keep my word when I give it."

Corvus gave a choking laugh. "You have no idea what's coming for you. I'd rather see you suffer than die a clean death."

"One hundred quid that he breaks in under an hour," Byrnes said.

"Mmm, I think it will take at least an hour. Lord Corvus is a war veteran, after all," Gemma replied. "Two hundred, and you have a deal."

"I can be very persuasive," Byrnes told her. "I once saw a man make another eat his own finger. I've always wanted to try it."

"Done."

Corvus's gaze flickered to the pair of them, and his nostrils flared.

"You will tell us the truth, Corvus. What condition you're in when you speak it, depends on you," Malloryn said. "You told Adele I had less than a week, which means Balfour is setting things in motion as we speak. I wonder though, whether the explosives were designed for the Ivory Tower? Or is it the Prometheus chip we should be wary of?"

Corvus paled. "How did you—?"

"Did you think you were the only target we went after?"

"You son of a bitch."

"Your little house of cards is toppling, Corvus. Just fill in the gaps, and I may make this swift."

"Don't drink too much of it," Ava warned as she liberally laced Adele's tea with brandy. "It'll go straight to your head."

"Thank you." Adele sipped at her tea, sighing with relief as the brandy warmed from the inside. She'd bathed the blood from her skin, and one of the other ladies had managed to find her a new nightgown and robe, but the chill of Corvus's hands on her skin still lingered.

"Ava is speaking from experience." Ingrid snorted, her long legs thrown over the chair's arms as she watched Ava fuss over Adele. "She gets *very* talkative when she's had too much liquor."

"And I'm sure you and Gemma weren't egging me on at all that night," Ava rebuked, slipping the glass topper back into the decanter.

"We didn't have to."

"Did I miss something?" Lark asked.

"Nothing," Ava replied promptly.

"*Battering rams,*" Ingrid coughed, almost-but-not-quite smothering the words with her hand.

The three women had gathered Adele into their confidences while Malloryn, Gemma, and Byrnes headed off to question Lord Corvus.

"Now I definitely know I missed something." Lark leaned forward in her chair, her hazel eyes glittering. "Confess."

"If you want to know more," Ingrid said, "then you'll need to drink up. One secret per glass. That's the way we played it." Her smile abruptly widened. "We can consider tonight Lark's and the duchess's initiation into COR."

"Oh, no. I don't think this is a very good idea. The duke would definitely not approve." Ava waved her hands in front of her. "Besides, Gemma's not here."

"She can catch up when she returns. And it's not as though you're at risk of blurting something inappropriate," Ingrid said, gesturing to Ava's rounded form and hence her inability to imbibe. No amount of ruffles could conceal Ava's thickening middle. "You can be our chaperone."

Adele drained her cup of tea. As much as tonight had been utterly horrid, a part of her liked the idea of making friends. It was the sort of gossip she might have enjoyed with Lena, but beyond that, she had very few companions, and the camaraderie she'd noticed within COR made her feel a little left out.

"I'm game," she said, setting her teacup onto her saucer with a clatter. "Though you must call me Adele."

Lark's eyes widened. "You are?"

"You do realize they're going to interrogate you about Malloryn," Ava said dryly.

"But not a word of what occurs here tonight leaves this room," Ingrid promised. "The gentlemen will remain oblivious."

Malloryn would kill her.

But then, Lord Corvus almost had, so really, what was she afraid of?

"As I said," she replied with an insouciant shrug, "I'm game. It sounds like fun."

And it had been so long since she'd truly enjoyed herself like this.

Ava sighed and poured them all a brandy, liberally

splashing it into Adele's empty teacup.

"To a lady's secrets, and a promise of friendship everlasting," Ingrid said.

"No Rogue left behind," Lark added.

The three of them clinked cups together.

And then Adele managed to choke down half the cup, while Ingrid and Lark drained theirs.

"The first time Gemma brought out a bottle was just after Kincaid started pursuing Ava," Ingrid said. "There may—or may not—have been a conversation about what precisely a lady may expect in the bedroom. Gemma and I were trying to restrain ourselves for poor Ava's innocent ears, when to our shock and horror she blurted out that our dear Kincaid is a man of stature."

Adele blinked, slowly working her way through "stature" and "battering ram." Then her eyes widened.

Ava groaned, burying her face in her hands. "I will add, neither Ingrid nor Gemma was shocked or horrified."

"Delighted, I presume," Lark said with a snicker.

"You know Gemma." Ingrid waggled her brows. "Your turn."

Heat flushed through Lark's cheeks. Though she wore men's attire, she'd been reticent enough until now that Adele didn't truly know much about her.

"Are you asking about Charlie's, ahem, girth?"

"He's a strapping lad. But you're quite welcome to volunteer any secret you wish. As long as it's naughty." Ingrid's eyes flashed intently. "Our sugarplum is such a sweet young boy, I'm sure he has no dark secrets."

"Not like Byrnes," Ava said.

Lark snorted into her brandy. "Bloody hell. I don't think I want to know."

"Well?" Ingrid leaned forward, and Adele started feeling a little nervous about what she'd be expected to share.

"Our first time was in Russia," Lark muttered.

"Our?" Ingrid arched both brows.

"He waited for me," Lark replied. "We were both virgins."

"Oh." Ava sighed. "That's so sweet. I adore Charlie. He's always so thoughtful."

"*Very* thoughtful, if one knows what I mean?" Lark said. She turned to Adele to explain, "We grew up together and were friends as children, though it took him a few years to realize I was a girl."

"And then he definitely realized you were a girl," Ava said kindly. "He was mooning after you all through Russia. Gemma wanted to shake him to keep his mind on the job."

"Your turn," Ingrid said as Ava topped up Adele's cup. "We're all dying to know... is the duke as cold in bed as he seems?"

Adele buried her face in the cup and drank swiftly.

"Technically," she admitted, blushing furiously, "we haven't yet made it to a bed."

"I knew it!" Ingrid punched the air. "You made love to the Duke of Malloryn on his desk!"

"Charlie owes you fifty quid," Lark pointed out, and then looked chastened when Adele shot her a sharp look. "He was adamant the duke had managed to seduce you earlier."

"What, precisely, do you count as seduction?" Adele murmured, muddying the waters.

Of all the things Malloryn expected to find when he walked into Hardcastle Lane several hours later, it was not a very drunk Duchess of Malloryn.

He'd been prepared for tears.

Prepared to gently tend to his wife's distress, as Gemma had given him a lecture in the carriage on the way home about the aftermath of the assault and how he owed Adele a shoulder to cry on.

But the second he walked in, he noticed Herbert's slightly horrified expression beneath his nightcap, and wondered, for the second time that week, what sort of hell had broken loose.

Malloryn tugged off his gloves. "No break-ins? No scheming duchesses trapped in my study? No bodies?"

"No, Your Grace."

A round of giggling floated down the stairs.

"What on earth is going on?" Gemma asked, slipping her cloak from her shoulders as they all glanced up.

"That sounds like Ingrid," Byrnes said with a faint frown as something smashed.

"I believe the ladies are in no condition to put themselves to bed," Herbert said discreetly. "They have... raided Master Byrnes's private stock of blud-wein for Miss Lark, and the duke's decanters seem to have vanished. I tried to fend them off, but they were adamant."

"And one does not stand between Ingrid and a bottle of brandy when she has a thirst." Gemma shook her head.

"Again?" Byrnes shook his head. "That woman owes me."

"I'm sure she'll reimburse you in private," Gemma drawled. "I cannot believe they started without me."

Malloryn didn't move. "The duchess is with them?"

"I believe Her Grace is currently leading the charge. She Duchess of Malloryn'd me when I asked them to be a little quieter." Herbert cleared his throat. "Clara had to retire. It was all she could do not to burst out laughing."

As if to prove his statement, Adele staggered onto the

landing, practically tripping on the hem of a green silk nightrobe that was too long for her. "Oh, it's my favorite husband!"

Malloryn realized his jaw hung slightly open.

"Don't break your neck on the stairs," Ingrid hollered. "Or the duke will have my head."

"But the duke is *here*!" Adele cried in delight. "And Gemma too! We waited for you, Gemma, but you—" A hiccup escaped her. "—have to catch up."

"My wife is a cool, rational creature without a heart," Gemma said, with a snicker.

"She would never make demands of me, the Duke of Malloryn," Byrnes added, getting in on the joke.

"She is the epitome of class and grace—"

"And would never dare cause her husband any uncomfortable displays of emotion—"

"The next person to open their mouth," he growled, "will be cleaning chamber pots for a month."

The pair of them tried to contain their laughter.

"Did you know I like your Rogues?" Adele started down the stairs, and he leapt up several steps, one hand braced to catch her, before realizing she'd hauled her nightrobe up past her knees. Slim, delicate, *bare* calves flashed before him as she took slow, careful steps.

"Where are your shoes?" he demanded. "And your stockings?"

"Where's your cravat?" she replied, shrugging flirtatiously. "I like your cravat. Especially when you use it to—"

"Jesus Christ." Malloryn eased Adele up into his arms, reeling at the scent of brandy that steamed off her. "Did you drink the entire bottle of brandy by yourself?"

"I tried to talk them out of it, Your Grace." Ava looked chagrined as she appeared at the top of the stairs with Ingrid and Lark at her sides. "They wouldn't listen."

"When does anyone in this house bloody listen?" he growled under his breath as he strode back down the stairs and set Adele on her feet.

"He wants to know where my shoes are!" Adele called back up the stairs.

Ingrid slid down the bannister. "But that's not the theory!"

"Bloody hell," Byrnes said, and exchanged a long-suffering look with him. "We are in for a night of it."

"What theory?" Malloryn demanded.

"No, no, no!" Adele shook her hands in the air. "Ingrid wants to measure your boots. Don't let her! I wouldn't tell!"

"I'm so sorry, Your Grace," Ava repeated.

"It appears your wife is as much of a lightweight as Ava," Ingrid added, swinging off the bottom of the bannister. "She said she'd imbibed before."

"The punch is never as strong at the balls." Adele hiccupped. She set a hand to her temples, swaying slightly.

Malloryn swiftly caught her arm. "Are you all right?"

"I am most... excellent. Exceedingly excellent. Did you kill Lord Corvus? You don't have any blood on you."

"No, I did not. Do you want to sit down?"

Adele gave a little burp, and pressed her fingers to her lips in horror. "Oh, goodness. I don't think I feel very well."

He gaped at her.

"You need to get her upstairs and get some tea into her," Gemma muttered under her breath. "I did warn you that no matter what condition you found her in, tonight you had a certain duty to perform."

Yes, but holding my wife's hair out of her face as she casts up her accounts isn't even on the list of things I anticipated.

Getting her back up the stairs would be more hassle than it was worth. He swung her up into his arms. "Good God, how much have you had to drink?"

She held both hands about nine or ten inches apart with a giggle. "About this much." A slight frown wrinkled her brow. "Or was that the other thing we were discussing?"

"Definitely that much to drink," Ava blurted in a high-pitched voice.

Something was going on. His eyes narrowed. "Does this have anything to do with the size of my boots?"

"No!" Lark and Ingrid chorused together.

He did not want to know.

Herbert snapped his heels together. "I shall fetch Your Grace a clean chamber pot and some tea."

"There, there, Malloryn." Gemma patted him on the shoulder, grinning at him unsympathetically. "This is one of the joys of marriage."

Adele awoke with a groan.

Oh. My. Goodness.

She pressed her hands to her throbbing temples. There was far too much light in the room. What had happened? Where was she?

"Why," purred a dangerous voice, "if it isn't my favorite wife. How are you feeling, Adele?"

Malloryn.

She was in Malloryn's bed at the safe house. Adele rolled onto her side, realizing she was naked under the covers. With a squeak, she hauled them up to her chin, and then clapped a handful to her mouth as her stomach rebelled at the sudden movement. "What are you doing in here?"

Light streamed through the curtains he'd just jerked open, highlighting the dangerous smile on his mouth. "Well, I certainly wasn't sleeping, unlike others."

She managed to sit herself upright. Very slowly. "Where are my clothes?"

"Clara has very kindly removed them from the room, along with the chamber pot."

The chamber pot?

She groaned. There was a vile taste in the back of her throat. Faint recollections rose of lots and lots of brandy. Had there been singing at one stage?

"Apparently I'm not as good at hair as she is, though I did manage to braid most of it out of the way."

"Braid it back?" she asked in a horrified whisper, as images of the chamber pot resurfaced to haunt her. "Oh, no."

"Oh, yes, my favorite wife." Malloryn's smile was pure evil. "It was quite an eventful night. I have learned rather a lot about you. Including what you ate for dinner last night."

The only way to deal with such a statement was to ignore it.

"Why am I your favorite wife? I thought I was your only wife?" The world was spinning too much for her to put the pieces together.

"Well, apparently, I am your favorite husband. I am a very good husband, indeed." He said the titles simply, as if speaking them to a three year-old. "Am I a good husband, Clara?"

"The very best," Clara said promptly as she stepped into the light.

Adele hadn't even realized she was there.

"I hope you're feeling better, Duchess." There was a faint note of sympathy on Clara's face. "I've bought you up some tea. I wasn't certain if you were quite ready for breakfast."

The very idea of baked kippers made her stomach revolt again.

"Tea will be fine," she managed to whisper.

"Clara, would you be able to assist my wife with her toilette this afternoon? I don't want her to drown in the bath, and we have an important meeting to attend downstairs. Some of us have been putting together the pieces of what we learned at Angel's Fall."

"Certainly, Your Grace."

Malloryn strode for the door, and then paused, one hand on the knob as he glanced over his shoulder. "You may have to wash her. Thoroughly. Along with my boots."

"Your boots?"

Please tell me I did not....

"My very big boots," he replied, a strange glitter in his eyes, "which are suddenly the topic of discussion among the female Rogues, though I can't quite work out why."

Memory repaid Adele with a sudden flash of Ingrid announcing, in all seriousness, *"It has some sort of correlation with the size of a gentleman's feet, I've heard."*

"That's ridiculous," Ava had replied. *"That's the least scientific theory I've ever come across."*

"Well, you're the scientist. In the interest of disproving the theory, you should test it," Lark had replied. *"Use Kincaid's boot size as your sample."*

"Kincaid?" Ingrid snorted. *"I'm going to examine His Grace's boots, since Adele is so unforthcoming."*

Ava looked dubious. *"To properly test a theory, one would need a larger field of data. And I am* not *going to go about measuring the size of the gentlemen's boots in the house."*

"Oh, no," Adele blurted.

What had she told him?

What had she told the other ladies?

"Oh, yes," Malloryn purred. "Bathe, drink your tea, and then meet me downstairs. Apparently, you're officially a Rogue now, which means we have schemes to plot. No matter what kind of condition some of us may be in."

CHAPTER TWENTY

"What have you got for me?" Malloryn asked as he followed Jack and Ava through the cellars the rest of the Rogues had affectionately called Dungeon II. "Have you two managed to decipher what this Prometheus Project is all about?"

The most reclusive member of COR, Jack spent most of his time down here, fiddling with strange devices and creating weapons for the rest of the Rogues to use. And Kincaid liked to tinker.

"It looks like schematics for the control chip the latest metaljackets have," Kincaid said, leaning over the design Gemma had sketched for them.

The former mech knew everything there was to know about automatons after years of being trapped in the Echelon's enclaves, where they had been created.

Gemma sipped her tea as she followed Malloryn. "Control chip?"

Light flared to life in Jack's eyes. "If these schematics are what we think they are, then they're designed to control an automaton of some sort."

"Each squadron of metaljackets required a handler with a control box. They were brutally effective in number, but severely limited in what they could do on an individual scale," Kincaid added. "So the prince consort ordered a new ceremonial model that could be programmed individually. The contract wasn't finalized by the time he died, but the design was in place. They're designed to patrol a specific section of a building. You plant frequency transmitters in the walls, which communicate with the receivers in the automaton's head, so the metaljackets don't patrol beyond their limits."

Jack gestured with his hands. "We think that if someone replaced the chip inside a metaljacket with another, somewhat like this, they'd be keyed to obey the new instructions."

"Which makes the tower's metaljackets a weapon to be used against us." Malloryn scrubbed at his mouth.

"But how does Balfour get inside the Ivory Tower and replace the implants?" Gemma placed her cup on its saucer with an agitated rattle. "When Obsidian was under his control, he spent weeks trying to work out how to get past the tower's defenses."

"Maybe that's why he needs Sir George?" A frown of concentration drew Kincaid's brows together. "Adele's father used to own several manufacturing factories, and I think he had shares in the Ironmonger Enclaves."

"Which produced automatons."

"Household automatons. Not metaljackets," Kincaid replied. "*They* were created in the King Street and Oldgate enclaves. But Sir George has mechwork knowledge, contacts, and access to the tower."

"Kidnap him?" Gemma suggested, glancing at Malloryn.

Which was precisely the sort of thing one wasn't

supposed to do to one's in-laws, though Malloryn knew Sir George didn't care for him.

The feeling was mutual.

"Not yet," he replied. "I'll need more proof if I'm to bring it to the queen and make it official. The membership rolls list our enemies, but if used in a court of law, then they may argue they are merely that. Membership lists. I need cold, hard proof."

He'd barely managed to get the queen's approval on Corvus, though considering it happened after he'd actually kidnapped the bastard, the queen had been in somewhat of a quandary. "If I start publicly arresting members of the Rising Sons, the entire Echelon will be up in arms. The queen wants everything to go smoothly for her celebrations."

"Bloody politics," Kincaid muttered under his breath.

"And unofficially?" Gemma joked. "I may know a *dhampir* who excels at making people disappear. He owes me a favor or two."

"I'll consider it."

"There's a slight problem with your theory," Ava interrupted. "This isn't the sort of thing that could be done in a short amount of time. And you have two hundred metaljackets in the tower. It would have been noticed. I don't think the metaljackets could have been tampered with."

"So back to the drawing board," Gemma grumbled.

Malloryn stared at the thin lines on the paper. "We can't afford to dismiss the fact it might have been done. Jack, I'll need you to work out how to detect if a metaljacket's been altered."

"You could just clear them out of the tower," Gemma suggested.

"And have Balfour know we're onto him?" Malloryn

arched a brow. "I want to lure him out, Gem. Not make him scuttle back into hiding. Or use another weapon against us that we won't see coming."

"But what is he planning?" she asked.

"An attack on the tower."

Gemma rolled her eyes. "Very droll, Your Grace."

"Before you head upstairs for the meeting, Your Grace, may I show you the latest batch of designs?" Jack asked.

"Ooh." Gemma clapped her hands together. "New weapons? You shouldn't have, Jack. You do know the way to a girl's heart."

"*You* are not getting your hands on anything. You ruined my blast shield. That thing took me months to create."

"I only tested it," Gemma replied. "It's not my fault the design was flawed."

The scarred inventor limped toward a rack on the wall. "I've been experimenting with several new bullets, using the same design as the Firebolts." He tossed Malloryn a bullet. "Full of colloidal silver. Burns a blue blood, burns the hell out of a *dhampir*."

"A Firebolt will tear a hole in an enemy," Malloryn pointed out.

"Then you had best make sure your aim is exceptionally good if you're surrounded by friends," Jack replied smoothly. "This way you won't kill anyone, but you'll incapacitate them." He grabbed a smooth orb made of brass. "Ava helped me with this design. It's a recreation of a Doeppler Orb, used by a group of humanists several years ago to release a toxic gas that could drive blue bloods mad. Ava's managed to create a means to transfuse the Black Vein serum into a gaseous state when the Doeppler Orb is activated."

"I managed to distil it into a perfume bottle too," Ava said brightly. "One spray and it's in the air."

"I can't see any potential problems with that at all." An injection of Black Vein was toxic to blue bloods, *dhampir,* and vampires, and deadly within minutes. "Except for the fact none of us can use it."

"That's why it's not for you," Ava chided. "I made it for your wife. A little 'Welcome to COR' gift."

It hadn't escaped his notice everyone was going out of his or her way to include Adele.

He didn't quite know what to think about that.

"And for anyone else," Jack said, tossing Malloryn a breathing mask. "This will do in a pinch."

"We managed to get some vital information out of Corvus," Malloryn said, as the rest of COR gathered around the dining room table.

Jack and Ava had spent all morning searching the room from top to bottom, and finally managed to find the listening device Balfour's agent must have set inside. He'd told them not to destroy it, just in case he wanted to send Balfour on a wild goose chase.

"We've confirmed Corvus, Devoncourt, and Sir George Hamilton are the three leading members of the Rising Sons, though Dido is the one who controls them."

He watched Adele's face as he mentioned her father's name. Though she paled, she didn't protest.

"Corvus admitted there's some scheme with the metaljackets that Balfour is hatching, though Sir George was handling it and Corvus didn't seem to know many of the details. He's mostly in charge of recruiting, since he owns the club and is the perfect lure for the disenfranchised. Devoncourt's in control of munitions."

"So they have explosives," Gemma mused. "But we need to get to Devoncourt to find them."

"Or Sir George to work out what this scheme involves," Jack murmured.

"Byrnes and Ingrid, think you can track our erstwhile earl?" Malloryn asked.

"Consider it done," Byrnes replied.

"We'll handle the metaljackets plot. Sir George is awaiting a final piece of information they need to get this scheme off the ground, though their informant is withholding it until a certain payment comes through. Apparently, Sir George is furious. Doesn't want to look the fool in front of Balfour. The informant's supposed to be in attendance at Lady Haynes's ball tomorrow night, where the transfer is intended to take place. He and Sir George had some sort of falling out years ago, and Mowbray doesn't trust him to hold up his end of the deal."

"Mowbray?" Adele lifted her head from her hands. "There was a letter to a Mr. Thomas Mowbray on my father's secret desk. He was an old business partner who part-owned one of the factories Father had invested in."

"The one and the same," Malloryn confirmed. "We need to attend Lady Haynes's ball, to see if we can get some eyes and ears on this transfer. Think you're up to it, Duchess? I believe we were both invited, were we not?"

Adele looked like she had a little color back in her cheeks. "I'm not the one who's going to turn heads. Lady Haynes is going to think it the coup of the year to have your illustrious presence in her ballroom."

"As well as my cousin, Lady Beechworth, and her husband, Dmitri Grigoriev, a Russian prince," he replied, gesturing to Gemma and Obsidian. "Think you can get them past the door?"

"Oh, please," Adele replied. "Give me a challenge, Malloryn. You may all be lethal in dark alleyways and gambling dens, but the Echelon and its ballrooms are my territory. I can get them in. Just don't kill anyone, or I'll never be able to show my face in society again."

"I'm sorry, my lord." Sir George bowed his head as Balfour lashed out, kicking the desk in his study over.

"Sorry?" Balfour snarled. "*Sorry?* I told you not to commit *anything* to paper."

"They didn't take anything," he growled out, "except for my bloody paperweight."

"And you're certain they were inside your *private* study?" Balfour demanded.

"Yes. The floorboard is rigged to alert me should anyone break in."

Balfour strode to the fireplace and depressed the sun symbol. This was what he got for relying upon others.

"Do you think they found the map?" Jelena murmured to him as they ducked inside.

"They couldn't have. I burned it yesterday."

Balfour made Sir George examine the room. "Nothing else's been touched?"

"Nothing. I've checked everything."

Jelena knelt in front of the desk, examining the lock. "Someone's picked it. There's a faint scratch on the lock."

His fingers curled into fists. "Then we need to move the explosives. Tonight."

"But they couldn't know what the—"

"They'll know," he snarled. "Move every stockpile tonight, or I'll remove your throat. And make sure all of those bloody automatons are in place. We're so close to completing our plans. I will not suffer any more incompetence." He turned on Jelena. "I want the Duke of Malloryn distracted. Keep him away from rest of the Rising Sons. I don't care how."

"Trust me," she purred. "I know exactly how to do it."

CHAPTER TWENTY-ONE

There was another body that night.

Malloryn made his way through the evening fog of Brompton Cemetery, his steps slowing as he saw the gathering around a familiar headstone.

Garrett Reed awaited him, the entire area cordoned off by Nighthawks. "Another message from your friend."

Malloryn flicked a glance toward the girl's body. White gown, bloodied gore spattered all over her chest, her body draped in front of the headstone like an offering.

Like a reminder.

Malloryn examined the familiar calling card that bore his name. He wanted to tear it into little pieces. Perhaps even burn it. Instead, he breathed out, forcing the rage from his lungs.

This was what Balfour wanted from him.

Pain. Suffering. Tormented memories rising to choke him.

He couldn't give in to it.

"Who is she?" Garrett asked. "Do you recognize her?"

"No." He knelt at the girl's side, reaching out a hand

to slowly close her eyes. This one hadn't died easily. Her face was a rictus of horror, her hands scratched and bloodied. She'd fought, even at the end. "Have you worked out the identity of the first girl?"

"Miss Millie Vane," Garrett replied quietly. "A butcher's daughter."

"Send me her details," he murmured, standing and tugging his gloves back on. "I'll arrange for the funeral to be paid."

And money to be given to the grieving family, to try and make their lives easier in some small way.

It would be the least he could do, for bringing this nightmare into the homes of an innocent butcher and his family. All because the girl resembled Catherine.

Malloryn glanced at the tombstone.

Miss Catherine Tate.

Along with her birth and death dates. Two simple lines that told no one of the horrors of her murder.

I'm sorry. I'll stop them.

There was no answer. There never was. Only the wind blowing through his hair and stirring his coat.

Slipping the bloodied calling card in his pocket, he turned toward the gate.

There was no point lingering.

He couldn't do a damned thing for Catherine.

But perhaps he could finally bring her peace.

And protect those who still lived.

Plans were in place, half the Rogues trying to track vital members of the Rising Sons—such as Sir George and Devoncourt—which left Malloryn with the silence of his thoughts as he returned to Hardcastle Lane.

He'd heard Gemma giggling in Adele's room about something to do with corsets—the pair were becoming thicker than thieves these days—and with the dead girl's body on his conscious, he'd chosen to avoid them.

He wasn't in the mood for giggling.

Nor his wife's company.

As much as her state last night had amused him, the ease with which COR had accepted her into their ranks bothered him a little.

She wasn't supposed to be a part of this.

And she wasn't staying.

But pointing this out to Gemma had only earned him an arched eyebrow and a little smirk. "Keep telling yourself that, Malloryn."

They all seemed to think something was happening when it wasn't.

He couldn't *allow* anything to happen.

Malloryn found himself in the training room, staring at the enormous padded automaton some of the Rogues occasionally fought. Stripping down to bare feet and trousers, he set the machine running and started warming up tight muscles as he ducked and dodged its swings.

He wasn't a complete bastard, but he'd always presumed the arrangement he and Adele shared suited them both. And if it didn't, then it didn't truly matter for they'd both been at odds. A cold war of words begun the day he slipped the engagement ring on her finger, which had only escalated the closer their wedding day loomed. While he certainly hadn't been entirely innocent, neither had she.

Yet....

It was almost as if he'd come to enjoy the daily trading of barbs, the swift uppercut he received in return. The second her face lit up with the intense flash of emotion when they sparred, he'd known he'd won, but there were moments when his jaw would clench and he'd be forced to concede the floor to her.

Their marriage was a battleground, a constant lingering tension, and yet he couldn't deny that Adele was the only woman of his acquaintance who wasn't afraid to go toe-to-toe with him. He'd even secretly respected her for it.

Everything had changed in the blink of an eye.

A single photograph.

His wife in another man's arms.

Or.... If he was being honest with himself, this shifting of axis—the complete skewing of his life with Adele—had begun the day she'd given him blood in the Tower.

Attraction simmered between them.

It always had, though he'd been forced to confront the truth of it that day.

To admit to himself that he desired his wife.

Try as he might, he'd never been able to stop his eye from lingering on her nape as he came across her dashing out some sort of correspondence in the library. Toying absently with her pearls, her fingers drawing his attention to the smooth curve of her breasts. Nibbling on the end of her pen, those soft full lips parted slightly. Sometimes he'd pause, and take the moment to peruse her while she was unaware of him.

In those moments, she seemed a different woman entirely, and it hadn't escaped his attention that he was curious about that woman.

Curious about the swift wit that flashed behind those expressive eyes. Curious about the soft gasp she'd made when he came back to himself in the tower, and found himself clasped between her thighs, her blood wet across his lips.

Curious about the whisper of silk behind the locked bedroom door that marked the edges of their respective territory.

The sound of her sheets rustling as she slipped between them chastised him each and every night. When he did sleep, he woke hard and aching, with her perfume in his nose.

And somehow, somewhere along the line, the bloody woman had begun to slip under his skin. No longer an enemy. Not quite a wife. Where then, could he place her?

Malloryn drew to a halt as the automaton ran through its cycles, his bruised knuckles slamming one last blow into its poor defenseless midriff. Who was he fooling? Certainly not Gemma.

And certainly not yourself.

Adele was proving dangerous.

He... liked her.

Quite a lot.

"Want something to hit that's a bit more lively?" drawled a quiet voice behind him.

Malloryn merely stared at the automaton. The former assassin made a cat seem sloppy, but he'd heard the faint creak of the door. Bloody Gemma. Sending Obsidian up here to nursemaid him, no doubt. "I think I'm still recovering from our last bout."

"You gave as good as you got."

Malloryn sighed, scrubbing a hand through his hair as he turned to confront his protégé's lover. "Did Gemma set you upon me?"

"No. She's distracted. She's been teaching your wife some self defense techniques and now she's trying to convince the duchess to wear something red tomorrow night."

"What is it with Gemma and red dresses?"

"I wasn't talking about a gown. It seems they share a fondness for fine undergarments."

His mind immediately pictured Adele in a flimsy little scrap of silk in vibrant red.

He didn't have to wonder about the precise color of Adele's nipples anymore. The softest, palest of pinks, imprinted in his memory as firmly as his signet ring into hot wax.

Knowledge he'd generally prefer not to have.

Just like he hadn't wanted to know what precise sound would escape her when she cried out with pleasure.

Malloryn punched the automaton's padded flanks, but though it might help alleviate the nightmares he fought, it did nothing to vanquish those licentious thoughts. "I did not need to know that."

Obsidian smiled faintly as he began stripping his coat off. "Consider yourself warned."

They'd been enemies once upon a time, and Malloryn had struggled to trust him, but all of that changed when Obsidian helped rescue him in Russia. Curiously, the assassin was the one Rogue who almost seemed to understand him.

Obsidian didn't push where he felt he wasn't wanted—unlike certain others. And he knew how to keep a secret.

It was becoming remarkably easy to deal with him.

"So you just happened to seek me out?"

"I knew where you'd be." Obsidian hauled his shirt over his head and folded it atop his coat.

"I'm growing a little weary of everyone nursemaiding me...."

"You're on edge and you're tired. That's the sort of combination that sees mistakes creep in. Considering you're the one in charge, you cannot afford to make mistakes."

Nobody else spoke to him like this. Anger flared. "You dare?"

"Technically, I outrank you, Your Grace," Obsidian said dryly. "So I'm not afraid of the Duke of Malloryn act."

"Do you want me to curtsy?"

"No." Obsidian padded toward him on bare feet. "I want you to fight."

They met in a flurry of blows.

Obsidian had an inch or two on him, and hence a longer reach. He was faster, stronger, and had trained all his life to be an assassin.

It was the only time Malloryn had ever found himself outclassed.

He took it as a challenge, each and every time.

The man who feared to face a worthier opponent was the man who stopped learning. Already, his bouts with Obsidian had tightened his reaction time, and taught him a unique style of combat he'd never known before.

He staggered back beneath a blow, and Obsidian pulled up to give him a chance to get his feet.

"Don't go easy on me," he warned. "If we go up against Dido and Jelena, then I cannot afford to be too weak or slow."

"You'll never match them for speed or strength."

"I know."

Which meant he had to be able to protect himself long enough to work out their weaknesses. Everyone had a weakness. Even him.

But his greatest strength was using his mind to dissect others.

The next time he and Jelena crossed paths, he would kill her. There was no other option.

He just had to master the tremors that lit through him whenever he heard her name.

They fought on, and Malloryn lost himself in the rush of blood and the slam of knuckles to ribs. This time, Obsidian showed no mercy. Malloryn hit the mats once. Then again. No matter how hard he pushed himself, his thighs were soon quivering, and while he saw the next feint coming, he couldn't move in time to avoid it.

Malloryn crashed onto his back, the breath slamming out of him.

"Enough," Obsidian said, leaning down to offer a hand to haul him to his feet.

"Not yet."

"You're exhausted. If you'd been taking better care of yourself, then I would not call this, but I am. You are done for the night."

"I am—"

"If Balfour attacked right now, he would defeat you," Obsidian said. "You never know when the next attack will occur. Don't let your pride push you too far."

Malloryn gritted his teeth as he shook himself off. "Sometimes I regret allowing you into COR."

Obsidian smiled faintly, pouring them both a glass of blood. "I'm sure you do."

Rolling his shoulders, Malloryn accepted the glass.

"Your mind was elsewhere tonight," Obsidian pointed out.

It left him an opening. If he wanted to talk he could choose to accept it, or not. Sometimes he appreciated the fact the assassin didn't pry.

Malloryn drained the glass, ignoring the faint prowling stir of the predator within him. It wanted more blood. "I thought I was prepared for Balfour's games. But he had Jelena kill another girl today." He could see the poor thing draped across Catherine's grave, both a desecration of human flesh and mortal memory. "I don't know what sort of message he's trying to send, beyond a taunt. I thought it meant the female Rogues were at risk—particularly as both girls he's killed look like Gemma—but he's not made a move against them."

"Don't worry about Gemma. She's dangerous enough to protect herself, and he knows he will have to go through me too." Obsidian leaned against the wall. "And maybe there is no message. Maybe he just wants you distracted."

Malloryn dragged a towel over the back of his neck and clung to each end. "That did cross my mind. Which means he's up to something. The dead bodies. The letter on my desk. He wants me to look close to home, rather than watch out for what he's doing."

"Which means you've uncovered something he doesn't want you to know."

"Sir George." He scrubbed at his mouth. "The explosives. The Prometheus Project. I just wish I knew which one."

"Be patient. Now we have a lead, we can explore them. This is what we do."

"I know." But he hesitated. God, it ached to admit it, but Obsidian had been right about pride and its cost. "I am not... at my best, right now."

"You need sleep."

How easy it sounded. He gave a faint, humorless laugh. "I know." The laughter faded as he looked the assassin in the eye. "I can't afford to make a mistake." The cost would be the lives of one of the Rogues, and the thought hamstrung him a little. "If you think I'm about to make a misstep, then tell me. You know him as well as I do. I won't like it, but I can't.... I can't wear the weight of it all alone."

It was the closest he could come to a confession.

Obsidian slowly nodded. "As you wish."

"And I would appreciate it if you wouldn't tell Gemma about this conversation."

"She worries."

Malloryn scrubbed his face with the towel, then cast it aside. "I've noticed. Maybe you can distract her."

It was a clear dismissal. Obsidian grabbed his clothes and headed for the door, but he paused there, one hand on the knob.

"You are not at your best," the assassin said. "I understand. But there is one thing you should know: This doesn't rest solely upon your shoulders. I know you fear for their safety, but you need to trust your Rogues. They are good at what they do, and they know the risks. They've accepted them, because the consequence is a world where Balfour once again pulls puppet strings.

"I never understood why Gemma's loyalty was bound so inexplicably to you. This. This is why. Because Balfour does not give a damn about those who work for him, and you do. You see it as a weakness—that you care for those around you, and he does not. He can be ruthless with his pawns and the cost of their lives is merely an irritation to him. He has more. He can throw dozens of lives at you without a care, until he overwhelms you. It makes him dangerous. But it is also a weakness.

"Because Balfour's play pieces know they mean nothing to him. They know they are disposable. And while he may offer the Rising Sons a vision of a future they crave, they'll turn on him without a second's notice if that vision goes up in flames.

"Balfour is not invincible. You see him as a threat because this time, you think *you* are the one who has everything to lose.

"But Gemma would set the world on fire for you, because she loves you. Every single Rogue volunteered to travel to Russia—the most dangerous place in the world—to rescue you. No Rogue left behind. It means something to them. It means something to you. It... means something to me. Stop thinking of it as a weakness, and start thinking of it as a strength."

Malloryn reached for his shirt, as he sorted through his feelings. "He will kill them because of me."

It was the secret that haunted his nights.

"He can try. But we're ready for him, Your Grace. And if our dear leader would get some bloody sleep, it would be a weight off all our minds."

Malloryn blinked in surprise.

"You're not the only one who worries," Obsidian said dryly, as he opened the door. "If you need to hit someone—or be hit some more—then let me know. Otherwise, I'm fairly certain there's a pair of willing arms waiting to greet you upstairs if you were to seek your bed."

If only it were that easy.

"Not you too." Malloryn grimaced. "I think you've been spending too much time with Gemma. Your brain's starting to rot."

Obsidian shrugged and glanced at the practice automaton. "I spent years on my own, hitting things that couldn't hit back, just to silence the voices in my head. I've since discovered a welcoming embrace can be far more therapeutic in some instances. You should try it."

And then he was gone, leaving Malloryn alone with his thoughts.

And the frustrating desire to see if Obsidian was right.

Malloryn sighed, and turned back to the automaton. He wasn't quite ready to concede defeat. Far better if he stayed away from Adele.

Because a part of him couldn't forget the sight of that poor girl draped across a grave.

Catherine. Isabella. Millie Vane. And now this anonymous girl.

All dead because of him.

No. He was better off staying as far away from his wife as he could.

"How is he?" Gemma murmured sleepily, as Obsidian slid between the covers and curled around her.

"On edge," he replied, brushing a kiss to the back of her neck.

Gemma rolled to examine his expression. "What did he say?"

"He asked me not to repeat it."

Which was vexing, but if Malloryn had reached out to Obsidian, then at least he was talking to someone. She had to trust her lover.

"I don't know what to do," she whispered. Despite all the years she'd spent at Malloryn's side.... "I don't know how to reach him."

Not with this.

The duke despised weaknesses, but he would not tolerate them in himself. And despite the fact she could pinpoint the precise issue that afflicted him, she couldn't seem to help him.

Russia had left scars on Malloryn's soul that she couldn't heal. She knew he'd been tortured at Jelena's hands, but not the extent of it. He was learning to control his flinch every time he heard the *dhampir* agent's name, learning to lock down his physical responses through sheer force of will.

It didn't mean she couldn't see the ghost of it written all over him.

He wouldn't talk to her about it.

He wouldn't even admit he had a bloody problem, despite the restless hours he spent prowling the night, or forcing his body to the edge of exhaustion. Despite the ever dwindling levels of brandy in his personal decanter.

Herbert wouldn't speak of it, not even to her, but she'd seen him look concerned when he refilled them.

"As much as I know you'll hate to hear it," Obsidian murmured, stroking the hair off her face, "maybe you're not the one who *can* reach him. He's spent years protecting you. He sees that as his role, and the idea of reversing it is simply incomprehensible to him."

"We can protect him too," she growled. "If he'd just let us."

"I know." Obsidian brushed his knuckles against her lips. "After what happened in Russia, he's more than aware of it. He's just struggling to admit it. You want a proud man to bare his soul, but it's entirely possible he won't. Or can't."

Gemma shivered at the sensuous touch. "How do I help him?"

"Be there," he murmured. "The way you were for me. He will come to you if he needs you. He loves you, Gemma. You're the sister he never had. He trusts you. And if he is on the verge of breaking he knows you will—"

"He'll never admit it," she said, knowing Malloryn all too well.

"True." Obsidian rolled onto his back. "Though there is one spark of hope."

She turned onto her side, to drape a thigh over his. "The duchess? You noticed that too?"

"I know what a man looks like when he's trying to pretend a woman hasn't captured his interest. I saw that look every day in the mirror for the last five years. Maybe he just needs to release some of that tension."

"I would say 'poor duchess', but then I was watching his face when Adele handed him a set down in the garden of Lady Rutherford's ball. You might be right. She's proved herself his match." A chuckle escaped her. "Oh, and he doesn't like it."

"Malloryn likes to control things." A finger traced over her thigh. "It baffles him when he can't."

"Like his feelings," Gemma mused, though she knew her gaze had darkened. She enjoyed those softer moments where she could lie in her lover's arms and merely talk, but the stroke of his hand was distracting. "And the duchess."

"Which are currently tied together," he pointed out, his fingers tracing up and down her thigh. "Are we done speaking about the duke?"

"Are you feeling neglected, my love?"

His eyes darkened. "Always."

"Then let me make it up to you."

Rolling over the top of him, she straddled his hips. Obsidian's lips quirked as he toyed with the flimsy hem of her nightgown. "Is there any point in wearing this when it's so fine I can see right through it?"

Gemma slid her palms up his bare chest. "That *is* kind of the point."

"Oh?"

"Don't think I cannot see how well you manage the duke. And me." She dug her nails in. "You think I need to release a little bit of tension too."

"I offer myself as willing sacrifice."

She leaned down and pressed a kiss to his chest. "How noble of you."

His hand slid through her hair. "I thought so too."

"Fine." She bit at his thumb as it rasped over her cheek. "I'll stop worrying about Malloryn if you'll shut up and kiss me."

"It's a deal," Obsidian purred, dragging her face down to his.

CHAPTER TWENTY-TWO

Lights glittered in the ballroom, like a thousand stars sparkling in the night sky.

Watching Adele glide down the stairs made Malloryn's breath catch in his tracks. She'd been caught up in the receiving queue with Gemma as she introduced her husband's "cousin from the country" and he'd been so focused on the mission at hand that the sudden shock of her as she appeared on the stairs momentarily stunned him.

She looked utterly ravishing in a raspberry pink gown that sat just off her shoulders and displayed her full curves to best advantage. Tendrils of hair hung from her elegant chignon and brushed against her collarbone, where her favorite pearls gleamed.

"*I'm saving my diamonds for you,*" she'd whispered as he handed her up into the carriage, and he'd spent the entire carriage ride trying not to think about her in just those diamonds.

Keeping his hands off her was becoming more and more difficult with each passing hour.

Someone coughed discreetly at his side. "You're

staring. And the lady is spoken for, I believe. You don't want to earn the wrath of her husband, as I'm told he's a cold, vicious bastard."

Malloryn glanced at Lord Barrons as his oldest friend paused at his side. They'd gone through Eton together, fought duels side by side, and wooed many a young woman in the Echelon before a minor argument had parted them for several years.

They'd managed to set aside their differences during the revolution. And then Barrons had played an integral part in his rescue from Russia.

The fact that so many people had risked their lives to save his still left him reeling at times.

"Barrons. Lady Haynes's standards must be slipping. I didn't realize she'd invited the riffraff."

"Oh, it's you," Barrons said, in mock surprise. A ruby earring winked in his ear. "From the way you were perusing your wife as if she were something to be consumed, I didn't quite recognize you."

"Bugger off," Malloryn replied, scanning the room for signs of Gemma and Obsidian. He'd set them to keep an eye out for Thomas Mowbray. "Haven't you got anything more important to do? Where's your wife?"

"Eviscerating Lord Carlyle. It was embarrassing to watch."

Mina did have that way about her.

"So what brings you out of your dark little hidey hole?" Barrons asked.

Malloryn paused, glancing around. Both Barrons and Mina were on the Council of Dukes who helped rule the city. They'd be mostly up-to-date with the situation. "I'm setting a trap."

"For?"

"Sir George," he murmured.

Barrons's eyebrows rose. "As in, Hamilton? Your father-in-law?"

Malloryn discreetly turned away from the ballroom. "It appears Sir George has been up to no good."

"Those *old friends* of yours?" Barrons murmured.

"Yes."

"There you are," Adele said, appearing at his side and rapping his arm with her fan. "You were supposed to wait for me."

"We were just talking about you," Barrons said, a teasing twinkle in his eye. "You look utterly captivating tonight, Duchess."

"Thank you, Lord Barrons." Adele seemed a trifle disconcerted by the compliment.

"Don't you agree, Malloryn?"

"Adele knows how lovely she is," he murmured.

"Yes, but I'll give you a word of advice from an old married man: It never hurts to remind them."

The last thing he wanted to do was betray his growing feelings for his wife in public. Too many eyes were watching them. One hint that the Duke and Duchess of Malloryn were no longer entirely at odds, and he might condemn her to a dangerous fate. It was one thing to know she was working for him, but Balfour's spies would be watching for any sign of weakness in him.

"I'll consider your advice," he replied, hoping she'd understand. "Right now, I need to keep an eye out for Mowbray."

Adele startled.

"Barrons is aware of what's going on," he told her, just as a familiar face caught his eye.

"There's my father by the orchestra," Adele said without moving her lips. "Thomas Mowbray is talking to Lady Agatha Callahan. He looks like a walrus."

"Found him," Malloryn murmured.

"Why, it sounds like the waltz is just starting," Adele said with a mischievous twinkle in her eyes.

"Perhaps Barrons would escort you?" Malloryn suggested, watching Sir George slip quietly from the room.

"Of course," Barrons replied promptly. "It will be my honor, Your Grace."

Malloryn noticed the slight hint of disappointment in her eyes as he tilted his head to them. They'd only ever danced that once, and it was clear she wanted to be in his arms again.

It had been clear this morning, when she asked him where he'd stayed the night that she wanted more than a dance.

"You'll be safe here," he murmured. "I'll be back shortly."

"It seems much has changed," Lord Barrons murmured as he swept Adele around the ballroom.

"Does it?" she asked dryly. "Or are you merely being charming again?"

"I'm being honest. You would have to know Malloryn as well as I do to see it," Barrons mused. "He doesn't like to reveal his inner thoughts in public."

"It seems as though he rarely reveals them in private either."

"You, however, are a little easier to read."

Adele looked away.

She couldn't help herself sometimes. Every time she saw her husband, the rest of the room faded into inconsequence.

"Be patient with him," Barrons murmured. "And

smile. You're dancing with me. You'll ruin my reputation if you continue to look so grim."

Adele *tsked* under her breath. "No wonder your wife never stood a chance."

He laughed. "I'll tell her that."

It felt like dancing with a dashing pirate. Barrons was ridiculously handsome and moved with the sort of dangerous grace that quite swept a young woman off her feet. She'd always had a certain partiality for brown eyes, but as she looked up into his, she realized the allure had faded.

All she could see were eyes the color of a stormy sky.

Eyes as piercing as one of her gray diamonds; their facets equally as reflective and fascinating.

"Don't let him push you away," Barrons continued, as the waltz began its last stanza. "He will, you know, but I think he needs you."

"It's not quite as easy as one might imagine." After all, he hadn't bedded her since that day on his desk.

"I'll tell you a little secret: Malloryn lives and breathes control, especially now, after Russia—"

"Why Russia?"

Barrons leaned closer, so he wouldn't be heard. "I don't know precisely what they did to him there, but it wasn't kind, Duchess. Jelena tortured him extensively, and I don't think he thought anyone would come for him. He won't talk about it. At least not with me. Probably not with others, either."

She considered that, feeling a little horrified at the thought. "He doesn't sleep very often."

"That doesn't surprise me." Barrons gave her a thin smile, and she realized he cared for Malloryn. "I can see the cracks in his surface. He holds himself together with pure willpower, but even Malloryn might break. I don't want to see that."

"What can I do?"

"You think he doesn't care for you. You think he keeps you at arm's length, no?"

She nodded. "We have reached a truce, but... Malloryn remains Malloryn."

No matter how much she pushed, she still woke alone.

"When you walked in here, he couldn't take his eyes from you." Barrons twirled her. "I have never seen him look at a woman like that in all the years I've known him."

"There is an attraction there."

"It's more than attraction. I saw longing, Duchess. The type you sometimes see in a man's eyes when he wants something, but does not dare reach for it. And we both know he won't reach for it. If you want more from him, then you must demand it."

To demand it meant wearing her heart on her sleeve, and Adele had her own demons.

"Thank you. For the advice," she whispered, as the waltz wound down.

Barrons led her to the edge of the ballroom. "Thank you for the dance. It was most enlightening." He gave her a considering look as he pressed a kiss to the back of her silk glove. "I wish you well."

And then he sauntered off, lords and ladies alike parting around him like the sea, as if they sensed a powerful predator in their midst.

Adele didn't know what to think.

Did she dare hope Barrons spoke the truth?

"Your Grace," said a footman, out of nowhere.

Adele startled. "Yes?"

"A message," he said, slipping a piece of folded paper into her hand before vanishing into the crowd.

Adele glanced at the paper, her breath catching when

she recognized the writing. It was Hattie's.

Please. I need to see you right now. Behind the stairs. Father's done something terrible.

Come out, come out, wherever you are....

"She's quite a catch, isn't she?"

Malloryn stilled as he recognized the voice, his hand sliding into his pocket and finding the small, hard lump there.

Lord Devoncourt stepped up beside him as Malloryn watched Adele dancing from the balcony. She seemed enraptured with something Barrons was saying, and the vibrant dark pink gown set her apart from the rest of the dance floor.

Not for him the art of espionage. Though he had more than enough experience at creeping about ballrooms unaware, he'd known there'd be too many eyes watching him tonight. He'd sent Gemma and Obsidian to follow Sir George instead, while he played decoy, wondering whom he'd lure out of the shadows.

And of all the people....

"Quite." He bit off the word.

"A bloom just ripe for the picking. It was remarkably easy to capture her attention, did you know? A few small compliments, a man's unabashed focus upon her—if you've ever seen her with Sir George, you'll understand why. She longs to be seen."

"Is there a point to this?"

Devoncourt's smile widened. "It bothers you, doesn't it? That my lips have known hers. That I could have had her if I wanted to."

It was far easier than expected to play the role of

jealous husband.

"But you didn't, did you?" He had his hands on the lapels of Devoncourt's collar before he even knew it. Devoncourt caught his wrist, and their gazes clashed, before Malloryn forced a smile. "And it wasn't for lack of trying."

"Careful," Devoncourt chided, his fingers digging into the nerves in Malloryn's wrist. "You wouldn't want anyone to know I struck a nerve."

Malloryn made a great show of glancing around, before he let him go and stepped back, straightening the rumples in his own coat, as if the altercation hadn't even occurred.

"And you're right," Devoncourt conceded with a smile. "She likes to play her own games. She's an elusive creature."

"Which seems to have worked to my favor. You may have offered her flattery, but Adele's quite good at baiting her own hook."

The faintest flicker of darkness flashed through Devoncourt's blue eyes. "I would never have guessed her to be working for *you.* Her animosity was quite convincing."

"Perhaps because it is." He couldn't afford to betray his feelings, and sometimes there were benefits to playing the Duke of Malloryn. Everyone knew he was made of polished steel. Ruthless. Indifferent. *Cold.* It was like slipping into another skin; one he'd mastered years ago. "You think her loyalty belongs to me? She has other buttons to push, beyond her father's indifference to her." His voice lowered. "It's just a matter of pushing the right ones to get what I want."

Devoncourt swallowed the lie. "You played the both of us."

He merely smiled. "I needed a weapon you'd never see

coming."

"Yes. It's strange how Adele vanished from Angel's Fall at the precise moment Corvus did."

There was no point prevaricating.

"He sends his regards," Malloryn replied. "Or he would if he could speak."

Devoncourt's lips thinned. "I hope he suffered. There's no love lost between Corvus and me, so your barb draws no blood."

"It wasn't intended to. Do you have anything of interest to say to me? Or are you merely tilting at windmills, when there's nothing either of us can do?"

"Too public," Devoncourt agreed.

"It's going to be private, one day."

"It will."

Their eyes locked on each other.

"Actually, I was merely meant to draw your attention," Devoncourt said, brushing lint from his sleeve. This time, it was he who held the upper hand.

Malloryn's gaze jerked to the ballroom.

Too late.

There was no raspberry pink anywhere to be found. He spotted Barrons immediately, laughing at something Mina said.

But Adele wasn't there.

"How interesting. You appear to have your own blind spot. You may not want her, but you do not want anyone else to have her either. Distractions are dangerous, Your Grace," Devoncourt said, with a faint smile. "I *do* hope you can find her in time."

Malloryn shot the man one last murderous look, teeth gnashing at the thought he may have bought into the game just a little *too* well, before he stalked along the balcony, hunting through the crowd.

Where would she have gone? She knew better than to leave the ballroom.

Slipping down the stairs, he found himself in a crush of people all looking to speak to him. Something about his face must have warned them, for suddenly his path opened up.

And then he paused as a prickling sensation ran down his spine.

And not just from Adele's disappearance.

Something had roused the predator within him and sent it hissing like a cat arching its back when another tom walked into its territory.

What had set off his darker side?

A hint of bergamot scented the air.

He looked around sharply.

It could have been in any perfume or cologne. It was a popular base scent, after all. But as the clammy sensation spread across the base of his spine, Malloryn couldn't help feeling as though someone had walked over his grave.

He didn't believe in coincidences.

His worst nightmare was here.

Somewhere.

And his wife was missing.

CHAPTER TWENTY-THREE

Gemma ran along the hallway at the back of Lady Haynes's house, holding her skirts out of the way.

She'd been caught between two drunken fools who were threatening fisticuffs, and had lost visual on Thomas Mowbray for a second.

"Obsidian?" she whispered, putting her hand to her earpiece.

"Yes?" said her lover.

"I've lost Mowbray."

There was a moment of silence. *"I've got Sir George in sight. He's prowling the garden folly."*

"Good. Stay on him. I'll find you."

Blood flavored the air as she turned a corner. All of Gemma's senses awoke, the hunger surging to the surface and darkening her vision.

"Oh, heck," she said.

"What?"

"I think I've found Mowbray." Turning another corner, she saw the elderly gentleman crawling across the marble floors, a bloodied trail behind him.

"Sir!" She slid to his side and rolled him over. "What happened?"

"There was a woman," he gasped, one hand clasped to his chest. Gemma could see hot, red blood spurting between his fingers in pulses. A human. He was not long for this world.

She tore his waistcoat off and wadded it against his chest, though there was little hope of staunching the bleeding. Heart blood, by the look of it. She could smell it in the air and her mouth watered as the predator within her awoke. "What sort of woman? Blonde? Was she very blonde?"

"Yes." Blood flecked his lips. "Hair like... snow."

Oh, heck. It had to be either Dido or Jelena. Gemma drew one of the knives attached to her thigh. "What did you give her?"

Mowbray blinked, as if his vision was fading. "Are you... an angel?"

"What did you give her?" Gemma shook him a little.

"The keys..." His breath started rattling in his throat as he clutched at her arm. "To all my... automatons. They're going to... burn it all... down. You have to... stop them." His breath started to wheeze and panic filled his eyes. "Stop them...."

"I will," Gemma promised as Mowbray's fingers loosened from her arm and he slumped to the floor. "Damn it."

Footsteps slapped on the marble as Obsidian sprinted around the corner, skidding to a halt when he saw Mowbray.

"Sir George was the diversion," she growled. "Either Jelena or Dido is here, and they took what they needed from Mowbray. Hurry. We need to find Malloryn. Because if it was Jelena, then she won't be able to stop herself from striking at him."

The first time Adele suspected she was being followed was as she made her way along the gallery behind the stairs.

There was no sign of Hattie, but several ladies laughed and twittered nearby, and a footman stood propped in front of the wall. The ballroom was mere feet away. So close, she had to be safe, didn't she?

It wasn't the first time she'd found herself stalked through ballrooms. And the woman behind her moved nonchalantly enough, passing laughing couples who'd sought some privacy in the hallway, pausing every now and then before a painting as if to examine it, that Adele almost doubted herself.

One could be forgiven for assuming she was just another guest, but there was a faint prickling sensation down Adele's spine. Something wasn't right, and she always listened to her instincts.

"Malloryn?" she whispered, touching the small auditory device in her ear. He'd told her not to use it unless strictly necessary.

Static shirred through it. *"Where are you?"* he demanded in his usual clipped tones.

"Behind the staircase. Hattie wanted to see me. You didn't happen to send one of your agents after me, did you? For protection?"

She could almost sense him pausing in whatever he was doing. *"No,"* he said slowly. *"Why?"*

"I think I'm being followed. It's a woman," she whispered, hoping he could hear her through the communicator. "She's wearing a swan headpiece and a white dress."

So were half the bloody debutantes at the ball. White denoted a young woman searching for a protector. But there was nothing innocent in the way the woman moved, her eyes radiating a particular sort of menace as her attention locked on Adele.

She was definitely moving faster now, as Adele froze in front of a painting. The footman had vanished. The three ladies slipped past the woman stalking toward her, fans fluttering.

And the woman was between her and the ballroom.

"Blonde—very blonde—and... I think there's something wrong with her mouth. A scar, perhaps. Or one side of it is pulled up."

Silence loomed through the device.

Then her husband's voice cracked sharply through the auditory device in her ear. *"Adele, where precisely are you?"*

There was something about his tone that made her heart skip a beat. "I'm behind the staircase, but she's between me and the ballroom. Should I try and circle around?"

"Don't go anywhere," Malloryn snapped. *"I'm coming for you, right now."*

"What's going on?"

"You just described Jelena."

The *dhampir* woman who worked for Balfour. Adele's heart pounded. "I can't stay. She's herding me away from the ballroom."

"Find someone. Find people. You're not safe," Malloryn said sharply. *"Gemma? Abandon Mowbray. I've got a possible sighting of Jelena near the back of the main staircase. She's following Adele."*

Her device was only linked to his, so she had to assume the other woman answered.

Adele stepped back as the woman smiled and advanced upon her. There was light to her left. Laughter in the distance. Safety, perhaps. "I have to move," she hissed. "The ladies' powder room is just in front of me. I'll lock myself inside."

"Ava wants to know if you have your perfume," Malloryn demanded.

Her perfume?

Clarity dawned. The pretty blonde scientist had doctored it with the Black Vein toxin. "Yes. It's in my reticule."

"If you're trapped, squirt it directly in Jelena's face. It won't affect you, but warn any other blue bloods in the area. She said she hasn't tested it directly, but it might be strong enough to incapacitate her."

Hemlock in her ring. Black Vein in her perfume.

Who did they think she was?

She was no Gemma or Ingrid.

"I'm coming, Adele. I won't let her hurt you. I promise."

Another woman stepped into the hallway ahead of Adele, gowned in vibrant green silk. Her silvery blonde hair was knotted back into an elegant coil, and her eyes glittered.

But it was the pistol in her hand, held low against her thigh, that caught Adele's attention.

Dido.

"There's two of them," she breathed. "Malloryn, I can't escape."

"Where are you?"

"She has *a pistol.*"

"Adele, focus. Where?"

Gaslights gleamed in their sconces. Doors lined the hallway. "Right outside the powder room."

"*Get inside it and lock the door.*"

The woman in front of her began stalking forward.

Adele burst into the powder room and locked it behind her, relief flooding through her the second she heard voices. A trio of debutantes laughed in front of the mirrors, patting stray curls into place and squaring necklines.

Safe.

She was safe.

But even as she said it, the handle turned. Someone twisted it violently, as if realizing it was locked.

"They just unlocked the door somehow," she blurted through the listening device. Then she froze as the lock gave a telltale click.

In the mirror's reflection she saw the door begin to open, and Adele turned to find Jelena slipping inside, one elegant shoulder bare and her painted mouth widening into a malicious smile.

Not safe.

Trapped.

"Duchess," Jelena murmured, closing the door behind her—and locking it again.

"Malloryn," she whispered, even as she knew her husband wasn't going to be able to save her.

"Unfortunately, your husband is... currently indisposed." The woman slunk forward, white silk skirts swishing around her ankles.

"What do you want?" Adele demanded, though her hands trembled.

"Malloryn's head on a platter. Or yours, if I cannot have his."

One of the debutantes looked around in surprise, even as a knife slid into Jelena's hand, half-hidden by her skirts. The swan headpiece was tossed negligently aside, revealing a gold-embroidered eye patch over the woman's missing eye.

The other two girls remained oblivious, chattering on about some lord and his padded shoulders, but the other girl was frowning, as if she sensed something amiss.

"Get your friends out of here," Adele told the girl, circling a padded velvet chair.

Jelena simply grabbed it and cast it aside. It hit the wall with a smash, pieces of timber tumbling askew.

And Adele had nothing else to hide behind.

All three debutantes screamed.

"Run!" she yelled to the nearest girl.

Could they not see how much danger they were in?

Adele shoved her hand inside her reticule as Jelena stalked toward her. Damn it, where was it?

White drifted into her field of vision, and Adele tried to dart to the side.

A hand locked in the back of her pearl necklace, and she fell backwards as she was drawn to an abrupt halt. She clutched at the necklace, but Jelena twisted her fist, and every single pearl dug into Adele's throat.

Suddenly she couldn't breathe.

"You poor, pathetic little bitch," Jelena taunted, her face coming into Adele's field of reference. "God, what was he thinking? Marrying cattle?" She gave another malicious twist of the necklace, and Adele's eyes popped as the pounding in her temples intensified. "He was given a gift. A near-immortal god, and he casts it all aside to bed down with the filth. I should make this bloody and slow, just for that insult."

So hard... to think. Adele tried to push at Jelena, but the other woman was choking her. Darkness blurred at the edges of her vision, and the pulse pounded in her throat, as if blood was trying to force itself through her starved veins.

The choker of pearls suddenly released as the thin strands broke. Pearls scattered all across the floor and her throat opened as Adele sucked in a rattling half breath.

"Maybe I will make this bloody," Jelena mused.

Adele's lungs pulsed, starved for oxygen, and she thought she'd burst into a coughing fit, but there was no time.

There was suddenly the tip of a knife in her vision, slashing down her cheek. Adele didn't bother screaming; she flicked the silver thorn on her ring out and stabbed it into the other woman's midriff.

Jelena gasped, and then smashed the back of her hand across Adele's face. Thrown onto her stomach in a tangle of skirts, Adele caught sight of her reticule on the floor. Behind her, Jelena made a horrible strangled sound in her throat.

"You fucking... bish...."

Hemlock might not be enough to incapacitate Jelena entirely—its effectiveness was limited by how high a blue blood's craving virus levels were, and a *dhampir's* CV levels would be stratospheric—but it slowed her down enough for Adele to reach her reticule.

A knee slammed into her back, the knife sliding across her shoulder. Adele screamed as she drove an elbow back into Jelena's ribs. The *dhampir* assassin was a heavy weight, her body clearly not working properly as she tried to grab a fistful of Adele's hair.

"Adele?" Malloryn's tinny voice in her ear.

He wasn't going to make it in time....

She was going to die. Right here. She'd never see her husband again. Never see Hattie. Never hold her baby in her arms—the one she'd wanted. Little Alex.... Little Alex, oh, God.... Lena.

Never kiss her husband ever again—

"You worthless scrap of nothing...."

Suddenly she was months in the past, as Lord Corvus clasped at his bloodied cheek and looked at her with fury in his eyes. "*You little slut—*"

And he'd come at her, knife swinging, before she'd darted under his arm and bolted through the gardens, fleeing directly into Malloryn's arms.

Corvus hadn't beaten her then.

And Jelena would not beat her now.

"If Malloryn wants you so badly, then he can have little pieces of you," Jelena whispered, the words barely penetrating the throbbing pulse in Adele's ears.

Like hell.

She was Adele Cavill, the Duchess of Malloryn, and she'd spent years fighting for the right to survive in this cursed world. Blue bloods had cut her and bled her and pinned her down. They had treated her exactly like the cattle Jelena called her. She was not going to be ended here, not like this.

Adele's hand curled around the small glass bottle of perfume. Her bloodied gloves slipped and slid, but she thought she had her fingers around the rubber bulb of the atomizer.

Another slash of pain—through her ear, this time.

A sweep of blinding heat went through her, and blood splashed wetly down her throat as Adele tried to scream.

In the distance, she could hear someone yelling. Fists pounded on the door. But she pumped a full dose of her perfume into Jelena's face, and then squeezed again. The liquid splashed across the *dhampir's* mouth and cheeks, and rage filled her eye and then—

Jelena jerked, sucking in an enormous mouthful of the perfumed poison.

She reared back, dropping the knife and clutching her throat.

Adele scrambled out of the way as Jelena thrashed on the carpets. Black veins spread across the other woman's cheeks, bloodied spittle spraying from her lips. Adele's ear throbbed, and when she clapped her hand there, she could feel hot blood pumping through her silk-clad fingers.

My ear.

There was a bloody knife on the floor right in front of Adele.

Jelena's knife.

Adele's hand locked around it, and then she threw herself atop the fallen woman and stabbed down. It went right through the other woman's chest, and Jelena's eye widened as black blood sprayed from her lips.

Adele lifted the knife again, seeing red.

This was for all the blue bloods who'd ever hurt her.

For this entire damned society that thought she was little more than cattle.

For Lord Corvus, who'd thought Adele his personal plaything.

For Hattie.

And her father.

And her ear.

"Adele! Adele!" Hands caught her by the wrist, and then Malloryn was there, forcing her to withhold her next blow.

"Let me go!" she rasped, clutching at the hilt.

"She's done for. She's not breathing." He held one sleeve over his mouth and nose, coughing through the superfine. "*Jesus.* What did you do?"

Thin threads of black began to wend through the capillaries in his cheeks.

Dhampir weren't the only ones vulnerable to Black Vein. And it was that fact alone that cut through her rage.

"You idiot!" Adele dropped the knife and shoved herself under his shoulder. "You shouldn't be in here!"

Together, they lurched toward the door.

Malloryn slammed against the wall, blood spattering

his lips as he coughed.

Gemma appeared, dangerous in bright blue silk with a pistol held low against her thigh. She took one look at Malloryn's face and jerked her reticule open.

"Here." Removing a thin syringe, she jabbed it into his upper arm and pumped its contents into him. "Ava's cure."

Malloryn coughed, dropping his sleeve from his face. He leaned against the wall. "How much... Black Vein did she put in that... bottle?"

"Enough to drop an elephant," Gemma said dryly. "You, of all people, should know better than to run into a room filled with atomized Black Vein."

"Sorry," he snarled. "I wasn't aware it was. All I saw was Adele with a knife, and Jelena on the floor beneath her."

Gemma eased the door open, protecting her mouth with her glove, and took in the room. Her eyebrows rose. "You killed her."

"Not me," Malloryn murmured, his attention all on Adele. "Are you all right?"

And suddenly it hit her.

How close she'd come to dying. That she'd *killed* another woman.

He must have seen it in her face, for his brows drew sharply together. Adele threw herself into his arms, burying her face against his chest.

There was a minute hesitation, and then Malloryn's arms closed around her. Palm spreading wide across the flat of her back, his voice roughening, he said, "You're safe. You're safe, Adele."

And she believed it.

The Duke of Malloryn was a force of nature. He'd helped drag the prince consort from power and ruined Lord Balfour's schemes. Every blue blood in the Echelon secretly feared him.

A hiccup escaped her.

"You're bleeding," he murmured, rubbing that hand up and down her spine. "I can smell it. Will you let me see?"

She wanted to stay right here in his arms, but her ear was a throbbing mess.

Malloryn captured her face in his hands, his pupils black with the craving as he turned her face from side to side. "Bloody hell. She's cut you a few times."

He tore his cravat free from his throat, wadded it into a bunch, and pressed it to her ear. Adele winced.

"N-no more earrings." Adele managed a weak smile as she touched the cravat. And then she remembered what had become of her grandmother's pearls. "Oh, no. My pearls. She broke them!"

Scattered all over the room inside like the pieces of her life.

She took a step toward the powder room, but Malloryn hauled her back. "Gemma will fetch them," he said. "You don't need to see that room again."

Tears wet her eyes as the loss finally hit her.

Her ruined earlobe could be hidden by a strategic curl. The scars on her cheek could be managed.

But those pearls were the only thing she had left of her grandmother—the only family member who'd ever given a damn about her as a little girl.

"That bitch," she said, trying to wipe the tears from her eyes.

"Here," Malloryn said, dragging her bloody gloves off and discarding them on the floor. "We need to get you home and out of that gown. Before people start talking."

Jelena was dead.

His heart wouldn't stop racing. The world around him flashed past in jerky vignettes as Malloryn sent for the carriage: Lady Haynes's face swam in front of him as he curtly made their goodbyes; he fought his way through flashes of garish color as every silk-clad aristocratic lady fought to say something to them; and then there was cool, blessed air washing over him.

Washing away the last cloying lungful's of Black Vein.

Sweeping the clinging tendrils of bergamot from his coat.

It couldn't remove the surreal sensation that he was finally free of those nightmares, or the worry that, even though she was gone, they would remain.

She was dead. Jelena was dead.

All these months of lying in bed, dreaming of what he'd do if he ever saw her again. Both fearing and hungering for that moment.... Craving the need to take back his power over her, and the way she'd broken him.

He felt cheated somehow.

Obsidian had gotten rid of the body, but there was no blotting the blood from the carpets in the powder room. No hiding the tremble in Adele's shoulders as she clung to the coat he'd draped over them.

"Are you all right?" he murmured, though his ears still rung. He needed to pull himself together, and now, but there was an odd dreamlike quality to the moment.

"Never better," Adele lied.

He caught himself before he reached for her. So much for sleight of hand. So much for manipulating Devoncourt. What a fucking idiot he'd been. Too busy playing his own games to keep his eye on the prize.

He'd nearly lost her.

Nodding curtly, he helped her up into the carriage, as Obsidian and Gemma swished down the steps behind him.

"What the hell happened in there?" Obsidian muttered. "I thought you were watching her?"

I made a mistake.

The muscle ticked in his jaw. "I left her with Barrons."

Obsidian searched his eyes. "Why? You were supposed to keep an eye on her. You were supposed to be the decoy."

"And I was." Malloryn pressed a hand to his earpiece, trying to force his body to control itself. "Byrnes?"

"*Yes?*" came the crackling reply.

"Have you got your tracking device upon you?"

"*Yes.*"

"Good," he said, ignoring the flare of surprise in Obsidian's eyes as he hauled himself up into the carriage. "Follow Devoncourt. You won't have to get too close. He'll be expecting a tail but I managed to plant the tracking device on him. I need you to find me those explosives."

CHAPTER TWENTY-FOUR

As Ava and Kincaid bundled Adele inside the safe house, Gemma stopped Malloryn, her gloved hand locking around his upper arm.

"A word?" she asked briskly.

He nodded to Herbert, indicating the butler should drive the carriage around back. The man snapped the whip with alacrity, and then Malloryn was standing there alone in the street with his protégé.

"What is it?"

"You didn't think to tell us about your plan?" she asked briskly.

"It was more of an opportunity taken, than a plan."

"You just happened to have a tracking device upon you? And Byrnes and Ingrid waiting?"

"You knew they were at hand should anything go wrong." Malloryn stared down into her eyes. "I expected to draw someone from the shadows. It's merely happy coincidence it was Devoncourt, and not Jelena."

"And what if it *had* been she who approached you?"

"Balfour knows her weaknesses. I was gambling on

the fact he couldn't afford to let her off the leash—"

"And yet, it seems he did." They broke apart, as Gemma paced. "You took a risk. You should have had someone watching *your* back. Watching Adele's. We both know you're targets. I should have insisted upon it. I didn't know you were planning to act independently."

"I'm more than capable of defending myself."

"Are you?" The flash of challenge in her eyes made his temper rouse. They both knew he wasn't operating as efficiently as usual. "I'm so sorry I give a damn, Malloryn. I'm so sorry you mean so much to me. To COR."

"You care too much—"

"And you don't care enough!"

The near shout took them both by surprise.

He stared at her. "Don't mistake control for indifference. I care about COR. I've risked my life for all of—"

"I'm talking about yourself," she said, anger thick and constrained in her voice. "Ever since we rescued you in Russia, you've been pushing us all away. Pushing yourself. You're callous and reckless with your own health and safety. Balfour's demise has consumed you and do you know what frightens me the most, Malloryn?"

He didn't have to answer.

"It's not the fact I don't think you can beat Balfour. It's the fact you're acting as though you don't think you'll survive the encounter."

It was true. He hadn't been himself in months. He could admit that. "Nobody knows the outcome of what's to come."

"But do you care? Do you honestly care whether you survive it?"

"Of course I want to survive it." His mouth twisted. "I won't let him beat me. Trust that, if nothing else."

A choked sound echoed in her throat, and then she was stepping forward, wrapping her arms around his waist.

Malloryn held his arms out in surprise, as Gemma pressed her cheek to her chest. She squeezed him so hard he thought she might intend to break one of his ribs.

"Promise me," she whispered. "Promise me you intend to survive it."

Malloryn rested his chin on the top of her head as he folded his arms slowly around her. "I promise. I can't just leave you all behind. Who else would provide Byrnes with so much amusement? Who else would curse you all, as you try to run roughshod over poor Herbert? Someone has to keep you Rogues in line."

A shuddery breath escaped her as she buried her face against his chest. "I am going to hold you to that promise, because if you let yourself be killed, I swear I will tell Society every damning secret you ever had."

"You don't know all my secrets."

"I'll make some up," she threatened.

A rough laugh escaped him. "Ah, Gem. Who would have ever thought we'd end up here the night Balfour sent you to kill me? You're a menace."

"And you're an arrogant ass," she muttered.

It made him smile.

"So much for being one of my most dangerous spies," he murmured, drawing back to look into her face. "Is this 'hugging' going to happen often?"

"You started it when you thought I'd gone missing after that incident at the tower."

So he had.

Maybe she wasn't the only one beginning to wear their heart on their sleeve. "Promise me one thing."

"Anything."

"If we survive, then you're going to set a wedding date

with Obsidian."

She looked up sharply, but he pressed a finger to her lips.

"No more excuses. London won't fall apart just because you took the chance to enjoy your own life for a moment."

"We've been so busy," she grumbled.

"Promise me," he repeated. "I want to walk you down the aisle. I want to see you happy, after everything you've done for me. Give me something to fight for, Gem."

Gemma's eyes narrowed. "I promise. But don't think I'm not aware you're manipulating me right now. 'Give me something to fight for' indeed."

He smiled.

"There is one last little issue to discuss," she said in a warning tone, as she drew away from him. "You've been clucking over Adele ever since we put her in the carriage."

"Of course I have. She was bloody injured—"

Gemma leveled a stern look upon him. "If I were a young woman and my husband was cooing over me the way you have been, I might be forgiven for misreading the situation."

"There is nothing to misread."

"Does Adele know that?"

Malloryn paused.

"I saw the way she looked at you when she hugged you." Gemma's mouth pressed into a thin line. "She has feelings for you."

"She was overcome in the moment. Adele knows the rules. She's hardly about to fall for me."

Gemma shut her eyes, took a deep breath, and then opened them again. "She is also a young woman married to a powerful man who's recently been playing seductive games with her."

"That ended the second she realized the truth."

"Yes, but who ended it?"

He opened his mouth. Then closed it. *I did.*

Gemma read the answer in his eyes. "Malloryn, I like your wife. And once upon a time, it amused me to see how easily she could get beneath your skin. No woman has ever riled you the way she has. I thought there might have been something there on your behalf—"

"You hoped."

"I hope," she replied boldly, staring him in the eyes. "But if there is not, then you need to make that very clear to Adele. Because I don't want to see you break her heart."

I have no intentions of hurting her.

"Are you finished?"

Gemma tipped her chin up. Only she could get away with speaking to him thusly. "I think I've said what needs to be said."

"Then perhaps we can focus on what hasn't been said: What happened with Mowbray?"

"I was too late. He was dead by the time I got to him. Either Dido or Jelena must have met with him, and Sir George was the distraction."

"So we have nothing."

"Mowbray did manage to confirm it has something to do with the automatons. He said London will burn."

"Damn it."

Gemma watched him with considering eyes. "Your ploy with Devoncourt may yet bear fruit."

"Despite the fact you disapproved of it?"

"I never disapproved of it. I disapprove of the way you handled it without informing me. Here are Adele's pearls," she said, handing over a bloody handkerchief knotted around a bulging lump. Turning with a flounce, she grabbed a fistful of her skirts. "Perhaps you can return them when you remind her there's nothing going on between the two of you."

He clutched the bloody things.

Adele wasn't the only one who needed the reminder.

"Here," Malloryn murmured, holding open the door to his bedchamber after Adele had obediently drank her tea. "You can stay with me again tonight. Just let me know if I need to remove my boots."

Adele slipped inside. "You're never going to let me forget that night, are you?"

"Considering the sad state of my boots... no."

Adele tried to smile, but she was simply too tired. Ava had tended to her wounds, and Malloryn assured her she wouldn't scar—he'd managed to swipe his saliva across her cheek—though she'd most likely be missing a piece of her earlobe.

His room at the manor was cold, crisp, and austere in its elegance. You couldn't enter the bloody place without being reminded that you were dealing with His Grace, the Duke of Malloryn. The enormous four-poster bed positively *loomed,* and she was quite grateful he'd never consummated their marriage in the monstrosity.

But this was... nice.

She'd been too ill the other morning to truly take note.

A handsome quilt stretched across the foot of the bed, and there were papers strewn across the small writing desk in the corner, as if he'd been working upon something when he'd been called away. Books were piled haphazardly on the side table, scraps of paper marking several spots in each. He liked to read. Even at their house, he was usually in the library at all hours.

Adele took a hesitant step forward, her slippers sinking into the soft rug. It felt like she was taking a peek inside the mind of Auvry Cavill, and not merely the Duke of Malloryn. She'd never realized until now that there were two of them.

A copper bathtub stood in the corner, filled with steaming water that smelled like lavender. Herbert, she presumed. The butler seemed to cluck over everyone in the house as if they were his personal tribe of ducklings, and had extended the notion to her, it seemed.

Malloryn turned her head from side to side, examining the purple bruises welting her throat. "Society's going to think I did this to you." His lips thinned as if he'd tasted something unpleasant.

They wouldn't be the first bruises she'd had to cover. "You'd be surprised. Diamond chokers hide all manner of sins. Nobody will suspect anything untoward."

He helped undo the buttons down her spine as Adele stood with her head tilted forward.

"You looked beautiful tonight," he murmured. "You understand I couldn't say it? I couldn't let the world know."

"You mean Balfour?"

"Yes." Malloryn eased the silk down over her hips, and it pooled around her ankles. He knelt behind her, starting on the tapes of her petticoat and the mesh cage of her bustle. "It's safer if he doesn't know how far our truce extends."

Adele stepped out of the mess of petticoats and froth of skirts. "I understand."

All she wore was her corset and chemise.

Malloryn's gaze dipped, caressing her figure with a heated look before he started on the strings to her corset. "That being said, I don't wish to give you the wrong impression. You are beautiful, but what lies between us cannot be pursued."

Adele stilled. The discrepancy between the look in his eyes and the words on his lips threw her for a second. "Ah. So even in the privacy of your bedchamber, nothing more is to come of this."

"Correct."

"He's not peering through every window, Malloryn. He's not hiding under the bed."

The next tug came a little sharper. "Maybe what I'm talking about has nothing to do with Balfour. I cannot give you more than I am."

Of course. "You think your skills in bed will turn my head?" *What was it he'd said?* "It's just a kiss, Malloryn. Just a moment of passion."

"I think this is becoming dangerously complicated between us."

"And you don't want any further complications."

The silence thickened, broken only by the whisper of his hands on the silk of her corset. "It wouldn't be wise," he finally said.

Adele closed her eyes. She shouldn't have expected anything else. Malloryn didn't like messy situations, or complex emotions. *Push him*, Lord Barrons had said, but she was so tired and her heart felt a little bruised by his declaration.

"I appreciate your straightforwardness," she whispered.

It didn't mean she wasn't going to torture him with the promise of everything he'd denied.

Once the strings were undone, he turned away. "I assume you can manage from here."

Adele removed the rest of her undergarments and stepped into the bath, sinking up to her shoulders in the bubbles with a soft groan. Various aches and bruises she hadn't recognized began to make themselves known.

He returned with a dripping piece of linen that was gloriously cool. "I sent Herbert to chip some ice."

The steam from the bath would make short work of the ice, but Adele took it and held it gently to her hot ear. The wound itself had healed, courtesy of his saliva, but the flesh sill throbbed.

Despite his words, he'd been tender with her tonight. It was confusing.

"Tell me something," she murmured. "You seem remarkably insistent upon avoiding affairs of the heart. Why?"

Malloryn sank into the chair near the bath, clasping both hands between his knees. "I wasn't aware we were on such intimate terms, to be speaking of our pasts."

Every time she thought he would let her in, he set a wall between them.

She flicked water at him. "I nearly died tonight."

"I *was* trying to keep you out of this mess," he pointed out. "As I recall, you insisted. Don't blame me, and don't try to use it to appeal to my gentler nature."

"I wouldn't. You have none. And considering what you did to me on your desk the other day, I'd have thought us quite intimate enough for such revelations."

His stare turned intense, and though it remained locked on her face, she couldn't help feeling particularly naked in that moment.

Then he closed his eyes and laughed under his breath. "You *always* have to challenge me."

"Driving you crazy *is* one of my favorite pastimes."

"I've noticed."

"And here I thought ignoring *me* was your favorite pastime," she said, with a careless shrug that belied the hurt inside.

He sensed it in some way. He always did. "How could I ignore you? Every time I went to read one of my bloody books, you'd moved the bookmark to another page. Your perfume was on my favorite chair. There were *crumbs* on my desk, and someone had tried to pick the lock on its drawer."

"You noticed."

A smile escaped her.

"Falling asleep in my library chair with your gown slipping from your shoulder. Stealing one of my favorite shirts and wearing it about your rooms *en dishabille.*" Malloryn leaned closer. "Kissing strange men who worked for my enemy. Yes, I noticed."

"If I'd known that would have bothered you, I'd have kissed one many months ago," she admitted, then saw his face. "Only a kiss. And only to capture your attention."

"It didn't bother me."

Adele flicked more water at him. "And yet, you keep mentioning it. I think someone is lying, but the question is, is he lying to me? Or himself?"

His eyes narrowed. "You have some sort of obsession with torturing me, I swear. Why?"

Adele slicked soap down her arms in a sudden nervous flurry. "Possibly for the same reason you keep mentioning that kiss. As if *your* mouth has been chaste since we married."

Stillness radiated through him. For a second, she thought he wasn't going to reply. "Technically... it has."

Adele blinked. "You expect me to believe you haven't touched another woman since our wedding day?"

"I haven't, no."

"It was a well known fact the baroness was your lover," she murmured, dipping her gaze to her legs as she focused on slicking soap along them. "And from what I can gather, she worked for you here in the same capacity Gemma does now."

"Isabella was a friend, though yes, we were intimate. I called off our arrangement before the wedding," he murmured, hands braced together between his thighs. "It wasn't fair to her, and…."

It clearly made him uncomfortable to speak of such things, but she couldn't hide the rush of blood through her veins. He'd been chaste since their wedding. It didn't mean anything, and yet, she wanted to suddenly capture his hair in her fist and drag his mouth down to hers.

"And?"

"I was trying to keep her safe. Balfour has a habit of striking at those closest to me. He wants me to suffer. I'd hoped—" A shake of his head. "I was wrong. She paid for it with her life." His voice roughened. "They all pay for it with their lives."

Suddenly, some of the mysterious puzzle pieces of what drove Malloryn began to fit themselves together. He'd lost Catherine Tate, and now the baroness. It made sense he'd wall himself away where nobody could ever reach him.

It wasn't that Malloryn didn't care.

He cared too much.

And he thought he couldn't afford to.

Perhaps Barrons had been right.

Perhaps Malloryn held her at arm's length because he was trying to protect her.

The revelation left her breathless. "I'm sorry. I shouldn't have bought it up."

"It's fine. Now it's your turn," he murmured.

"My turn?"

"To share a secret." His eyes glittered as he reached for the washcloth and slowly lathered it. "Lean forward."

Adele complied, and the hot flannel slid across her

back. "What sort of secret?"

"Tell me why you can't resist tormenting me."

Adele rested her chin on her knees sleepily. Most of the ice had melted, so she cast the cloth aside. "I always knew you hated me for trapping you—"

"I didn't hate you."

A laugh escaped her. "I thought we were to speak only the truth tonight?"

"I didn't hate you," he repeated.

Slowly, she turned her head.

Their eyes met.

"I disliked the way you manipulated me that night. There's nothing I despise more than being twisted into a situation beyond my control, but the truth is, there are ways I could have managed our engagement so it ended."

A rush of breath escaped her. "Then why did you...?"

"Marry you?" Dark lashes shuttered his eyes. "Because I realized you suited my purposes. It was expected that I would marry at some point, but I've never wanted a wife. The lifestyle I lead... it doesn't lend itself to being a husband. I have no time for a wife. And I did not wish to give some young woman the wrong impression—that ours would be any sort of match beyond contractual. I gave my heart once, Adele. There is nothing left for another woman."

"And here I was," she whispered, understanding exactly what he meant. "A wife who would be content to accept a match in name only. Someone who would make no demands of you, nor one who... who wanted your heart."

"Exactly."

She felt a little ill.

Because while she might have portrayed such an impression to the world, it wasn't what she wanted at all.

Water dripped over her shoulders as Malloryn continued washing her back. "And so you provoke me because...?"

Because I want you to look at me. Because you frustrate me. Because you attract me. Because there's a part of me that wants to know what it feels like to wake in your arms.

Because I want what Lena has.

She rested her chin on her knees, closing her eyes briefly. God, what a mess. How was she to obfuscate the truth now?

"My father ignored me all my life," she admitted. "I've always been his greatest possession, but he never truly valued me for me. But you.... You were distant and cool, but occasionally I would see your eyes light up when we sparred. And it sounds ridiculous, but you gave as good as you got, and sometimes you'd almost smile at something I said and it felt like a compliment."

"You enjoyed torturing me."

"I hate it when you ignore me."

"Then I won't ignore you." He hesitated. "You're going to fall asleep in the bath if you continue."

"Don't let me drown."

He laughed under his breath. "Never. Here." He reached for a towel. "Stand up."

Adele didn't bother to argue. She slowly unfolded herself and let Malloryn wrap the towel around her.

Bubbles sluiced down her thighs as he tucked the edge of the towel between her breasts to anchor it. Then his hands came to rest upon her waist.

Where they stayed.

Adele set her palms on his shoulders, as his gaze dipped to her breasts. Despite her pain and exhaustion, she felt that heated gaze like a caress.

"Malloryn?" she whispered.

When he looked up, his irises were flooded with pure black—a sure sign the craving had him in its grip.

Her breath caught.

Only blood thirst, sexual hunger, or the sheer possessive nature of the predator roused that sort of look.

But which one was it?

"For all your fancy words, I'm going to start thinking you have wicked intentions if you keep looking at me like that," she said.

"I don't."

Liar.

Adele arched a brow. She could feel the towel slipping free from its hold. "And yet, your eyes are black. Do you want me, Malloryn?" She brushed her thumb to the base of his throat. "Do you want my blood?"

There. The muscle ticked in his jaw. "No."

"Liar," she breathed. "That is one problem with the craving virus. It betrays itself when the predator rises. You want my blood, don't deny it."

"I thought you sought to avoid such predators?" His lips thinned. "And I was trying to be considerate, what with your past. It's merely a result of my not drinking enough today, and the consequences of the ball. It will pass. Or I'll send for some blud-wein."

It wasn't the bloodletting she had a problem with. Husbands and wives often shared blood privileges. "I trust you. I never thought I'd say that about a blue blood, but I trust you. You wouldn't hurt me. And it would be my choice to allow it."

"No," he said, as if the only lifeline he had in this moment was to repeat the word.

Damn him. "You're such a stubborn bastard."

"And you're a distraction I cannot afford."

A distraction, am I? Her eyes narrowed. "Better than

being a coward."

Oh, that earned her a heated look. "No one has ever dared say that to my face before—"

"Well, I'm not afraid of you. And you can lie to yourself all you want, but you know I speak the truth. Maybe you didn't want a wife. And maybe I'm not asking for your heart. Just your presence in my bed. Why are you so determined not to touch me? You keep saying it's dangerous, that this might cause complications between us, but do you know what I think? I think you're afraid if you touch me, you won't be able to stop."

Heat blazed in his eyes. "I told you—"

"You've told me a lot of things. Perhaps we should test my theory?" Lifting her arms, Adele felt the towel slip loose.

He caught it at her waist, but the damage was done.

A harsh exhale escaped him as he glanced down at her bare breasts, all flushed and pink.

"What the hell are you doing?" he demanded. "You're injured."

"Then be gentle with me."

Make love to me.

The blackness was back in his eyes. "I don't think I can tonight. There. Is that the truth you desire? That I want your blood? That I want to take you to bed and make sweet use of that body you flaunt in front of me? All night long. In every way you can possibly imagine, and some you probably can't." Sweeping his arm behind her knees, he lifted her out of the water as it dripped from her legs. And then he was setting her on her feet and toweling the water from her skin with rough, insistent hands. "Don't push me. Not tonight. Because I won't be gentle, Adele. And you need gentleness. I am doing my duty."

Duty. Oh, how that word burned. "Duty as my

husband?"

Tugging the nightshirt down over her head, he met her eyes. "Yes."

His own were dark, the hunger eating up all the light in his world. Not immune. No matter how much he pretended to be.

"Then I have been remiss in my *duty* as your *wife*. Let me make it up to you."

She lifted on her toes and pressed her mouth to his. It had been days since he'd kissed her. Days of heated looks that belied the cool words that kept her at bay. Days of frantic yearning.

A desperate sound escaped him.

But he didn't push her away.

And his mouth softened beneath hers, before he surged against her with a furious claim.

Adele slid her arms around his neck, hungry for more. The nightgown clung to damp patches of her skin, a thin barrier between her soft curves and the hard planes of his body.

Firm fingers dug into her waist, and then one hand splayed over the curve of her bottom, drawing her against him.

God, it felt good.

Adele bit at his lip, her hands sliding down his chest. She wanted to rouse the passion she knew he hid deep inside him, but he kissed her jaw in that moment, his stubble rasping over her ear and—

A pained gasp escaped her.

It broke the moment, broke her hold over him.

"Damn it, Adele. This is precisely why this shouldn't happen." Malloryn caught her wrists and held her at bay, his breath whispering over her lips. "You're hurt."

"I'll be fine."

But he shook his head. "No."

A third and final time.

She wanted to reach for him so badly.

She wanted another kiss.

But he was locking himself down visibly, right before her eyes, and she didn't understand it.

"I don't think it wise to stay here with you tonight, Adele."

"Would you just stay... until I fall asleep?" It was the only sign of weakness she'd allow herself. "I don't want to be alone in the darkness. Not tonight."

"I shouldn't."

She hated herself for saying it, but she did. "I won't touch you."

Malloryn stared at her for a long time before nodding. "As you wish."

But when he lay down behind her, curling his arm over her waist, he remained dressed and atop the covers.

Adele closed her eyes, burrowing into the pillows and blankets as she laced her fingers through his.

She wouldn't push him further. Not tonight.

But she was Adele Cavill, and she was determined.

After tonight's revelations, the Duke of Malloryn didn't stand a chance.

Adele's breathing softened as she fell asleep, her body relaxing against his.

But Malloryn did not soften. Nor did he relax.

Instead, he held her in his arms as he tried to analyze their previous encounter and work out precisely what had gone wrong.

He'd meant to set her at bay, the way Gemma has

suggested. He didn't want to break her heart. He didn't want to hurt her. He couldn't offer her anything more of himself....

They were all truths he'd long believed, and yet somehow, they felt *wrong.*

And to make matters worse, Adele had seen right through them.

She'd routed him with all the ease of a master general.

It felt like another opening in their game.... But if this was war, then he was badly outflanked. Adele seemed to hold every ace in her hand.

He had no real clue how to deal with her.

Why?

Malloryn brushed a lock of hair from her cheek with soft fingers as he examined her in the dark. He could admit he found her dangerously intriguing. No woman had ever stood up to him so brashly, nor refused to back down when he arched a cool brow. Crossing wits with her felt like dueling, only, he was never quite certain of the outcome.

And worse, he enjoyed the uncertainty.

She was clever, cunning, and dangerously sensual. Beautiful, and yet callously dismissive of it—unless it suited her needs. Fiercely protective of those she loved—like her sister, and her friends—but also wary and guarded.

He'd walked a dark path alone for so long, he'd thought he'd never encounter a woman who wouldn't flinch at the shadows of his soul, but Adele bore her own shadows.

And she trusted him with them.

Malloryn sighed as he buried his face in her hair, breathing in her perfume. *Oh, you vexatious woman. What have you done to me?*

What was wrong with him? Why could he not deny

her?

Was it something within *himself* that left him so unsure of her?

He kept finding himself with a smile on his lips at the oddest moments, when he thought of her. The memory of her giggling as he tried to wrestle her into bed the night she'd imbibed too much sprang to mind.

"*Did you know,*" she'd said seriously, lying flat on her back when he knelt at her feet and slipped her stockings off, "*that I like your Company of Rogues very much. I like you very much too. Not the duke, mind you. I like Auvry though.*"

"*You do realize I am one and the same person,*" he'd mused, discarding her stockings.

"*No, you're not. The duke is cold and serious, and keeps everyone at arm's length, whereas Auvry argues with me, and flirts with me, and he kisses me when he can't help himself. He's my favorite husband. I like torturing the duke, but I adore Auvry. He does wicked things to me on his desk.*" She'd pressed her finger to his lips. "*Don't tell the duke though. He'll lord it over me forever if he thinks I like him. He'd wear this sanctimonious expression on his face the whole time too, as though he thinks he's won. Like this.*"

And she'd pulled a face that had made him burst into sudden laughter.

"*The duke doesn't look anything like that.*"

"*Oh, yes he does!*"

He'd kissed her then, and he hadn't meant to, and somehow her hands had woven through his hair and he'd been crawling over her when she suddenly pushed him aside.

"*Oh, no,*" she whispered, a horrified look on her mouth. "*Chamber pot!*"

He hadn't managed to get to it in time, though she'd somehow managed to find one of his boots propped beside the bed.

Afterwards, she'd groaned as she knelt at the foot of the bed, resting her head on the mattress. "*I think I like your boots too,*" she'd said. "*Though I'm afraid they're not going to be* your *favorite boots anymore. I will buy you new ones though. And I won't let Ingrid measure them.*"

He'd never laughed as much in his life as he'd laughed that night, helplessly charmed by Adele when she had all her guards lowered.

Imagine what it would be like to spend a lifetime with her, without those walls?

All year they'd tilted at each other, lances shattering on each other's shields and savaged armor.

But his armor was thin and cracked.

Fractures slithered through his façade.

He didn't want to fight her anymore. He didn't want to push her away. He simply wanted to stay in bed beside her and bury his face in the soap-scented mess of her hair.

To let himself touch her and make love to her, without having to protect himself. He wanted to let himself be Auvry again, the husband she preferred. He wanted—

Malloryn froze, as he realized he was musing in an almost daydreaming manner about a future with his wife. A violent spasm of *something* gripped his insides as he finally realized what it all meant.

It wasn't her.

It was *him*.

He suddenly knew exactly what was wrong with him, and why she set him so at odds.

"Malloryn?" Adele shifted in her sleep, almost as if she'd sensed his sudden shock.

"Shush," he whispered, squeezing her fingers. "I'm here. You're not alone."

The breath eased out of her as she relaxed back into his arms, snuggling her face into his biceps. His heart gave a horrifying little squeeze at the sight.

She'd been right.

He was lying to himself.

The Duke of Malloryn did not dare kiss his wife and it had nothing to do with Balfour, and everything to do with the fact that, for the first time in seventeen years, a woman had slipped beneath his guard when he wasn't looking and started carving her name on his heart.

CHAPTER TWENTY-FIVE

Dawn edged over the horizon, though the fog was so thick it was difficult to see the sun. After last night's revelation he'd barely slept a wink, and when Byrnes returned with news of Devoncourt's destination, it had been almost a relief to sneak from Adele's bed.

Malloryn crouched beside Byrnes as they surveyed the pair of warehouses down by the docks. Old. Decrepit. Seemingly abandoned.

"This is where Devoncourt went before he returned to his house," Byrnes muttered, his hard blue eyes locked on the target.

It wasn't much, but it would have to do.

From what Malloryn's sources had managed to discover, the warehouse belonged to the False Dawn Corporation, which was a front, if ever he'd seen one. Thomas Mowbray had once been listed as director, though the position had been transferred ten years ago and the records were currently obscured.

"Think this is where Balfour is hiding?" Gemma asked, squatting on the other side of Malloryn.

Instinct stirred. Too easy. By far.

He couldn't help hungering for it though—an end to this cursed game.

"One can hope." He cracked his knuckles inside the black leather of his gloves. "Kincaid, are you, Charlie and Lark in place?"

Static *shirred* in his ear. "*Ready,*" Kincaid replied gruffly.

"We're going in," he replied, then made a swift gesture with his fingers to Obsidian and Byrnes.

The pair of them slipped through the fog, taking up position on both sides of the nearest door.

Malloryn gave the gesture, and then Obsidian kicked open the locked doors and disappeared into the shadows inside, his pistol tracking the room. Byrnes, Malloryn and Gemma were right on his heels, plunging into the shadowy confines of the warehouse.

A pair of guards materialized out of nowhere, and Malloryn put a bullet directly between the eyes of the nearest, as Gemma handled the other.

Shouts echoed.

Only one or two more guards, by the look of it. Obsidian dispatched them coolly, and then glanced around at the pile of crates.

"Not enough guards," Obsidian said.

"Agreed." There was a faint light in the overseer's office and a shadow moving up there. "Watch your backs."

Byrnes grabbed a crowbar and jammed it beneath the lid of a crate. The second he pried it off, he whistled under his breath. "Someone's planning one hell of a party."

"Explosives?" Malloryn glanced inside the box, his eyebrows shooting into his hairline. There was enough dynamite there to destroy half of London.

"I think we just found Balfour's stockpile," Byrnes replied, with a grin.

Seconds later, an alarm blared through the facility, and a pair of eerie red eyes lit up at the far end of the room.

"What the hell is that?" Byrnes demanded, clenching the crowbar in one hand.

"Ask questions later." Malloryn shot it, but the bullet ricocheted into the wall.

A click sounded and a small flicker of fire ignited somewhere around the shadowy figure's waist. It had to be nearly ten feet tall.

"I think you just... irritated it." Byrnes took a step back.

The small spark suddenly ignited into a gush of flames, and then it was streaming toward them.

They all threw themselves aside, heat stealing the oxygen from the air.

"Jesus Christ!" Gemma rolled out of the way. "It's a metaljacket. One of the older spitfire models."

Which should have all been destroyed following the revolution.

The enormous automaton clanked forward, its breastplate stained with soot and slightly dented. That didn't make it any the less dangerous. No. A single spitfire could burn a street to the ground and was virtually unstoppable.

"Draw its attention," Obsidian commanded, tugging a small grappling hook from his belt. Both he and Malloryn had managed to take cover behind a larger crate several feet behind the other two. "I can take it down if it's not locked on me as a target."

"Anyone volunteering?" Byrnes drawled, staying exactly where he was.

Gemma sighed. "You're faster than me."

"You're prettier."

"What's that got to do with anything?" she demanded.

"It's a *machine.* It's not going to be staring down my bodice."

"You do realize," Malloryn snarled, "that you're both hiding behind boxes of explosives?"

"Fuck," Byrnes cursed under his breath as his thighs bunched. He was the closest to the automaton. "I hate fire."

Then he was darting forward, trying to engage the metaljacket's motion sensors so it would lock on him as a target.

Fire spewed across the factory floor as Byrnes skidded behind another set of crates. It licked at the crate, and Byrnes seemed to realize his predicament and bolted further into the darkness. The monstrosity followed, each clanking step echoing on the cement floors.

Malloryn glanced up at the warehouse's office, noting the light there had been swiftly snuffed. The metaljacket was merely a distraction. The office was where he'd find whoever was in charge.

"Go!" Gemma told him, watching her lover slip behind the metaljacket. "You can't let whoever that is escape."

He'd given her command of COR upon their return to Russia, but as he slipped away, he wondered if she realized she'd just told him what to do.

Moving like a ghost through the darkness at the back of the warehouse, he headed for the office. Shoes rang on the stairs as the overseer escaped into the morass of rooms at the back of the building.

And a figure loomed nearby—

"Don't shoot me," Kincaid called, materializing out of the shadows, as Malloryn jerked his pistol up at the last second.

"Follow me," Malloryn commanded, moving to cut

the bastard off.

Charlie and Lark were presumably cutting off the rear, as instructed.

Sure enough, the overseer had returned, clearly sighting the trap. Footsteps pounded down the hallway. Malloryn pressed his back to the nearest wall, holding a finger up to his lips.

Kincaid vanished into the shadows with a nod.

Someone cursed under his breath, and Malloryn could hear his target panting. Not Balfour. Whoever it was, they weren't used to running.

Malloryn coolly stepped out of the shadows, his pistol locking on his target's chest.

Sir George Hamilton skidded to a halt, the tails of his coat flapping.

They both stared at each other in shock.

"Malloryn," Sir George spat.

"Sir George." This was an unexpected boon. Caught red-handed with his fingers in the till. "Fancy finding *you* in a warehouse full of explosives."

Sir George's eyes darted this way and that. "You son of a bitch. You have no right to be in here."

"I have every right," Malloryn told him as he advanced. "My men tracked a dangerous suspect who has ties to a dangerous organization to this building last night. My information tells me a group of terrorists are planning an attack on the queen, and they have enough explosives to level the tower. The only anomaly—as far as I can see—is your presence. But surely you can explain."

Sir George's mustache fair quivered with rage. "I don't have to explain anything to the likes of you!"

Malloryn stared along the top of his pistol. "You don't. But you will. Eventually."

"What are you going to do? Shoot me?"

A part of him would like to. He'd spent years dealing with belligerent fools like this, who thought themselves entitled to do anything they desired. They'd sneered at him at Eton, and spat behind his back when he first ventured into society.

And they still sneered, even now he'd climbed to the top of the tree.

No matter how many "Your Graces" he heard in a day, he would never truly be one of them.

And he'd never truly cared.

But something about Sir George rubbed him the wrong way—as if Malloryn's loyalty to the queen and his country was little more than the lip service of a social-climbing monkey, when it was one of the few things he cherished most.

"I should." Malloryn hesitated. "But I won't."

This was Adele's father.

And while he knew there was no love lost between the pair of them, she might look askance on him putting a bullet in Sir George's skull.

"You're under arrest," Malloryn said, putting up the pistol.

"You can't arrest me! I'm a peer of the realm!"

"And I have been granted the queen's authority on this matter. *Anyone* who is suspected to be part of this conspiracy is subject to my authority, no matter their rank. Put your hands in the air."

Sir George tore something from the pocket of his waistcoat. "You're the traitor! You're a traitor to your class and I'll be damned if I'm brought down by someone like you! Rot in hell, Malloryn!"

He held up a small device, thumb hovering over the red trigger.

"Get out! He's got a detonator!" Malloryn screamed,

turning and catching sight of a nearby window.

Kincaid stood directly in front of it, his eyes widening in shock as Malloryn sprinted toward him. Slamming into the burly mech, he heard glass shatter as they both went through the window.

A whoosh of sound lit up the warehouse behind him, heat and light exploding into being as they hit the docks and rolled. Slashes of pain speared through him. Glass stabbing into his sides, and splinters of timber slicing lethally through the air. Flame seared the air, stealing all the oxygen around him, until he thought—for a second—that it was all over.

That this was the end.

Then he and Kincaid were skidding to a halt as the enormous fireball rolled over the top of them. His leather body armor saved him from most of the intense heat, but he could feel his skin cracking and drying. His sleeve was on fire, but Kincaid slapped it out as they both scrambled to get to safety.

Malloryn rolled behind a nearby pillar, tearing the earpiece from his ear as the high-pitched whine threatened to rupture his eardrum. He threw it aside, staring with horror at what remained of the warehouse.

"Jaysus fuckin' Christ," Kincaid breathed, staring up at the enormous fireball. The color drained from his face. "Who was inside?" He scrambled for Malloryn's cast-aside earpiece, and fiddled with the transmitter. "Gemma? Byrnes? Charlie? Can anyone hear me?"

Malloryn pushed unsteadily to his feet as Kincaid kept repeating the message.

He and Kincaid had escaped, but the others.... They would have been inside. Somewhere.

And the fuse must have been set in the center of the warehouse.

All those crates....

"Stay here," he told Kincaid. "Keep trying to contact them." Licking dry lips, he stared at the far end of the warehouse. "I'm going back in."

The front door burst open, and then Malloryn hauled Obsidian inside the safe house.

The tall *dhampir's* face was blistered and what remained of his shirt clung to him in charred strips. Raw, reddened skin peered through the gaping fabric, but it was the look on his face and the trembling in his hands that caused the most concern. Behind them, Gemma looked like she'd been in the same fire, half her hair singed, and her cheeks black with smoke.

Adele found her feet abruptly, her mouth falling open. "What happened?"

A swift glance assured her Malloryn was bloodied but otherwise unharmed, and she managed to suppress the sudden flurry of panic she felt.

"Byrnes?" Ingrid quivered beside her. She'd been left behind to help Herbert protect the safe house, while the others went to check on this Devoncourt lead.

"He's alive," Malloryn said curtly.

Ava hurried into the parlor, gasping as she saw the damage. "My surgery! Now!" She glanced over their shoulders. "Kincaid?"

"Safe," Kincaid growled, lumbering through the door with Byrnes's arm slung over his shoulder. Byrnes's other arm was tied in a makeshift sling around his neck. "We're all safe."

"Though it was touch and go there for a moment," Charlie corrected, as he and Lark shut the door behind them. Of them all, they appeared to be the least the worse for wear. "Malloryn managed to break the door down, so we could get Gemma and Obsidian out."

Malloryn helped Obsidian into the small room off the parlor, which Ava had claimed for her surgery.

"Blood and ashes," Ava exclaimed, as she used a set of tweezers to pry Obsidian's shirt from the slick burn down his side. "What's wrong with Byrnes?"

"Broken wrist," Byrnes replied, with a wince. "Maybe ribs."

The pretty young scientist glanced between both Obsidian and Byrnes, as if trying to work out who needed her the most.

"Treat the burns," Byrnes replied. "I'll manage."

"If I wait too long, I'll have to break that wrist again and set it," Ava warned. "You heal too fast now."

"If I may, Miss Ava?" Herbert asked, gesturing Ingrid and Charlie out of the way. "I have some experience with wartime injuries. I can set the wrist."

It was all happening so swiftly.

Adele didn't know what to do, or how to help. And from the look on several of the others' faces, neither did they.

Malloryn turned and almost walked directly through her.

"What happened?" Adele whispered.

His face shut down. Amazing, to think there'd been any hint of emotion on it before, but there must have been, for there wasn't now. "This way," he said, grabbing her arm, and leading her toward the parlor.

Clara appeared with a jug of steaming water, linens and bandages. "Do you think you can tend the duke?" she asked Adele bluntly, which was an abrupt change in the dynamics between them.

"Put it on the table there," Adele instructed, and then turned to examine her husband, momentarily at a loss as Clara vanished.

"I'm fine," Malloryn said.

Blood dripped sluggishly from a gash on his arm, and if it were still bleeding after all this time, then she'd hate to think what it had looked like earlier.

"Sit down," she said, "and let me look at it."

"I'm—"

"Only going to get in the way in the surgery," she retorted, picking at the mangled remains of his leather body armor. One of the metal buckles looked like it had almost melted into his flesh. "Does that hurt?"

Malloryn ground his teeth together and tore it free, sending dark blood flooding to the surface. Adele swore under her breath, and then hastily pressed a piece of clean linen to the bleeding. "Hold this."

He must have been tired, for he didn't bother to argue as she set about prying the other buckles loose, and then lifted the molded leather carapace of his chest-piece over his head.

Though this was entirely outside her experience, she focused on cleaning the blood and soot from his skin, her heart aching at every sign of injury.

"What happened?" she whispered.

And he told her of breaking into the warehouse and handling the guards.

"I'm glad you're all safe. At least no one died."

Malloryn seemed to take a deep breath. "Adele, there was a casualty."

The way he said it made tension slither through her. She looked up. "Who?"

"Your father was in the warehouse. He was the one who set off the explosion."

Adele staggered back a step, cold shock slamming through her.

"There's no way he could have survived it," Malloryn said quietly, capturing her fingers. "We barely did."

The world came back to her with a sucking pop of noise. "My father is dead." Strange, how coherent those words sounded.

"I'm sorry. I told him he was under arrest, and he must have decided dying was worth the risk of taking me down with him. It appears his hatred of me was stronger than his sense of self-preservation."

It didn't surprise her.

Her father had been twisted up with hate and bitterness for years.

But what did surprise her was the loss she felt.

Sir George had never been a kindly man. Or a father. He'd dismissed her, ignored her, used her, and abused her.

But his death somehow felt as though her nice, safe world was imploding. She shouldn't shed a single tear for the bastard. She shouldn't. But there was one sliding down her cheek all the same, though she didn't know if it was sadness, hatred or rage at her father that fuelled it.

Hattie.... Good God, she'd have to tell her sister.

And worse. *Treachery*. The sentence would *destroy* her family, and her sister's prospects.

"Adele?" There were rough hands on her shoulders, holding her upright. Thumbs stroking her skin. "I'm sorry."

"Don't be." She managed to press her hand to his bare chest, noting again the bloody slashes and marks that marked his skin. "You're hurt. He tried to hurt you. He deserved to die."

"I'm fine." Malloryn captured her chin, forcing her to meet his eyes. "I have the power to suppress word of his involvement. Several of the council members owe me a favor. Nobody has to know he was a traitor. It doesn't have to affect your sister."

That he understood exactly what bothered her eased the burden.

"Thank you."

Relief flooded through her and she stepped forward, wrapping her arms around his waist and pressing her tearstained cheek to his chest. He tensed, but then his arms wrapped slowly around her, and it felt like she could finally catch her balance again.

"Thank you," she repeated.

For everything.

"What the hell are you doing?" Lady Hamilton demanded, as Malloryn and his Rogues splayed out through the foyer of her home. "You cannot simply shove your way in here! Richards! Richards! Remove them at once."

Adele paused on the lintel, silently steeling herself for this encounter.

"I'm afraid it's not that simple, Lady Hamilton." Malloryn held up a piece of paper. "The queen has signed a warrant to have your house searched. Your husband, Sir George, has been accused of treason against the crown, and there is enough evidence to suggest he kept vital documents of a plot against the queen in his study. I've been authorized to search it."

Lady Hamilton snatched the warrant, and then swiftly tore it into shreds. "My husband is not a traitor. You have no proof! Get out!"

"Was not," Malloryn said coolly.

"*What?*"

"*Was* not a traitor. Your husband is dead. He set off

an explosion with himself inside the building."

All the color drained out of her mother's face.

"Get out, you son of a bitch!" Lady Hamilton hissed. "Get out of my—"

"For God's sakes, Mother!" Adele hurried inside. "It's done. Father made his own choices and he has paid for them."

Lady Hamilton lashed out, her hand slapping Adele's cheek. "You treacherous snake!"

The shock of the blow sent her reeling, but then Malloryn was there, capturing her mother's wrists.

"I would urge you to think of yourself and your other daughter, Lady Hamilton," he warned, in a cold, deadly voice. "The only reason your house isn't swarming with Coldrush Guards and journalists, is because your eldest daughter has convinced me to keep word of Sir George's treachery quiet. Thank all the gods she has some familial affection for you and her sister. But if you *ever* lift a hand against Adele again, I may not be so inclined to protect you."

Adele pushed past Lady Hamilton and crossed to Hattie's side. Her sister's wide eyes darted back and forth, and she trembled. "Adele?"

"Are you all right?" Adele asked.

"What's going on?" Hattie whispered, as Adele hugged her.

"You're safe. You're finally safe." She closed her eyes as Hattie's slender form molded to hers. Then she looked up, locking eyes with her mother. "My husband is now your official guardian, and all thrall or consort offers must be officially signed by him. Nobody can force you into any match you do not willingly accept. And once this mess is all sorted, you'll be coming to live with me."

Lady Hamilton's lips pressed thinly together, but as

she took in all the movement in the foyer, she finally seemed to concede, her shoulders shrinking in upon herself.

It was as if she aged twenty years in a single second.

"Search the house," Malloryn barked, granting Adele a nod, before he turned and followed Charlie up the stairs toward her father's study.

CHAPTER TWENTY-SIX

The scent of brandy filled the air as Adele made her way down to the library that night.

The second Malloryn saw her, he stiffened. A nearly empty glass hung from lax fingers, and his cravat was undone and draped down his chest. It was as close to disheveled as she'd ever seen him.

"How are you feeling after your nap?" he asked.

Lonely. She hugged herself. "I keep thinking I'm going to wake up and it will all have been a dream. But then I pinch myself, and I'm not asleep."

"Your sister is well settled with your aunt," he murmured. "She'll be safe there."

"I know." Adele crossed toward him. "How are you feeling?"

It had been an eventful day, and he'd only just returned from the Ivory Tower. She'd seen the carriage from her window.

Malloryn scraped a hand across his jaw. "Frustrated. The queen is on edge and there's nothing incriminating in your father's study anymore. He must have burned everything, for the grate is full of ashes. And now he's dead—"

He suddenly stopped as if realizing what he was about to say.

"And you cannot question him," she whispered.

"Forgive me." Malloryn reached forward to capture her fingers. "That was unforgivably rude."

Adele squeezed his hand. "It feels strange. I should be grieving, but I'm not. I just feel... so empty."

They stared at each other, fingers linked.

Try as he might, he'd never convince her he didn't want her—every time their gazes met, she could feel the spark igniting between them. Malloryn looked like he wanted to haul her into his lap.

Even as he denied himself.

So be it.

This stalemate had gone on long enough. Perhaps it was time to take matters into her own hands?

"Why don't you come up to bed?" she whispered. "You look tired."

"And you look like you have no intentions of luring me to bed to sleep."

"I could stay with you," Adele murmured, the hem of her robe draping over the chair as she knelt on it. "We could grant each other sweet dreams."

Malloryn brushed his knuckles up her thigh and then slowly looked up, his lashes stained copper in the lantern-light. "I don't think I would be very good company tonight."

"That's nothing new," she said, with a smile and a twitch of her brow.

"Adele."

"You've barely slept in days."

Please. Tell me why.

His head lolled back in the chair, roughened stubble darkening his cheeks. "Not tonight. It's… the anniversary of Catherine's death tomorrow."

Adele's hand froze on his cheek. "Oh. I'm so sorry."

"Don't be," he said with a sigh, turning his face into her hand. "It's been years. I barely remember her sometimes. But I cannot help thinking it an ominous occasion. Balfour's going to do something, strike out somehow. I can just feel it."

"You're as prepared as you're going to be. You'll defeat him, I know it."

Malloryn kissed the back of her hand. "Go back to bed. One of us should get some rest."

"And you?"

Malloryn lifted the glass. "Maybe I'll come up in an hour or so."

Push him.

Adele slid into his lap.

Malloryn shot her a challenging look.

"You owe me a kiss," she murmured, sliding her hands up his chest. "You cannot simply kiss me on a rooftop and then pretend nothing more is going to come of it. You cannot simply wash my back, and then not touch me again."

"We shouldn't."

"I don't care what we should or shouldn't do. I want you. I want your kiss."

There was a long, slow pause, as if he fought some inner battle.

And then finally conceded.

"Then take it," he whispered.

Night marked his eyes with shadows, and she traced her fingers over the thin curve of his upper lip, ignoring the way he watched her. Ignoring the questions in those eyes.

Instead she leaned down and replaced her finger with her mouth.

The kiss was softer than anything they'd previously shared.

The faint teasing caress of his tongue against hers. The startled intake of his breath, closely followed by the dart of her own tongue. Every time she kissed him, she grew a little more intoxicated with the taste of his mouth and the way he threw himself into each kiss with a passion that defied his cold reputation.

Sweetness turned to hunger. Adele shivered as his hand slid up the back of her neck, fingers tangling in the fine hairs there.

He reached for the ties of her robe, but she batted his hand away, captured his wrist.

And then placed it, quite firmly, upon the arm of the chair.

"My turn," she whispered.

And he let her.

Malloryn's gray eyes heated as she reached for his cravat.

And then she was dragging it free from his neck with slow, sensuous tugs, their eyes meeting as the cravat fell free.

Leaning forward, she brushed her lips against his throat. His pulse kicked, and Adele slid her tongue out of her mouth to lick him there. A tug of her fingers and his top button was undone. Then the next, and so forth, until the hard, muscled planes of his pectorals gaped through the linen. She slid her hands beneath his parted shirt, pushing it wide. Cool skin met her palms, the thump of his heartbeat an intimate drum against the fleshy pad of her hand.

But it was the hollow groove of his collarbone that drew her lips.

And then the satiny skin at the base of his throat as he arched his head back to give her access.

Sweet gods, but she liked this.

And he did too, judging by the corded tension in his powerful thighs.

"*Adele.*"

One word.

Tight with need.

She'd never wanted to hear him say her name like that before, but now that she'd heard it once, she wanted to hear nothing else.

Forever.

Adele let herself suckle at his throat, her thighs clenching slightly in need. He hadn't made a single move to touch her, but her body ached, as if merely being in control of him wielded some sort of pleasure inside her.

She felt powerful.

Glorious.

And completely in control.

"Just what are you planning?" Malloryn murmured, turning his face to hers as she came up for air. The coarse rasp of the stubble on his jaw sent a shiver through her.

Adele captured his face in both hands. "I thought I'd ruin you."

"Oh, really?"

"*Yes.*" She breathed the word into his mouth. "It's always been my intention. Hadn't you realized?"

And then her tongue was stroking against his, her newfound confidence blooming within her as she pressed her breasts to his chest, her thighs straddling his lean hips.

If not for the faint tightening of his fingers over the ends of the armchair, she'd have thought him unmoved.

But that was the challenge, wasn't it?

To break through Malloryn's hard steel walls.

To shatter his almost insurmountable control.

One hand came up, almost hesitantly, to cup her backside.

And then he was urging her against him, the firm length of his erection grinding right between her thighs.

Adele gasped. Only two pieces of fabric separated them.

Malloryn's teeth nipped at her jaw, his other fist clenching in her silken nightgown as the tides between them began to shift.

Oh, no.

No, that wouldn't do at all.

Adele drew back, breathing hard.

The cravat. She needed the cravat. She'd had plans for it, after all.

Malloryn palmed her breasts through her bodice, brushing his lips against—

"Don't even think about it," she growled, grabbing a fistful of his hair and denying him.

He responded with a self-satisfied, utterly masculine smile that made her want to kiss him again. And then his thumbs traced teasing circles over her nipples.

"You seem to be losing control of the situation, my dear."

Capturing both wrists, she set his hands firmly on the arms of the chair again.

"I told you once," she said, sliding the tie of her robe free with a slow, stealthy glide, "that this wasn't over. Tonight, you're mine."

"And tomorrow?"

"We deal with tomorrow when it comes," she

whispered. "As long as you remember not to fall in love with me, we should be safe. All I want is your body."

A startled laugh escaped him.

This bloody woman.

She defied all of his expectations of her, constantly forcing him to reassess. Adele was both a force to be reckoned with, and a siren who lured him down reckless paths. No matter how hard he tried, he couldn't seem to resist her, and now he knew why.

Giving him a wicked smile, she bound one of his arms to the chair with his cravat, and the other with the tie on her robe. His breath came a little more harshly.

"If you have some idea of rousing me like this and then leaving me here, I warn you to think again," he growled, a little flustered by the vulnerability of the situation.

He was always the seducer.

Never the seduced.

"Why ever would I leave you here when I have you at my mercy?"

At my mercy....

Bound to the chair.

This was not to be borne.

And yet....

He couldn't deny he was curious as to her full intentions. "I could free myself if I wanted."

"I know," she teased, as she went to her knees before him. "But are you sure you want to?"

No. No, he was not.

"Tell me to stop." Sliding her hands between his knees, Adele pushed them wide. And then her palms were skating up the inside of his thighs, thumbs digging into the muscle there. "Tell me to go back to bed. Tell me you don't want this. Me."

It made him feel a little vulnerable, which was ridiculous.

He could read her intentions, after all.

But he'd never given himself over into another's hands.

"I want this. I want you."

Adele's wicked green eyes promised a wealth of pleasure ahead of him as she settled between his parted legs. Those deft thumbs found the firm outline of his engorged cock, and then she was stroking up the length of him, eyeing the hard length of his cock with a curiosity that made him *ache*.

"I had been doing a little bit of research before I realized you thought me a spy. I was planning on starting a new campaign against you. But all my knowledge is purely theoretical." Her eyes laughed at him as she found the placket on his breeches and freed the last button. "You'll allow me to indulge, I'm sure?"

"It will be my pleasure."

His cock sprang free, slapping against the hard planes of his stomach. The widening of her eyes almost made him smile. This was the Adele he was most curious about: the one who shed her untouchable exterior and revealed a softness that both intrigued and surprised him.

It was also the Adele that threatened him the most.

Because he should not be curious about her.

He should not yearn to unearth her so often.

Adele reached out and traced down the thick, veined length of him. She gripped him with curious fingers.

"Harder," he breathed, and she tightened her grip obediently.

She rewarded him with a smooth stroke, and he told her how to continue. Her fingers curled around him, her eyes a promise of ruin and sin. Up and down, until his lip curled up and he gasped through clenched teeth.

He couldn't restrain himself then. He closed his eyes and sank back into the chair, leaving her to it.

And then there was something wet and hot circling the head of his cock, the weight of her hair tickling his hip.

Malloryn looked down in shock, every ridge of his abdomen standing out in stark relief. Adele's lips were wrapped around him, all plump and pink, and he could feel the rasp of her tongue flicking up beneath the swollen head of him. Tasting that salty bead of him.

Fuck.

He tossed his head back, hands sinking into the chair. Urging her lower. Lower. Telling her to replace her hand with her mouth, until he thrust up into her throat, encouraging her to fuck his cock. Harsh, panted demands as he fought to keep his hands in place.

The heat of it hit him suddenly.

The room swam with shadows, and he realized the hunger had risen, stealing all the color from the world. Making its own pressing demands on his flesh.

"It's all right, Malloryn," Adele whispered, her warm breath stirring over his wet cock as she drew back with a low, smoky laugh. "Just close your eyes and think of England."

And then her head lowered again, her blonde curls bobbing over his lap as the heat of her suction enveloped him, clamping around his prick with devastating consequences.

A shiver of pleasure licked its way up his spine.

Fuck.

"That's enough," he rasped.

As if to defy him, her lips lingered, her tongue stroking slowly up the back of his shaft and caressing the arrow-shaped groove beneath the head of his cock.

"*Adele.*" Part growl. Part plea.

And she bloody well laughed, her mouth vibrating around his swollen prick.

He was seconds away from spilling. Moments away from losing all sense of control.

His right hand tore free from her makeshift binding and Malloryn captured a fistful of her hair, lifting her away from her enthusiastic ministrations and dragging her up to meet him.

Capturing her mouth in a slow, drugging kiss, he tightened his fingers in her hair, and steadily tugged.

Adele was forced to either crawl into his lap or fall to her knees.

"Think of England," he growled as he captured a handful of silk nightgown and ass. "I swear to God you're going to be the death of me."

Then he was hauling her into his lap, pressing her thighs on either side of his. He claimed her mouth, breathing hard. Adele wound her arms around his neck with a low moan, and he ground her hips against his.

Kissing her, long and slow, he gripped both edges of her nightgown and tore it right down the middle.

"Malloryn!" A gasp.

Another jerk, and all that lovely skin was bare to his gaze, to his touch. Pushing the remnants from her shoulders, he watched as silk pooled in a mess about her waist.

Then his hands were back on her, brushing the long blonde curls over her shoulder so her breasts were no longer hidden.

It was a delight to behold.

Adele had been made for a man's gaze. She was all smooth curves and pale, creamy skin. Capturing a handful of her bottom, he lifted her toward him, his mouth clamping over the hardened nub of her nipple. Adele gasped, her fingers sliding through his hair.

"Are you wet?" he demanded, drawing back with a harsh breath.

Adele sank her teeth into her swollen lower lip as she dug her nails into his shoulders. "Yes."

"Good."

He thrust up into her, and her eyes widened. Then she was throwing her head back and sinking down on him, the hot clamp of her flesh sending him right to the edge again.

"Like this," he whispered, leaning his head back against the chair and watching as he guided her to rise and fall.

There was something to be said for letting her find her own stride.

Languid pleasure made her eyelashes flutter as she bit her lip and rode him. Adele threw her head back, her hips rolling as he found the spot inside her that made her quiver.

Blood and ashes, she was perfect.

He licked his thumb and slid it between them, finding the seat of her pleasure. Instantly, she clenched around him. Adele's fingers dug into his biceps.

He licked the sweat from her throat, teeth grazing sweet skin as she moaned.

"Malloryn!"

"What's wrong?" he purred.

Nothing was wrong. He could feel her body trembling and couldn't resist pressing his lips to the flickering vein in her throat. He held himself there, right on the edge of danger, forcing himself to control the beast inside him. It wanted blood. Wanted to claim her in every way possible. A savage, irrepressible part of himself he'd never known existed.

"Oh, God." She arched her spine. Begged him.

"Auvry!"

Adele came apart in his arms, a soft cry escaping her as she clutched at his shoulders. Malloryn slowly stroked his palms up and down her spine as her heartbeat raced.

He needed the respite. He was so close to spilling it wasn't amusing.

But Adele wasn't done yet.

"How do you always managed to turn the tables on me?" she gasped.

He laughed.

"This time I will not be thwarted," she said in a determined voice as she began to ride him again.

"Faster," he urged, fingers clamping around her hips.

Her eyes locked on his. "But you're not the one in control."

It was a devilish smile on her lips.

Taking his hands, she set them quite firmly on the arms of the chair. "Don't move," she whispered. "This is my moment. I want to bring the Duke of Malloryn to his knees."

"Think you can?"

His gaze was on hers as she rose up and down, glorying in this moment.

His fingers locked around the ends of the armchair. Oh, God. He wanted to reach for her, wanted to urge her faster. Heat flashed behind his eyelids as he threw his head back.

And then soft lips were at his throat as her hips rolled, grinding against him, clenching hard.

He broke his promise as he came, one hand lashing out and clutching at her. *More. Harder.* He thrust up into her, blunt teeth sinking into the soft flesh of her shoulder. Ecstasy pulsed through him, and he gave himself over to her, spilling deep inside her.

Panting hard, he dragged her against his chest as she wilted against him. Their heartbeats merged as Adele pressed her forehead against the crook of his throat.

A quiet moment, eased by the caress of his hand down her bare skin as they both came back down from the heavens.

She shivered, her body clenching around him, and Malloryn shifted.

Good lord. There was a smile on his lips as he slowly opened his eyes and stared at the ceiling. He couldn't help himself.

"What's wrong?" Adele demanded, slowly lifting her head from his shoulder as if she sensed his smile.

Malloryn shook his head.

Everything.

"You've ruined my study for me," he told her, "and now this.... How the hell am I supposed to focus on a book when all I'll be able to think of is my lady wife having her way with me in this chair?"

The smile that spread across her mouth momentarily transfixed him.

"That's precisely the point. You're not supposed to be able to focus. Come to bed," she whispered.

The urge to obey her was incredibly potent.

Then she'd be in his arms all night, whether he chose to enjoy the taste of her skin further or merely fall asleep curled around her. He was so fucking tired, his head ached at the thought. Release. Relief. A moment of respite against the harsh reality of day, a moment in her arms.

She'd give it, if he asked for it.

But there was too much to do.

There always was.

He couldn't rest until Balfour was dead.

And he couldn't afford to let himself weaken even

further, for somehow Adele ignited a piece of him he'd thought long-since buried. Every kiss was a dangerous trap that beckoned him down a long, seductive road.

"Maybe later," he said, and she slipped from his lap, a flash of chagrin crossing her face. "I need to return to the safe house. Now I have proof Devoncourt was at the warehouse, I can arrest him for questioning."

"Do you want company?"

He paused. "As you wish."

Adele sighed. "Give me twenty minutes to wash up."

Slipping into a clean gown, undergarments and boots, Adele pushed open the door to the bedroom, her skin all soft and dewy with the heat of her bath water. She'd cleaned up as best she could, but she could still feel the ache of his possession on her body.

He'd set his walls back into place the second they'd finished, but she'd seen the look in his eyes.

What was it going to take to break through those walls?

Patience, she told herself.

She was getting to him.

She just had to continue pushing.

The moment Adele set the lantern on the dresser in her room, she turned, lifting her hands to her damp hair to pin it. Malloryn would be waiting for her. Her shadow stretched out in front of her, growing rapid wings that seemed to swallow her whole.

She suffered a moment of confusion, before realizing the shadow was too big to be hers.

Adele half-turned, but it was too late.

A hand slammed over her face, wet linen smothering

her mouth and nose. She tried to cry out, but the familiar scent of ether swam through her head. It was like déjà vu. Her wedding day happening all over again. Chemical crawled down her throat, its choking fingers slipping lassitude through her veins.

Lifting a foot, she stomped on her attacker's instep as Gemma had taught her, but the world started spinning. All she could do was lash out, hoping to grab something, anything, off the dresser….

Malloryn!

"Sorry, cherub," whispered a familiar voice, as the world started going dark around her. "But you picked the wrong side."

A thunk sounded above him.

Malloryn lifted his head as he set the sticky glass on the drinks table, and stilled. Heart suddenly beating faster, his hearing intensified as he focused outward.

All he could hear was the slow, steady shuffle of the butler moving about the house and throwing the locks. The tick of the enormous clock in the front hall. A carriage clattering past in the streets outside.

Where was she? She said she'd be twenty minutes.

Climbing the stairs, he set out toward her bed-chamber.

Moonlight streamed through the windows ahead, painted in a grid across the runner. The curtains fluttered in the breeze—

The curtains fluttered.

Time suddenly slowed around him. He reached for the knife up his sleeve, but the hollow retort of a dartgun firing stole his attention.

Too late.

Malloryn froze as he reached down to touch the dart embedded in his chest. A tremor of shock ran through him, slow creeping numbness stealing through his fingers. Not Black Vein, thank God.

Hemlock.

He'd been hemlocked.

"Adele!" He staggered sideways, slamming into the wall.

A shadow separated itself from all the others. Despite his well-trained staff, despite the sentries he had posted throughout the property, the enemy had somehow invaded.

But how?

The doors and windows were all equipped with special locks that would blare an alarm if someone tried to break in. The only way to do it was to have someone on the inside....

His knees went weak, feeling flooding out of his limbs first as the poison ravaged through him. A horrified sound echoed in his dry throat, but he couldn't stop himself from hitting the ground, one knee at a time, as a tall, slim woman stepped out from behind the curtains, holding her dartgun on him the entire time.

"Hello, Malloryn," Dido purred, as he lost his fight over his unresponsive body and slumped face-first to the ground. "I have an invitation from Lord Balfour. He wants you to attend an exclusive viewing. You'll have the best seats in the house for when the fireworks start."

There was nothing he could do. Nothing he could even bloody well say, as one of his servants scurried out of the shadows and rolled him onto his back.

"Where to Lady Dido?" the footman whispered.

Of all the things Malloryn had prepared for, he'd never expected himself to be the target.

CHAPTER TWENTY-SEVEN

By the time sensation returned, it was too late.

Malloryn let his head fall back against the stone wall of the dank cell where he was chained, blood wet against his split lip. Dido didn't share Jelena's enthusiasm for pain and suffering, but she'd been methodical. He was fairly certain at least one of his ribs was broken, and his left eye threatened to swell shut.

He could feel the craving virus swarming through him in response to the injuries, but there was nothing he could do right now.

Each wrist was clamped in a steel manacle two inches thick. Both were soldered directly to the wall above his head, leaving his chest splayed wide and vulnerable.

The only thing he could hope for was that one of his household staff—or even Adele—would notice him missing, and the Rogues would track him using the beacon inserted at the base of his skull.

Once again, he was forced to rely upon others.

Keys clanked in the darkness, and then the cell door opened. Light bloomed, forcing him to look away as his vision slowly adjusted.

Balfour stepped out of the shadows, his gloved hands curled around his cane. Snowy white lashes flickered over his coal-black eyes as Balfour took a slow, considering look at him.

The instinctive curl of fury and rage knotted tight inside his gut, and Malloryn strained at his shackles.

Twice now, he'd found himself at this man's mercy.

He could only expect to escape once, and he'd already used up that life.

"And so we meet again," Balfour murmured as Dido strode into the cell with the lantern. "Sometimes I wonder if fate is determined to throw us against each other until one of us breaks."

"You've tried to break me before," he rasped, slumping his head back against cold stone. "And you didn't succeed. What makes you think you will this time?"

Balfour slowly knelt, a smile stretching over his lips as he leaned on the cane. The action brought them to eye level. "Because I am patient. And I am determined. I will find the means to destroy you, Malloryn. No matter how long I must wait, or what I must try. Do you understand? You took everything from me."

His manacles clanked as he jerked forward. "I wanted you to know what it felt like. I wanted you to suffer."

"It seems we are of like minds."

Dido set the lantern on a nearby table, where several items lay covered by a velvet cloth. Something to torture him with, no doubt.

Malloryn steeled himself. He'd survived what they'd done to him in Russia. He could survive this.

But he couldn't escape the physiological effects. His body tensed, his heart starting to race. The worst thing was knowing what was to come. Expecting it. Knowing how much pain his body could bear before he'd begin to scream for mercy. He'd begged then. He'd never thought he would, but Jelena had managed to find every little weakness he owned and exploit them.

Ever since she'd died, he'd thought himself free of this fear, but the simple clank of whatever was on the table put him right back there in Russia. Right back there in those dark, dark moments, where not even a scrap of light could reach him.

Balfour was saying something.

He fought to break free of the panic, forcing himself to breathe. One slow breath in, and one slow breath out. And again.

Until his ears were no longer ringing and he could see through the narrow tunnel he'd found himself in.

"This time, we will have our end. This time, only one of us will survive," Balfour promised.

"Then do it," Malloryn taunted. "Kill me. I know you want to."

At that, a faint smile touched Balfour's lips. "You arrogant little cur." He began stripping off his gloves, one finger at a time. "Did you think it would ever be that easy? I don't want you to be a martyr. I want you to suffer. Death is too easy. Death is a release. No. I want to make you hurt. I want to destroy each and every aspect of your life... the way you destroyed mine. I want to break you."

You already broke me.

The boy that he'd been—the arrogant youth who'd thought himself above punishment—had died a swift, merciless death as he held the bloodied form of the girl he loved in his arms and begged her to come back to him.

From the second Balfour put a bullet in Catherine's chest, he may as well have started digging that boy's grave.

Auvry was dead. Buried. Gone. Only Malloryn

remained, a thin veneer of civility straining over the ligaments and bare bones of his rage.

And he laughed.

The sound filled the cellar, making Balfour flinch back in surprise.

"Do you think there's anything you can do to me that hasn't already been done?" he breathed, when the laughter choked in his throat. "You already killed the woman I loved."

And he'd never dared love again.

"Did I? We're here to test that theory."

A chill ran through Malloryn as Balfour whisked the velvet from the table, revealing a pair of objects. "I'll even give you a clue as to what I plan."

The heat drained from Malloryn's face as he recognized the threat.

Not torture.

But something designed to cripple, all the same.

Two miniatures. Two women, their oval faces gleaming on darkened canvas. One as blonde and radiant as the sunlight, and the other dark and smiling a secret, sensual smile.

This was his Achilles heel.

"I must admit, it's been difficult to decide who to hurt first. I couldn't guess which one held your affections more, so I took both. On one side we have the glorious soprano, Mrs. Danner, and on the other, we have the calculating duchess, Adele."

That noise he'd heard.

He'd been right all along. There *had* been someone in his house.

"Which one will you choose to save?"

The breath exploded out of him.

Pain screamed through Malloryn's wrists as he tore at

his restraints, but there was no way of escaping. Horror flooded through him. *No*. "You bastard! They're both innocent. This is between you and me—"

"It has never been solely between you and me. You made sure of that when you stole my blasted thrall. Killed my puppet prince. Ruined my power base here in London. So now I will return the favor. You *might* have enough time to save one of them," Balfour promised. "Even now your Company of Rogues rides to your rescue, guided, no doubt, by that beacon in your head."

Balfour wanted them to find him.

"Or perhaps both will die," Balfour mused. "I would enjoy that, I think."

"You son of a bitch. You—"

"Now, now, Malloryn. Mind your temper. You wouldn't want me to think I'd actually scored a blow." A smile stretched thin. "You can pretend you don't have a heart all you like. I will always find it."

"They are *innocent*."

"Are they?" Balfour examined his pocket watch, and then exchanged a slow smile with Dido. "Ready to enjoy the fireworks, my dear?"

Dido gave Malloryn a long, narrow-eyed look. "You should cut his throat now."

"But that's not half as much fun," Balfour chided. Grabbing his cane, he headed toward the door. "I am being generous, Malloryn. You have half an hour to find and rescue both women. Or fail. Sweet Adele is at the Ivory Tower, where you first laid eyes upon her. And your mistress is at the opera where you met. Both sites are loaded with enough dynamite to blow the entire room—and each woman—to pieces. Alas, you only ruined half my stockpile. You have half an hour until the fuses light."

Dido put a small clock on the table, its hand ticking

one minute past half-eleven.

"I am interested to see which choice you will make. The soprano? Or your wife? I guess we'll soon find out."

Loud shouting echoed above them.

Balfour gave him a sinister smile. "Looks like the cavalry's arrived."

"No!" he screamed, as Dido opened a secret door in the wall.

"Tick, tock, Malloryn." Balfour faded back into the shadows. "Make your choice. When the clock strikes midnight...." His voice lowered as he began to vanish into a secret tunnel behind a tapestry. "*Boom.*"

"Are you all right?"

Byrnes tore his shackles open, but Malloryn shoved him out of the way, fighting free of the ropes around his ankles. Everything hurt, but there was no time for that now.

"What is it?" Byrnes asked sharply.

"He's got Adele and Giulia Danner." Malloryn raked his hands through his hair. "How many Rogues are with you?"

"Only me and Ingrid. The others are working in pairs across the city, trying to track you. We heard the tracking device start clicking a half mile away."

Two of them. It might work. "Giulia's at the opera house. Find her and get her out. Balfour said there's enough dynamite there to blow the room to pieces, so be careful. And hurry." He turned on Byrnes. "I need a weapon."

Byrnes tossed him a knife and a pistol. No doubt he had several others.

"You're going after Adele?" Ingrid asked breathlessly.

It had never been a choice.

"I'll take the Tower. If you can get in contact with any of the other Rogues, tell them to head in my direction. I may need help finding her."

The Ivory Tower.

Of course.

This was where it all began. Where it all ended.

Malloryn galloped into the courtyard, his horse's flanks foamed with sweat. He'd hired it from a startled hack driver by the simple expedient of tossing one of his gold rings at the man.

Several guards lowered their stunners, recognizing his face—and the look upon it.

"Your Grace?" Halstead, the new Master of the Coldrush Guards, asked. "What is it?"

"Is the queen here?" he demanded, swinging his leg over the horse's bare back and hitting the ground.

"No, she's—"

"Lock down the tower and start evacuating people. I have credible news of a threat. There may be explosives on the grounds."

He barked orders as he surveyed the grounds. Ivory Tower stood at the heart of the walled compound, soaring into the heavens like a marble finger pointing directly toward the stars. There was no way Balfour could have gotten explosives inside it, was there? Malloryn had changed the guard rotations, virtually locking it down after he received the letter from Balfour.

But then, it wasn't the only building in the complex.

Four towers stood at each corner of the heavy stone

walls that circled the bailey: Thorne, Oak, Shield, and Crowe.

Adele could be anywhere on the grounds. But where, damn it? He didn't have time to search the entire keep. He needed a location.

Halstead reported back.

Nobody had been seen entering the grounds with any large shipments. No one had been admitted to the tower in twelve hours who hadn't been expected.

That didn't mean Balfour's agent hadn't been able to get in.

But he was running out of time.

Think, damn it. Malloryn turned, his gaze locking on Crowe Tower, where an open clock face loomed. It had been rebuilt in the wake of the revolution but was little used. A couple of minutes until midnight. Adele had to be here somewhere. The second hand ticked toward—

There was a faint light in the window up there, behind the open clock face, almost like someone had lit a candle.

Of course.

He was running before he thought about it. The enormous brass minute hand ticked closer to the hour. Two minutes. At most. That was all he had.

Bursting through the door, he found himself at the base of the tower.

Malloryn flew up the stairs. He shoved open the door into the first level, and a string tied to the door jerked, a flash of light igniting in the corner. As he watched, fire raced along the trail of gunpowder. Hell. Malloryn started sprinting, following the trail.

Up more stairs. Thighs straining and lungs burning. The gunpowder led to a cask, and the second it hit the cask, everything went white.

BOOM—

The concussion smashed him off his feet, slamming him back into the wall behind him. Pain exploded through his head, his ears ringing. Somehow he crawled onto his hands and knees. The hallway loomed ahead. Another trail of gunpowder ignited, leading higher, higher....

A small charge set at each station, as if Balfour wanted him to get close enough to taste success.

"I don't want to kill you, Malloryn," echoed that hated voice from their confrontation in Russia. *"I want to destroy every single thing you ever loved. One by one. Until you are crippled and alone, with their deaths on your conscience—"*

"Adele!" He staggered up the stairs, trying to fight off the wave of double vision that afflicted him.

The trail of gunpowder hit the closed door ahead of him, vanishing beneath it. A series of pops and crackles suddenly exploded behind the door. *No.* Malloryn threw his shoulder against the timber, rebounding sharply. Again. This time the lock shuddered. A scream echoed within as smoke began to creep out from beneath the door.

The fury ignited in him. The craving. Suddenly the world was nothing but shadows, and he could feel his sight and hearing sharpening, his mouth suddenly aching for the taste of blood. *Adele.* She belonged to him, and damned if he knew what was going on between them, but he wasn't about to lose her.

Malloryn bellowed in rage and threw himself at the door.

It burst open, sending him rolling through flames and smoke. The entire room was on fire. Her wedding gown hung in the corner, flames chewing their way through the fabric.

"Adele!" he yelled, fighting through the smoke. "*Adele?*"

Flames licked at the walls, revealing a half dozen

barrels stacked around the room. His heart stopped in his chest—

—and then someone coughed.

A figure was bound to a chair in front of the open clock face, slumped behind the thick hood.

No time to think. The flames had almost reached the first of the barrels and the second they went up there'd be nothing on this earth that could stop the tower from burning to the ground.

Malloryn drove into Adele, his arm locking around her waist as they plunged toward the open clock face. The pulley mechanism that opened and closed it flashed past his eyes, and at the last second he grabbed hold of it, the two of them swinging out into the open—

Not a second too soon.

The entire top of the tower exploded.

Heat seared his back, burning straight through his coat. Then he was falling as the pulley's rope suddenly cut off, Adele screaming in his arms, her hands bound behind her back. The ground flashed up toward them, and Malloryn stuck his feet out—

He hit, the impact jarring through his left ankle and flipping him forward. Somehow he bore the brunt of it with his shoulder, pain screaming through him as the joint popped from its socket. Adele slammed against him, and then they were rolling head over heels until they finally came to a stop.

He could barely move. Barely lift his head off the cobblestones. His ankle and shoulder were on fire. But Adele gasped in a sob, and somehow he managed to scramble across to where she lay, his useless arm hanging in its sleeve.

Once again his vision turned to shadows as the heat of the craving swept through him. Safe. She was safe. He'd never wanted to kiss her so much in his life.

"You saved me," she sobbed.

"I've got you," he gasped as he tore the ropes from her wrists.

Malloryn yanked the hood off her face with one hand—

—and stared directly into the terrified eyes of Mrs. Danner as she threw her arms around him.

CHAPTER TWENTY-EIGHT

His heart jacked through his chest, kicking behind his ribs as Malloryn caught Giulia's arm. He couldn't move. Couldn't breathe. *Giulia....* What was she doing here? What was—? Where was Adele?

"You came for me," Giulia gasped, bursting into tears.

And that was when he knew how Balfour had played him.

Suddenly he could move again, pushing her away from him. *No.* No, not this. Anything but this.

Somehow Malloryn staggered to his feet, aware that dozens of Coldrush Guards were streaming from the Ivory Tower, watching as Crowe Tower burned. He felt weightless. Distant from his body. Unerringly, his head turned toward the east, toward the opera house where he'd first met Giulia.

The opera house, where he'd sent Byrnes and Ingrid to rescue the soprano at his feet.

And as he watched, an enormous mushroom cloud of fire suddenly bloomed into the sky.

Adele wriggled in her ropes.

She couldn't see a damned thing, and there was a hood over her face. First thing first. Using her teeth and her shoulder, she managed to get hold of the edge of the hood and then painstakingly drag it off her head. It hit the floor beside her, and Adele took her first blessedly cool breath of air even as light blinded her.

Where on earth was she? As her eyes slowly adjusted, she took in the stage around her, the red velvet curtains—and the spotlight shining directly upon her.

"Hello?" she called.

Adele began to notice the elegant chairs and the sumptuous carpets. She'd been here. Many a time. The opera. She was tied to a chair on the opera stage.

"Devoncourt?" she yelled, and her voice echoed through the room.

That rat bastard.

He'd kidnapped her, and tied her here and—

There were half a dozen barrels all around her, marked ominously with painted green flames, but no sign of anyone else. Clearly, nobody expected her to escape, and the barrels.... There was a good reason she might be here alone.

Adele swallowed hard. She knew the symbol for Greek Fire when she saw it. And judging from that ticking sound, there was some sort of explosive device stacked among the barrels.

Devoncourt had left her here to die.

And he'd done a jolly good job of tying these knots.

I am not going to die in the bloody opera house.

And certainly not at Devoncourt's hand.

If she couldn't loosen her ropes, then she would have to cut them, or abrade them. She glanced down, at the coiled spring attached to the chair she sat in. Any sharp jerk might trigger the mechanism there. So, not only would she have to cut her ropes, but she'd have to do it gently.

Not a great deal of time to lose then.

It was a good thing she'd come prepared.

Adele gritted her teeth and tried to force her blood-starved fingers to work. They flapped uselessly against her lacy sleeve. She couldn't remember much of her kidnapping, but as her fingers groped blindly, she hoped whoever had been behind it hadn't thought to search her.

Almost there.... Her fingers brushed the hilt of the small knife she always carried up her sleeve. *Come on.* Sweat dripped down her temple. Then she caught hold of the hilt with her fore and middle fingers.

It took her perhaps ten minutes, but Adele finally gasped in success as she managed to tumble the hilt into her palm. Her fingers snapped closed around it.

Time to get out of here.

Before those barrels exploded.

"Where is she? Where is she?"

Malloryn shoved through the smoky crowd outside the opera, finding Byrnes and Ingrid sitting on the steps of the palladium opposite the burning opera house. All he saw was blood and ash marking Ingrid's face, and Byrnes's protective arm around her shoulders.

The world started buzzing again. Malloryn staggered to a halt. "*Adele?*"

There was no sign of her.

"Adele?" Byrnes's frown drew his eyebrows together, and Malloryn watched as the other man suddenly realized exactly what had happened.

Ingrid looked up, her nostrils flaring with pain as she held her arm across her chest. "I'm sorry."

"It went up just as we breached the opera house door," Byrnes said gently, but Malloryn didn't hear any of it. "We were too late. I'm sorry...." A gurgle died in his throat. "It was all I could do to get Ingrid out of the way in time."

Malloryn finally managed to take in what remained of the opera house. Rubble lay strewn across the square, fire licking at what was left of the building. Men manning water pumps seemed to be streaming from nowhere, and as he watched, an enormous column of marble toppled, shattering across the cobbles.

"*Stay back!*" someone called.

There was no way anyone inside could have survived.

This was his fault.

And suddenly Malloryn was on his knees, the heat—what there was of it—draining from his face, and the world rushing away from him.

"Malloryn?" Byrnes caught him by the arm, and the duke groped for his hand blindly.

Adele.

That was when he knew what she'd meant to him.

CHAPTER TWENTY-NINE

Adele surfaced from the Thames with a gasp, filthy water streaming down her face, her skirts threatening to suck her under.

There was a boat nearby, and she kicked toward it, going under a couple more times before her hand finally caught in the mooring rope.

It took an enormous amount of effort to draw herself onto the banks of the Thames, and she collapsed there, shivering with cold.

Fire raged and bloomed in the distance. She was somewhere near the base of Waterloo Bridge. Slowly she sat up, staring at the opera house. It was on fire... or what was left of it was. It struck her then. How close she'd come to being inside that building when the explosion occurred....

A wave of trembling broke over her. Somehow she forced herself to her feet, her teeth chattering.

This was the third time the Opera House burned.

She could barely remember escaping. All the doors had been locked, and she'd returned to the stage, somehow managing to open one of the trapdoors by pulling on several of the ropes. Then she was working her way through the bowels of the building, ending up in a tunnel below it.

And from there, the river.

She took a step toward the opera house, and then paused.

Devoncourt had put her inside it for a reason.

Perhaps she would find help there, but who knew if the perpetrator lingered behind?

She couldn't go to the opera house. She couldn't go home to Malloryn Court, just in case it was being watched.

There was really only one place left for her.

Shivering with cold, Adele pushed her way inside Hardcastle Lane without bothering to knock. Some man by the river had given her his cloak and a ride to Hardcastle Lane in exchange for one of her rings.

The house was oddly silent.

Subdued almost.

She'd expected Herbert to pop out of nowhere to offer her a "spot of hot tea," but even he was nowhere to be seen.

"Hello?" Adele called softly, swinging the damp cloak from her shoulders.

Had something happened?

Where was everybody?

Sharp heels rapped on the floors to her left, and then Gemma burst out of the parlor in a hurry. She slammed to a halt, her mouth falling open as she clapped a hand to her lips. "Adele?"

"Alive," Adele managed, her smile trembling.

Gemma became a blur of movement and then her

arms were around Adele and she was gasping softly. "Oh, my goodness. Oh, my goodness. You're alive. He's going to— He's— Oh, you have to see him!"

"Malloryn's here?"

"He thought you were dead." Gemma looked like she wanted to cry. "I've never seen him like this before. He arrived at the opera house too late. And it was burning, and.... Oh, my goodness."

"Wait." Adele tried to capture the other woman's hands, tried to make sense of what she was saying. "Malloryn thinks I'm dead?"

"I sent the others away for the night. All except Obsidian. He's distraught—"

"Obsidian's distraught?"

"No! Malloryn." Gemma suddenly examined her. "He's in his study. Just go to him, please. I'll pour a bath and fetch some tea, and.... Well. They'll be ready when you are."

"Thank you," Adele whispered, glancing upstairs, toward the study, as she finally realized what state of mind she'd find her husband in.

"I will not add your name to that list."

Oh, God.

It hadn't really hit her until then. If Malloryn thought she was dead, he'd be blaming himself.

Someone opened the door.

"Get out," Malloryn said flatly, one hand resting on the mantelpiece as he stared into the flickering flames. A half-empty glass of scotch dangled laxly from his fingers. He was barely aware of it. He felt nothing.

Nothing but hollowness.

There was a rushing roar in the distance, as if *something* threatened to sweep over him and roll him under, but he'd kept it at bay so far. Or perhaps shock was protecting him from that screaming roar of darkness.

"I want to take every single thing you ever loved away from you."

"You already killed the woman I loved," he'd taunted.

God, he'd been so blind.

The person behind him didn't leave. And suddenly Malloryn couldn't take it anymore. "Get out before I kill somebody—"

"Is that any way to speak to your wife?" demanded a very familiar, very not-dead voice.

Malloryn spun around, dropping the glass of scotch. Glass shattered, but he didn't even flinch.

Adele stood in the doorway.

Adele.

He barely had time to take in her bedraggled state and her wet skirts before his heart punched right into his ribs. Malloryn's jaw dropped open. No. There was no way she could have— But he could hear her breath and if Adele were going to haunt him, it wouldn't be wearing half the Thames, by the look of it.

"You're alive," he rasped, taking a step toward her.

"Well, of course I'm alive," she replied with a faint, hesitant smile. "You didn't think I was going to let Devoncourt do away with me so easily?"

"Devoncourt?"

"He's the one who kidnapped me. And then he tied me to a chair on the opera stage and left me there along with over a dozen barrels of Greek Fire, and—"

One stride. Two. Then he was in front of her, capturing her face in his hands.

His lips met hers, and they were real beneath his

caress.

The heat of her skin filled his chilled hands, her tongue slick beneath his as he kissed her to hell and back, drowning in the realness of her warmth beneath his touch.

Alive.

Alive, and safe, and wet, and...

Perfect.

Adele reared back, meeting his gaze. She held on to his wrists, as though he'd almost knocked her over. "*Auvry?*"

"I thought you were dead," he somehow managed to say, and his voice was a mess of raw emotion that even he heard. "I thought—I thought you were gone, and he'd won, and I was never, ever going to be able to tell you...."

A thousand thoughts danced across her expression: uncertainty, disbelief, shock, confusion, hope.... But the one that finally settled was an odd sense of understanding, as if she *knew* what he was trying to say.

"Tell me what?" she whispered.

He closed his eyes to avoid the way she sought the truth of him with her own gaze. The truth he'd barely begun to recognize himself.

This wasn't supposed to happen.

He wasn't supposed to feel this way.

He wasn't supposed to want her.

To crave her.

Not just physically, but her smile, her teasing flirtations, the way she would link their fingers and rest her head against his chest, as if listening to his heart beat.

Her affection.

Adele was a dream he'd never expected to dream again.

He couldn't say it.

Instead, he kissed her again.

Poured everything he had into that kiss, his hands curling through her tangled hair, his body meeting hers and bending it back until she practically lay in his arms. He ravished her mouth, breathing in the taste of her, hungry for each and every little part of her. Hungry to consume her, though it was not merely passion he sought, but her.

Her.

I thought you were dead, and I did not know until that moment what you meant to me.

Somehow, her smiles had become a gift he lingered over. Somehow, without him even realizing, Adele had crept into his heart—into his arms—and started to lure him out of the darkness of his world.

He'd been granted a second chance. And this time, he wasn't about to waste it.

They staggered.

Then the desk was there, and he hitched her up upon it, sweeping a hand across the desk to clear it. Paperwork cascaded across the carpet like fluttering moths. But the center of his awareness was locked on her. On the fistful of skirts he held. The cold, clammy feel of the fabric against him, as he yanked them out of the way, stepping between her parted legs. Of the taste of her mouth as she kissed him back as if she had nothing more to lose.

And maybe she didn't.

"Adele—" He kissed her again, a slow, soul-shattering kiss. Caught both hands in her bodice and tore. Then he was burying his face against her throat, tracing his lips across the smooth slope of her breasts. The puckered bud of her nipple slipped over his lips, and he sucked hard, finding life in her gasp, feeling heat blooming beneath his hands and mouth—

Alive. Alive and so beautiful.

Her heart pounding beneath his touch.

Warmth flooding to the surface, stealing away the chill of her skin.

Alive. Alive. And it made his heart beat too. Made him realize that he'd been many years dead in some ways, until she forced her way into his life and made his heart beat for the first time in seventeen years.

"Malloryn," she whispered, fingers threading through his hair as she arched against him, offering him all of her. "I want you. Inside me. Now."

He freed himself from his trousers and then grabbed her by the hips.

"I thought you were dead," he said again, filling her with one smooth thrust.

But it was heat that surrounded him.

A living woman in his arms, one who gasped in shock and threw her head back as he took her. He tried to be careful. Tried to restrain himself. To maintain some sort of grip over the passionate demands of the craving as his bloodlust rose, threatening to overwhelm him.

Mine.

She is mine.

Adele moaned and bit his lip, and then he couldn't restrain himself any longer. Hips flexing, he captured her face between both hands as he plunged his tongue inside her mouth, consuming her, devouring her, thrusting so hard the desk inched across the floor with a groan.

Each stroke punched through him, a shiver of heat licking up the base of his spine. Adele's hands ran down his back and over his bare buttocks, clasping there, her nails digging in even as her hips locked around his. "Malloryn!"

And then, a little softer, but far more dangerous, "*Auvry.*"

He could feel the edge of orgasm quiver through her, and then his hand was between them, thumb grazing over the slickness between her thighs, determined to push her over the edge first.

Adele convulsed around him, her body clutching at his in spasms of pleasure that left scoring marks across his back from her fingernails.

And then he was tumbling into oblivion himself, throwing himself into headlong pursuit of the physical, and giving himself over to the mind-shattering relief of a pleasure so violent it burned him up from the inside out and tore from his lips in a soft cry that sounded like her name.

Malloryn collapsed against her, his breath coming in great, heaving gasps even as gentle hands rubbed his back, as if she knew exactly how much he needed her touch right now. A wounded-animal sound echoed in his throat, and he clung to her, soaking in the heat of her skin as he buried his face against her throat.

Balfour had lost this round.

But only because of Adele's ingenuity.

And yet it didn't feel like they'd won. Because now Balfour had the key to Malloryn's complete destruction.

He'd revealed everything—including his heart—when he went straight for the location where he'd thought Adele was being held. If Balfour wanted to cut his heart out of his chest, now he knew how to do it.

"I'm never letting you out of my sight again," he whispered.

Ever.

CHAPTER THIRTY

"I'm so glad you're all right," Lena told her, throwing her arms around Adele and nearly squeezing her breathless. "Will heard some strange story about you being injured in the explosion at the opera, and I came straight over."

"To Hardcastle Lane?"

"Well, you certainly weren't at home. So I had a little suspicion this might be where you were hiding." Lena turned in circles, examining the foyer as she tugged her gloves off. "Though I must admit, I am decidedly curious. The last we spoke, you were marching here to confront your husband. I quite feared for his life, but then I didn't hear from you...."

Malloryn was going to be furious if he realized his secret little safe house wasn't so secret anymore—though he'd already claimed there was no point moving again, as Balfour had found his safe houses twice.

"Wait." Adele frowned. "How on earth did Will know I was in the explosion?"

"Blade may have been curious about the explosion, and saw your husband there. Your name was mentioned,"

Lena said. "I wasn't sure if you were the one setting the charge, however, considering your recent vendetta against certain opera singers."

"I did not burn the opera down." Adele tried to rein in her thoughts. She had to be careful what she said. Lena was her dearest friend, but how could she even begin to explain.... "And I don't have a vendetta against any opera singers."

"No?"

There was something about the way her friend said it.

"No." Adele didn't even know where to begin, but she couldn't deny it was lovely to see her friend. And the rest of COR seemed to be running about at Malloryn's beck and call, which left her alone with her thoughts. "Here. Come and sit in the parlor. We'll have some privacy."

Lena wasted no time. "You haven't been in society for some days now. There's... a lot of mention of the opera."

"I haven't really heard," she admitted. "I've been resting, and Malloryn's been busy for the last two days...." Her voice faltered.

Matters of the realm.

Dealing with the queen and the council.

She knew that.

And yet, as much as something had changed between them the night of the explosion, some things hadn't changed at all. He'd practically avoided her all day yesterday.

Lena glanced down.

"What is it? I can see you have something on your mind. Tell me," Adele demanded.

"Will said.... He said your husband saved Mrs. Danner from Crowe Tower before it blew up." Lena tried to keep the words light. "Everybody in the Echelon's talking of it—quite the rescue, according to all reports."

That she hadn't heard.

"*Mrs. Danner?*"

A chill ran through her. But it made no sense. The night she'd returned home, when he'd thought she was dead, Malloryn had been almost inconsolable. The way he'd made love to her on that desk had been proprietary, and then he'd spent all night in her arms.

"I'm sorry." Lena squeezed her hand. This was the way it had always been between them. Friends didn't lie to each other. Nor did they keep devastating secrets like this.

"No," Adele said, her heart giving a little squeeze in her chest. "I needed to know that. I thought...."

"You thought?"

I thought he cared for me.

But why had he not told her?

"I didn't realize Mrs. Danner was also kidnapped."

Even as she said it, her mind—that blasted devious little thing that drove her mad sometimes—began working. He'd said Mrs. Danner was only a friend and never a lover, and she'd trusted him. But both Adele and the opera singer had been kidnapped. And Malloryn had arrived at the opera too late to save *her*.

All of the blood drained out of her face.

A choice.

He'd been given a choice.

She just knew it.

"Adele." Lena bit her lip. "I'm the only person you'll never be able to fool, remember?"

It was instinct to protect herself, but Lena was right. They knew each other too well. And Lena could no doubt hear the rapid beat of her heart.

"When I came home, he was so shocked to see me. He thought I was dead. And he... well..." She pressed her hands to her burning cheeks. "He was quite demonstrative of the fact he was pleased I was alive. I'm so confused."

Lena's amber eyes softened in distress. "You care for him."

The sudden surge of tears took her by surprise. "No. I—I—" *Yes*, said her heart, giving another brutal twist in her chest. And suddenly she understood what it all meant: the way she watched him; that dance at the ball; the hungry way she turned for his kisses.... Malloryn, the icy duke who pulled the strings of everyone he knew. "Oh, no."

Practical, ruthless Adele. Where are you now when I need you most?

"It could be nothing," Lena said hurriedly. "Maybe he was given the wrong information? Maybe he thought he was rescuing *you*?"

Adele forced herself to face the facts, dashing the tears from her eyes. She stood, pacing to the fireplace, but even though the grate was warm there was no heat there. Not for her. "Malloryn doesn't make mistakes. He's not stupid enough to fall for the wrong information—"

"Unless he was emotionally compromised?"

And Adele made herself laugh, feeling utterly miserable. "My husband doesn't know the meaning of the words."

Or did he?

One moment she was dealing with Malloryn, who remained impenetrable, and the next she saw hints of something else. The man behind the mask.

Yet it wasn't enough.

He'd slipped into bed with her last night when he'd thought her asleep, and Adele had curled in his arms, but *not once* had he mentioned that Mrs. Danner had been kidnapped.

What did that mean?

"I need fresh air," she said. "I've been cooped up in

here for two days."

"A stroll in the park outside?" Lena suggested.

"Perfect." She needed sunshine on her face and the day's heat on her skin. She needed to breathe the scent of grass, and smile and laugh, and remember she was alive. Regardless of whether her husband had made a choice or not, she was still alive. That fact could not be discounted.

She could heal from a broken heart.

And never let herself suffer such a risk ever again.

But it was not to be.

Herbert appeared out of nowhere in the foyer and stepped between the pair of them and the door, clasping his hands behind his back. "Sorry, Your Grace. But you're not allowed to leave the premises."

Adele stared at him in shock. "What? Why?"

She knew the *who*. Not a damned thing happened in this house without Malloryn pulling its strings.

"The duke's orders."

Suddenly she saw red. "I see. Is my husband due anytime soon?"

"He is expected momentarily."

"I'll wait." Adele locked all of the hurt deep inside herself as she gave Lena another hug.

Lena squeezed her firmly. "If you need me...."

"I know."

At least she had this one thing she could count on. A friend.

"And talk to him," Lena suggested. "Maybe it's all just some vast mistake."

But Adcle didn't dare let herself hope.

The expression on Herbert's face warned him.

Malloryn tossed the man his hat and coat, and then paused with one foot on the staircase. "Something you want to tell me?"

He had the eerie suspicion he'd watched this entire scene play out already.

"I believe Her Grace is upset," the butler replied.

Thank God. He'd thought someone had died. "Not unusual," he replied, continuing up the stairs, "She's been through quite an ordeal—"

"With you," Herbert stressed, and shot him *that* look again.

Malloryn's step on the stairs slowed. "With me?" That made little sense.

"Her friend, the verwulfen ambassador's wife, was here," Herbert volunteered. "Your wife wanted to take a walk in the nearby park, but I suggested most emphatically she remain behind."

Lena Carver. Malloryn began to draw the scarf from around his neck. What had she said to Adele to upset her? Or was it locking her inside the house? "Send for a light supper. But perhaps give us a half hour before you bring it."

Enough time to soothe Adele's ruffled feathers and remind her he was doing this to keep her safe.

One step inside the study, and there she was.

Sitting in the window seat, the late afternoon sunlight streaming over her and gilding her hair. Her hands lay in her lap and she may as well have been a statue. There was no sign of her smile. No sign of the wicked glint he'd begun to recognize in her eyes.

Malloryn's eyes narrowed. Now he was coming to know her, he could sort through her moods relatively easily.

Her Grace was not just upset.

No. Not a single sign of tears afflicted her, and she wore that cool, disaffected mask he knew so well. *Walled up*, her expression told him. *And you are not welcome here.*

This was beyond upset.

What the devil had he done?

Balling the scarf in his fist, he considered his options. He'd been avoiding her since the explosion—so many things to see to, buildings to clear, Balfour to hunt—and that was as good an excuse as any he had available. But the truth was the night of the explosion had affected him greatly, throwing an ungallant truth in his face. Exposing his heart and scraping it raw before he managed to disengage and retreat to shore up the walls that guarded it.

"Should I remove anything breakable?" he asked. "Herbert said you weren't happy about being kept inside."

"I'm not going to throw anything. It's not the sort of thing well-bred ladies do."

Trouble, his instincts warned. *Definitely trouble.* And it had nothing to do with being contained.

"Did you miss me?" he asked. "I thought you'd prefer to recover here after the situation, and I had many things to see to. I'm sorry if I haven't been around of late. I didn't want your nerves to—"

"Did I look like I was suffering from a bout of nerves? As I recall, it wasn't I who was undone." Those green eyes narrowed dangerously. "Unless that was just another pretense too."

No, she'd been remarkably well-balanced after all of the exhilaration. His gaze strayed to the desk, and he could sec himself again, fucking his way into her like a mindless animal. Desperately kissing her, his hand sinking into her hair so he could press his lips to her throat and feel the thready kick of her pulse there.... The one that told him she was alive.

Alive and not burned in the opera attack.

Alive and not a charred mess of bones.

He slammed his way back out of the memories of how he'd felt when he stared into the flames of the opera house and thought she'd been inside. It had woken him last night, a new nightmare to add to the collection.

And the easiest way to deal with nightmares was to ignore them.

Moving slowly, he considered her as he crossed to the decanter and poured himself a brandy, tugging at his cravat. It felt tight.

"No," he said. Her eyes glittered, as if she were daring him to work her out. "No, you didn't succumb to nerves. And I'm not certain what you mean by 'pretense.' You could simply tell me what the matter is."

"It's the game that counts, isn't it?" They sounded like his own words, though he wasn't entirely certain when he'd said them to her. "And you like games. Guess."

"You're angry."

"I would have to care to be angry."

The faint press of her lips together betrayed her, as if something violent wanted to spill over the top of them. Not unflappable, after all. He focused on the faint sign of distress. If he couldn't control himself, then he'd damn well break her down to his level and bring whatever this was to the surface.

Pushing away from the desk at last, he began to tug his cravat free, feeling a little more composed now he wasn't the only one afflicted. "Oh, I think you care. I think you care far too much, *Adele*."

She flinched a little at the sound of her name, so soft on his lips. "Aren't you tired of the lies?"

"I wasn't aware I'd been lying. Do you have something to confess, my dear?" He wrapped his cravat around one of his knuckles, drawing the material tight.

And her gaze dropped to the silk.

He could almost see the memory strike her, those wicked green eyes warming. Adele sucked in a sharp breath, and Malloryn emphasized the moment, stroking his thumb softly over the tension in the cravat; a sensual rustle he felt inside him as his callused thumb snagged on the silk.

It felt like her skin beneath his touch.

It felt like her surrender.

The last time they'd played this game, it had been her hands bound by the cravat.

Her arms tied above her, pinning her wrists to the bed.

Her pleas soft in the air as he buried his face between her thighs.

And they were both suddenly there in that moment, his cock hardening behind the placket of his breeches.

"You son of a bitch," she whispered, moving in a sharp flurry of skirts.

He stepped between her and the door. "Now that," he said, "is a rather unkind assessment of my mother."

"*Assessment*?" she hissed, trying to step around him. "That's all you have to say? You think you can come in here and seduce me and I'll forget everything?"

Sometimes it seemed like the only way he could breach the distance between them. "It's never bothered you in the past."

One fist lashed out toward his chest, and he captured her hands, holding her there with minimum force. A storm of anguish broke her cool mask, and his gut clenched, for he'd never, *ever* seen Adele so undone before. He wanted to take it all back in an instant. *Why* had he said that?

I don't want to hurt you.

But he didn't know how to say it, not in any way she

would understand. All he had was this.

And he captured her face with one hand, his mouth slanting to capture hers. Adele's mouth softened momentarily, and a flood of relief swept through him, his tongue darting out—

Then her hurt was gone, obliterated by rage as she fought him. Malloryn found himself with a wildcat of pure fury in his arms, one that fought only to free herself. Silk ripped as she twisted, and he let her go, unnerved by the maelstrom of emotion on her face. Adele staggered back into the wall, one hand splayed over the wallpaper, her face shocked as their eyes met.

No, her gaze said. And it wasn't in the playful challenging way she sometimes looked at him.

It was in a *game over* kind of way.

The *no* echoed through him like a knife. He had this horrible feeling he was losing her, but that made no sense, because had he ever had her? Malloryn moved, but the second he lifted his hand, she scrambled away and he was left frozen and awkward, not quite knowing where to put his hands.

They ended in some sort of stalemate, with her trapped in the corner and Malloryn staring helplessly at her.

"You win," she gasped. "You win. I can't do this anymore."

"Can't do *what*?"

"This.... This marriage!"

A tear slid down her cheek, and *fuck*, his gut plummeted to his feet, because Adele didn't cry. Adele didn't break. And yet, somehow he'd pushed her too far and he didn't have a fucking clue how he'd done it, or what precisely he'd done.

"Adele," he whispered.

"Don't touch me!"

Malloryn sucked in a sharp breath, his hands in the air in a sign of surrender. Again he felt that punch to the gut. Or maybe it was higher. "What do you want from me?"

"The truth!"

"I'm telling you the bloody truth! I don't know what this is all about. Why are you so angry with me?"

"It's all through the Echelon!" she cried. "Your brave, dashing rescue of Mrs. Danner! They say you leapt out of the tower with her in your arms."

It had been in the papers too, but.... "Well, yes. I thought—"

"You chose *her*!" Her voice became a whisper. "You chose her."

A crushing, helpless little voice that ripped him open from the inside.

"Don't think I cannot put two and two together." Adele's fists shook. "The opera singer at the Ivory Tower? Me at the opera. Your guilt when you thought me dead. And I've overheard enough of what Byrnes and Ingrid were saying about how Balfour captured you. He gave you a choice, didn't he? About who to save. And you rode straight to the tower."

"Of course I did! I thought *you* were there. He said it was you! I made a choice, yes! And I picked you!"

"You don't make mistakes."

"Jesus Christ, Adele." He raked his hands through his hair. "I'm not infallible. There was fire blazing and every time I took a level of the tower, it set off another small explosion. I finally got through the fucking door at the top and there you were—or what I thought was you. She was wearing a gown similar to the one you'd worn that afternoon and there was a hood over her face. It wasn't until we landed in the courtyard that I knew what he'd done. Do you have any idea what that *felt* like?

"That's the way Balfour plays. He *wanted* me to make a choice, and he wanted me to rescue one of you. And then he wanted me to realize I'd saved the wrong woman as I watched the other one die."

"Then why didn't you tell me he made you choose? Why did you not tell me about *her*?"

"Because she's not a threat to you, Adele. I told you I ended our agreement."

"Yes, but—"

"Giulia prefers women," he barked.

Shock rocked her. "What?"

"Giulia and I have never been intimate. I wasn't in a place to take a lover when I returned from Russia. I needed a cover. We were only ever friends and it was only ever an arrangement that was mutually beneficial for the both of us. My name granted her protection from predators and men who won't take no for an answer, and I was free to come and go as I wanted."

"Why didn't you tell me?"

"Because it wasn't my story to share. All you needed to know was that it was over." His voice hardened. "But you didn't trust me enough to believe it."

"How can I trust you when you keep so many secrets? You keep me at arm's length all the time. You only ever reveal just enough. How am I not to leap to assumptions when I don't know what is going on in your mind? Explain it to me."

"I thought I had." The words came out a little rougher than either of them expected. "I'm not the only one who hides, Adele. You take your hurt and you lock it down deep and pretend it's not there. You were about to cut me from your life, weren't you? Without even knowing the truth. I am not your father. If you want to know something, ask. I gave you my word I would end my so-called relationship with Giulia, and I meant it. My honor is the one thing I have left. Don't throw it in my face."

"I *didn't.*"

"Trust goes both ways. You think I didn't let you in? The second you saw my maps and guessed what I was up to here, I told you more than I've told anyone in years. I let you help me. I gave you my trust, and let me assure you, that is not a thing easily won." He advanced upon her with brisk strides. "Despite my best intentions I allowed you to go undercover at Angel's Fall. Tell me how that is not *letting you in*?"

Adele set a hand to his chest, refusing to retreat. "Oh, your plots, yes. I'm talking about here." She thumped his chest. "Right here. I'm talking about you, Malloryn. Not your schemes. I don't even know where you've been for the last two days!"

"You needed rest and quiet—"

"I needed *you.*"

The words shocked the both of them.

They ricocheted around the room like a cannon blast.

"Well, maybe *I* needed time," he admitted. "After what happened at the tower.... It rocked me too. I just painted a damned target on your chest, because Balfour *knows* I chose you. And now he knows how to hurt me."

"Because my death would compound your guilt." She searched his face for the truth of it.

"Because... your death would cause me pain." He brushed his fingers against her cheek, and even though she allowed his touch she turned her face away. "It's not easy." Heat filled his voice. "I am not used to.... You want my thoughts. You want my presence. You don't think I don't know why? I told you: Don't fall in love with me. I warned you from the start."

"You also told me you'd never kiss me. Never share a

bed with me." *Never share your heart* went unsaid. "You broke those promises."

"And I shouldn't have."

Because this was the result.

Each kiss seduced both of them into... emotions he didn't have time to explore. It confused matters. Made it harder to work out where the line between them needed to stay.

Gemma had warned him.

He tried to make her understand. "For seventeen years, I have lived this life. Revenge. Power. They were the only things I ever wanted, the only things that have kept me going at times when my world was burning around me. I walked this path alone. I had to. I had nothing else to give to another. I couldn't give them my heart."

"*Have*," she pointed out. "For what has changed? You're still walking your path alone. You're still striving to bring him down."

"I have to end this. Because he will not stop coming for me."

"I understand that." She squeezed her eyes shut, as if fighting to work her way through these feelings. "You're trapped in this vicious cycle that will not end until one of you is dead. It's too dangerous to leave him alive. I *understand* that."

"Adele." He cupped her face, willing her to look up and meet his eyes. "What do you want of me?"

"Nothing," she whispered.

Nothing that you can give, remained unspoken.

He stroked his thumbs across her cheeks, across her mouth. "What do you want me to do? I will try to let you in."

"All I want is for you to talk to me. I want to share your secrets. I hate feeling like an outsider in this world.

You all have your places here. You all know what you are doing, but I don't. I hate these doubts that afflict me."

"Then I will try. But you have to grant me some trust. You have to talk to me too."

Adele slowly nodded, the tension in her shoulders easing.

He leaned down, brushed his mouth against hers.

It was the only thing he could give her.

And yet, when he drew back, it was clear it wasn't enough, for her glorious eyes held shadows that stole the sparkle from them.

CHAPTER THIRTY-ONE

Malloryn paced his study in the aftermath of the argument, raking his hands through his hair. She'd accepted his apology, but there'd been a distance within her, as if some sort of gaping wound still existed.

As if she was determined not to let him get too close to her again.

For once, he found himself on the other end of such a situation, and he had a swift insight into how others had felt dealing with him over the years.

Adele's words stabbed at him over and over again.

You're still walking your path alone.

And it was true.

Revenge. Power. Balfour. What was left of his life?

The sad fact was: Nothing.

There was no set of welcoming arms to greet him at night. No soft smile in the morning as he woke. No laughter ringing in his ears.

But there had been a chance for it.

Until he ruined it.

He'd pushed Adele away, and for what?

Balfour had still tried to kill her. He'd nearly fucking succeeded, and the thought carved out something hollow within Malloryn's chest.

And he would try again. Malloryn had never been so certain of anything in his life.

So why not let himself have her, before it was too late? Why not… let her in? All the way in?

What are you so afraid of?

He was already losing her.

Malloryn found himself in front of the brandy decanter, but the second he lifted the stopper he paused. There was no answer to be found there either. It was merely another means to hide, to avoid facing his demons.

If he wanted a chance to make something of this marriage with Adele, then he had to confront them. He had to splay himself wide, to admit she'd managed to unearth the very heart of his vulnerability. Not drown his sorrows.

Glass clinked as Malloryn slowly stoppered the decanter.

He refused to let himself think about it as he hurried up the stairs to the bedchambers they shared at Hardcastle Lane.

There was no sound of anyone within the room, but he could sense her perfume. Malloryn eased the door open and belatedly rapped with his knuckles.

"Adele?"

She lay tucked up in bed, a blanket splayed over her hips. Dressed in her nightgown, her hair unpinned and draped across the pillow.

Tension lingered in the curve of her spine, which faced him, and he could hear the soft intake of her breath as she heard the door click closed behind him.

He'd never been uncertain of his welcome in this room, but he was now.

"May I speak to you for a moment?"

"I thought you had matters of the realm to see to."

He sighed and eased onto the edge of the mattress. "I think this is more important, right now. Isn't it?"

Adele's head turned as if he'd said something intriguing, the pillow rustling. But she didn't answer.

And it was clear she didn't intend to.

No. This time it was his turn to extend the olive branch.

"I have a confession to make," he murmured. He reached out, brushing his finger down her cheek. It came away wet.

He'd been right.

Even here, in the silence of her bedchambers she'd been afraid to give voice to her sadness. He would have heard her sobbing. And each sound would have felt like a lash against his soul, but the fact that she'd been determined to keep him from hearing her cry only hurt him more.

"You scare the hell out of me," he admitted, rubbing her tear between thumb and forefinger. "You always have, and sometimes it's easier to keep you at arm's length, where I don't have to confront the way I feel about you."

Adele rolled onto her back, as if surprised. "How you feel about me?"

He traced the curve of her lower lip. "You are an amazing woman and I see it every day. And I want it. I want you. I want to make something of our marriage. I want.... I want a child with you. A future. Even as I dare not take it. To reach for it is to risk losing it, and I don't know if I can bear its loss. Not again. I have lost enough."

"Catherine," she whispered.

He bowed his head. "Catherine, yes. But more than that: Everything. Myself. My father. The concept of love.

The very core of who I was, who my mother raised me to be. I feel as though I somehow destroyed myself. Not Balfour." His mouth tasted like ash. "*Me.*"

"I don't understand."

"There was a child," he whispered. "In a way, it's what started this entire mess. I was careless and Catherine found herself in a delicate way. It was the one thing Balfour could not tolerate. If I had walked away from Catherine, then she would still be alive. My father would still be alive. But I could not, because I was too proud. I challenged Balfour directly, again and again, because I could not be patient. If I blamed Balfour for Catherine's death, then I did not have to confront the part I played in it."

Adele's eyes were very big and round. "You didn't pull the trigger."

"I may as well have. It should have been me. He was pointing the pistol at me, and Catherine begged for my life. It was the last thing he could tolerate." His mouth felt dry. "She died because she tried to save me. She died because she loved me."

A warm hand cupped his cheek. "She didn't die because she loved you, Malloryn. She died because Balfour chose to shoot her, because he could not tolerate another man owning a piece of her, even if it was just her heart. She died because an oppressive society took away her choices. She was given as chattel to a man who used her for blood. Sold, as if she was virtually livestock." Adele's hand slid behind his neck, and she drew him down onto the bed beside her. "Perhaps her love for you was the one defiance she was allowed. Perhaps it was the thing that kept her warm at night, that made her smile, even at the end. Perhaps that child was her joy, even if she didn't live long enough to hold it in her arms. Honor that memory, if nothing else. Honor her love. Don't let Balfour take that away from you."

"It's not memories I'm afraid to lose," he slowly admitted, brushing his thumb across Adele's mouth. She didn't understand. He'd fought so hard to hide it from her. "Not this time."

It's you.

Adele's breath caught.

"I swore on Catherine's grave that I would never love another woman. I would never dare." He brushed the strands of hair that clung to her damp cheeks out of the way, a breathless feeling filling him. "And I'm afraid I'm breaking that promise every time I look at you."

The clock on the mantle ticked in the silence as a hundred thoughts raced through those green eyes. Shock, mostly. Doubt. Wariness. Need.

And a furious desire for what he spoke of.

Her mouth opened, but nothing came out.

"I shouldn't be here," he whispered, brushing the back of his knuckles down her cheek. "I shouldn't let thoughts of you consume me. I shouldn't seek you out, even for a moment, because it makes me feel alive. I shouldn't remember what it feels like to live. I should lock myself away in the Duke of Malloryn's mantle and pretend that Auvry no longer exists, that you don't tempt him in so many ways. Because you are his equal and he knows it. Because he wants a child with you, but he does not dare, because he's not certain if he could survive its loss. He's not certain if he could survive your loss, if he lets himself care. And he's not certain if he's going to win."

He buried his face in the crook of her neck, breathing in the familiar scent of her perfume. Adele's heart pounded through her chest, and he felt it echo against his own.

"My love is a terrible thing. I would not wish it upon my worst enemy," he whispered. "And so, the Duke of

Malloryn does not dare love you."

"Then he is a fool," she breathed, "for his wife would give him the world, if he dared."

Adele turned her face to his and captured his mouth, and then he was pressing into her, trying to steal the promise that beckoned on her tongue. Shuddering beneath the stroke of her hands up his back and spine, as if her very touch had the power to destroy him.

Mine, said the dark, forbidden part of his soul he kept locked away.

And just this once, he let it loose.

Let himself dream of what they could conjure between them, if they both allowed themselves. A future where no shadow loomed over them. A future where he *did* dare. Where he *could* grant her all that her heart desired.

All that *he* might desire.

Her hands went to his shirt, and somehow she had it undone. Then there was nothing but skin beneath her touch as she stripped him bare. Hot little hands wreaking havoc on his cock as he thrust into her palms, begging her for more. The drag of her nightgown as he tore it up over her head, barely breaking the fusion of their mouths to cast it aside.

Naked flesh beneath his.

The pounding of both their hearts.

And need.

Fierce, furious need.

He used teeth and tongue to bring her to the brink, and raptured in the shuddering of her body as she cried out in pleasure. He could spend a hundred nights in her arms, just like this.

A thousand.

Then he was crawling up her body, the hunger demanding that he claim her, as he kissed his way up her throat.

Adele's hips arched beneath him, and he could barely deny the ache of his cock or the slickness of her body. There was no finesse as he drove himself inside her. Merely a meshing of tongues, and bodies and breath.

Hard and furious and desperate. It felt as if he came alive, for the first time in years, as he held nothing of himself back.

And Adele was just as demanding, her nails digging into his spine as he rocked within her, the bedhead hammering the wall. He could feel her clinging to him as if to stake her claim upon him. Fusing their palms together, he pinned her wrists to the bed, meeting those glazed green eyes.

"I knew you were trouble the moment you ran into my arms," he whispered, fucking slowly within her. "You ruin me, but it feels as though there is redemption in ruin." Malloryn bit his lip as her body clenched around his. Sweet Jesus, she was close. "And I want nothing more than to let it consume me."

Adele threw her head back, coming with a soft cry.

He rode her through the aftermath, watching each and every unshuttered emotion cross her pretty face. And somehow, within that moment, he felt himself reborn like a phoenix.

Mine. Forever mine.

He came with a soft cry, collapsing down into the warmth of her arms, and burying himself there. Shuddering, he clung to her, feeling her chest lift with each surge of breath, her heart pounding beneath his.

Hands slid through his hair, her fingers massaging his temples, as he kissed her chin, her jaw, her lips. He eased his weight off her, though he didn't remove himself entirely. He wanted to stay within her body as long as possible.

"We're not going to lose," she finally whispered.

He bit her fingers. "You give me hope."

"I won't let him hurt you."

Malloryn shut his eyes. "I'm the one who's supposed to be protecting you."

"And you have," Adele admitted. "Trapping you into marriage was the best mistake I ever made."

He couldn't help laughing. "I wish I could go back to that moment and tell myself not to be so bloody stubborn. We've wasted too much time."

"Well, you'll just have to promise me forever, so we can make up for it," she replied archly.

"Make up for it, huh?" He nuzzled at her throat, enraptured by the kick of her pulse against his lips. His cock was hardening again, and he felt the urge to explore her body. To revel in the simple affection of her touch. "You are very demanding."

"I'm a duchess, didn't you know?"

"My duchess." *My hopes. My dream.* Rocking against her, he felt her breath catch again.

"Didn't you call a meeting?" she whispered.

"The Rogues can wait. It will give them something to bloody gossip about. Besides, Charlie's not back yet."

And Adele laughed as he palmed her breast and bent his head to her nipple, the sound piercing straight through his heart.

Surrendering to his fate had never felt more right.

Dawn bloomed, bringing with it the hope of a new day.

And a certain sort of focus and determination Adele hadn't seen on her husband's face in weeks.

"Mowbray practically confirmed the metaljackets are the key to Balfour's attack," Malloryn began, the second all the Rogues were gathered around the table.

Adele frowned. "There are barely two legions of them left. The queen had most of them destroyed after she overthrew her husband, and maintained only an elite ceremonial guard."

"Jack?" Malloryn turned to the masked man who spent most of his days tinkering with his devices down in the cellars.

"Her Grace is quite correct. The populace disapproved of the metaljacket legions, and rightly so, considering they were once used to crush any dissenters. Her Highness had most of them broken down into scrap as soon as she took the throne." Jack leaned forward and sketched something on the sheet of paper in front of him with swift, brief strokes of his pencil. "What remains are the Firebird Legion and the Celestial Legion. The Firebird model is an updated, improved version of the spitfires that used to wreak havoc. Their flamethrowers no longer use Greek Fire, however.

"The Celestials are mostly ceremonial. Gold-plated and carry a saber attached to their mechanical arms. They're somewhat reminiscent of the Imperial Legion in China. Pretty and useless in a pitched battle. Too lumbering and slow, with no long-range weapons."

"Corvus said Balfour plans to tamper with the Firebirds." This from Malloryn. "He'll turn them against the queen."

"Of course he would," Byrnes drawled. "Why not set fire to everything? Everybody likes a good bonfire. It's not as though it could escape his control and burn half of London to the ground."

"I don't think he cares if half of London burns to the

ground," Malloryn pointed out.

Adele watched as COR bantered back and forth about the best way to stop Balfour's latest scheme. She reached slowly for the pile of papers in front of Malloryn. The list of Rising Sons leapt out at her.

"It has to be the Prometheus Project," Gemma said, pushing forward the schematics she'd drawn from memory. "He's going to use this chip to assert control of the metaljackets."

"How does he plan to get at them though?" Kincaid mused. "I imagine they're stabled in the Ivory Tower and kept under lock and key."

"They are," Malloryn replied.

Jack frowned as he examined the schematics. "This isn't the sort of thing that can be simply removed and inserted. If Balfour's replacing the metaljackets' chips with this one in order to control them, then it would take him at least a week. He'd need a half dozen bio-mechanical engineers with a degree from the Royal Mechanical Academy, or a master smith in the least. It's not something your average blue blood lord could do. And someone would see it."

"It's complicated." Malloryn scrubbed at his mouth. "Time-consuming. Difficult. And the more difficult a plot is, the harder it is to pull off. It makes no sense."

Adele watched his mind ticking over. "Are you certain this is how he means to attack?"

Malloryn swore under his breath. "No, I'm not certain. This seems too easy for Balfour. It's practically gift wrapped."

And that was the problem.

"Devoncourt's known we had Corvus for days, and they'd be aware of the depth of his knowledge. So why would they continue with this plan if they thought we knew about it?" he demanded.

"It could bc a decoy." Which, from what the Rogues had told her, sounded much more like Balfour's style. "Maybe he wants us to focus on the metaljackets?"

Malloryn started pacing, his hands clasped behind him. "So what is he hiding? What is he really planning?"

"Why wouldn't he use both metaljackets and Rising Sons?"

"He most likely will," Malloryn replied. "I expect a coup attempt, in the least. A two-pronged assault. We know who they are now, so the second they make their move I can arrest them."

"You have to convince the queen to cancel her celebrations," Gemma said. "I know you want them to make their move where you can see it coming, but you cannot control everything. One stray bullet and we lose her…."

"Convincing the queen may be easier said than done. I've practically locked down the tower," Malloryn growled, "and it's still not enough. She refuses to be cowed by the threat. Insists that the people need to see their queen hold her head high."

"This is madness, Malloryn," Gemma said. "The Ivory Tower's immense. There's not enough of us—or those Coldrush Guards we know to be loyal—to cover the damned thing."

"Then we focus on Balfour's potential targets," Malloryn countered. "You and Ingrid are going to make some excellent ladies-in-waiting."

"The queen can barely look at me after I nearly killed her," Gemma argued.

"If she wants her ball, then she will have you in her retinue. It is not negotiable."

They argued back and forth, voices growing more and

more heated.

"Why not set a trap for him?" Adele suggested. It made perfect sense to her. If they couldn't counter the threat, then they could contain it.

Every head in the room swiveled to look at her.

"How do we set a trap?" Gemma asked. "What do we bait it with? Malloryn?"

"We could tie a target to his chest," Byrnes drawled.

"Paint him pink," Charlie added.

Malloryn focused on her, his mouth thinning with displeasure. "If you're about to suggest yourself, I'll warn you to save your breath."

"Well, technically, not myself."

"Technically?" His voice dipped several octaves.

"We use the queen."

CHAPTER THIRTY-TWO

Her Highness was not amused.

"You want me to do *what?*"

Malloryn stood before her in the Council Chambers, his hands clasped patiently behind his back. "I want to use you to set a trap for Balfour. And to do that, I need the real 'you' to disappear."

"So you're going to replace me with a body double?" she repeated, as if to confirm what he'd said earlier.

"While I'm certain I can lure Balfour to his doom, I'm not about to put you at risk. Especially since the realm has no heir."

If anything, Alexandra's eyes narrowed further. It was a point of long-standing contention between them. While he could understand her reticence in refusing to take a consort following her disastrous marriage, the country didn't have the luxury of it.

The rest of the Council of Dukes hastily averted their eyes.

Cowards.

"But what about my anniversary?" she demanded.

"The parade? The ball? I've been planning this for nearly a year now. The people need to see—"

"And they will see *a* queen," he replied smoothly. "Unless…. We can make it a state funeral, if you wish? Though I'm sure Balfour will have the final say on that, not us."

Faint color mottled her cheeks.

"I cannot overemphasize the risk, Your Highness." Malloryn knew he had to push now, or risk losing her. "Balfour wants every single person in this room dead. At this point, I don't even know if he's concerned about who he will replace them with, or whether vengeance has completely consumed him. He's not acting the way he usually does."

"You think you've finally pushed him over the edge?" Rosalind Lynch asked.

"I think he's lost enough to make him dangerously unpredictable." He shot the duchess a look. "I have a half dozen threads of his schemes at my disposal, but I don't know precisely where the push is going to come from."

"So you give him a chance to make his play," Barrons mused, rubbing at his jaw. "You gift wrap him an opportunity too irresistible to pass up."

"We shall still have our parade. Our ball. But the queen will be spirited away before it's all begins. Balfour will know it's a trap, but he's always thought himself smarter than I am. He'll take the opportunity, just to prove he can. And we will be prepared for whichever thread he chooses to play."

"You're playing dangerous games, Malloryn," the queen warned.

"Aren't they all? I cannot give him the chance to slip away and escape. Not this time. This confrontation must be the end. All I need is for you to play your role."

Queen Alexandra pushed to her feet slowly, her silk skirts hissing as they fell around her ankles. "And just who did you have in mind to sit on my throne?"

The doors opened behind him, right on cue.

"Your Highness." He gestured to the woman who entered the Council Chambers behind him. "Please meet Her Highness."

The queen's mouth dropped open as she beheld the woman who entered.

Adele's bearing was as regal as any royal's as she tilted her chin toward her monarch. They'd dyed her hair yesterday to the rich, sleek brown of the queen's. A pair of colored occipital lenses—used by most of his agents at some stage—turned her green eyes the same hazel as Alexandra's. They were of a height. Of a similar build.

And Adele lived and breathed court etiquette when required.

"Forgive me, Your Highness," Adele murmured, "for my poor imitation."

It was not a poor imitation at all.

With the right powders, jewelry, and gowns, Adele could easily be mistaken for the queen unless one was particularly close or knew Alexandra well.

And if he played his cards right, Balfour would never get close enough to realize the mistake.

"Your wife?" The queen's eyebrows almost hit the roof. "Are you insane?"

"Adele volunteered," he replied.

Insisted, despite his best arguments, if he was being honest.

"Then where am I to go?" the queen demanded. "What am I to do?"

Sir Gideon Scott leaned back in his chair. "That is where I come in. I have a small country estate very few people know about. You and I are going to slip out of the tower via one of Malloryn's secret passages and vanish to the country until Balfour is brought to heel. I have a carriage awaiting you as we speak."

"You planned this?" she gasped.

Scott scrubbed at his jaw. "I happen to agree with Malloryn on this matter. Balfour needs to be dealt with, and Malloryn has proof confirming the Ivory Tower is a target. The Coldrush Guards are compromised. The Echelon is full of Rising Sons. So we either remove the lot of them while we try to ascertain which of them are Balfour's, or we tempt them to make their play."

The queen looked at all of her councilors in turn, but Malloryn had spent half the night in secret meetings. They needed to present a united front.

"How intriguing," the queen drawled. "Not a one of you is protesting this idiot scheme. Do I even bother calling for a council vote? Or have you already had one?"

"It's for your own protection, my dear," said Mina, the Duchess of Casavian, as she circled the table and took her dearest friend's hand. "Think of it as a holiday. You *were* the one who was saying how you wish you'd been born a commoner just the other day. Well, now you get to be one."

"Mina and Barrons will be staying here," he told the queen. "Nobody would believe the Duchess of Casavian would abandon you. Sir Gideon will accompany you and play the gracious host; and Lynch and his wife, Rosalind, will be in your retinue for protection. We don't expect the ruse to be discovered, but we cannot be too certain. The fewer people outside this room who know you're gone, the better."

"I see," she said. "I'm leaving my country in your hands, Malloryn."

"I will protect it as if it were my own."

She sighed. "Don't destroy my city. Don't ruin my tower. And for God's sake, don't get yourself killed. You and I haven't had the last word on this subject."

He winked slowly at her. "As my queen commands."

The queen slipped away in the middle of the night with her small retinue of trusted guards.

Malloryn smuggled Adele into Alexandra's chambers, where he checked all the wardrobes and under the bed with a small mechanical apparatus that sensed listening devices before pronouncing the room clear. The rest of the Company of Rogues was interspersed among the guest chambers on the floor below them, and he'd requested a handful of Coldrush Guards he knew to be loyal to take guard duty.

Now it was just a matter of waiting.

"Well," Adele murmured, easing the queen's crown from her head and holding it reverently. "Life at your side is certainly entertaining. And touching this is better than holding an entire case filled with diamonds." She closed her eyes for a moment. "I am touching the queen's crown. I was *wearing* it on my head."

"Do you need a moment alone with the crown?"

"I think I'm going to sleep with it on," she whispered, sharing a conspiratorial smile with him.

"I've been replaced, have I?"

"Who said you'd ever earned your place in my bed?"

Her husband shook his head. "It's the diamonds, isn't it? If I glue one to my forehead, will I have your entire focus?"

"If you glue one somewhere else, you might."

He gave her a swat on the bottom. "I've created a monster."

Adele burst into laughter, and he shook his head at her. Opened his mouth to speak, and then closed it with what could only be described as a flash of chagrin darting across his expression.

"You have something to say," she interpreted.

"How do you do that?"

"See right through you?" She quirked a brow. "We embarked upon war, Malloryn, and the first act of engagement is to know your enemy. I think I'm finally starting to get a handle on how you think."

"Well, that makes one of us. You always seem to catch *me* by surprise."

Adele reached out and captured his fingers in hers. "You could just tell me what it is, you know? Someone once told me trust is an art that soothes the waters of marriage considerably."

"Sounds like a smart fellow." Malloryn said. "Turn around."

Adele obediently faced the mirror.

Malloryn loomed over her shoulder, his expression tightening, which was a sure sign of his emotional state.

"I'm not very good at this." Reaching around in front of her, he moved to put something around her throat. "But I wanted to give you something."

"I adore presents."

"I noticed," he murmured. "This is our last night together. Tomorrow, we set our trap and it wouldn't be wise for me to stay with you at night."

"That's all right. I have the crown."

A soft laugh escaped him. "I swear to God, Adele. I'm trying to be serious."

"So am I."

"I never thought I'd resent a hunk of gold and gemstones so much. With all the Devoncourts of the world flirting with you, it's a fucking crown that tempts you."

"*The* crown," she teased. "Every little girl dreams of being a princess. I could almost kiss you right now for making my dreams come true."

"Almost? Well." He leaned his chin on her shoulder as he examined her in the mirror. "Now you're making me wonder if my paltry gift is even worth it."

A heavy weight settled against her throat.

And despite her giddiness, she couldn't help feeling a little nervous. "You went shopping for me?"

"No."

Adele's smile slipped off her face as she saw what he was draping around her throat. "Oh, my goodness. My pearls."

"I had them fixed for you," he said as he gently worked the clasp. "They were your grandmother's. I know how much they meant to you."

Adele touched the pearls as if to make certain they were real. Her heart started thumping. "How did you know they were my grandmother's?"

"You told me. On our wedding day. For all your talk of diamonds and precious gems, you chose to wear your sentimental favorites."

He'd remembered?

Tears glittered in her eyes. They were perfectly put back together. If she hadn't been there when Jelena broke them, she wouldn't have believed they'd even been ruined.

And how had he...? With everything that had been going on, he'd remembered her pearls and gotten them fixed. The thoughtfulness shocked her.

"Better than a crown?"

Emotion thickened in her throat, choking her. All she

could do was nod.

"Good. Because while we have this chance, I wanted one last night with you. And I want it to be perfect." Malloryn's voice turned soft and teasing. "Good gods, are you crying?"

Adele turned and slid a hand into his hair as she dragged his face down to hers. Their lips touched and then Malloryn kissed her. Truly kissed her. Lazy and slow and heated in all the good ways.

This was the Malloryn she desired.

The one who claimed her mouth without a single hesitation.

The one who stole her breath—her thoughts—with the heated, slick dart of his tongue.

The one who tenderly brushed her cheek with his thumb as he slowly drew back, looking down into her eyes with an expression she couldn't read.

Her Auvry.

"Thank you. Thank you for fixing them."

He rested his forehead against hers, his breath stirring against her swollen lips. "We've come a long way together. Who would have thought?"

"From threatening castration to stolen kisses," she joked.

"From doing everything to avoid going home, to trying to find where in my house my wife is hidden," he said, his mouth softening into a smile.

"Preferably in your bed."

"Preferably," he agreed.

"Can I tell you a secret?" she whispered, biting her lip.

"I have an entire network of spies at my behest. There's nothing I enjoy more than secrets."

You might not enjoy this one. Adele closed her eyes. "I love you."

He drew back sharply, the humor fleeing from his eyes. "Don't tempt fate—"

She put a finger to his lips, shaking her head. It was time to be brave. "I know *why* you don't want me to tell you that. You see it as a burden, as one more weight on your shoulders should I fall."

"Adele—"

"You said it yourself," she whispered. "This is our last chance to be together before we confront him. And I cannot help thinking, what if I don't ever get a chance to say it? I love you, and I'm not afraid to say it. I want to say it."

"It's not a burden," he whispered, cupping her face between his hands. "Never that."

And then he kissed her again.

There was a desperation to his actions; not merely hunger or desire, but something almost frantic.

One hand cupped her bottom, dragging her firmly against him until they were chest to chest, groin to groin.

"You're not going to lose me," Adele promised, the moment he let her come up for air. It haunted every line of him, his hands clinging to her as if he was afraid to let her go, even for an instant. "We are going to defeat Balfour and make him wish he'd never happened upon either of us."

"I just wish he was dead." A shudder ran through him as he stroked his thumb longingly down her side. "I've carried that bastard like a noose around my throat for almost seventeen years. I want to live in a world where his ghost no longer haunts me. I want to...." He clearly sought the right words. "I want to tell my wife how much she means to me."

Those words.

They ricocheted through her like an arrow given flight.

"Does she?" Adele's heart hammered. "Does she

mean something to you?"

Malloryn stared down at her, his heart splayed wide in his eyes. And she realized he could not say it. Could not force the words past his lips.

"*Everything*," he said simply.

Just that.

A word that held so much more in it.

She'd thought him cold, once upon a time, but it was merely a mask. One she recognized, for she'd worn it too. If you didn't let anyone in, then you couldn't be hurt again.

It didn't mean you didn't feel deeply.

It didn't mean you couldn't be hurt.

And it didn't mean you couldn't love somebody, even if you couldn't bring yourself to say it.

"I love you," she whispered, saying the words he couldn't. It set her free in some way. Unfurled something within her that had been so tightly guarded for so long. Adele leaned onto her toes and pressed her lips gently against his. "And I will love you for as long as we both live. I will love you, even if you think you are not worthy of it. I will love you even when you are too afraid to tell me the same."

A shudder tore through him. "Adele."

"I will love you when you push me against bookcases. And throw me over your shoulder." She felt his mouth soften against hers, and eased her tongue against his. A soft, petting caress as she breathed into his mouth, "I will love you when you threaten to lock me away for my own good. And I will even love you when you are being your arrogant best and clearly wrong."

His eyelashes stirred against her cheeks as he drew back, cupping her face with an expression she couldn't name. "And when you throw books at my head?"

"Especially then."

He breathed out a laugh. "I'll consider myself a lucky man as I'm dodging glassware and curses."

"That's the spirit," Adele whispered, and then smiled. She felt the smile blaze within her, lighting her from within. Happy. In this moment, all she knew was happiness.

Malloryn's breath caught in his chest, as if she'd somehow knocked him for six. "You ruin me. You always have. You're like a cannonball that's obliterated every aspect of my life."

"We're going to have to work on your delivery," she said. "You're severely lacking in poetry."

"Adele."

She bit his finger. "I know."

And then he was laughing helplessly, as if her happiness was contagious. He stole another kiss, and the roughness of his hands was a little unsteady on her skin.

This time it was long and slow and deep, holding the promise of everything he wanted to do to her. He pushed her back, toward the bed, and Adele went with a shiver.

"Are you planning to ravish me in the queen's suite?"

"Yes." He captured her mouth again, hands stroking down her sides. "A thousand times, yes."

"Do you—" She gasped. "—think I could wear the crown?"

Malloryn bit her lip sharply, a growl echoing in his throat as she burst into a cascade of laughter.

Reaching down, he slung her up over his shoulder and strode toward the bed. "Why did I ever think you were going to be a cool, biddable bride?"

"I don't know," she replied. "The idea baffles me too."

And then she gave a squeal of laughter as he tossed her onto her back in the middle of the queen's bed and followed her down with a smile.

CHAPTER THIRTY-THREE

The day of the queen's parade arrived.

This was it.

Adele nervously smoothed her borrowed finery into place as Malloryn barked orders and snapped commands.

Tension etched his hard frame as he sent the Rogues scurrying. Gemma saw her watching and rolled her eyes behind his back. Far below them, the carriage was brought out, its gilt edges twinkling in the sunlight, and Adele could hear people chanting the queen's name, the sound floating up to the heights of the tower on the breeze.

"Are you ready?" Malloryn asked, finally turning to her.

No.

It had been easy to commit to this before she'd realized she had a target painted on her back. Easy to jest about the crown jewels when thousands of people weren't out there calling the queen's name. Someone had to realize she was a fraud. Someone would notice.

Or worse, they'd put a bullet in her head.

"Breathe," Malloryn warned her, cupping a gentle

hand against her cheek. "The parade route is patrolled by so many Nighthawks, nobody's going to get near enough to take a shot."

"This corset is too tight."

Of course, said his eyes. "It's the steel inserts. I won't let anyone hurt you."

She didn't care who saw them then. All of the servants around them knew of the ruse, and Gemma wouldn't care. Adele grabbed a fistful of his shirt and hauled him down for a kiss.

A kiss to catch her balance.

A kiss to ground her.

One last chance to touch him before she had to perform.

Malloryn drew back, breathing hard. He rested his forehead against hers. "You're going to ruin my reputation. If anyone sees us, they'll think I'm having an affair with the queen."

"I'm fairly certain Sir Gideon Scott might have something to say about that."

He looked at her sharply. "Scott?"

"You haven't seen the way he looks at her? And she at him? They're besotted with each other, though neither dares make the first move."

It was clear he hadn't.

"Oh, Malloryn." Adele slid her hands inside his coat, resting her forehead against his chest, where she could hear his heart beating. "How can you be so all-knowing, and yet so blind to what's happening right beneath your nose?"

"*The queen?*"

"I thought that was why you sent her off to his estate with him." All those little plots, and he'd missed the most delicious one. "A masterful stroke, I thought."

"Suffice it to say," he grumbled, "but I don't always

see what's right beneath my nose. Especially when it comes to people wearing their hearts on their sleeves. Scott and the queen? Who would have guessed?" He frowned. "I've been pushing her to consider a European prince."

"Do you think she'll accept one of their proposals?"

"Considering she practically snarled at me when I suggested it, my hopes remain low." Malloryn stepped back, a considering look on his face.

Adele recognized it. "You have your 'meddling' face on. I shouldn't have told you."

"Scott might make an ideal consort. He's the head of the Humans First party, a councilor, and decidedly conservative in his decisions."

"You mean, he listens to you?"

Malloryn flashed her a smile. "Sometimes. More importantly, he talks her around when she's being irrational. The humans of London would rejoice, though this will cause problems among the Echelon. A human queen and a human consort? Even those blue bloods who've accepted the new way of doing things will grumble about it."

Adele fixed his collar. "It's nice to see you plotting the future of the realm again. But perhaps this can wait until we kill Lord Balfour and hang his remaining Rising Sons."

"I never knew you were so bloodthirsty."

"Dead enemies don't cause future problems."

"You practically read my mind sometimes." Malloryn captured her hand and lifted it to his lips. "Do you know, if we survive this, I think we're going to make a formidable pair."

"Oh, Malloryn." She rolled her eyes. "We've been a formidable pair ever since you surrendered to me."

"Did I surrender?"

Adele shot him a wicked smile. "Many, many times."

The parade through the streets was a nerve-wracking affair.

Adele waved at the crowd from a closed carriage with Gemma, Ingrid, and Lark, whilst Malloryn rode at the head of the column and deployed his teams of Coldrush Guards with a stern hand. Adele forced herself to smile, buoyed by the throng of humans and mechs who swarmed the parade route, waving the queen's colors in the air.

Nothing had been left to chance.

Charlie and Jack were working with a scrambling device Lena had created during the revolution in order to counteract any automaton attacks; Obsidian, Byrnes, and Kincaid made dashing Coldrush Guards; and the Nighthawks' dirigible prowled overhead. Several nearby contingents were prepared to whisk her out of the way the second any signs of danger erupted.

Balfour, curse the man, declined to accept the opportunity they'd presented, though an assassination attempt during the parade had been the lowest of Malloryn's suspected possibilities for the day.

Gemma eased a sigh of relief as they rode beneath the arches of the gate towers that guarded the Ivory Tower. "Well, ladies. It looks like tonight is going to be the night."

Adele breathed a sigh of relief. "Thank goodness. I can't wait to get out of this armored corset."

"I'm sure Malloryn will assist you." Gemma looked completely innocent.

"But then we'll never get to the ball."

Everyone who was anyone in the Echelon was invited.

Especially those on a certain membership list.

Malloryn wanted nothing left to chance. He wanted them to take their shot at him when he dictated, not when they did.

The ballroom practically glittered, there were so many lights, and the mirrors that lined the chamber made it seem as though there were thousands of guests.

"What the hell is Balfour waiting for?" Adele murmured as she accepted a glass of watered-down wine that Malloryn provided for her. Her husband was carefully managing the aristocrats who attempted to get close to her, keeping them at enough distance to maintain her subterfuge, but her nerves were frayed around the edges.

"A chance," he murmured, surveying the ballroom and the Nighthawks who were wearing the Coldrush Guards uniform. They surrounded the ballroom discreetly.

"Maybe you scared him away?"

"He'll be here. I can feel it."

There was a slightly feral gleam to his eye, and black bled through his irises. Every inch of him quivered with the intense desire to finally get his hands on Balfour.

Out of everything, it was this fact that bothered her the most.

She couldn't help feeling as though their time together was slowly ticking to an end.

People danced. Debutantes laughed. Lords watched her with glittering eyes.

She recognized several of their faces as men to be wary of. They circled the ballroom in small droves, and Adele tried not to stare at them. Sweat dripped down her spine. Thank goodness she'd told Lena and Hattie to avoid the celebrations tonight. She could almost feel that target painted between her breasts.

But when she blinked again, only friendly faces smiled back at her.

Barrons started a toast to the queen. "...and as we usher in a new day, so do we celebrate a new era of..."

She could barely make out what he was saying. "Where have they all gone?"

Malloryn had been pretending to laugh at something the Duchess of Casavian said, but he turned to her sharply. "Who?"

"The Rising Sons," she said through her teeth. "I can't see any of them anymore."

He raked the crowd with his gaze and reached up, very slowly, to tug at his earlobe. Several Nighthawks noticed Malloryn's signal and straightened.

The enormous clock began to chime midnight, sending a portentous shiver down Adele's spine.

Its peal rang slowly; *one, two, three, four, five—*

"If we could charge our glasses?" Barrons called.

A choreographed wave of glassware glittered in front of her. She couldn't help looking for a malevolent stare, but all she could see was the flash of gleaming white teeth. No Rising Sons anywhere.

"*Malloryn,*" she whispered sharply.

"To her Majesty, Queen Alexandra!"

—six, seven, eight, nine—

BOOM.

BOOM.

BOOM.

It sounded like fireworks, but they weren't scheduled yet, were they? There was supposed to be some grand conflagration just before dawn to herald the rising of the sun in some sort of symbolic gesture.

Every guest in front of her froze.

Malloryn's hand locked around her upper arm, prepared to haul her to safety if need be. "That." Malloryn clasped the hilt of the sword sheathed at his hip with his other hand. "He's been waiting for that."

"What the hell is going on?"

"We're under attack," he replied grimly, pressing a finger to the earpiece in his ear. "Ava? Jack? What have you got for me?"

Another explosion ricocheted through the night, and this time it felt as though it detonated nearby. The entire tower seemed to shudder.

Adele screamed as a chunk of the roof crashed down, sending a pair of debutantes sprawling. Lords and ladies fled the center of the dance floor in a panic of silk and velvet.

Plaster dust rained down, painting Malloryn's coppery hair white. He looked up, tensing as he listened to the information clearly relayed through his earpiece.

Another explosion rattled the tower. Adele staggered into him.

"Where is that coming from?"

"Protect the queen!" he bellowed, shoving her behind him into the waiting arms of Gemma and Ingrid.

The cacophony of sound continued.

Another detonation shattered every window along the north side of the ballroom. Glass spewed into the ballroom. Screams filled the air.

"Sound the alarms!" Malloryn bellowed, for the sake of the crowd. "And find out where that noise is coming from! Someone's setting off explosives."

"Where's the source?" Gemma demanded as she put herself bodily between Adele and the crowd, her pistol held low, hidden in the folds of her diaphanous skirts.

"I don't know yet," he snarled. "Clear the room!"

Several guards surrounded her, forming a bodily mass. The rest started pushing the frightened guests through the doors. Until they could work out where the explosions were coming from, there was no point fleeing.

Adele slid her little knife into her hand, though she was trembling so badly she didn't know what she'd be able to do with it.

"He knows where we are." Malloryn's face tightened with strain. "He's going to drive us out of the ballroom."

Gemma whirled her skirt away from her waist, revealing tight leather trousers and half a dozen knives strapped to her at various places. "We need information," she said as Obsidian appeared at her side. "Obsidian and I can work out what's going on. Ava and Kincaid may not be in the right position."

Malloryn hesitated only a second before he nodded curtly. "Watch your back. Dido's still out there."

"Yes, Father." Gemma rolled her eyes again. "Please. Tell me how to run reconnaissance again."

"Haven't you been doing this since you were off short strings?" Obsidian drawled, loading bullets into a dangerous-looking pistol.

"I don't know," Gemma replied, mock seriously. "Weren't you once the most feared assassin in Europe?"

"Ha. Ha," Malloryn said. "I don't know why I even bother, some days."

But Adele knew their banter had a purpose.

"I'll watch her back," Obsidian promised, as if could sense Malloryn's concern.

Then the pair of them vanished.

Malloryn turned to her. "Are you ready?"

Adele nodded at him.

"Good." He glanced toward Ingrid. "On my signal, prepare to get her out of here."

CHAPTER THIRTY-FOUR

"Your Grace, it appears to be coming from Thorne Tower!" One of the guards told them after a swift glance through the ruined windows. "They're firing on us!"

"The headquarters of the Coldrush Guards," Charlie said, pausing by the windows to get a better look.

"Stay there," Malloryn told her. He pressed a hand to his earpiece, trying to tune it. "Kincaid? Are you there? The cannons in Thorne Tower are firing on us. Can you find out what the hell is going on down there? Have they breached the walls? Is there any sign of anyone approaching?"

He listened intently to the tinny reply, and Adele watched his face tighten.

"It's one cannon," he said.

"What's its range?" Charlie asked. "Because those explosions are happening too frequently for one cannon to manage, and I doubt it would have hit us up here."

Malloryn relayed the information through the communicator, and then looked up. "Ava said she thought it was coming from the servants' quarters."

"What the hell is going on?" Byrnes snapped.

"So it's coming from both inside and outside the tower." Malloryn spoke his thoughts out loud.

Adele was so intent upon him, that she almost missed the movement at the corner of her eye.

The nearest metaljacket turned and lifted its arm cannon, the round end locking directly upon her. Adele froze. Her husband had assured her the two metaljackets in the room were defunct and purely there to lull the Rising Sons into a false sense of security. He'd had Jack check the chips in their heads himself.

"Malloryn?" she called.

He glanced across the throne room at her, seeing the threat immediately.

"Protect the queen!" Malloryn bellowed, and then he was sprinting directly toward her.

Heat flared to life deep in the heart of the spitfire's cannon. Adele stood mesmerized, her heartbeat ticking out the seconds as the press of her corset strained against her agitated ribs.

And then fire bloomed, a gush of it spewing directly toward her.

Malloryn drove into her like a freight train, and she slammed into the marble tiles as fire gushed overhead. It licked against the tapestries behind the throne, curling up the walls as the metaljacket maneuvered slowly, trying to find its target with its sensors.

"Stay down!" Malloryn said, lifting his head to see what was going on. "Byrnes! Charlie!"

Both of the enormous, ceremonial metaljackets lumbered forward, iron-plated boots striking the marble. These were the Firebird models, and virtually unstoppable without water cannons or arm cannons.

Adele screamed as the fire bloomed again, spraying

over the top of her and Malloryn. Heat blistered her skin, but Malloryn shoved his body over the top of her and grunted as the stink of burning wool filled the air.

His weight suddenly shifted as he tore his coat off, tossing it aside before pushing her in the back. "Move!"

Adele scrambled toward the throne, peering out from behind it. "What's *wrong* with them?"

"I don't know!" he yelled back. "Someone must have tampered with them."

"But Jack checked them!"

Everything was happening all at once.

Malloryn drew his pistol, crouching by her side as he surveyed affairs.

Byrnes tried to kick one of the metaljackets behind its knee joint, before it swung its massive fist at him. Ingrid drove her knife between the fine gap of its chest plate, cursing under her breath as the blade stuck.

"Get clear!" Byrnes yelled, wrenching her out of the way as fire bloomed from its flamethrower.

"This big bastard is mine!" Charlie yelled, sprinting toward the other automaton.

He slid to his knees beneath a gush of fire as it turned on him, and rolled a handful of golden orbs toward the metaljacket. The orbs quivered as they changed course, rolling toward its steel boots as if magnetized.

Each orb split in two, little spindly legs erupting in an insect-like fashion as the orb rearranged itself into a carapace. Tiny golden spiders. And then they were crawling up the metaljacket's boots, sparks erupting between their pincers as they found the connecting wires in the knee joint.

The metaljacket's glass eyes flashed a warning as sparks spat out of its joints. And then it was sinking slowly to its knees and landing on its metal face with a clatter.

There was nothing she could do except stay out of the way.

"Stay here," Malloryn demanded. "Lark!"

The young woman backed away from the fight, knives held at the ready. "Last line of defense," she repeated, as if they'd had this conversation several times already.

Malloryn grabbed a stunner that one of the Nighthawks tossed toward him. The long poles had thin metal loops on the ends of them that could be electrified with a push of the button. He swung it at the last metaljacket, hooking the loop around its steel-plated head. The monstrous metal beast jerked and spasmed as current arced through it.

The second he released the trigger, Byrnes launched a flying kick at its face, metal crunching around his boot as the steaming hulk slowly toppled with the clatter.

Both metaljackets were down.

"Nice work, Your Grace," Byrnes said, breathing hard.

Ingrid yanked her knife out of the breastplate, leaning all her weight on the metaljacket to do so. "How did Jack miss it?"

"This might be the problem," Charlie called, having rolled one of them over. He yanked a small, magnetized device off the back of the metaljacket's head. "It looks like some sort of frequency-altering device that must have overridden the control chip. I can pull it apart later when we get a chance, but I daresay it's the cause."

Adele eased her way out from behind the throne. "Now what?"

"Evacuate Adele," Malloryn said to both women.

"We don't know which parts of the tower have been compromised," Lark replied. "The tunnels might be nothing more than rubble by now."

"Then go to Plan B. There's a bloody reason I

approved the funding for that damned dirigible. It wasn't so the Nighthawks could take scenic flights in it."

Ingrid glanced at her. "Care for a flight, Your Grace?"

"Go with Lark and Ingrid," he told her, a smear of soot across his cheek.

"What about you?" she demanded.

The line of his jaw tensed. "I have to finish this, Adele. I have to make sure he dies this time."

"The entire tower's on fire! He's called your bluff."

As if to punctuate her words, something else exploded.

"He's here somewhere, I know he is—"

"Please," she whispered. "Please come with us. Come with me...."

Malloryn turned his face away from her touch. "I can't." Capturing her hand, he pressed it to his lips, his eyes raw with unspoken words. "I'll see you at home."

Then he turned, heading into the smoke.

Adele stared after him, her heart in her throat, aware of all the eyes watching them.

Just before he was about to vanish, he paused.

And then he was striding back toward her. Capturing her face in his hands, he pressed his lips to hers. Adele wrapped her arms around his neck, clinging to him as he kissed her, long and slow and deep. She didn't want this moment to end, for the second it did, he'd walk away from her again, she knew it.

This was goodbye.

All the things left unspoken between them poured into a moment of perfection. Of need and desire, and a thousand little secret confessions.

And then Malloryn finally drew back, carefully disengaging her arms from around his neck.

"I love you," he whispered, his eyes gleaming bright

gray in contrast to the soot on his cheeks. "I have tried not to. I knew I was breaking every single promise I ever made myself when I looked at you. But I couldn't help myself. You drive me crazy, Adele. But you also give me back a piece of myself I thought I'd lost."

Another kiss, her arms locking around his neck.

And then he was capturing her wrists, lowering her hands in front of her, his expression grim. "And so I want you to go. If I don't make it, go and live your life. Be happy. Be free."

She knew what he was saying.

He didn't think he was going to survive.

"Come with me!"

"I can't." Malloryn cupped her hand against his cheek. "This needs to end, Adele. One way or another, one of us has to die. If I walk away, he'll scuttle free, and then there'll be more dead girls in the streets. More explosions. More killing. He'll come after the queen again. He'll come after you. I can stop it. I have to stop it."

"None of this was your fault!" she cried.

"*Adele.*"

The way he said her name always cut right through her. But this time, there was a slight pleading undertone.

"Know this," he said. "I want that future we spoke of. I will fight for that, if nothing else. And I will come home to you if I can. But you need to go now, before the tower goes down." His mouth softened into a smile. "Be brave."

And let me go....

She didn't want to go.

Heavens knew what Malloryn faced. But if his attention was focused on protecting her, then he'd be at risk himself.

She couldn't afford to distract him when he went face-to-face with Balfour.

Adele steeled herself, drawing on years of experience to swallow down the fear inside her. "Go and kill him. And you had better come home to me, Auvry, or I am going to be most put out."

"As you wish. Fall back," Malloryn commanded, pushing her toward Lark and Ingrid. "Keep her safe for me, please."

"*I love you*," she mouthed, before she turned away from him.

Before she could linger any further.

"This way, Your Grace," Lark said, gesturing her to the back of the throne.

Ingrid tore a burning tapestry from one of the walls, revealing a secret passage behind it. "I'll go first. Cover me."

The three of them fled along the corridor and appeared outside on one of the enormous spiral staircases up the center of the tower. Each staircase twined around the other, so you couldn't see anyone travelling up or down the other staircase.

Another loud explosion sent them all sprawling.

Smoke poured up through the hollow of the tower, and Adele lay winded as the entire structure shook. "Is Balfour insane? He's taking out the base of the tower!"

Perhaps, after all this time, he'd finally given up on taking power and merely sought revenge.

Ingrid hauled her to her feet. "Keep moving! We need to reach the top of the tower and signal the *Nightingale*."

A second explosion sounded closer. Nearby. Adele screamed as she was slammed into the wall. Pieces of shrapnel flew past them, landing with a tinny bang against the wall. One large piece clattered down the stairs toward them.

"What the hell was that?" Ingrid demanded, spinning

in that direction with her knives drawn.

Lark bent to pick up the domed helmet, flinching from the heat of it. "It looks like some sort of—"

"Oh, my God. It's a Mowbray!" Adele cried suddenly, recognizing the piece of machinery. All the facts suddenly rearranged themselves inside her head. The Prometheus Project had never been about the metaljackets. They were merely the distraction.

"What in bloody rot and ruin is a Mowbray?" Ingrid demanded.

Adele took the domed helmet from Lark and shook it. "*This* is a Mowbray! Or part of one. They're in almost every aristocratic home!"

Recognition dawned in Lark's eyes. "Household automatons."

"The best on the market." Adele wanted to slam her palm to her forehead. "Of course! There was some sort of shortage fault discovered in the previous models the tower used. A Paxton Elite burned the Earl of Ardmore's townhouse down, and the bloody council ordered their Paxtons all replaced six months ago. It was a major scandal in all the papers and sent the other manufacturer broke. The tower scrapped the other contract and went with Mowbrays. Balfour didn't need to smuggle explosives inside the tower! They were already here, packed inside each Mowbray in the tower. He must have been waiting for this day for months. I'll bet my best diamonds they're all full of explosives."

"And now they're exploding," Ingrid said, her eyes growing distant. "They're destroying the tower from the inside."

Lark put her hand to her earpiece. "I'll tell Ava."

"And then we need to go," Ingrid warned. "Who knows how many bloody automatons are strewn throughout this section of the tower."

Lark relayed the message, and Ingrid pushed Adele in the back. "Move."

But Adele skidded to a halt on the next curve of stairs.

A tall, slim figure stalked through the smoke, a pair of swords held at her side. She wore tight trousers that showed the muscles in her thighs, a leather overcorset, and a long bloodred coat that flared around her calves as she slowly made her way down the stairs toward them.

"You're not the queen," Dido said, her silvery brows drawing together. Then she suddenly smiled as she drew both swords. "Malloryn's little wife. This is even better."

"Do you think the women got clear?" Malloryn demanded as he, Charlie, and Byrnes staggered to a halt on the staircase.

It had taken the three of them to defeat a second set of metaljackets who'd turned on them the second they left the throne room. Blood dripped down Charlie's shirt, though the lad had been singlehandedly responsible for taking both automatons off their feet and giving them a chance.

"Can't hear them," Byrnes said, his head turning to-and-fro. "Ingrid will know the way."

"What is Balfour thinking?" Charlie demanded, leaning on the edge of the bannister and peering down the hollow core of the tower. "How are we going to get out of here?"

Malloryn joined him, squinting through the smoke. The entire ground floor of the tower must be on fire.

"Gemma?" he demanded, pressing the tuning button on his auditory device.

A long, staticky silence dwelled.

"Little... busy... right now," she finally gasped. "Rising Sons overrunning... Thorne Tower. Obsidian's helping me... take out the cannons, just in case they get... hands on another one. Kincaid and Herbert with us."

"Right." He depressed the button, turning to the other two men. "Gemma's team is handling the crisis at Thorne Tower. Ava said something about explosives being packed inside every household automaton in the entire building." Of which, there were hundreds, always sweeping unobtrusively or removing household waste. You barely even noticed the damned things anymore. "We've got to find Balfour and get out of here before this entire bloody place goes up."

The queen was going to kill him.

She'd deliberately stressed that he not get her tower destroyed.

"Come and find me, Malloryn."

The words ghosted down the stairs, almost on the edge of hearing.

He paused. "Did you hear that?"

Byrnes looked up grimly. "Sounds like a dead man to me."

There was one more level to the tower: the atrium, where blue blood duels were fought and won, and rogue blue bloods had been executed in the past.

"Malloryn?" Charlie asked.

His body moved as if some invisible puppet master tugged on his strings. "He's here," he whispered, looking up. "Balfour's here."

Ingrid shoved Adele through a pair of double doors into what looked like a sitting room as a knife buried itself in the frame.

Behind them, Lark was ducking and weaving, using every inch of her speed to avoid Dido's deadly swords.

"Keep out of this," Ingrid snarled, her eyes lighting with fierce bronze as she turned toward Dido and drew her own knife.

The *dhampir* woman was a whirlwind of steel as she kicked Lark firmly in the chest. Lark staggered back into Ingrid, and then Dido was turning on Adele, her eyes alight with maniacal glee.

"I'd like to extend an invitation, Your Grace," the assassin purred. "Lord Balfour would very much like to meet the woman who's captured Malloryn's heart."

It wasn't the sort of encounter she'd survive.

Adele turned, yanked a vase off a pedestal, and threw it at the woman as she advanced. Dido deflected it with an arm, but it didn't slow her.

"As for me," Dido murmured, fingers caressing the hilt of both swords. "You killed my sister-at-arms. So I thought I'd just bring Balfour your head. We can put it in a pretty box for your husband and tie a bow on it."

Adele scrambled over the daybed, the sword slashing through her skirts.

"Adele!" Lark screamed.

And then Ingrid threw herself at Dido, driving both of them to the ground. The tall Amazonian woman drove a pair of staggering punches into Dido's ribs, and the pair rolled as they wrestled for supremacy.

"Adele!" Lark tossed something toward her.

Adele snatched it out of the air.

A Doeppler Orb.

"I can't use it," Lark cried, "but Malloryn made sure

we all had one."

Hope flared.

"Cover your mouth!" Adele yelled, cupping both hands around the Doeppler Orb.

Lark fell back as Ingrid took a blow to the ribs, jerking the filtration mask up over her mouth and nose. Every blue blood in the Company of Rogues had one tucked about their person somewhere, what with the dangers of Black Vein.

Adele twisted both halves of the orb as Ava had shown her, and then threw it toward where Ingrid and Dido were grappling. Diffused steam hissed out from it as the orb clicked apart, tendrils of fine mist curling around Ingrid and Dido, where they fought.

It wouldn't affect Ingrid, but Dido was another matter.

Ingrid lashed out with both knives and Dido leapt up on the daybed to avoid them. She'd lost one of her swords somewhere.

Adele kicked the daybed.

Hard.

The *dhampir* shot her a murderous look as it jerked beneath her feet, and Ingrid managed to bury one of her knives in the woman's side. Dido hissed through her teeth and slammed an elbow into Ingrid's head, sending her staggering.

The mist from the Doeppler Orb started to stutter. Black capillaries bled through Dido's face, but perhaps the room was too large? It didn't seem to be having the same effect as it had on Jelena.

"Get her out of here!" Ingrid yelled, her eyes flashing a fierce bronze.

Lark hauled her toward the door.

"Not without Ingrid!" she insisted.

"Malloryn's orders," Lark replied grimly.

"Bugger Malloryn and his orders," she insisted. "No Rogue left behind. Isn't that the COR creed?"

Lark hesitated, and Adele cursed herself for being so spectacularly useless in the face of violence.

As if to taunt them, Dido drove her knife between Ingrid's ribs.

"Ingrid!" Lark cried, moving forward and then hesitating.

"Go!" Adele told her. "I'll manage."

Arms locked around Dido, Ingrid staggered back as Dido knifed her again.

It was all happening so fast. Adele didn't know what to do.

Lark reentered the fray as Ingrid staggered back a step, one hand slapped to the bleeding wound at her side.

Adele could see what was going to happen.

With Ingrid injured, Lark was no match for the vicious assassin.

Turning around, she grabbed an enormous Chinese urn off a nearby pedestal and lifted it over her head.

She slammed the urn down on the back of Dido's shoulders. A hand lashed out, knuckles filling the center of Adele's vision, and then she was staggering backward, dropping the urn on the marble tiles. Heat spread across her face, her eyes watering. Good God, was her nose broken?

Ingrid's eyes flashed bronze as she shot both Lark and Adele an anguished look. "Tell Byrnes I love him."

And then she muscled Dido to the side, throwing her back against the window. Glass shattered, and Dido's eyes went wide as she clawed at Ingrid's shoulders.

Locked together as they were, Ingrid had no chance of saving herself.

Lark and Adele screamed in horror as the pair of them vanished through the window.

"Ingrid!" Adele yelled, sprinting to the window and peering through its broken remains with Lark wedged against her.

Ingrid lay flat on her back on the marble colonnade that circled the ballroom three floors below them, groaning as she tried to roll onto her side—and failed.

Dido pushed to her hands and knees, swaying badly.

"Will this bitch not die?" Lark snarled. "Get up, Ingrid. Come on, get up."

But Ingrid couldn't move, and Dido was the one with the weapon in hand.

"We have to do something," Adele gasped.

"Come and find me, Malloryn," whispered that ghostly voice.

Malloryn tracked it up the stairs, a pistol held low against his thigh and a knife in his left hand. He reached a corner and heard Balfour chuckle. Pressing his back to the wall, he put one finger to his lips to still Charlie and Byrnes, and then eased out his breath.

Rolling out into the hallway he aimed the pistol and—

There was no one there.

"All these years," Balfour murmured, somewhere to the left of him. *"I've been waiting for this moment."*

A pair of open doors awaited him.

Tension crept through him as he put one foot in front of the other, crossing the carpets. He slipped through the doors, pistol tracking the room. A sitting room, by the look of it. One of the guest chambers.

"Revenge shall be so very sweet."

Left again.

Near the windows.

But surely no one could fit behind the curtains?

Malloryn yanked the curtain aside, his stomach falling as he saw a small ECHO recording device he'd seen the Nighthawks use on occasion. It's clockwork mechanism wound through the prerecorded reel of Balfour's voice.

As if to mock him, the words repeated, *"Come and find me, Malloryn.... All these years...."*

He jammed his heel down on the brass device, cogs spewing from its body as the recording cut off. "Son of a bitch."

"It's a trap," Charlie said, spinning around.

"Yes." Malloryn sheathed his rage. "But who is it designed for?"

"Can anyone hear something ticking?" Byrnes asked. "Or is that just my ears ringing?"

They all froze.

Tick. Tick. Tick.

There was no clock on the mantle.

"Under the sofa," Byrnes breathed, and as one, they all looked at it.

The ticking sped up.

"Move!" Malloryn yelled, yanking Charlie toward the door.

They were barely through it when a blast wave went up, slamming him in the back and sending him sprawling across the marble floors. Charlie hit the railing of the staircase, his eyes widening as he started going over it.

Somehow Byrnes managed to grab him and haul him back to safe ground.

"*Thanks,*" Charlie mouthed.

Malloryn shoved to his feet, his ears ringing. Little bits of shrapnel had shredded his arms, and he could feel the craving rushing through him as it sought to heal him.

Bit by bit, the whining in his ears stopped. Behind him, the doors were gone. Half the wall had vanished. Smoke billowed from the remains of the sitting room and flames licked at what was left of the furnishings.

And there was still no sign of Balfour.

Byrnes frowned behind him. "Malloryn?" He had his fingers on his communicator, his face paling.

"What?" he barked.

"It's Ingrid," Byrnes said, and took off sprinting before either he or Charlie could stop him.

"Damn it! Byrnes!" Malloryn went after him, but as he rounded a corner, he slowed to a halt.

Half a dozen blue blood lords were sprinting up the stairs toward them, heavily armed, as Byrnes burst right through the center of them.

Every single one of them wore a golden sash over their court attire, with a pin jabbed into their breasts: a rising sun in stylized gold.

Devoncourt was in the lead.

"Tell Byrnes I love him…."

The words echoed through Byrnes's head as he sprinted through the tower, trying to find his wife.

The second he'd heard them through the communicator, he'd known.

Ingrid was verwulfen to her core, and Malloryn had given her an order to protect his wife. It didn't matter what Ingrid had to do, she would give her life for that command.

He had to find her.

Before it was too late.

"Here's my pistol." Lark gave it to Adele. "Don't go anywhere. Shoot anybody you don't recognize."

Here goes nothing.

Putting her knife between her teeth, Lark caught hold of the velvet drapery and ran at the gaping window.

Leaping through it, Lark sailed through the air, trying not to look down. They were nearly at the top of the tower, and for a second she could almost hear Charlie telling her there were at least a thousand stairs from the base to the top, which was not what she needed to be thinking about right now. The second she started swinging back toward the tower, she gauged the drop and let go.

Air whistled past her ears.

Her heels slammed right between Dido's shoulder blades, and Lark turned her fall into a roll, coming up with her knife in her hand. She crouched over Ingrid protectively.

"Get up," she said, never taking her eyes off the assassin. The woman was backlit by the flames burning in the ballroom.

"I can't," Ingrid growled. "I can't move my legs. I landed on my back—"

There was no time to examine her.

Lark drove to the side as Dido lunged for her, steel flashing in the night. A hot line of fire rose along her arm as she lashed back with her own knife, feeling it bite into flesh.

She was no match for the dhampir by herself. All she could do was lure her away and hope Ingrid could get to her feet.

Dido slowly stood, blood streaming down her leg from where Lark had cut her. "Irina Grigoriev. We meet again."

"This time, you don't have any vampires on a leash."

"Yes." Dido smiled. "But there's only one of you."

A boot drove into her sternum, and Lark flew backwards, crashing to the marble and sliding several feet. The air was driven from her lungs, but she'd been hit before. Many a time.

Muscle memory forced her to roll back over her shoulder, and Dido's sword spit sparks off the marble as it cut down exactly where Lark had been mere seconds ago. She ducked the next swing. And the next. Every inch of her was focused on Dido's movements, but she was simply too damned slow.

Lark's knife flew to the tiles as Dido smashed it from her hand. And then she was throwing herself back beneath the sweep of the blade and fetching up against the broken windows of the ballroom.

Nowhere to go.

No weapon to protect herself with.

For the first time in her life, Lark froze, wondering where Charlie was and hoping against hope that he got out of this mess safely.

"You put up a good fight," Dido said. "I respect that. A shame it had to end this way. I could have made something of you."

She took a step forward, lifting her sword.

Lark threw her arms up in front of her face.

BANG.

Lark froze, lowering her arms as Dido looked down in shock at the enormous gaping wound in her chest.

BANG. BANG. BANG.

Dido staggered back against the balcony. Blood sprayed across the floor as Byrnes came out of nowhere, drilling holes in the dhampir assassin. Or tearing chunks of flesh from her torso, to be more precise.

He had to be packing firebolt bullets.

"You hurt my wife," he snarled, his eyes pure black with the craving.

And then he pulled the trigger one last time.

Dido catapulted back over the railing, and Lark slammed her hand over her mouth to swallow her gorge, the after-image of Dido's ruined face remaining with her. Too close. That had been far too close.

Byrnes looked over the edge, then put up his pistol and slid to his knees beside Ingrid. "Are you all right?"

"You came," Ingrid whispered.

"Always." His hand shook a little as he cupped her head. "I swear my heart stopped in its chest when I heard you through the communicator. What the hell happened? What did you do?"

"Had to stop her. Somehow." Ingrid winced as she tried to drag herself into a sitting position.

"She threw the pair of them through a window," Lark said.

"Good thing you knew the balcony was below," Byrnes growled, and then paused. "You did know the balcony was below?"

"Absolutely."

Lark hauled herself to her feet and glanced over the edge of the balcony. No sign of Dido in the dark of the night, but considering Byrnes had put that last bullet right between her eyes, Lark didn't think she need be concerned. All the king's horses and all the king's men wouldn't be putting the assassin back together again.

"Where's Charlie and Malloryn?" she demanded.

"Fighting on the stairs last I saw them. It seems the Rising Sons finally found their balls and are pressing for the top. There's a contingent of Coldrush Guards there with them," he said. "Where's the duchess?"

Lark looked up at the broken window above them. There was no sign of Adele.

"Adele?" she called.

No answer.

She'd lost Byrnes's attention. He was cursing under his breath, fussing over Ingrid.

"Adele?"

Silence.

The duchess wouldn't have vanished. She was barely armed and wouldn't have left the pair of them behind without assuring herself of their safety.

Grabbing Byrnes's shoulder, she knelt to see the damage to Ingrid. "We have a problem."

"Can't be any worse than it already is," he snarled, hoisting Ingrid up into his arms. "Ingrid can't feel her bloody legs."

"Adele's not answering me," Lark said. "She was in that room above us when Ingrid went through the window. I told her to stay put."

Byrnes's face paled as he looked up.

"Then where the hell is she?"

"I don't know," Lark replied grimly.

CHAPTER THIRTY-FIVE

Swords clashed as Malloryn drove Lord Greenwich down several steps. Greenwich had always been a mediocre duelist at best, but the Rising Sons had the numbers here. It was only he, Charlie, and three Nighthawks who'd burst out of nowhere holding the stairs.

Lifting his pistol, he shot Baron Carstoke in the face, giving Charlie some room to move, and then he disengaged Greenwich's next thrust and slammed the butt of the pistol into his lordship's nose. Blood splashed as he drove the rapier in his hand through Greenwich's chest to the hilt.

Greenwich slid off his sword, dead before he hit the ground.

No mean feat, but Malloryn was a trifle vexed at the moment.

The Rising Sons had swarmed out of nowhere.

And somehow three of them stood between he and Devoncourt.

"*You and me*," Devoncourt mouthed, and then winked.

A sword came at him. Malloryn dodged and grabbed the newcomer's wrist, throwing him aside. He shoved forward, but there were too many other people between them. Damn it.

He caught a glimpse of Devoncourt's blond hair as the Falcon vanished through a side door. Not today. He owed Devoncourt a bloody death. Malloryn kicked the Earl of Hargreaves in the face, and the blue blood slammed into three of his fellows, sending them toppling down the stairs.

"After me," he said grimly, trying to catch his breath. It was getting harder and harder to breathe with all the smoke funneling up through the center of the tower.

Charlie hauled him up short. "Look!"

There were more Rising Sons on the stairs below them, clashing with a group of Coldrush Guards and Nighthawks, that appeared to be led by Barrons.

Malloryn stripped the blood off his blade with his fingers and nodded his thanks to Barrons. As grateful as he was to have someone at his back, he couldn't help wondering if any of them were going to get out of here. The explosions had stopped—thank you, Gemma—but hot orange flames licked up the center of the tower. Barrons had a wife and a daughter and—

Don't.

Don't think about the what-if's.

Focus on Balfour.

"Where did Byrnes go?" Charlie demanded.

Malloryn looked around. "He said 'Ingrid.'"

"Do you think the ladies are in trouble?"

He understood Charlie's worry.

If Ingrid was in trouble, then it stood to reason that Lark and Adele faced the same peril. A whisper of dread slid through him.

There was no point going after Devoncourt. Vengeance could wait. He had to make sure Adele and the other women were safe.

"*Hello, Malloryn*," Balfour's voice said in his ear.

Malloryn froze, pressing his fingers to the earpiece in horror. "Balfour?"

The only way his nemesis could have gotten his hands on one of the communicators was to take down one of his agents.

But who?

"What the hell do you want?"

"Your lovely wife would like to say something to you," Balfour murmured.

"You're bluffing. You don't have Adele."

He'd gotten her clear of this entire mess, hadn't he?

Maybe it wasn't a communicator? Ava's transmitting device kept them on the airwaves, but there was no guarantee Balfour hadn't somehow manipulated the system. Perhaps he'd found the correct radio frequency—

"Here, Adele. Tell your husband how much you love him."

"Auvry?" came a tremulous voice.

Her voice.

The bottom of his stomach dropped. What had happened? How had Balfour gotten his hands on her?

The seconds ticked out in time to his heartbeat.

"Hello, Adele," he managed to say. The last thing he needed to do was panic. He couldn't betray his feelings right now. He couldn't. "Are you all right?"

"He has a knife to my throat," Adele admitted, though he could hear the tremulous quiver in her voice.

"Where are you?"

Static whined in his ear.

And then Balfour was back. "I'm where it all ended last time."

"The throne room," he said, loudly and clearly, so anyone listening through Ava's communication device would hear him. "You're in the throne room."

"You have five minutes to find me, or I'll cut her throat."

Malloryn went cold.

He'd cut her throat anyway.

"If you hurt her in any way," his voice came out hard and cold, "then I will not simply kill you. I'll destroy you."

But he knew Balfour.

The bastard wouldn't hurt her until Malloryn was there to watch it happen.

"Tick, tock, Malloryn."

He had five minutes to rescue Adele.

Heat seared the air as Malloryn fought his way through gusts of fire.

Lark and the others had appcared just as he and Charlie cleared the stairs. He'd taken one look at Ingrid in Byrnes's arms and swallowed the hot lash of fury inside him. This was Balfour's doing. They'd done their best.

"Get out of here," he'd said curtly. "Get to the rooftop and evacuate."

And Ingrid must have been hurt badly, for Byrnes didn't bother to argue.

Lark and Charlie exchanged a slow look.

But they didn't follow him.

Smoke nearly stole his breath as he climbed the stairs once again, the intensity of the heat drying his lips and skin. His eyes stung. Only long-time familiarity with this place allowed him to make his way toward the throne room.

Balfour would be waiting for him there.

He knew it.

Shoving his way through the enormous double doors

that led into the throne room, he found small respite from the updraft of smoke and flames that licked at the hollow core of the tower.

He wasn't alone.

Balfour turned to face him, his boots crunching on the broken glass that had fallen from the atrium roof. He had Adele's back against his chest, his knife held tight against her throat. Smoke poured up through the ceiling, leaving the room clear enough to see.

They stared at each other for a long moment, Malloryn's pistol trained on Balfour's head.

Then his gaze cut to Adele's, and it felt as though he lay splayed on an altar before Balfour, his chest cut open and his heart exposed for all the world to see. He'd never meant to let her in. He'd never meant to fall. But somehow, Adele had slipped beneath his guard when he least expected it.

It was like reliving the past; Catherine begging for him to leave, and Balfour turning the pistol from Malloryn's chest to hers.

This time it was Adele on the sacrificial altar.

Not her. Please not her. He'd only just started to realize how much he loved her.

"Hello, Malloryn."

"Let her go."

Balfour gave him a thin smile. "I don't think so. Put the pistol down."

The second he did, she was dead.

Malloryn's gaze focused through the sights of the pistol, narrowing between Balfour's eyebrows. Could he take the shot? All those years spent practicing for this moment, and suddenly he wondered if he was good enough.

Not to kill Balfour, but to save her.

"I'll kill her," Balfour warned, the knife tightening just enough to make Adele squeak. A thin trace of blood slid down her throat.

"You'll kill her anyway." He saw Catherine overlaid on the scene. Her face begging him to rescue her.... But when he blinked, all he could see was Adele, and she begged for nothing. She *believed*, her eyes shining as she stared at him with utmost trust. "It's what you do. Just to prove you can."

"*Do it,*" Adele mouthed, and his hand stopped shaking as his resolve firmed.

"Adele." He focused on Balfour's forehead. "Do you remember what Gemma taught you?"

"Yes," she whispered, tensing.

"Good."

He took the shot.

The bullet ricocheted as Balfour jerked to the side. Adele drove her palm up into Balfour's wrist, jarring the knife from her throat and stomping on his heel. Balfour tried to jerk her back in place, but she flung herself to the side and Balfour was forced to dive for cover.

Malloryn strode forward, firing on Balfour with every step. Blood splashed on Balfour's shoulder, and then Malloryn clicked empty.

He flung the pistol aside and scrambled to where Adele lay clutching at her throat. Blood dripped between her fingers, and his heart hammered, but when he looked at the wound, it was superficial. *Thank God.* Relief burst through him.

"I'm fine," she gasped. "Go!"

"Get to the roof," he told her.

"Not without you."

"You don't understand." He didn't want to try and explain. Time was running out. The chance for either of them to escape this mess was rapidly narrowing. He could feel the building shuddering beneath his feet. The air was growing hotter, thicker.

He couldn't let Balfour escape, but nor could he deny that if he stayed, his own chances faded.

Adele lifted her chin stubbornly, her cheeks stained with soot and her eyes red-rimmed from the smoke. Dark bruises circled beneath her eyes, as if she'd taken a blow to the face. She'd never looked more beautiful. "I understand perfectly. Not. Without. You."

Malloryn pressed his forehead to hers. To grant her this meant making a huge concession. But he had to accept, just this once, that he couldn't sway her. "Then stay out of this."

"Go and kill him."

Years of hate and fury turned into a cold, hard lump in his throat as Malloryn stood and faced his enemy. Endless games stretched out in the past, battles over the council table when the prince consort held power. Secrets. Lies. Espionage.

And revenge.

He'd thought once that seeing Balfour dead would finally ease the burden of debt from his shoulders, but it hadn't. There'd been a cold, hollow nothingness within him the day he helped cast the prince consort down and slit Balfour's throat. An emptiness he couldn't seem to slake in the years that followed.

And then Balfour returned, and Malloryn had realized he'd spent so long striving to destroy this man that he was still trapped in that vicious spiral. It was almost a relief to start the game afresh. To know there was something to tilt his lance at.

This man had ruined his life.

But Malloryn had allowed it to happen.

And worse, he'd allowed it to consume him.

Until Adele had finally shown him a path clear of this bloody spiral. He didn't want to die here, with the promise of their relationship so newly unfurled before him. He wanted time, damn it. Time to explore it.

Time to learn how to be Auvry again.

"And so it ends," Balfour told him.

"And so it ends," he replied, sliding the rapier at his side free of its sheath with a steely rasp.

"You have been a thorn in my side for far too many years." Balfour drew his sword also. "I should have ended you the day I shot Catherine."

"Then why didn't you?" He circled Balfour, knees flexing as he watched for the first sign of a lunge.

"Because you were a pup. You'd been beaten, you just didn't know it. Power isn't about those you crush beneath your heel. It's about those you didn't crush when you could have."

"A mistake on your behalf," he said coldly. "I am very, very good at surviving. You underestimated me then, and you underestimate me now."

"I'll grant you this," Balfour conceded, "I did not expect the ruse with the queen. I didn't realize you'd be cold enough to set your own wife as bait in a trap for me."

Malloryn breathed a laugh. "Then you don't know Adele. It wasn't my plan."

"Ah."

"You know me too well. As I know you. But you didn't account for her."

"I didn't think you'd ever be able to cede control to those who surrounded you. I wouldn't have."

"But I'm not you."

Another smile. "You're more like me than you care to think. Even if you survive—even if you beat me here—you'll never escape me. I molded you into the man you are.

In a way, you're the heir I never had."

The words tasted like bile in Malloryn's mouth. "I am nothing like you. Maybe I could have been, but I have something you've never had. I have people that love me and keep me human. And Christ"—he shook his head with a breathless laugh—"they're infuriating and drive me insane, and disobey me, and...." He stared at Balfour as he realized the truth. "And yet, they risked their lives to come rescue me in Russia. They've risked their lives to help bring you down. And they're the reason I will win.

"I'm nothing like you, Balfour. You've never seen the value in the people who serve you. You've never put their lives first, you've never cared. They've always been tools for you to use." He stepped forward, the tip of the sword in his hand rising. "All I ever wanted was to protect those I loved from you and your machinations."

Balfour stepped back into a duelist's stance.

"And so it comes to this, after all these years...." Balfour gestured with his sword, a faint smile on his thin lips. "Why don't we finish it?"

Smoke clung to the ceiling, pouring through the open hole where the glass ceiling had been. "Neither of us is getting out of here."

"Then we die together."

Balfour suddenly lunged forward.

Steel clashed on steel.

They'd only ever dueled twice.

The first had been a foolish clash when he'd been barely a man and Balfour had years of experience with a sword. All he'd wanted to do was avenge Catherine's death, but Balfour hadn't even had the decency to kill him. No. He'd earned a thrashing then—an abject exercise in humility—but he wasn't that young man anymore.

He'd hired the finest sword masters. Spent hours

perfecting his form.

Learned hand-to-hand combat. Pugilism. Batitsu.

Every hour he'd ever spent in the ring had been aimed at this moment.

The second time had been a brief skirmish as the revolution raged against him and he'd cut Balfour's throat in a moment of distraction.

Once again Balfour had the advantage, now that he'd metamorphosed into a *dhampir*. But Malloryn had spent months testing his reflexes against both Obsidian and Byrnes. He was as prepared as he was ever going to be.

They drove together, steel ringing on steel. Firelight flashed off both blades like whips of lightning as they riposted and lunged, working through each other's defenses.

Balfour's face showed strain when they broke apart.

"You've spent too many years pulling puppet strings," Malloryn warned him. Whipping past Balfour in a lunge that caught the other off guard, he slashed his knife across the bastard's ribs and spun to face him.

Balfour winced, pressing his fingers to his bloodied side. He looked up with a smile. "Your form's improved."

"Thank you. Nothing like a good motivator to really inspire."

"A pity it won't be enough."

Balfour drove forward, and this time it was all Malloryn could do to keep the bastard off him. The tip of Balfour's rapier flicked across his arm, leaving a burning lash in its wake. And then it was under his guard again, skewering through his side.

Malloryn gritted his teeth and fell back.

"That's just a taste of what is to come."

Back and forth they went, his eyes stinging from the smoke. It was growing thicker in here, and he could hear

Adele coughing. Having her here distracted him, but he couldn't do anything about it.

"Where are your precious Rogues now?" Balfour sneered as he scored another slash along Malloryn's shoulder.

Safe. Hopefully safe.

"Your precious Gemma and her lover? Your pair of thieves? Your mech and his wife? And the verwulfen bitch and her lover? Have they left you here to die?"

No. I made them go, so they would not.

He ignored the taunt as Balfour suddenly intensified his attack. Behind Balfour, he could see a shadowy figure emerge from behind a tapestry that hung on the walls; a secret passage only he was aware of. Relief burst through him as he recognized the familiar mask.

"Watch out!" Adele cried.

A pistol suddenly echoed behind him.

Heat burst through his right shoulder, a shooting numbness jolting down his arm. Grinding his teeth together, he tried to hold Balfour's sword at bay with both hands on the hilt of his own rapier, but it felt as though someone was slowly sliding a hot poker through his upper back.

He went down on one knee, his arm giving way beneath Balfour's pressure. Behind him he could hear Adele grunting with exertion.

"You son of a bitch."

A quick glance showed a familiar figure wrestling with Adele, his pistol still smoking. *Fucking Devoncourt.*

"Always have an ace up your sleeve," Balfour told him, almost fondly. "You should have learned that lesson by now."

Then a knee was driving toward his face.

Pain burst through Malloryn, and he slammed onto

the marble tiles, sliding back several paces.

Balfour drove his sword down, but Malloryn managed to parry it. And again. He kicked out, aiming for Balfour's knee even as his nose throbbed. Broken, possibly.

"I did," he managed to grind out as he rolled onto his knees. Behind him, Adele went sprawling as Devoncourt threw her aside.

Balfour paused. "Pardon?"

Malloryn slowly pushed to his feet. "I said, I *did* learn that lesson. You weren't the only one who brought a friend. You missed one of my Rogues."

Balfour stilled.

Behind him, the pistol lifted.

Devoncourt didn't even see his death coming.

There was a swift retort and then a dart stuck out of his chest.

The false earl looked down in shock, plucking at the dart, but it was too late.

"A taste of your own concoction," Malloryn sneered as Adele escaped the earl.

Balfour snarled as he spun toward Malloryn's last ace.

And then he froze.

"Hello, Father," Jack rasped, his facemask strapped into place and his green eyes glittering mercilessly as he took a threatening step forward.

It had been an agreement Malloryn had conceded weeks ago. *He's mine,* Jack had claimed.

Balfour seemed taken aback. "You shouldn't be here."

If there was anyone in the entire company who deserved revenge more than Malloryn, it was Jack. Balfour had twisted him to his use as a child, molded him, and then shunned him when his sister, Rosalind, proved the more dangerous.

And then he'd punished Jack for Rosalind's betrayal.

"You and I have unfinished business," Jack replied. Then he pulled the trigger on his dart-gun.

The dart slammed into Balfour's chest, but it only quivered there, stuck by its point.

Something was wrong.

Balfour smiled at the pair of them, and then yanked it out. "Did you think I didn't come prepared for Black Vein?"

He rapped his knuckles on his chest, and the sound echoed hollowly. No wonder all of Malloryn's strikes had skittered harmlessly off him.

It happened in an instant.

Balfour glanced at Malloryn as if to say *what can you do?* And then his left arm flicked out, a flash of silver spinning from his fingers.

"Jack!" Malloryn yelled, but his agent staggered back, the knife hilt-deep in his chest.

Jack's face paled behind the mask, and he went down on one knee.

And then, dart in hand, Balfour turned back to him. "Perhaps a taste of your own medicine?"

Devoncourt thrashed on the floor as Black Vein wreaked its damage. Adele took one look at this face—mottled with dark veins—and knew he was no longer a problem.

She scrambled for the knife at his side.

But as Devoncourt began gasping his last breath, she saw something better hanging from his belt. He must have found one of the Doeppler Orbs Lark had dropped.

Adele wrenched it away from him, glancing at Malloryn.

"Do it!" he yelled at her.

Adele twisted both halves of the orb and threw it at Balfour's feet.

The orb sprang open, gas hissing from its internals in an inky cloud of pure death—for any blue blood or *dhampir* in the room.

Malloryn draped his shirt sleeve over his mouth as Balfour sucked in a startled gasp. He turned on her, Malloryn's blood still dripping off the end of his rapier.

One step.

Two.

Black veins mottled through Balfour's face.

He clutched at his throat, clawing at the skin there.

"Auvry!" Adele slid to his side, grabbing two handfuls of Malloryn's shirt and trying to haul him away from the deadly hiss of atomized Black Vein. Where the hell was his gas mask? He should have had it strapped at his belt. She managed to drag him three feet, but he was coughing in earnest now, and she had to presume he'd lost the mask in the melee.

Something nudged her foot.

She looked down, and found Jack dragging himself toward them, holding out the filtration mask he wore to help him breathe in London's smoggy air.

"Take it," he rasped.

Adele tore the mask from his bloody fingers and slapped it over Malloryn's mouth and nose, holding it there. "Breathe," she told him, praying to every god in the sky that it would filter the poison from the air.

Malloryn sucked in a heaving gasp, tiny little black capillaries spreading through his cheeks.

"Don't you dare die on me," she rasped through a raw throat.

A hand came up. Slid through her hair.

Then he was pushing her away.

"Never. Need… to… move."

Adele wiped her weeping eyes. There was no time for relief. No time for tears. The entire tower was on fire now, though the flames were the least of their problems. She burst into a coughing fit, trying to keep her head low, below the roiling cloud of smoke. Sweet heavens, it was getting worse.

"Jack?" he asked.

"Alive," Jack rasped, one hand clamped to his chest. He must have jerked the knife out, but as they watched he burst into a coughing fit, his ravaged lungs no match for the smoke-tainted air.

Adele tore strips of silk from her gown and hastily fashioned a makeshift bandage for him. Hot red blood wept over her hands, startling her. She was so used to a blue blood's cooler, darker blood.

"Thank you." Jack's head slumped, but he turned to look at the fallen man nearby. "Is he dead?"

Malloryn tried to roll onto his side, still gripping the mask. "Came back… once."

Balfour stared sightlessly at the ceiling, his entire face ravaged.

Malloryn crawled toward him, bloody knife in hand.

"This time, I'll make sure he stays dead," he promised, and Adele turned her face away as he set about removing Balfour's heart.

The air was so thick with smoke that Adele couldn't see a damned thing as she heaved Malloryn to his feet.

For a second, panic bloomed. How were they going to get out of here?

A rope suddenly dropped through the open hole

where the atrium's glass roof had once been.

Then a figure in black was sliding down it, wearing a similar mask over his face as the one Malloryn wore. A second figure followed the first.

"Over here!" Adele screamed, waving one arm.

She sucked in a lungful of smoke and started coughing as both figures turned toward them.

Nighthawks.

She recognized the hard leather body armor and the golden striking hawk embossed on the chest of the lead figure.

Then Malloryn's weight was being eased from her shoulders, and the leather-clad figure hooked some sort of harness around her husband's waist.

A breathing mask was clamped over her face as the second Nighthawk strapped Malloryn to him and gave a tug on the rope still attached to him.

"Adele first," Malloryn insisted, but the taller man by her side made an impatient gesture with two fingers, and suddenly Malloryn was vanishing up through the hole in the ceiling with the second Nighthawk.

"Your Grace," the stranger said, his voice echoing through the mask. He clipped a harness around her waist, and she barely had time to realize one of his arms was made of metal.

Jack presented a problem, but the Nighthawk solved it by offering the looped footstrap at the end of the rope to Jack. He lashed the pair of them together.

"You're not coming?" Adele screamed.

The handsome stranger winked at her, drawing a grappling gun. "Don't worry about me, Your Grace. My wife would have my hide if I did something foolishly heroic. I'll be on the roof."

And then she and Jack clutched at each other as the

rope suddenly retracted.

The last she saw of the Nighthawk, he was pointing the grappling gun through the hole.

The pair of them swayed on the rope as it was winched toward the solid hull of the dirigible. The sudden lack of smoke and heat felt like a blessing that left her lightheaded. If she hadn't been harnessed to Jack, she'd have probably fallen.

Adele caught her first glimpse of the tower below.

Flames licked through every opening and window. Smoke circled its brow like a crown. Despite the hundreds of tiny figures in the yard around it, there was clearly no hope for the Ivory Tower.

She blinked, and then voices were shouting.

People hauling at the rope, leaning through a pair of retractable doors to snatch hold of her and Jack.

Somehow she found herself in the hold of the dirigible the Nighthawks owned. The *Nightingale*, Malloryn had called it.

Adele slumped against the steel hull as someone held a glass of water to her lips. She slurped at it, her dry, cracked lips raw and painful.

"Here." A cool, wet cloth wiped her face and eyes, and Adele finally got a good look at their rescuer.

The woman was tall and leanly muscled, her blonde hair braided tightly. Something about her appearance spoke of a quiet, solid sense of power, as if she'd faced the worst the world could throw at her and survived unscathed.

Lady Peregrine of the Nighthawks.

Which meant the Nighthawk with the bio-mech arm had most likely been her husband, the Guild Master himself.

"How did you even… know we were there?" she whispered hoarsely. Every inch of her hurt.

"Don't talk," the woman replied. "Byrnes waved us down from the rooftop. When we brought them up, he was beyond frantic. Said the duke was battling Balfour in the throne room and required assistance. If we didn't offer it, he was going to go back down himself."

Stoic Byrnes, with his callous shrugs and sarcastic rejoinders. "Is Ingrid all right?"

"We've got her in one of the bedchambers. They're trying to keep her immobile, but Doctor Gibson is hopeful that the loupe will repair the damage if given the chance."

Adele saw her husband then, pushing irritably at a pair of Nighthawks who were fussing about him. Lady Peregrine saw her attention shift and helped her to her feet.

"Your Grace, I believe you're upsetting Her Grace," Lady Peregrine told Malloryn. "Please let Fitz and Dr. Gibson see to your injuries."

"I'm fi—"

"That wasn't a request," Lady Peregrine cut in. "Don't make me hemlock you, Malloryn. It would be undignified."

"Though she'd probably enjoy it," said her husband, Guild Master Reed, as he was winched through the trapdoor.

Malloryn subsided with a thinning of his lips.

And then Adele was in his arms, and Malloryn gave her a gentle squeeze and a sigh as if to say, fine, he would submit this one time. For her.

The doctor finished checking Malloryn over before pronouncing him fit as a fiddle. "Your wife, on the other hand, is going to require rest," Dr. Gibson said firmly, and started reciting a list of herbal remedies and honeyed teas she would need for her throat and lungs.

Adele slumped against Malloryn's side as he slid his arm around her. Jack's ventilation mask hung undone around his throat, but the mark of it remained on his skin, as smoke had blackened the top half of his face.

She'd hate to know what she looked like right now.

A pair of Nighthawks was hastily bandaging Jack's wound. Adele couldn't believe it. They'd escaped.

"Balfour is dead," Malloryn said incredulously, his head slumping back against the hull of the airship. "And we survived. We both survived."

"Good," she rasped, then clutched at her throat and winced. "You owe me… future."

"And I plan to live it with you for a very long time."

CHAPTER THIRTY-SIX

"What now?" Gemma asked, bustling around his bedchamber at the safe house. "Barrons has called. Twice. The queen's demanding to know what happened, and they're trying to set a council meeting. What should I tell them?"

Malloryn shook his head as he slumped in the armchair by the bed. "For the first time in years, I don't give a damn, Gem. I just want some peace and time alone. Tell them I nearly died and I will be with them as soon as I can."

A faint smile crossed her mouth.

"What?" he demanded.

"The Duke of Malloryn taking a moment for himself? My, my, what is the world coming to? One would almost think you a changed man."

Malloryn scowled at her. "Peace, Gemma, includes you."

She glanced at the woman asleep in his bed, her lips curving in a secretive smile. "It seems the mighty have fallen."

He sighed. "I'm never going to hear the end of this, am I?"

"Love is for fools or those who want to punish themselves," Gemma said, pitching her voice to match his. "'Love clouds your judgment,' 'love is a weakness people like us can ill afford,' 'love is a disease that afflicts even the most rational-minded of individuals and turns their brains to mush.'"

"I never said that last one."

"I beg to differ," she said, crossing her arms over her chest. "And considering I've been on the receiving end of many of your lectures over the years, I do feel as though I have them virtually memorized by now."

"So is that a no, I will never hear the end of this?"

"No, you will never hear the end of this." Her smile could have warmed the world. "Byrnes is going to rub your nose in it until both of you finally cease drawing breath. And Kincaid will be beside himself."

Byrnes he understood, Kincaid.... "Why?"

"Because," Gemma told him, "it seems Ava won the kitty. She was the only one of us who gambled on the duchess stealing your heart. She scoops the entire pool."

Malloryn tossed his crumpled cravat at her. "Get out of here and leave me in peace. Some of you need more to do in your lives."

"Haven't you realized yet, Malloryn?" she teased, crossing to the door. "The Company of Rogues is family. And if there is one thing family does best, it's meddle. You may as well accept it, for you're not getting rid of us now."

He groaned as he collapsed back against the headrest of the chair and heard the door snick shut.

"What have I created?" he asked himself.

"A monster," Gemma called through the door cheerfully. "Give our love to your duchess when she finally wakes. Herbert and I will bar the door."

"And so the Ivory Tower fell," Adele whispered as Malloryn carefully tucked his coat around her shoulders in the predawn chill and rested one hand there.

It was several days after the city's fire crews and Nighthawks had managed to get the fires under control. Malloryn had only allowed her out of bed this morning, as her coughing had finally subsided to the occasional bout, and Adele had insisted upon getting out of the house.

One small carriage ride, she'd begged.

Which suited his purposes perfectly.

They stood before the ruins of the tower, watching as workmen cleared the rubble under harsh lights. It would take months to clear the worksite completely, and they'd been working through the night.

"Do you know—despite the verbal thrashing I received from the queen—I actually think I'm quite glad to see its fall," Malloryn murmured as a sliver of light lit the east. From the ashes, a new London could be rebuilt.

All those who'd held back its progress were gone.

He'd handed over the membership lists of Angel's Fall to Barrons, and the few remaining members of the Rising Sons had been rounded up and either executed or imprisoned.

Balfour was finally dead, and his schemes with him.

And Malloryn could finally lay to rest the ghosts of his past.

Adele glanced up, resting her gloved hand on top of his, and he sensed her quick mind trying to chase down his reasons.

"Because it was a product of the prince consort's

reign?"

"Precisely. He had it built—he and Balfour—to remind the citizens of London that they were forever in its shadow. When we overthrew the prince consort, his legacy ended, and yet it somehow remained. Watching. Looming. I could never walk the tower's halls without seeing his and Balfour's hand in every piece of it."

"How utterly phallic of them."

He flashed her a smile. "Men do that, I'm told."

"Worship their manhood?"

He brushed a kiss against her cheek. "As for myself, I'd prefer to leave such adoration in your capable hands."

Adele blushed.

They hadn't been intimate since she'd woken, as the doctor had warned Adele against exertion until her lungs had fully healed, but he was enjoying this newfound affection between them.

He hadn't felt this free in years.

"My hands?" she whispered. "Or my mouth? As I recall, you seemed to enjoy that very much."

"Behave," he teased. "We're in public. And such behavior is only to be found in the bedroom."

"Or the carriage. Or the library. Or your study...."

"Yes, well. When one's wife is pushing you to the brink, you make do with what you can."

"I hereby promise to push you to the brink on a regular basis."

"What more could any husband desire?"

Malloryn stepped down over an immense block of white marble, then turned and reached up to lift her down. Dawn was definitely on the horizon, which meant he'd have to hurry.

Adele's hands slid over his shoulders, and when he set her on her feet she lingered there, her skirts caressing the tightly pleated folds of his trousers. "What now? The queen has forgiven you?"

"It seems she's in a forgiving mood," he replied, enjoying the brisk whisper of the breeze through his hair. "Something to do with her holiday to Sir Gideon's house. Though I'm not quite certain what precisely went on there."

Adele's laugh was low and husky.

"Will she rebuild?"

"Alexandra's uncertain. She's taken up residence at Windsor Castle for the moment and seems in no hurry to return to the city."

"I wonder why?" Adele mused.

He had to hand it to her. He'd been watching the queen's face when he made his report, and the glance she'd bestowed upon Sir Gideon Scott… had been unexpectedly warm. "It has absolutely nothing to do with the fact I placed Sir Gideon in charge of her loyal Coldrush Guards and insisted he watch over her until the city was safe."

"You're trying to play matchmaker," Adele accused, "and steal my idea."

Malloryn lifted her knuckles to his lips. "I never look a gift horse in the mouth, my dear. You ought to know I cannot resist meddling. Though I shall grant you half the credit for it."

"*Half?*"

Malloryn rolled his eyes. "Three quarters of the credit."

"That's better. And what do *you* intend, now your ancient foe is vanquished?" she asked, sliding her arm through the crook of his elbow as he led her along the Thames embankment. "I've noticed you haven't been attending to 'business' quite as often as you did."

"Even a duke needs a holiday."

"Does he?"

"And he has plans."

"What sort of plans?"

Malloryn shook his head. "Always trying to ruin the surprise."

Adele shot him a startled look. Then her eyes narrowed. "You are up to something. I wondered, when you insisted upon leaving before the crack of dawn."

"I am always plotting something," he purred.

"Will I like this surprise?"

Fine. Here ought to do.

He paused and clasped both of her hands in his. "Perhaps. I thought—for so many years—that only vengeance could save me. I thought it was the only thing worth living for. And then you ran into my life—right into my arms as a matter of fact—and turned everything on its head.

"Love ruined me once, and I've never wished its acquaintance again. But it seems even the Duke of Malloryn is not entirely immune." He took a deep breath. "You saved my life, Adele. You have plagued me and vexed me and engaged in marital warfare with me... but you brought me back to life. You made this"—he pressed a hand to his chest—"start beating again, even when I wished it was not. Even when I wished you to the devil because I could not take my eyes from you.

"I love you. I love your devious mind. I love the way you challenge me and the way you refuse to back down when anyone you love is in danger. I love the way you tease me and remind me of what it's like to be Auvry again. We make an exceedingly good pair."

"That was almost the nicest thing you've ever said to me," she whispered.

"I'm not finished yet."

"Oh?"

"I have a proposition for you," he said, reaching insidc his coat, his hand closing over the small leather box there.

Adele tried to pretend her eyes weren't gleaming with unshed tears. "A proposition? Does it involve something ridiculous, like an intention to seduce one's wife? Or an act of war?"

"No. Gemma wanted to unleash doves, but I told her to stop being ridiculous."

"Doves?" He could see the sudden confusion in her eyes.

"And Kincaid threatened to dump a barrel of flowers over the top of you."

Confusion turned to outright suspicion. "What on earth are you talking about?"

Malloryn went to one knee, clasping her left hand. He eased the wedding ring he'd once placed there off her finger. "Adele Cavill, our marriage started under dubious circumstances, and I once told you I resented it. I lied. It's the best thing that ever happened to me, but I want there to be no more doubt left in your mind." He presented the small box with a flourish. "Will you do me the honor of renewing our vows?"

Adele's luscious rosebud mouth dropped open, and for once, it seemed he'd rendered her speechless.

"Is that a yes?" he teased, as a single tear slid down her cheek.

"Oh, my goodness. Yes!"

He eased the new ring onto her finger, and she splayed her fingers wide to examine it.

"Emeralds," he said, with a wicked smile. "To match your eyes. And a pair of pearls I kept from your necklace. You keep prattling on about diamonds, but I think, in a secret little part of you, there's a sentimental woman."

Adele burst into laughter.

And then a tear slid down her cheek, and she flung her arms around him as he pushed to his feet. The sweet crush of her body against his eased some small tension he'd been carrying. He'd known she'd say yes, but there was something nerve-wracking to be said for doing this when it actually mattered.

"That was almost romantic," came a very small whisper.

"Believe it or not," he whispered back, burying his face against her throat, "I planned it all myself. I win our war, Adele. I have you right where I want you."

Her laughter lifted his heart as she drew back with twinkling eyes. "I would call it a draw, Your Grace. Considering I finally brought the arrogant Duke of Malloryn to his *actual* knees."

"Let's start a new game," he said, sliding a hand up to cup her nape as he lowered his head. "This one lasts forever. And we both win."

And then he kissed his wife as a new dawn broke over London, promising a brighter future.

For all of them.

COMING SEPTEMBER 2019

PROMISE OF DARKNESS
DARK COURT RISING

Princess. Tribute. Sacrifice. Is she the one prophesied to unite two warring Fae courts? Or the one bound to destroy them?

In a realm ruled by magic, the ruthless Queen of Thorns is determined to destroy her nemesis, the cursed Prince of Evernight.

With war brewing between the bitter enemies, the prince forces Queen Adaia to uphold an ancient treaty: she will send one of her daughters to his court as a political hostage for three months.

The queen insists it's the perfect opportunity for Princess Iskvien to end the war before it begins. But one look into Thiago's smoldering eyes and Vi knows she's no assassin.

The more secrets she uncovers about the prince and his court, the more she begins to question her mother's motives.

Who is the true enemy? The dark prince who threatens her heart? Or the ruthless queen who will stop at nothing to destroy him?

And when the curse threatens to shatter both courts, is she strong enough to break it?

A fairytale twist inspired by the Hades and Persephone myth.

Want to know more about Promise of Darkness? Make sure you sign up to my newsletter at www.becmcmaster.com to be the first to know its release date, read exclusive excerpts, and see cover reveals.

ABOUT THE AUTHOR

BEC MCMASTER is a writer, a dreamer, and a travel addict. If she's not sitting in front of the computer, she's probably plotting her next overseas trip, and hopes to see the whole world, whether it's by paper, plane, or imagination.

Bec grew up on a steady diet of '80s fantasy movies like Ladyhawke, Labyrinth, and The Princess Bride, and loves creating epic, fantasy-based romances with heroes and heroines who must defeat all the odds to have their HEA. She lives in Australia with her very own hero, where she can be found creating fantasy-fueled worlds, where even the darkest hero can find love.

Read more at www.becmcmaster.com

Printed in Great Britain
by Amazon

46048784R00272